REANIMATORS

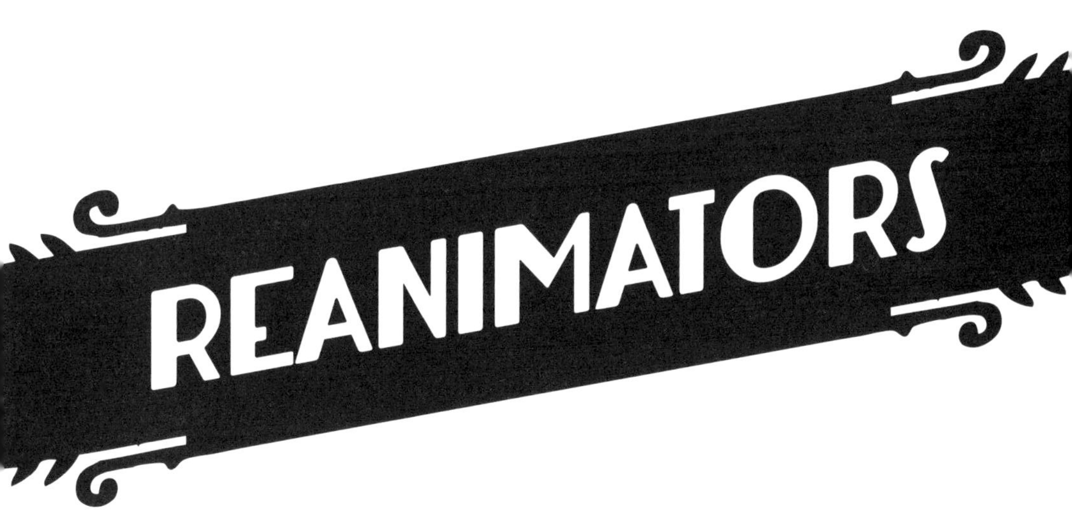

PETE RAWLIK

NIGHT SHADE BOOKS
SAN FRANCISCO

Night Shade books may be purchased in bulk at special discounts for sales promotion, corporate gifts, fund-raising, or educational purposes. Special editions can also be created to specifications. For details, contact the Special Sales Department, Night Shade Books, 307 West 36th Street, 11th Floor, New York, NY 10018 or info@skyhorsepublishing.com.

Night Shade Books™ is a trademark of Skyhorse Publishing, Inc. ®, a Delaware corporation.

Visit our website at www.nightshadebooks.com.

10 9 8 7 6 5 4 3 2 1

Library of Congress Cataloging-in-Publication Data is available on file.

ISBN: 978-1-59780-478-3

Cover art by Anthony Palumbo
Cover design by Victoria Maderna and Federico Piatti
Interior layout and design by Amy Popovich

Printed in the United States of America

For Mandy,
who gave me the time and encouragement to do this,
and deserves more credit than I can possibly say.

"Who amongst us carries the seed to transcend the mundane? Which of us has the potential to transform into something wondrous or terrible? What price to learn the mysterious forces that change men into gods and monsters?"

—Robert Harrison Blake

PROLOGUE

That I was arrested on four counts of murder is well known. That I was responsible for the deaths of four men, I have confessed to the authorities. So I am sure that it came as a shock to many when on the advice of my doctors, the district attorney chose not to press charges, satisfied revoking my license to practice medicine. Some say that the Commonwealth of Massachusetts has suffered enough of late, the city of Arkham, indeed the whole of the Miskatonic Valley is tired of tragedy and scandal. The federal government has cast a long dark shadow over Innsmouth, and a strange catastrophe has plunged the Dunwich area into a horror unmatched in our history.

I am grateful for such events, for they served to draw the faculty and students of the university away, leaving the grounds nearly empty. Had the campus not been all but deserted, the malignancy that had festered amongst the citizenry of Arkham might never have been contained. Even now if the events of that night were publicly known, the residents of this city would likely rise up to form a mob intent on slaughtering fully a tenth of their neighbors, and I would likely be the first victim. I know this because while the terror came to light in October of 1929, it began long before then. I was there in 1905 when it was born, and it is I who have nurtured and directed its cancerous growth for the last two and a half decades!

CHAPTER 1.

THE ARKHAM TERROR

For the record, my name is Stuart Asa Hartwell. I reside and work at Number Twenty-Nine Crane Street. The expansive three-story house with its basement and sub-basement has served the Hartwell family as both home and storefront for generations, though not always in a medical capacity. My father, like my grandfather and his father before him, were butchers and it was through his hard work that I was able to attend nearby Miskatonic University from which I obtained a degree in medicine and became a doctor. Given the heinous acts of which I am accused, it is perhaps better that my parents were lost in the summer of 1905, victims of the madness and typhoid fever that had enveloped Arkham. Shortly before that dreaded year my sister married a man named Kramer and moved to Boston. I have not heard from her or her family in more than fifteen years. Once again, perhaps it is better this way.

My involvement with the creeping horror would begin in that dread summer when even the lowliest of medical students were pressed into public service. The typhoid fever that had come to the city had grown to such an epidemic that both physicians and morticians were overwhelmed. The practice of embalming was forgone and services for the deceased were held en masse. In some cases, a single oversized grave and a hastily erected stone were the only niceties that could be mustered to mark the passing of entire families. Miskatonic University itself had shut its doors. Every member of the medical faculty was in service battling the plague, while non-medical faculty and staff were likewise pressed into carrying out the most menial but necessary tasks. It was not uncommon to see freshly graduated medical students or even nurses directing seasoned professors of literature in the fine sciences of sterilizing medical instruments or changing linens. It is my understanding that in a precedent-setting coup, the entirety of the Miskatonic's science faculty commandeered the kitchen facilities of the student cafeteria and through the careful rationing of stores and application of modern manufacturing was able to supply not only the university but both the staff and patients of St. Mary's Hospital for more than a month on a supply that was estimated to meet the needs of less than two weeks. Of all the acts of sacrifice that occurred during those sick days, those of Dr. Allan Halsey, the dean of medicine, were particularly distinquished. A skilled physician, Halsey walked where others feared to tread, taking on cases that appeared hopeless or that had overwhelmed lesser men. Driven to near physical and mental exhaustion, Dr. Halsey recruited me apparently at random, to serve as his driver and assistant. For the whole of July and the beginning of August the two of us crisscrossed the city to treat victims of all stations from the lowest of dockworkers to the daughter of the mayor. Dr. Halsey refused no one, and no act, whether administering injections or cleaning bed pans, was beneath him. That summer I am proud to say I learned much about being a doctor, and I am even prouder to have learned it from Dr. Halsey.

It was on the twelfth of August that Halsey, complaining of exhaustion and a migraine, promptly collapsed into the passenger seat of our commandeered Pierce Arrow automobile. We had spent the last sixteen hours administering to the thirty or so occupants of a rundown tenement on the south side of town, so the fact that he quickly fell into a deep sleep was to be expected. At his home on Derby Street, I could not rouse him from his slumber, and was forced to carry him from the Arrow to his bed. After a brief repast of water and bread, I took up my usual position on the couch in the parlor and quickly fell into a dreamless state of exhausted sleep. It was only the next morning, when I found Dr. Halsey unmoved from the position in which I had left him, that my concern was raised. Unresponsive to my verbal or physical attempts to rouse him, I quickly discovered his breath to be shallow and his heart rate dangerously low. I sent his houseboy, a young lad named Soames, to fetch help, but Doctor Waldron could do nothing but confirm my own diagnosis. Dr. Halsey had suffered a cerebral hemorrhage, apparently brought on from the stress of the last several weeks. He lay silent and immobile for the whole of the day, and in the wee hours of the fourteenth his body succumbed to the injury and the great Dr. Allan Halsey passed away.

A funeral service was hastily assembled for the next morning and the entirety of the medical school faculty and remaining students attended. Flower wreaths and other tributes were sent by a number of Arkham's elite as well as by the city administration. Following the service, the body was allowed to rest within the receiving vault, while the attendees tromped morosely through the streets to the Commercial House and held an impromptu wake that lasted through the afternoon and well into the evening. It was a somber, respectful affair punctuated by bouts of drunken melancholy that served only to drive our mood deeper into depression.

Most vociferous was the newly graduated Herbert West. Over the last two years, as the young West carried out the final phase of his education, years in which the student determines his own course of independent study, research and specialization, he and Halsey had clashed vehemently. West had become an adherent of certain theories, gleaned from the writings of certain European researchers, most notably Gruber and Muñoz, but not widely credited beyond a small circle of eccentrics. Halsey had attempted to counsel West on the futility of such radical theories, and when such warnings went unheeded, had banned West from carrying out experiments involving the administration of various reagents into the bodies of recently deceased animals. At the time West had called Halsey overly sentimental, but the entire campus understood that Halsey was by no means an anti-vivisectionist, but had prohibited West's experiments on the grounds that his voracious use of subjects as outlined in his experimental design would have quickly devoured the entirety of available subjects, leaving none for use by other students.

West was a charismatic figure and had attracted a small cohort of similarly minded researchers including the weak-willed Daniel Cain, the flamboyant and adventurous Canadian Eric Moreland Clapham-Lee, and the diminutive Geoffrey Darrow, who despite his tendency to spend his days sketching anatomical details revealed during autopsies, was considered by many to be one of school's most eligible bachelors, being the sole heir to the prestigious Darrow Chemical Company. Also present were Paul Rigas, Henryk Savaard, Richard Cardigan and Maurice Xavier. Like West, this band of miscreants had all come into conflict with Halsey or with Arthur Hillstrom, the president of the Miskatonic Valley Medical Society, but in a series of magnanimous gestures, all proposed toasts to the good doctor, and none denigrated his good name. Even West took time to praise the man, though in the same breath he espoused a course of action which hinted at blasphemy and spawned a low and uneasy murmur throughout the room. It was then that I and my sometimes companion Chester Armwright, finding the atmosphere of the room suddenly unsavory, bade our farewells and departed for the evening. Given events to come, our departure was perhaps the most prudent of actions.

The next morning I slept in, the last several days having apparently taken their toll on me, and it was only the smell of my mother's hash brown casserole that stirred my weary mind and body into action. Over breakfast my father and I listened as the radio announcer reported on two tragic events that had transpired in the night. The first detailed a gruesome discovery. Sometime after midnight the watchman of Christchurch Cemetery had been viciously assaulted and dismembered; a trail of blood led from the body to the gate of the receiving vault where it formed a small pool. A fainter trail led away from the tomb and into the woods where neither man nor dog could follow it. Police had questioned the proprietor of a traveling circus currently in Bolton, but all of the exhibits were quickly accounted for.

The second news report, while not as ominous, struck closer to home. At approximately three in the morning, the police had been summoned to a disturbance at a Water Street boarding house. After forcing a door, the police discovered Herbert West and Daniel Cain unconscious, the victims of a brutal attack from an unidentified stranger that the two claimed to have met in a downtown bar. After an hour, the stranger had suddenly turned violent and began pummeling, clawing and biting his two hosts before vandalizing the contents of the room. While West and Cain had sustained minor injuries, the police wondered how their assailant had fared after leaping from the second-story window to the lawn below.

This then was the beginning of the horror that would come to eclipse that of the typhoid plague. For while neither the police or the newsmen had drawn the connection, it was obvious to me that the stranger that had so brutally assaulted my colleagues was the same person that had so mercilessly slaughtered the cemetery night watchman. That night the streets of Arkham were filled with a preternatural howling, and something monstrous leapt from rooftop to rooftop shattering windows and breaking down doors. That night the beast invaded eight houses, butchering fourteen, and gnawing at the already deceased bodies of three plague victims. Those who had seen the killer, those who had lived, swore that while the thing stood on two legs it was not a man but some sort of hairless and malformed simian with sickly pale flesh and blazing red eyes.

The human mind can tolerate only so many traumas, and the creature that actively hunted through the streets of our fair city had overshadowed the massive but equally passive horrors of the typhoid plague. And so they were pushed aside, ignored, forgotten to make way for this new terror. In the light of day the able-bodied men of the city made plans. A net of volunteer telephone stations were established throughout the city and search parties were organized, armed, and in the evening deployed. Each search party was comprised of a single police officer and four men from the neighborhood in which they were stationed. Thus the searchers were not unfamiliar with the streets that they were patrolling, and I as one of those searchers was not far from my family home.

I remember that night. I remember the hot dry breeze rolling down the streets carrying with it the stench of humanity, and the stink of death. It was low tide and even in the college district I could smell the river. Insects, mostly mosquitoes, gnats and moths with the occasional beetle, were thick that night. They swarmed about the street lights, at windows, and around our heads like clouds of dust, drifting purposefully into our ears, our noses and our eyes. The howling that had filled the night before was gone, replaced by a thin drone that worked its way into my teeth, through my jaw and finally drilling down to the deep recesses of my brain. As time progressed the denizens of the night revealed themselves: a pack of thin feral dogs marched down the street as if it belonged to them; cats, black cats, fat cats, thin cats, calico and tortoiseshells that stalked unseen prey in front yards and along the sidewalks; and then came the rats, lean grey things that skittered and skulked along the curbs and sewers, seemingly unapologetic as they rummaged through the refuse that had accumulated there. Watching these creatures go through their nightly routines, wandering amongst our streets, our yards, and between our homes, made me wonder how much more went unseen in the streets at night, and how much of it impacted our lives during the day. Given time and effort, how much of the plague could be traced to the actions of these unseen and ignored residents of Arkham?

The alarm was raised just before midnight. Something large had scratched incessantly at the second-story windows of a house just a block from our patrol, methodically testing each of the windows, sending the residents of the home to seek shelter in the fruit cellar. The windows had been shuttered and so the beast had not only been deterred but had remained unseen as well, but it had whined in frustration, and slate had tumbled to the street below as the thing dashed across the roof.

By the time I and my fellow hunters arrived, the thing had moved on, but it had not traveled far, for we could hear the faint distant sound of wood splintering and a woman screaming. We ran down the street in the general direction of the disturbance. While my companions paused to gain a sense of direction, I sped on, fully cognizant of where we should be going. The screaming, which I recognized, and which drove me to new heights of frenzy, grew pitched and then suddenly ceased. Reaching the house which was the source of such terrified vocalizations, I cleared the front porch in a single leap and dashed through what remained of the shattered door and frame. Those brave men who followed me stumbled in the dark, tripped up by the furniture and lost in the dark inner rooms of the house. I had no such problems and weaved my way through with practiced grace.

It was in the kitchen that the final tableau was to play out. The gaslight sputtered, giving me only brief glimpses of the scene. On the floor, an older man, the owner of the house, lay in a bloody pulp. His head lolled horribly to one side, and though any semblance of life had long left that body, arterial blood still sprayed rhythmically from the place in which his left arm, the hand of which still held a large cleaver, had been ripped from its socket.

I screamed in outraged denial and was greeted by the sudden movement of another shape in the room, which as the lamp flickered back on was revealed as two figures, one clasped by the other. That the woman was dead was not in doubt, for she was held so tightly about her neck that if she had not died from asphyxiation, she surely had died from trauma to her spine or those fragile arteries that supply blood to the brain. The claws that clamped about her tender throat were pale monstrous things with broken nails caked with blood and filth. As I watched, the face of the beast rose up from behind the dead woman. There was a horrid ripping sound and the woman's head fell forward as the monster's own head jerked backwards, tendrils of bloody flesh and chunks of bone clenched between its teeth. It saw me then and I saw it for what it truly was. It dropped that poor woman, casting her aside as one would casually dispose of an apple core, and crouched back. It leapt through the air and I fired my revolver, hitting it squarely in the chest, all the time screaming and cursing the name of the man who had so obviously unleashed this monstrosity.

Though it took a bullet to the chest, the beast, the Arkham Terror, did not die that night. In truth I think it may not be capable of death, nor can it ever be truly alive, not as we know it. It was not until the next day, when nurses and guards at the asylum hosed the thing down, that they learned what I already knew, though they have tried to keep it a secret. Some, the bolder of our city officials, have called for an investigation; have gone so far to suggest a disinterment, to prove the matter once and for all. Most however are content to confine the Terror to the asylum and let the events of that summer become just another part of Arkham's strange witch-haunted past. But I know the truth, for even in the flickering lamplight I recognized the face of the Arkham Terror; after spending so much time with its owner, how could I not? I do not blame the Terror itself; I curse Herbert West for what he did that summer, for regardless of his intentions, the results were a brutal uncontrollable beast that killed without need or mercy. It was a bestial thing that was once human which broke into my family home and killed my parents. A monster which, as it chewed hungrily on my mother's cracked skull, I recognized as the late great Dr. Allan Halsey, reanimated by the mad and inept experiments of the deranged Dr. Herbert West!

Chapter 2.
A Rebirth in Ice

My quest for vengeance festered like an infection, tolerable at first—the wound need only be scratched to bring relief—but as time wore on, it was inevitable that more drastic responses were required to bring comfort. It is not often that a doctor must conceal the motivations which guide his decisions on how to manage his life and career, yet that was the position I found myself in. My medical degree obtained and the plague burned out, I found myself courted by the most prestigious of hospitals throughout the country, including Boston, New York, and Philadelphia. I was even offered a partnership in a practice located in the distant and exotic locale of Key West. To the chagrin of my colleagues and mentors I eschewed all of these offers, and instead set up a small general practice in the family home, renovating what was once a butcher shop into receiving and examination rooms and even a small surgery. As I was something of an accomplished carpenter, most of the renovations were made by my own hand, and thus in a matter of weeks I was easily able to conceal the presence of both the basement and sub-basement, the existence of which was my primary reason for staying in my horror-haunted family home.

For all public appearances, I was a simple town doctor, but in the secret chambers beneath my offices, I plotted against the man who had murdered my parents. It was true that the Arkham Terror, the plague-demon that had brought death to Arkham, was locked away in Sefton Asylum, but towards this malformed creature I felt no malice, for my vitriol was directed at the man who had created that poor beast. Though none but I had made the connection, I knew without doubt that it had been Herbert West and his companion Daniel Cain that had stolen the body of Dr. Halsey from the receiving vault of Christchurch Cemetery, and it was these two that had so shockingly murdered the night watchman who had must have disturbed them in their foul exploits. West and Cain had formed queer ideas about the nature of life, and of death, and their theories had allowed them to develop some biochemical process by which they could reanimate the recently dead. The reanimated and demented Halsey was obviously the horrid result of one of their gruesome experiments. That the two madmen had been attacked by the creature was justly deserved, for their creation had gone forth and terrorized the city, over two nights slaughtering and partially devouring sixteen innocent victims, including my own parents in the very house I called home. In the basement of my family home I plotted vengeance, maintaining a sort of covert surveillance of West and his sycophantic companion, all the while constructing a laboratory in which I could understand the process that West had invented.

The first task I undertook was to isolate and then reproduce the process by which reanimation was achieved. I initiated my investigation by first examining samples I had ready access to, namely the blood and tissue samples I had gathered from the walls and floor of my kitchen, the remnants of my shooting of the reanimated Halsey. I had collected and stored these samples, not with any forethought, but rather in accord with the cold methodical processes used by trained medical researchers. The skills I had learned at Miskatonic University had developed into reflexes that automatically recognized the value of such samples regardless of the horror with which they were associated. Thus I had an adequate supply of samples to at least begin my studies of the strange compounds that coursed through the blood and tissues of Dr. Halsey.

Being cautious and rationing my supply, I was able to discover that the samples all contained high concentrations of a compound that I was able to identify quite easily. Derived from a byproduct of the Leblanc process for the manufacture of alkali salts, the chemical whose name and formula I shall, for obvious reasons, not reveal, was relatively easy to synthesize. Chemical experimentation showed remarkable properties, similar to some qualities of both dimethyl sulfoxide and hemocyanin, the principal component found in the blood of mollusks and arthropods. Readily bonding, transferring and becoming saturated with oxygen, the compound revealed itself to be chemiluminescent, producing a strong blue-green glow visible even in daylight.

It was not until early December of 1905 that I began to experiment on animals. Initially I had thought to breed and use rabbits, but while their procreation rates were sufficient, their size and dietary needs quickly eliminated them as test subjects. After much consideration I settled on the ubiquitous laboratory rat which I could breed quickly, feed kitchen waste, and if need be handle with a single hand. In the sub-basement I built separate cages for both experimental animals and breeding stock. My breeders consisted of ten females and three males, which I routinely culled and replaced with their own progeny. In this manner I made sure that my animals were as homogenous as possible.

As I expected, my first few experiments were qualified disasters. The discovery of what dosage was required to elicit a response was a matter of trial and error. Too little reagent and there would be no reaction, or the reaction would be limited to the tissues immediately surrounding the injection site. Too much reagent and the subject would suffer uncontrollable seizures as all the nerves in the body seemed to react simultaneously. These reanimated rats were inherently violent and voracious, and refused to eat anything but live prey, and the cannibalism of live rats was carried out without pause. Strangely, these monsters would not ever attack one of their own reanimated kin, even when all other sources of sustenance were denied.

Yet through all this hardship, through tedious nights of failure and limited success, not to mention numerous rat bites, I slowly discovered the secrets of the reagent and soon had developed a procedure by which the bodies of recently dead rats could be effectively reanimated. Moreover, I was able to incorporate certain steps that prevented the animals from turning violent. However, as these were simply animals, I had no manner in which to discern whether or not any higher functions were retained. Thus I was forced to begin studies on the social behavior of both normal and reanimated rats. In this I discovered a marked variation, for out of every twenty rats that I successfully reanimated only one seemed capable of being reabsorbed by the general population. The others would cluster together with their own kind, and eventually develop a sort of malaise. Their food and water intake would decrease and eventually cease, and they would simply expire from a combination of starvation and dehydration.

It was on the basis of their behavior that I began to classify the various states of the rats in my basement. Those that had returned as violent uncontrollable monsters I called revenants, while those that returned but slowly lost the will to live earned the title morbids. Those rats that reanimated and successfully reintegrated into the warren, I called the risen. From all three classes I learned much. While morbids would die from starvation within weeks, revenants could linger for months before their systems would collapse. Similarly, morbids suffered from death like any normal rat, while revenants would only cease functioning if a significant portion of the brain or upper spinal column were destroyed; this however was not without complication, for on occasion the body of the monstrous little beasts would continue to function even after the head was severed from the body. Such revelations propelled my studies forward and as my knowledge grew so did my desire for revenge.

While my skills at using the reagent grew, an ability to reproduce West's reagent and his results was not the only course of action in my vengeful plot. At least once a week I would take the morning train for the short trip from Arkham to the nearby mill town of Bolton where West and Cain had established their practice. I would spend the day in the potter's field that was so conveniently located next to their residence and offices. From a concealed position I would observe the comings and goings of both my quarry and their patients. When it came to securing their home and laboratory, Cain and West were careless, and often failed to lock their front door. This presented an opportunity I could not resist, and one November evening I hit upon the most brilliant of strategies. I waited for West and Cain to make their usual error and then cautiously entered through the unlocked door. I made my way to the kitchen and carefully searched through the drawers until I found a ring of spare keys. It took only moments to locate one that fit the back door, and even less time to slip it off the ring and into my pocket. Then with great care I made my way into their secret basement laboratory, where careful not to disturb anything, I proceeded to carry out several tasks. First, I took minute samples of any new versions of the reagent that West had developed; this was relatively easy as he would methodically label each minor modification with a letter, while major advancements warranted a new Roman numeral. After securing sufficient samples, I would then systematically contaminate the remainder, assuring that any results obtained from its usage would be wholly irreproducible. Finally, I would scour the contents of West's experimental journal, learning what I could from his successes and failures.

With the key in hand, I gained the ability to enter the home of my dreaded enemy, and to learn the most marvelous of things about him. In this way I discovered West's weakness, for despite his genius, he had made a fatal miscalculation when he decided to forego experiments on animals to work exclusively on men. For where I could easily carry out thirty or forty experiments a week, West could only use those bodies which readily availed themselves. Thus, while West had more experience with how humans responded to the reagent, I had achieved greater success with my rats; West had only succeeded in using his reagent to create the human equivalent of my revenants, yet he had never produced a human risen, nor even the equivalent of a morbid. At this revelation my mind snapped, all pretense of caution was cast aside as my head whipped back and my cackling laughter filled the air. As I made my way through the woods towards Bolton I continued to chuckle and my laughter only grew louder as I walked down the long road toward Arkham.

In February of 1906 I came to the realization that I had learned all I could from the rats. I resigned myself to the fact that if I were to continue my march towards vengeance, my experiments needed to progress from animals to men. It was a realization that shook me to the core, for it bore with it the implication that I must become involved in an event that would serendipitously bring a recently deceased body into my possession, or manufacture some such event. Thankfully, I was spared the need to engineer any macabre accidents, for I soon found myself surrounded by the dead and the dying.

February was bitterly cold, with sleet falling from the sky in sheets for three days straight, leaving the sidewalks and roads nearly impassable, covered in thick glittering sheets of ice. Arkham came to a near standstill, with even the postal service foregoing their daily rounds. The only people foolhardy enough to brave the frigid air and the frozen landscape were those with no worries or fears. Thus the winter streets of Arkham became filled with children: children on skates, children with sleds, children building snow men and snow forts. In retrospect the accident was inevitable, for while children filled the streets, the public servants, policemen and the like had shunned the temperatures and stayed close to their warming fires. So when the municipal trucks and their loads of salt left the garage, there was no one there to tell the children. When municipal truck number seven reached the top of the hill, there was no one there to clear the children. When municipal truck number seven, driven by Virgil Potter, began to roll down the hill, there was no one to warn the children. And when municipal truck number seven began to slip on the ice, and Virgil Potter turned the wheel, municipal truck seven lurched sideways first to the left, and then to right, no one on the street below was there to hear it and alert the children. Potter swore as the front left tire clipped the sidewalk, but no one heard that either. It was only when municipal truck number seven turned on its side, tossing Virgil Potter into the street, and dumping its load of salt onto the road in a crashing wave of glittering rock, only then did anyone, meaning the children, react.

Virgil Potter rode the wave of salt down the street screaming in fear and pain. The salt swallowed up the road in front of it like a wave on the beach. Before it children scattered like seagulls, jumping to the sidewalk or into yards and even up trees or light poles. It was young Sally Moore who they say stumbled on her scarf and then tripped, taking down with her three others, including one of my neighbors, the eldest Peaslee boy. They were swallowed by the salt, devoured, chewed and smothered by it.

I was on the street in seconds, for I and everyone else on the block had heard the truck overturn. Moreover, there was the screaming, that high-pitched mournful sound that was coming from Virgil Potter as he clutched his severed leg in his arms. I yelled for one of the unscathed children to run to St. Mary's for an ambulance and I saw three boys take flight like the devil himself was after them. Reaching Potter, I ripped the scarf from around his neck and tied the wool garment tight around his leg to stay the flow of blood. His screaming was unbearable and as he turned towards me to beg for help I cold-cocked him across the chin, sending him instantly into unconsciousness. It was as I began to drag Potter that I saw little Sally's boot sticking up out of the salt. I grabbed that tiny foot with two hands and in a supreme effort pulled the tiny girl out of her pebbly tomb. Crystals caked her face and packed her nose. Clearing her mouth, I immediately determined that the young child was not breathing. Cradling the girl's head I carefully carried her from the street and into my offices. Laying her on an exam table, I began application of the Silvester Method, alternatively lifting her arms above her head and then compressing them against the chest. Sadly, several minutes of this activity produced no results, and I collapsed in a combination of exhaustion, frustration and despair.

As I sat there listening to the siren of the approaching ambulance, I was suddenly conscious of the opportunity that had presented itself. Rising with a jolt, I dashed down to the basement and quickly prepared a syringe of reagent, basing the dosage on an estimate of the girl's weight. Climbing the stairs, I carried the syringe before me as if it were the fabled philosopher's stone itself. Pulling back the girl's hair and sweater, I adeptly inserted the needle into the base of the skull and penetrated the deeper tissue. In a second action I depressed the plunger and injected the glowing green fluid into her brain.

I fell back into a chair and rolled backwards into the wall. Through the window I could see the events transpiring outside. The first ambulance crew was loading Virgil Potter and his severed leg into the back of their vehicle, while a second crew was busy excavating poor Sally Moore's lost companions from the salt that was still slowly spreading down the street. Tears welled up in my eyes as I watched the rescuers drag body after small body out of the debris. Even from a distance I could see that only a handful of the other children had survived the accident, and once more I collapsed back into my chair.

It was then that I noticed that changes had taken place in the formerly cold dead body of Sally Moore. As I watched, her eyelids snapped open and her eyes darted back and forth. I watched her pupils dilate, and then her back arched and her mouth opened, and from it issued forth a soul-shattering scream that rivaled that of Virgil Potter. She convulsed wildly, thrashing her arms and legs about and knocking me to the floor, shattering cabinets and raining glass down upon both of us. As she sat up her mouth opened wide, wider than I thought possible, and then the air was filled with acidic fluid and partially digested food as she vomited forth the contents of her stomach. The stench of bile and other bodily fluids permeated the room and I retreated backwards across the floor.

She spun herself sideways, finding the edge of the table which she grasped firmly with both hands. Her eyes continued their frantic motions, but I somehow felt that they were no longer uncontrolled, but rather purposeful, for the look that had taken over her face was not one of madness but rather of fear and confusion. Before I could act, young Sally Moore bolted from the room and out the front door, leaving me stunned in silence. It was nearly twenty minutes before I rose up from the floor and methodically began cleaning up the shattered glass and other evidence of Sally Moore's violent reanimation. In the middle of sweeping up, the events of the last hour suddenly caught up with me and I let loose a resounding exclamation of joyful accomplishment.

Over the course of the next week I kept tabs on the girl, making sure I caught sight of her at least once each day. Her mother and father doted on the child as well as her two siblings, an older brother and a younger sister, and all seemed unaware of any change in their Sally. The only family member that seemed disturbed by the risen child was the family cat, which hissed incessantly at the girl. Besides this one problem I quickly came to believe that my first attempt at human reanimation had been a resounding success.

Eight days later my joy turned to dread as a representative of the city's police department disturbed my evening repast. Earlier that evening, the officer related, a child had gone missing; now normally the police would not involve themselves so early, but given that temperatures were expected to drop well below freezing the local constable was convinced that immediate action was required. I had not been out of the house all day, and consequently had seen no children, which I readily told the officer. He thanked me for my time and bade me a good evening. I retired shortly after that, but my sleep was restless, for endless worrying possibilities nagged at my mind. I woke with the dawn and dressed quickly, determined to check on young Sally's welfare.

I had not even left my own yard before all doubts were removed. The missing child sat on the sidewalk in front of my house. She must have arrived sometime after the police officer had left. She was frozen there; crystals had formed in her hair and a small icicle hung from her nose. She was obviously frozen to the ground and there was no doubt in my mind that she was dead. I had made a critical error; I had let an experiment begin and end in uncontrolled conditions, and as a consequence had leapt to a tragically incorrect conclusion. It was true that I had successfully reanimated Sally Moore, but I had no reference data with which to understand her life prior to her death; thus when I saw her with her family, I assumed that she had successfully reintegrated, that she was the human equivalent of a risen. Now I knew better, for the frozen child who sat before me was indeed Sally Moore who had returned from the dead not as a risen but as a morbid. Like all morbids, Sally had succumbed to an organic malaise, and in the end she did the only thing that made any sense to her melancholy mind. Unable to function with her family she returned to the last place that seemed to matter to her, the place where she had died. The place she now sat frozen, staring accusingly at my home and laboratory, the place where I had robbed her of that death, and dragged her back into a perverse imitation of that life.

CHAPTER 3.
A DEATH IN BOLTON

It had been just over six months since the death of both my parents at the hands of what had once been Dr. Allan Halsey, who had been brought back to a semblance of life through the reckless actions and research of Herbert West. I swore then in those horrid days that I would wreak vengeance on West, and I spent my nights studying, experimenting, understanding and then finally even surpassing West's research into reanimation. As West had limited his experiments to men alone, his progress had been horrendously slow, hampered in part by my own not-infrequent sabotage of his work. In contrast, I had begun my work with rats, and such experiments, so many experiments, had moved my knowledge of reanimation beyond even West's understanding, so much so that in my first attempt to use the reagent on a human I succeeded beyond anything West could have hoped for. Sadly, the subject, a child of just eight years, fell victim to a terminal malaise that seemed a common affliction of my rodent subjects, an affliction I had not yet been able to avoid.

As February had been bitterly cold, March was unseasonably warm, and I seized the opportunity such mild weather presented to make the trip from Arkham to Bolton to spy on West and, if possible, tamper with his laboratory and reagent. For the most part, the train trip was uneventful and the only thing worth noting was the presence on the train of a most curious individual. According to a helpful steward, the Negro was "Buck" Robinson, an amateur pugilist, and a magnificent specimen of a man, standing nearly seven feet tall and weighing in at over three hundred pounds. The train was crowded, and while many of the passengers were obviously afraid of the fighter, I held no such prejudices. When I asked if I could join him, he graciously adjusted his not inconsiderable frame to accommodate me.

He was a congenial fellow, and he had a way of speaking that was warm and inviting. His name was James Buchanan Robinson, named by his grandfather who had been an admirer of the president who had worked so hard to balance his desire to abolish slavery and maintain his Federalist views on the Constitution. Robinson, however, was not overly fond of his namesake; he had studied law and politics at Lincoln University in Pennsylvania, and greatly disagreed with how Buchanan had administered his presidency. The current Republican administration was, he felt, much more progressive, making great strides in curbing the power of corporations, while supporting unions and workers.

After nearly twenty minutes of conversation I suddenly smiled and let loose a little chuckle. I apologized, and explained that I was surprised that such a well-spoken and educated man would be involved in fisticuffs. Robinson nodded. In college he had run into money problems, and turned to fighting to pay the bills. After a half dozen fights, it became apparent that he had some aptitude. A promoter recruited him, dubbed him "The Harlem Smoke"—despite the fact that he was from Atlantic City—and when he was between semesters or on college breaks, he would schedule a few fights to earn some extra cash. It had been years since he had finished law school, but no matter how hard he tried, he couldn't get out of the habit of picking up a fight every now or then. Not for the money, but for the thrill.

I shook my head and expressed my concerns, as a doctor, over the dangers of such a risky hobby, but Robinson just laughed. It was a hearty, belly-busting laugh that was loud and infectious. "Dr. Hartwell, by my estimates I've had over a hundred fights, and broken a dozen bones, including my jaw and cheek. A man named Towers brought his heel down on my left foot and broke all my toes. I've been hurt, I won't deny it, but look at me; I'm big, with a reach and speed other men can't match, and a punch like a sack full of bricks. Do not misunderstand me, sir, I'm just as human as the next man, but in the ring, when I go up against another fighter, I'm damn near invincible, immortal even."

In Bolton, both I and Robinson disembarked the train and bade each other farewell. I trailed behind him, his massive stride quickly putting distance between the two of us. Outside Robinson was greeted by several well-dressed men who hustled him into a waiting car, while I continued by foot. Bolton is a lovely little town, and I spent the rest of the morning and early afternoon browsing several shops and having a fine lunch of fresh fish and winter vegetables. From a local delicatessen I bought a selection of meats and cheeses, and by the early evening I had secreted myself and my supplies in the woods on the far side of the cemetery across from the house where West and Cain resided and worked.

As the night deepened, I moved from the woods through the crumbling monuments and neglected graves to my favorite vantage point beside a statue of a weeping angel. No sooner had I settled in when two burly figures walked somberly up to the house and sheepishly rapped on the front door. After a brief conversation between the occupants and the visitors, both West and Cain donned heavy coats and followed the two visitors down the road. Delighted at my good fortune, in moments I was at the back door, into the house and down the stairs to their secret laboratory.

After liberally contaminating the most recent batch of reagent, alternatively diluting some components while increasing the concentrations of others, I casually settled in to reading and copying portions of West's journal and notes on his experiments. Thrilled was I to discover a number of facts, most notably that West was growing increasingly frustrated with his lack of consistent progress, for he wrote extensively on the failure to be able to obtain reproducible results. Indeed, West went so far as to speculate that Cain, despite his training, might be wholly incompetent, and the failure of the reagent to produce consistent results might be wholly attributable to Cain's inability to properly prepare the mixture. At this I chuckled, knowing full well that his failures were the result not of Cain's incompetence, but rather a product of my own deliberate interferences.

Furthermore, West confessed that he had lately become victim of a growing sense of preternatural dread, as if someone or something was following him, shadowing his every movement. It was, he wrote, as if a dark entity had begun plotting against him, aligning events and forces so that when the time came the strike would be swift, fatal and unstoppable. West traced such feelings back to his earliest experiments, prior to the fall of 1905, well before I began secretly hounding him. Still, I couldn't help but wonder if the dark entity that West felt was rallying against him was not in fact my own self.

After finishing with my amused investigation of West's lamentations, I proceeded to copy his notes on new directions and changes to the reagent formula. While such misappropriations added little to my own knowledge, they were instructive in their own way, insuring that I would not repeat such errors. Similarly, when West had succeeded in some minor breakthrough, I was able to quickly envision how such a modification could be integrated into my own reanimation process, sometimes making vast prescient leaps beyond the current procedures either one of us were currently using. Indeed, had I not been so hell-bent for revenge, I might have considered revealing myself and collaborating with West, for such an arrangement would surely propel the progress of discovery to new rates of achievement.

Suddenly, my acts of scientific espionage were interrupted by the most disturbing of events. Though muffled by the walls and distance, I distinctly heard the sound of footsteps tramping through the gravel walkway. I had spent too much time reveling in my success and transcribing notes. West and Cain had returned and I was still inside the house! I made for the cellar door, intent on making my way to the nearby safety of the cemetery, but as soon as I mounted the stairs, I knew it was too late. Desperate, I plunged for the darkness underneath the stairs that led to the first floor of the house. There, crouching behind a blind of crates and tarps, I observed as West and his mealy assistant Cain came down into the laboratory with yet a third man between them.

As they came into the light I recognized the third man as the man on the train, the boxer James Buchanan Robinson. Apparently despite his assurances to the contrary, he had not been invincible. Listening to West and Cain talk, I learned that the referee was unable to maintain control of either fighter, and the unsanctioned match had degenerated into a bloody slugfest. Robinson had suffered massive head trauma from multiple blows delivered by his opponent long after he had collapsed onto the floor. Being an illegal fight, there was no doctor standing by, and Robinson had been motionless for more than an hour before West and Cain had arrived. That he was already dead was a stroke of luck for the two ghouls, and what was more, the owner of the seedy warehouse at which the fight had taken place, a man named Durden, had paid West fifty dollars to take care of the matter.

The thing that was once James Robinson was poured onto the exam table, which given his great size he immediately overflowed. The great man's hands fell limply, his fingertips brushing back and forth across the cold concrete floor. I had never seen West work before, never seen how he treated his patients, his subjects, and the sight of it now was a revelation. Watching the man now, watching him move, prepare syringes, sterilize instruments and prepare for his experiment, I realized something about the man I had never known before. For all his knowledge, all his skill, all his mad genius, Herbert West was a horrible doctor. He was clumsy and unorganized, his technique was laughable and his methods crude. If it had not been for the tidy and meticulous ways of his assistant, nothing would have been done properly. Daniel Cain may have been a sniveling, sycophantic toady, but he was a competent doctor and understood the rules and limits of experimental design. West may have been a genius, but it was Cain that transformed that genius into brilliance and kept it on track. My analysis, my need for vengeance that had so focused on West, suddenly seemed so wrong. West was not to blame, at least not alone, and once more I swore vengeance against Herbert West and the unassuming Daniel Cain.

With all the skill of a butcher's apprentice West went to work on his specimen. He and Cain were earnest in their work and watched with rapt attention for the first response from their subject, not knowing that my tampering had irrevocably destroyed any chance of Robinson reacting to their reagent. It took hours for the two to accept that Robinson was not going to respond. When they finally conceded and dragged their failure up the stairs and into the woods, I made my way cautiously up and out of the cellar. My first reaction was to flee down the road and into town, but something made me stop, and soon I was stalking through the woods watching as West and Cain buried Robinson in a shallow, leaf-covered grave.

I cannot remember how long I sat there in the woods staring at the place where Robinson was buried, but the sun rose and the birds were singing when I finally took action. I used my hands to clear away the leaves and loose dirt to reveal the cold still form of James Robinson. In death, the blood drained from him, his face destroyed by the fight, he was terrifying, almost inhuman. Grabbing him underneath the arms, I pulled with all my might and dragged the body out of the dank earth. As the light of the sun slowly filled the forest, I knew that the instrument of my vengeance was at hand.

From my coat pocket I pulled out the small leather kit that I carried for emergencies and removed the small, glowing vial that was secreted in the bottom. I carefully estimated my subject's weight and then wracked my memory for the amount of contaminated reagent that West had already injected. Ultimately I filled the syringe with a volume that was as much guess work as it was science, and in a purposeful and direct act injected the dead body with my own superior reagent.

Afterwards, I fell back and watched as Robinson's body rapidly responded to the reagent coursing through his body. Like my previous human subject, Robinson's mouth opened wide and his screams filled the quiet forest. His body arched backwards, driving his head and heels into the frozen ground. Suddenly he was flapping about like a fish out of water. I winced as his hands beat against the frozen earth, and I heard the distinct crack of bones breaking. Then, as suddenly as they had begun, the convulsions ceased and the giant of a man slowly rose and, although unsteady, stood upright, staggering as he walked a few cautious steps.

I called out to him, called him by name, and he jerked his head and torso around to face me. His eyes were wild and filled with blood. Drool mixed with bile spilled uncontrollably from his mouth. His arms reached out and he lunged towards me, but only succeeded in falling pathetically to the ground. I knew then that I had failed, that my estimates of how much reagent to use in combination with the contaminated reagent had been woefully wrong. Watching what was once a man crawl about on the forest floor, I did what any man would do. I picked up a convenient branch and, raising it above my head, I prepared to put the poor thing out of its misery.

Tragically, I acted too slowly. For suddenly we were no longer alone, and I had no choice but to flee through the woods in terror. I did not stop running until I was safely at the station and onboard the train back to Arkham. In the car I hid in the lavatory, shattered, begging forgiveness for what I had done. Once again my desire for vengeance, my lack of caution and proper care, had ended horribly. The memory was more than I could bear, and try as I might, I could not stop the scene from being replayed over and over again.

The reanimation of James Buchanan Robinson had gone wrong, terribly wrong, and I stood above the poor man with a makeshift club ready to rectify my mistake and send him back into the oblivion he deserved. Yet as I readied the killing blow, a terrified voice broke the silence, a voice that was not Buck Robinson's. Standing there at the edge of the clearing was a small child who couldn't be more than five years of age. The boy was terrified and yelling, begging me not to do it, not to kill that man. He begged me, he begged me in the name of God not to kill that poor black man. I dropped the branch, and as I did the thing beneath me sprang forward, moving on all fours like a monstrous bear. The revenant, for surely that is what I had created, tore into the boy who released such a torrent of agonized vocalizations, that I clamped my hands about my ears and ran as fast as I could. I do not know what happened to the thing that had once been Robinson, but I know what happened to that little boy, for as I ran I turned back, and my last fleeting glimpse was of that giant of a man beating the bloody child with his own ersatz club; a club that was thin and pale and terminated in five delicate fingers.

CHAPTER 4.
THE SHADOW FALLS

After my disastrous experience in Bolton, I found myself in the most desperate of states. My mind was shattered and my spirit broken. My quest for revenge had not only faltered but had led me to take risks and commit acts that had ended in the murder of an innocent child, a murder I held myself responsible for. In my rash attempts to revenge myself on Herbert West for the accidental death of my parents, I had followed in his footsteps and descended to the same depths of depravity. The irony was not lost on me. In the week immediately after the horrid day in which I reanimated the amateur pugilist James Robinson, and he tore a small child to pieces before my eyes, I shut myself away, canceling all my appointments and seeing no one.

My only solace in those days was the evidence of my previous successes in the field of reanimation, the dozens of rats that occupied the cages hidden in my sub-basement laboratory. I had long ago slaughtered any revenants, and likewise the morbids had all since expired from their terminal malaise, leaving only untreated specimens and those rats that I called the risen, individuals that had been exposed to the reagent and showed no negative side effects. Attending to this community of normal and risen rats was the only thing that gave me any modicum of peace, and I devoted hours to the care and feeding of my charges.

April came, and though I had once more begun seeing patients, my melancholy showed no signs of waning. Such was my state that even my neighbors had noticed and apparently decided to take action, for early one evening there came to my door Wingate Peaslee, the young son of my neighbor. My presence, he informed me, was required, and his mother had told him not to return home without me in tow. Assuming the worst, I grabbed my medical bag and quickly followed the child home. Mrs. Alice Keezar Peaslee, a lovely woman with flowing locks and a shapely figure, greeted me as I came through the kitchen door, and immediately handed me a large knife and fork. On the kitchen table was a large roasted chicken, and she kindly asked me to carve the bird. For the moment I was dumbstruck, but I quickly conceded to her request. Within a few minutes I had filled the serving plate and with the help of the three Peaslee children the table was set just as their father came through the door.

Nathaniel Wingate Peaslee was a professor at Miskatonic University, primarily teaching economics and some business courses, of which I had been fortunate to benefit from. A decade or so my senior, his family and mine had been friendly since they first occupied the neighboring house in 1897. A serious but amiable man, Nathaniel Peaslee was a pillar of the community and was well loved by those who knew him.

Dinner was a casual affair, with idle chatter about the children's lessons as well as local and current events. It was only after the children had been dismissed, and Mrs. Peaslee had served coffee and then retired to the kitchen, that I learned the real reason that I had been summoned to the Peaslee home. Peaslee had learned that his personal physician, Dr. Arthur Hillstrom, was planning on retiring, and had yet to establish a successor to his practice, which consisted primarily of several dozen faculty members and their families. Similarly, Peaslee had also learned that many of his colleagues were significantly unhappy with the fees being asked by my old classmate Chester Armwright. All in all, suggested Peaslee, there were more than forty faculty members and their families that Peaslee believed he could deliver to an enterprising young doctor. That doctor, Peaslee believed, was myself.

Slightly stunned, I had to admit that Peaslee's proposal was intriguing, but frankly I was already serving a client base that was nearing my capacity; to take on another hundred or so patients would strain both my own sensibilities and the quality of care I could maintain. Peaslee took this in stride, and suggested that with minor changes, the addition of a second but not yet established physician, as well as a full-time nurse receptionist, for example, would result in a practice that could increase its client load, while maintaining quality. I agreed that such an arrangement could work, but that I knew of no such prospective candidates. Peaslee nodded politely, and inquired if I was free the next evening. As I was, he quickly invited me back for dinner the next night.

That next evening, after an excellently prepared ham, Nathaniel and Alice Peaslee formally introduced me to their other dinner guests, Francis Paul Wilson and his new bride Mary, Alice's younger sister. Francis had just finished his residency at St. Mary's Hospital where he had met Mary, a junior ward nurse. Nathaniel proposed a trial partnership. Wilson and I would work together for the next month; if we were compatible, I would give my existing part-time assistant notice and Mary would become our receptionist and assistant. During the trial period, the two would live in the Peaslees' carriage house apartment so both would be readily available.

I gladly agreed to the arrangement, with but one reservation. I have always had a keen memory, and as a student in Peaslee's class I had learned that it is a rare person indeed who does something for nothing. What, I asked, was Pr. Peaslee getting out of this arrangement? Peaslee congratulated me on my astuteness and confirmed that there was a charge for his services. In return for directing patients towards our practice, Pr. Peaslee and his wife would never be charged for any services provided by either Wilson or myself. This arrangement would extend to the three children as well, but only to the age of their majority. I quickly weighed the financial factors and, finding the arrangement mutually beneficial, I agreed to Peaslee's terms.

Over the next two weeks it became apparent that Wilson and I were a good combination, both in work ethic and style. He was punctual and diligent, clean and careful, thorough, efficient and conscientious. Had it not been for the secret laboratory hidden in the basement beneath my offices I would have had no concerns about Dr. Wilson whatsoever. When, after ten days, it became obvious that the practice of Hartwell and Wilson was inevitable, I knew precautions had to be taken. Once again I used my carpentry skills to full advantage, making sure that the basement itself appeared completely normal, and that the entrance to the sub-basement was completely hidden.

The practice of Doctors Hartwell and Wilson officially began in June of 1906 with a client list that consisted of the cream of the academic community, including Henry Armitage, Laban Shrewsbury, and a score of others. By the spring of 1907 it became clear that we had taken all the patients that we could handle and resigned ourselves to success. Wilson and his young wife moved out of the carriage house and into a small cottage just down the street. In time we became so busy that even Mary could no longer find the time to prepare meals and we had no choice but to take our evening meals with the Peaslees and then finally even had to have our lunches walked over as well. Suddenly, in the course of two years I went from being a man consumed by revenge and doubt, to a happy and successful physician surrounded by an improvised family. Were it not for my secret laboratory, my life would have achieved a complete state of normalcy.

My time in the lab working with my rats had dwindled to a few hours each night, consisting primarily of their feeding and upkeep, with very little time for experimentation. My efforts were not completely abandoned, but they were severely curtailed. This slow cessation of my research into reanimation was the result of a combination of factors, not the least of which was the overwhelming success of my practice. I had made astounding progress in the reanimation of rats, but I had failed miserably in translating that success to humans. This failure had seriously impacted my desire to continue any experiments, whether human or rat. Still, this failure-driven frustration was overshadowed by the results of my two human experiments, which had both ended in the tragic death of an innocent child. Given all of these factors, it was not surprising that my drive to understand the reanimation process had waned. The fires of revenge that had fueled my experiments in reanimation had been doused by failure and disaster, while at the same time my career as a physician was fueling feelings of wondrous accomplishment. This new direction slowly stultified my need to keep my secret laboratory and associated activities, and by the spring of 1908 I resigned myself to the destruction of my reagent, the termination of my rats, and the wholesale dismantling of my secret laboratory. Sadly, or serendipitously depending on your point of view, the dismantling of my laboratory and my research was derailed by events beyond my immediate understanding, but events that would nevertheless cascade through the next two decades of my life.

On the morning of May 14th Pr. Nathaniel Peaslee, my neighbor and the principal architect of my financial success, appeared on my doorstep. He was suffering from a massive headache, which I diagnosed as a migraine and administered an appropriate analgesic. Peaslee also complained of disturbing mental images that had seemed to haunt his dreams of the previous night, but had not dissipated with his waking. These chaotic vistas were coupled with a gnawing sense of alienation or displacement, which he had difficulty expressing. He was, he related, reminded of his childhood when the family dog would gently whine and scratch at the kitchen door, before eventually jumping up and with full force pop the lock on the door and barrel into the house in a clumsy and uncontrolled chaos of paws and fur. While such feelings were unusual for Peaslee, they were not inconsistent with the symptoms of a migraine, the victims of which often suffer delusional feelings of persecution, alienation, paranoia or emotional sensitivity. I made sure that Peaslee had a sufficient supply of painkillers and suggested that if the pain continued that he curtail his daily schedule, and regardless of his condition, visit me in the early evening. When Peaslee left my care, he was feeling somewhat better and appeared fully cognizant of his own condition and whereabouts. Consequently, it came as a great surprise to me when at approximately 11:00, I and Dr. Wilson were summoned to the Peaslee home to attend to the head of the house, who had summarily collapsed while giving a lecture.

Professor Nathaniel Wingate Peaslee was unresponsive to a variety of stimuli, and Wilson and I quickly realized that our friend had somehow slipped into a profound state of unconsciousness. I feared at first that Peaslee's condition had been initiated by an overdose of the analgesic I had given him. Fortunately, I found the bottle unopened. Wilson quickly ran through the other possible causes of coma including diabetic response, stroke or physical trauma, all of which were quickly rejected. Peaslee's condition was consistent with exposure to a high level of carbon dioxide, but the inability to locate a source, and the lack of similar symptoms in his students, made this an unlikely causative agent. In the end we physicians were left with little to do but collect blood and tissue samples and make the professor comfortable.

Mary cleared our appointments for the rest of the day and the next as well. Early in the evening, when it became apparent that there was to be no improvement in our patient's condition, we moved Nathaniel from the master bedroom to a smaller guest room. This allowed Alice some measure of privacy while still permitting Wilson, Mary and I to keep watch on Nathaniel. Mary took the first shift, Wilson the second and me the third, which started at three in the morning. Thus it was that I found myself stumbling through the Peaslee house with a lamp in one hand and a thermos of coffee in the other. I consulted Wilson in the hallway who reported no change in our patient's condition.

As I came into the room I made myself comfortable in the overstuffed chair beside the bed. Setting my thermos down on the nightstand, I adjusted the wick on the lamp so that I could take in the entirety of my comatose patient. His condition had not improved and I saw no course of treatment that could be a benefit to him. In a state of despair I turned to the only thing that came to mind. Perhaps the reagent, not a full dose but a diluted one, would have an effect. I prepared a 10% solution and with care injected Peaslee in his left arm. I laid him back down and watched for a response.

It wasn't long before I saw the eyelids of my patient flutter and then open wide. Almost immediately Peaslee began to speak, and though I was keen to hear his words, I quickly leapt to the door and called for the family. Within moments Alice and the children were gathered around their father and watching with hopeful eyes. Sadly, those hopes were quickly dashed.

As Peaslee spoke it became apparent that he had suffered a significant change in his psychological makeup. He did not recognize, nor could he name, his wife or any of his children. He did not even know his own name. Even his speech patterns were altered; once an elegant speaker, Peaslee's speech was now slow and stunted, reminding me of the cadence of brain-damaged patients I had studied in medical school. Even the way he unconsciously held his face had changed, revealing a psyche that seemed to hold no trace of compassion or empathy for his wife and family. Thoroughly frightened, Alice gathered her children and ushered them out of the room and back to their own beds.

I spent the next several hours alone with my patient, and it was only after the children had left for school that I was joined by Wilson and three other doctors. Over the course of the morning it became apparent that Peaslee was trying desperately to convince us that he was not suffering from any mental lapse whatsoever. Yet with nearly every sentence the man that once was Professor Peaslee provided clear evidence that he was no longer the man I knew. What was particularly upsetting was the curious usage of idioms that were long outdated or lacked clear meaning. At one point he called Mary a "flapper" and during a light-hearted moment suggested that three of us could have some fun during the weekend by "putting on the Ritz". These were terms that held no meaning to us, but would decades later be recalled with terror as they gained actual currency in both England and the United States.

Eventually, Peaslee admitted that he had suffered a complete lapse of his former self and was suffering from a profound case of amnesia. Such a state was readily accepted by his doctors, but Alice and the children expressed extreme discomfort with the situation, generally fearful of the man they once called Father. Recognizing that Peaslee was in need of strict medical care, but also needed to be in familiar surroundings, I moved him and some of his clothes to a spare bedroom in my own house. I had no reservations about taking Peaslee into my own home, for I had known him for many years, and strongly believed that despite his sudden transformation the core of the man, his morals and values, must still be intact. After making my housemate comfortable I retired to my bedroom and, exhausted by the events of the day, quickly fell asleep.

My slumber was disturbed just after midnight by the sound of someone moving about on the first floor of the house. Grabbing my dressing gown, I made my way down the hall and carefully poked my head into the guest bedroom. I was not surprised when I found the room and the bed vacant. I traveled down the stairs and into the kitchen, expecting to find my friend sitting at the table with either a drink or a late night snack. This time I was surprised, for the kitchen was empty, but the door that led to my offices was ajar. Quickening my pace, I found the office lights on, but the doors all securely shut and no trace of Peaslee.

Suddenly a most dreadful thought occurred to me. Cautiously I opened the concealed door to the basement, and to my horror the single bulb that lit the stairwell was on. I dashed down the stairs, only to discover that the secret door to my sub-basement laboratory was wide open. At a full run I took the stairs two at a time and reached the lab in mere seconds. In the full light of my laboratory I found Peaslee standing over my cages peering at my rats, swaying back and forth like a tree in the wind. I took a moment to catch my breath and then, still gasping, inquired firmly what he was doing.

That he had been caught in what was an obviously a private, and even secret, portion of the house seemed to have no impact on Peaslee. With an obvious conceit he responded that he had wanted to see how my work on human longevity and reanimation was proceeding. I laughed and informed him that I had never carried out any experiments on longevity and that my work on reanimation was all but over. The fact that Peaslee had accessed my secret facility and apparently knew about my experiments was puzzling, but frankly of secondary concern.

As I spoke Peaslee shook his head and seemed highly disappointed. "I thought you would be further along, but it seems you have followed too closely in West's footprints. You have made a critical experimental error and it has blinded you to any chance for success."

Insulted and slightly enraged, I professed that I had broken with and even surpassed West's methods and surely had produced a reagent of superior quality. To this Peaslee nodded, but at the same time expressed disdain. "Your reagent is superior, but you have failed to understand how to use it. Like West you continue to think of death as a condition that must be treated, responded to like any other trauma. You have failed to consider the alternative."

I was suddenly intrigued, and it was then that my desire to experiment on the reanimation of the dead returned and was directed into a totally new avenue of research. It was Peaslee, or the man who was once Peaslee, that would guide me now, for it was his words on how death should be treated, not as a trauma but as a disease, were a revelation. For like traumas, diseases can be responded to, attacked with antibiotics and other treatments, dealt with after the fact. However, unlike traumas, disease can also be prevented; infectious agents can be avoided or prepared for. My experiments on rats had been limited to those that I had already euthanized. I had never developed a control group, which in this case would have required the application of the reagent not to dead specimens but rather to living ones. It was a direction I had not considered, but a concept with which I and every other doctor in the western world were completely familiar; it only needed to be applied to the problem of reanimation. Could it be that simple? Could I use the reagent to develop a vaccine against death? Peaslee's strange but strong assurances seemed to imply that such a thing could be. Right then and there, I resigned myself to renewing work on the reagent, and it was then that Professor Nathaniel Wingate Peaslee revealed a syringe full of reagent and, using his right hand, inserted the needle into his arm and injected its contents into his own bloodstream!

I screamed then, for I didn't know how his body would react to a full dose of the concoction that I had created for, and to date had only used on, the dead. I kept screaming as Peaslee revealed a second syringe and walked slowly but deliberately in my direction. As he grasped me by the arm, I struggled desperate to pull away, but I failed. "What are you doing?" I screamed, but Peaslee never responded. With strength I would have thought inhuman I was flipped around, my shirt collar torn down and my hair shoved up.

There was a sudden, sharp pain at the base of my skull, one I recognized from years of practicing my skills at venipuncture. The needle penetrated my skin, and I gasped as I felt the shaft move through my flesh. Peaslee had plunged the syringe into the base of my own skull, and I could feel the pressure of the reagent spreading through my tissues and into my brain. The pain was excruciating but was accompanied by a strange moment of peace and resignation. Eventually, the pain overwhelmed my senses and I fell into merciful unconsciousness.

CHAPTER 5.

THE MAN WHO FORGOT HIMSELF

That I and Peaslee both survived the injection is quite obvious, and my fear-driven collapse was only momentary. When I awoke, Peaslee was laughing at my lack of fortitude, which he said the injection would quickly remedy. He had not, as I had thought, injected us with the reanimation reagent, but rather a derivation of the formula of his own devising. According to Peaslee, the formula would greatly increase stamina and disease resistance, while at the same time decreasing the need for sleep and rest. Given regular doses, the new formula would even extend lifespan well beyond the norm. What's more, Peaslee even offered to supply me with the formula for this concoction, though not without cost.

In the coming years Peaslee planned to travel and study extensively. He would have no time for the routine tasks of maintaining his house and other day-to-day affairs. In exchange for the formula I would serve as his factotum, arranging travel and lodging, and managing certain business affairs. His needs in these areas would be extensive, and he doubted that the funds currently held by the Peaslee family would be sufficient. My first task, therefore, was to make certain investments that would provide both short-term and long-term gains. Enraptured by the lure of the proven reagent, I readily agreed.

The next morning, I mediated a short conversation between Peaslee and his wife in which both agreed that he should move out of the house and take up residence in my home where medical supervision could be constant.

In order to lessen the strain on the children, who were all extremely disturbed by their father's new personality, the family itself would move into her sister's home. The day was therefore spent moving Peaslee's clothing and implements from one house to the other. Personal effects such as photos and the like held no meaning to Peaslee, and were unceremoniously left behind.

With Peaslee in residence and seemingly adjusting to his new persona and lifestyle, my house and time were quickly divided amongst competing projects. The medical offices were as busy as ever and I and Wilson spent our business hours tending to the manifold needs of our patients. Peaslee, whose condition had made him almost entirely unaware of current and historical events, spent his day reading national and international newspapers, and whatever nonfiction books, particularly historical reviews, he could acquire. The basement became Peaslee's refuge and he soon filled it with stacks of periodicals and books from the local library and university. It was from here that he also began a vast campaign of letter writing to addresses both nearby and far across the world. I routinely posted letters to Innsmouth, Kingsport, and Providence, but was just as likely to handle missives being sent to Madrid, London, Hong Kong and Perth. It wasn't long after such letter writing began that similar packets were received as well.

Over the course of the next several weeks, Peaslee and I met with a lawyer named Hand whom we retained to handle any legal issues that the family might face. The first such task was to set up a series of monetary trusts. Peaslee divided the family money into three parts. The first, and largest, was for the upkeep of the family itself—Peaslee's spouse and three children. The second, and smallest, portion was set aside for the future education of the children. The third portion, which amounted to several thousand dollars, was developed into a trust with Peaslee and I as co-executors. Much of this was invested almost immediately in several newly formed companies including the Burmah Oil Company, Briggs and Stratton, and General Motors. Instructions were also made to invest in specific companies that were on the verge of forming, including the Converse Rubber Shoe Company and First Union Bank. The vast majority of these business ventures were newly forming, and I had strong concerns that Peaslee was taking huge risks in such unproven companies. Peaslee chuckled and reminded me that he was after all an economist: who would be more fit than he to make investment decisions?

The month of July found Peaslee becoming more comfortable in his surroundings and confident in his ability to navigate the city on his own. He began a daily walk to the University Library and even began to attend seminars as well as a class on European history. His appearance in the outside world did not go unnoticed, and in September our little clinic began to receive visits from journalists, physicians, researchers and the curious, all desperate to speak to Peaslee, or, as *The Arkham Advertiser* had billed him, "The Man Who Forgot Himself". While Peaslee met with as many visitors as he could, most were quickly dismissed. One exception to this was Travis Marriott of *The Arkham Advertiser*, who would visit almost weekly, and to whom Peaslee had promised to send regular accounts of his observations of the world when he began his travels in the spring.

The other exception was a most curious visit of a wholly unique individual, of the most sober, almost dour, of appearances. He was an elderly gentleman, perhaps an octogenarian who, despite his age, spoke in a voice and language that was almost commanding in nature. He introduced himself as Ephraim Waite, and although he did not state it, I knew that he resided in Innsmouth, a nearby coastal village of ill-repute, as I had seen his name many times amongst both the incoming and outgoing mail. As with all of his visitors, Peaslee greeted the elderly man with a complete lack of visible emotion, though in this case I detected some level of nervous energy that was normally absent from his demeanor. Stranger still, Peaslee had always carried out his previous interviews and discussions in the parlor on the main floor. In this case the man was quickly whisked down the stairs to Peaslee's make-do study, with the door closed quite purposely behind them.

Peaslee never revealed the subject of their conversation to me. Thus my only knowledge of what was discussed for more than three hours was the fragments of sentences that wound their way up through the floorboards like whispers in the wind. Mentioned often was the small village of Dunwich, and a farmer who apparently dwelt there named Whateley. Both the village and the farmer were apparently held in contempt by Waite, though how he had been slighted was unclear. Much also was made of a foreigner who was apparently in league with Whateley; while invoked often, this man's name remained unclear, although it was often associated with a place called Tunguska. I have no other substantive memories of that conversation. Whether that is because the conversation itself was unimportant, I failed to understand any other snippets of discussion, or my memory has faded through time, I cannot say. I do however know that the conversation itself set in motion a series of events that would forever change not only my life, but how I would view the entire world around me.

One day, in the late afternoon, Peaslee bade farewell to his guests and immediately demanded that I arrange to meet with representatives from an engineering firm and a travel agency. I complied and placed several calls arranging appointments for the next day. At Botchner's, a reputable agency used by University staff for both academic and personal excursions, Peaslee negotiated a complex itinerary beginning with his departure from Boston in early August. From this date he would travel extensively throughout Europe including visits to London, Paris, Madrid, Sicily, Rome, Venice and Hungary. His final stop in Europe in March of 1909 was to be Constantinople, from which he would make arrangements for travels into Asia, Africa or the Middle East. Peaslee's travels included dates for lectures and courses at various universities and museums that were immutable and as such required a demanding schedule of trains, hired cars and the occasional boat. Additional expense was incurred when Peaslee revealed that he would be taking significant amounts of baggage with him. Such a revelation shocked me, for I recalled that the man had abandoned all but the essentials of his previous life. Peaslee explained that the majority of his baggage was to be cameras, surveying tools and specialized scientific equipment of his own design.

It was the design and construction of this equipment that was to consume most of Peaslee's remaining time. Entire days and vast quantities of nights were spent in consultation with engineers and metallurgists employed by the firm of Upton and Klein. Peaslee had paid the company a significant sum to have full run of the staff and facilities, including drafting staff, smelters and machine shops. Each day Peaslee would deliver to the drafting team rough sketches of an oddly shaped tool or part, while at the same time delivering the formula for the needed alloys to the metallurgists. By the afternoon of each day both teams would meet the machinists who would then begin the production of a dozen identical copies of the piece. Following the completion of each set, Peaslee would take his original sketch and the drafted versions and summarily destroy them in one of the kilns. Similarly, once manufacture was complete, the set of finished products was removed from the shop and never brought back again. Once, an enterprising draftsman recognized how two distinct pieces were related and casually made a sketch of the process of fitting them together, hypothesizing in the process the additional pieces needed to complete the attachment. On seeing the sketch, Peaslee immediately confiscated it, shredding hours worth of work into a metal bin before setting it ablaze right there in the drafting room. Peaslee then grabbed the man by his collar and hauled him out of the room, ordering him off of the project.

All of this was done at a breakneck speed, so as to allow Peaslee to make his departure date of August the seventh. Peaslee made his departure, leaving for England on the White Star Line steamer *Miskatonic,* and I received my first letter from him toward the end of the month. In London, he had established himself in a small rooming house near the museum at which he was attending a series of lectures on evolutionary theory presented by disciples of Charles Darwin. In addition, he was spending much time studying at the museum itself and amongst a small group of occultists who had, he felt, just grazed some of the universal truths. Included with the letter were several photographs of Peaslee in the museum as well as two with a rather serious-looking gentleman wearing a strange triangular headdress bearing a radiant triangle. On the back of each photo Peaslee had written a brief description of the subject, though given the state of Peaslee's handwriting I quickly abandoned all attempts to decipher such details. As requested, once I was finished with the letter I forwarded it on to Travis Marriott at *The Arkham Advertiser*. Days later I was shocked to open the paper and find one of the photos of Peaslee splashed across the local page beneath a banner that read UNIVERSITY PROFESSOR MEETS WITH WICKEDEST MAN IN THE WORLD. The caption of the article identified the man in the strange headdress as none other than Aleister Crowley, a notorious hedonist and mystic who had on more than one occasion been at odds with authorities both religious and secular. Shocked and amused, I clipped the article, along with several other stories, and posted them to Peaslee's address in London.

The next letter arrived in mid-September and Peaslee was in Paris. He had been amused by Marriott's article and promised to send even more inflammatory pictures when the opportunity arose. In the meanwhile, the rooms he had rented in Montmartre were filled with the most eccentric of persons, including many Americans who had embraced the bohemian lifestyle of the area. Oddly, the enthusiasm the other American guests had for baseball had wormed its way into Peaslee's brain. According to Peaslee, one of the other guests at the hotel had an uncanny ability to predict the outcome of various games. So accurate was the man that he had inspired Peaslee to request of me the placing of a small wager. Toward the end of the month, there was to be a baseball game in New York, and it was on this match that Peaslee wished for me to place a wager in the stunning amount of five hundred dollars. However, the wager was not that the favored New York Giants, nor that the opposing team, the Chicago Cubs, would win, but rather that the game would end in a draw.

You can imagine the laughter when I met the small grey man who acted as a bookmaker to place that bet at odds of fifty to one, and you can imagine the outrage when he came to see me on September 24th. For against all odds, in the bottom of the ninth inning, with the score tied, with two outs, and runners at first and third, the most preposterous thing occurred. The next batter, Al Bridwell, produced a bouncing hit into center field and ran for first. In the meanwhile, Moose McCormick ran from third and easily beat the ball home. Thinking the game over and the national pennant won, Giants fans rushed the field and Fred Merkle tragically aborted his run from first to second and walked into the dugout. Realizing that Merkle had never touched second base, Cubs first baseman Frank Chance ran for second base and called for the ball. Once in possession, Chance got the attention of the nearest umpire and casually touched second base. The umpire, a man by the name of Hank O'Day, had no choice but to call Merkle out and nullify McCormick's winning run. Unable to clear the field of thousands of fans, night fell and the game was called on account of darkness and officially declared a tie. Peaslee's bet had netted him $25,000, and when I asked if I could place a second wager on the outcome of the World Series the little bookmaker walked away without a word.

In late October Peaslee left Paris for Madrid, where he stayed till mid-November. In late December I received a letter from Sicily containing many photos and describing his journey in and around the island, including a climb up Mt. Stromboli, the active volcano just north of the island. In addition to the photos of his trip to the volcano, also included were images of Peaslee on a small trawler. Surrounding him on the expansive deck were a dozen identical mechanical devices the exact purpose of which I could not identify, but which were surely the specialized scientific equipment that Peaslee had spent so many days designing and manufacturing. In the background of the picture were several crates labeled DYNAMITE. Accompanying his letter was a notice to Botchner's Travel Agency that a large quantity of his equipment had been lost during his work in the strait and that his future travels would not require any cargo beyond his few suitcases. Referring to the photo of Peaslee standing amidst those strange devices with their spiraled metallic cones, thick hexagonal shafts and oddly shaped gears, I could only guess how much such equipment could weigh, never mind what it could be used for. Struck by the photo, I removed it and placed it on my desk, and then, as was my habit, I casually placed the rest of Peaslee's correspondence in another envelope and sent it on to *The Arkham Advertiser*.

It was three days later, on the morning of December 29th, that I once again picked up the newspaper and found Peaslee in the headlines. This time the headline beneath the photo of Peaslee on Mount Stromboli read UNIVERSITY PROFESSOR FEARED LOST IN SICILIAN DISASTER. According to the post, in the early morning hours of the previous day a catastrophe had devastated the ancient city of Messina, destroying more than ninety percent of the buildings, including the venerable Cathedral of Messina, and killing an estimated one hundred thousand people. The earthquake and resulting tidal wave had originated just offshore in the small Strait of Messina between Sicily and the Italian mainland. According to geologists, the area had been experiencing small tremors since December the tenth when a minor quake had been detected in the shallows of the strait. Prior to this event there had been no evidence or warning of impending seismic activity for many years.

Out of either fear or dread, I threw the newspaper to the floor and dashed to my desk. There amidst the detritus of bills and correspondence lay the photo of Peaslee on the deck of the hired trawler, surrounded by that strange, suddenly ominous, equipment and the stacks of crates labeled *dynamite*. My hand trembling, I picked the image up and slowly flipped it over. In an instant dread filled my chest and I dropped the print as I panicked and fell to the floor. Crumpled on the carpet, I had no doubts that Peaslee, or the thing that now wore Peaslee's face, was alive. No, there could be no doubt that Peaslee had left Messina and the island well before the devastation had been wrought. My anguish was not for that single man, nor was it for the tens of thousands that had been killed in that horrid catastrophe. My pain was self-directed pity, for it was apparent to me that I played no small part in this disaster. For it was I who had helped Peaslee with his financial affairs, it was I who allowed him to work with the engineers and draftsmen, and it was I who allowed him the freedom to travel from Arkham to Europe and Sicily. I did these things, so I am to blame as much as Peaslee for the deaths of all those people. For without me, Peaslee would have never been on that boat, a boat loaded with strange equipment which my friends at the university identify as a sort of geological boring drill, a boat loaded with dynamite, a boat in the photo on the back of which Peaslee had written *In the Straits of Messina, December Tenth, 1908*!

CHAPTER 6.

A RETURN TO BOLTON

It was early in 1909 when I received yet another letter from Peaslee. After the catastrophic events in Sicily, and my belief that Peaslee had somehow caused the deaths of nearly 100,000 people, I had come to dread any further involvement or communication with the man who had once been my friend and business partner, but who now seemed so inhumanely alien. The small packet of letters and photos had been posted from Constantinople, and included a summary of his time in Rome, as well as instructions for his agents at Botchner's. In March he would depart for India where he would travel north to Nepal and spend some time in the Himalayas. In the summer he would travel to Hong Kong, from which he would travel throughout Asia until at least May of 1910. The address that he provided in Hong Kong I recognized as that of Dr. Hu, one of the many people he had extensively corresponded with.

Unbeknownst to me at the time, Peaslee's Asian adventures were to mark a significant decrease in his correspondence, both in frequency and content. At first I took no notice of the lack of a regular missive, but as January turned to February and then to March I realized that a great burden had been lifted from my spirit, and the general malaise that I had been subjecting myself, Wilson, and our patients to, seemed to retreat. In April, I began a series of simple reanimation experiments, seeking to discover for myself the formula which Peaslee had hinted at by which death could be prevented outright, and although the experiments produced only negative results and my population of rats plummeted, it was fulfilling to once more be working towards some goal.

So content was I with my life and pursuits, that when in June, the inevitable package from Peaslee finally did arrive, it had virtually no impact on my mood whatsoever. Indeed, after skimming through his letters and photos relating his travels in the Himalayas, I forwarded them on to *The Advertiser* without delay. When a few days later the paper ran an article detailing how Peaslee had become only the second westerner to ever gain audience with the Dalai Lama of Tibet, the whole town became alive with tales of Peaslee's adventures, and I was pressed by patients and friends for details, all of which I rebuked, saying that I would not betray the confidence of my patient.

There then came over my life a period of great calm during which I settled into a routine that focused on my own projects. As Peaslee had suggested when he had injected me with his variation on my formula, my need for sleep had decreased and my stamina had increased. Thus it seemed that my practice benefited from my increased time and energy. Soon even Dr. Wilson was commenting on the new sense of verve and dedication that filled my days.

Emboldened by my new outlook on life, I made a bold decision to once more pay a visit to my hated rivals Doctors West and Cain. It was not until mid-July that I found the time to take the short train ride from Arkham up to Bolton to spy on those I blamed for the death of my parents. Once there it was easy to once more secrete myself near the remote farmhouse that served as home to their practice and secret laboratory. It was not long before I learned that West was not in residence, and inquiries revealed that he had been away for several weeks, and was not expected back for several days. Thus I learned that Daniel Cain was alone in the remote farmhouse and therefore vulnerable. It was then that my furtive mind hatched a most devious plan.

Leaving the farmhouse in the late afternoon, I traveled to the far side of Bolton and quickly located a church where I introduced myself to the resident priest. Portraying myself as a man of pious faith, I pleaded with the aging and feeble clergyman to aid me in my quest for penance and charity. Who amongst his flock was both poor and sickly? The priest had no shortage of candidates and soon together we identified a family whose patriarch had recently suffered an accident at the mill and was now racked with pain and fever from the infected wound. I gave the priest a crisp twenty-dollar bill and made it clear that he was to use it to pay for the services of Dr. Cain that very evening.

I made haste back to the cemetery next to West's house and waited for my plan to unfold. It was less than an hour later that a young man made his way down the rutted road and up the walkway to Cain's office door. Moments later the young man reappeared with Cain in tow. Together they climbed into Cain's automobile and soon motored out of sight, leaving only a cloud of dust hanging over the road to mark their passage. As the sputtering sound of the engine faded I slyly made my way from the graveyard to the back of the house.

I used the key I had stolen years ago to enter through the back door, and soon I was once more in the underground laboratory of my nemeses. West's notebooks revealed substantial progress in his goal of reanimation, though it was apparent in his writings that West had become frustrated by a lack of experimental subjects which he amusingly called a "drought". Experimenting instead with animals, West had hit upon a strategy of dividing his reagent into two parts. The first part consisted of a preservative that acted to halt the various processes of decay and place the body in a state of stasis. The second part of the reagent was comprised of three distinct components including a preservative counter-agent, a generous portion of the reanimation reagent, and a chemical stimulant designed to enhance the body's own healing factors. It was a bold and brilliant strategy but one that West had yet little success with, and I could easily see why. West's preservative was itself a problem, for while it acted to halt the processes of decay, it also served to halt normal biochemical processes, processes that had to be restarted, some simultaneously, some sequentially.

As I made my way back to Arkham, my mind was filled with new and exciting possibilities of the most macabre nature. Experiments that would horrify even the most seasoned of vivisectionists were outlined and quickly filed into the recesses of my mind. In retrospect, such thoughts and notions should have outraged my puritan sensibilities, but instead all these years later, I now find myself repulsed by the actions of a young doctor slowly being seduced by the false promises of a forbidden science, and becoming the exact thing he set out to destroy. For it was on that journey back to Arkham that I am certain that I abandoned my quest for vengeance against West and Cain, and decided to become not their nemesis, but their rival. I am sure that it was on that very train ride that I convinced myself that in the proper hands, in my hands, the science of reanimation had value and could be a boon to mankind. It was then that I accepted the inevitable and adopted the mantle of reanimator!

CHAPTER 7.

AN UNINVITED GUEST

In the fall of 1910 my practice and research were interrupted by Peaslee's return. Ostensibly to finalize his divorce, Peaslee stayed only briefly in Arkham, just long enough to meet with his attorneys and review certain documents in the Miskatonic University holdings. We spent several days together and he seemed pleased with the direction of my studies but also disappointed with what he termed retrograde progress, and my devotion to strict heuristical thinking. When I balked at his suggestion that I begin human trials using inmates at the state penitentiary or the factory workers in Bolton, he shook his head and made slanderous comments concerning the short-sightedness of human morality and ethics. With some cajoling, he agreed to place me in contact with someone who could aid in my work and mentor me through the difficult moral crises that would inevitably arise from my work.

In November Peaslee enlisted my aid, and together we set about closing down his expansive and now empty home. Where once a family had lived in this house, now only muslin-covered furnishings stood like specters in a still and silent landscape broken only by the occasional shaft of light that pierced the shuttered windows. On the twentieth, Peaslee locked the doors and handed me the key. Over the course of the next week or so, he told me, several parcels would be arriving and these could be forwarded to the Jekyll Island Club in Georgia where he would be residing through March. I casually asked when he would be returning. With his small valise in hand, the man who was once Nathaniel Wingate Peaslee turned and walked down the street without saying a word.

Peaslee's packages came and I dutifully shipped them back out, never knowing or wanting to know what resided within. Winter and spring were uneventful, and though I made some progress in extending the lives and health of some of my specimens, the treatment regime was only successful in a small percentage of cases and only barely was it distinguishable from no effect whatsoever. Meaning that out of every hundred rats I treated, only one seemed to have a positive reaction and develop an increased metabolism, resistance to disease and injury. Also, by treating some of my older individuals, I had found that my treatment appeared to effectively increase longevity, and had several individuals that had surpassed the control group average lifespan of three years and were now approaching almost four.

In May I received a brief missive from Peaslee, who had relocated to Barcelona, Spain. He was preparing for a summer expedition into the Arabian Desert, to be followed by an exploration of the Congo with the Baronet Arthur Jermyn sometime in the early part of 1912. More importantly, Peaslee informed me that he had encountered a gentleman, a physician, whose work was particularly relevant to the path of research that I was pursuing. What was more, the political situation in Spain following the disastrous Rif War was such that the learned gentleman had good reason to fear for his continued well-being. According to Peaslee, Spain, particularly Barcelona, was a powder keg waiting to explode. Consequently, Peaslee was making arrangements for the individual to be spirited out of the country and to the safety of the United States. Such plans were not as straightforward as they seemed. The man in question suffered from a condition that required specialized medical equipment and attention. Such equipment would arrive shortly, and I was authorized to withdraw what funds I needed to install it in the upper basement where Peaslee himself had once spent so many of his hours. A slight pang of distress welled up in my chest as I realized that I was still Peaslee's to command, but it was overwhelmed by the hope that Peaslee had found for me an ally in my war against death and the men who had caused the death of my parents, my rivals in the science of reanimation Doctors West and Cain.

It was high summer when the first truck arrived and unloaded its cargo of oddly shaped crates and boxes. I had to hire several men to help me move them into the basement, and then begin the prodigious task of opening, unpacking and then disposing of each crate. The contents were staggering, consisting mostly of vast amounts of insulation, large metallic cylinders, radiators, pistons, and valves. Flabbergasted, I quickly accessed the funds needed and hired the firm of Upton and Klein to handle the installation.

The foreman on the project was a young man named Truman who explained to me the actual function of the equipment, which was a modified reverse heat engine. Normally, heat engines convert heat energy into mechanical energy by exploiting the gradient between a heat source and a cold sink to drive a piston. As a byproduct of this process, energy is also transferred from one area to another, creating a cooling effect in one and a heating effect in another. In a reverse heat engine, mechanical energy is applied by a motor and the resultant transfer of energy is used to cool or heat a room. In the case of the current installation, the engine was going to be driven by a small electric motor, and the result would be to cool the basement to under sixty degrees. The transferred heat would be passed to a series of coils, which could be used to provide hot water for the house, but mostly would be sent to a copper pipe buried in the back yard where it would then dissipate into the ground. The insulation, which was to be applied to the walls, floor and ceiling, would help keep the temperature constant.

Installation of the insulation and equipment began in September and continued through October. During this time Wilson and I, along with our patients and staff, endured a barrage of hammering, sawing and digging that made the cabinets rattle and our teeth ache. At one point the construction became so distracting that we stopped receiving patients and began making house calls. Through it all I had to placate Dr. Wilson with the promise that the new equipment would be a boon to our practice. At the same time I had to be sure that none of the workmen discovered the secret passage to the lower basement and the secret laboratory that resided there.

On October 20th I received a telegram from Peaslee who was in Morocco.

Guest to arrive Arkham November 12.
Equipment must be operational
If any delay notify immediately
Rent icehouse similar facility.

Inquiries to the foreman assured me that the equipment would be operational by the required deadline, and sure enough, on November 5th, with little fanfare, the bespectacled engineer called me down to the basement, and with a flick of a single, albeit large, power coupling, the engine hummed to life. In a matter of moments the temperature in the room had noticeably dropped, and within the hour had stabilized at fifty-five degrees Fahrenheit. Ecstatic, I thanked the young man for his expertise and after obtaining from him an emergency phone number in case of the need for urgent repairs, I wrote him a check for the balance of the job, including a hefty bonus for him and his crew.

The morning of November 12, 1911, was bitterly cold; a blast of arctic air had worked its way east, sending temperatures plummeting around the country and setting new records in cities throughout the Midwest. Wilson and I conferred by telephone and agreed to have all of our appointments cancelled. As I puttered about the house trying to stay warm and busy, it dawned on me that the chances of my guest arriving on schedule had been greatly diminished. Just as such thoughts crossed my mind, there came a firm and steady knocking on my door, and as I entered the foyer I could hear the unmistakable sound of a truck engine idling in the street.

I rushed the two delivery men standing on my doorstep inside, sealing the door behind them in a desperate futile attempt to keep the frozen knife of wind from following them. The two were underdressed for the weather and stood in my hallway shivering. Against their weak-willed protests I dragged them into my kitchen and made sure that both had fair helpings of fresh brewed coffee and oatmeal. As we sat over our breakfast, the conversation naturally turned to the beastly weather, and I expressed my amazement that they had chosen to brave such conditions to make deliveries.

The two exchanged furtive, knowing glances which were followed by an awkward silence, finally broken when one of the two explained that all other deliveries had been cancelled, and the other men sent home, that I was to be their only stop of the day, before they too sought the comfort and warmth of their own kitchens. "The foreman, he came over on the boat with that crate, been with it since Barcelona. He says that box stinks, a funny smell that reminds him of his father's funeral home, like the stench of death hidden beneath the scent of flowers and incense. He says whatever is in this box; it makes noises; that something inside it moves. The foreman, he does not like that box, does not want it in the warehouse. He tells Joe and me to bring it to you first, and then go home after."

That my soon-to-be houseguest's belongings could be the source of such creeping fear made me chuckle at first, but then as I thought about it I began to develop a sense of dreadful wonder at what was inside the rough-hewn crate. Given the direction my own studies had taken, as well as Peaslee's equally strange predilections, the disturbed foreman may indeed have had reason for disliking the crate; anything at all could be inside. I could only hope that the contents and their delayed owner would be able to aid me in my research.

Suddenly, uneasy with the presence of the two men in my home, I politely waited for them to finish their meal and then took them down into the basement and showed them where to put the crate. They seemed not to notice that the lower level was much cooler than the rest of the house, and I suppose given the conditions outside, one might expect for the cellar to be colder. Regardless, within a few minutes the rough-hewn wooden box was off the truck and working its way through my front door and foyer.

It was a large oblong crate, some eight feet long, three feet wide and three feet deep. The wood was untreated, pale and cracked. There was a distinct odor, reminiscent of turpentine and insecticide, and I realized that the box had been made from camphorwood. When the shipping foreman said that this box reminded him of his father's funeral home, he was closer to the mark than he knew, for camphor has long been a primary constituent of embalming fluids.

As we moved through the house and down the stairs, it became clear that the crate itself was merely a container for another only slightly smaller object which would shift around inside as the two delivery men negotiated the stairwell. There was the sound of wood sliding against wood, and of metal springs creaking, as well as a hollow sound not unlike that of a can or bucket being struck. In addition to all of this, there was a whirring noise, like that of a distant summer locust or perhaps a watch while it was being wound. While I could understand why such things might disturb an uneducated man, I was utterly fascinated by the potential of the contents of the enigmatic crate.

Once the crate was deposited horizontally on the floor of the basement, I hurried the two delivery men out of my home and rushed back down the stairs. I paused only briefly to consider what I was doing, but so overcome was I with curiosity that soon I was holding a hammer and crowbar in my hand. With ease, the nails with which the long lid was secured to the rest of the box were removed and the lid was off. Excelsior filled the interior, and although such material is usually made of poplar, I was surprised to find that this selection seemed to have been made from sandalwood. With utter joy I began removing the woody packing material, desperate to reveal the prize hidden beneath. It was only after the entirety of the stuffing had been removed that I understood what had been uncovered.

There still inside the crate, but now cleared of packing material, was a massive trunk carved and assembled from ebony. Glossy black and decorated with carved flowers and vines, the object was held in place by a set of four large springs, one on each side, wedged between the ebony trunk and the outer camphorwood crate. At either end, between the spring mechanism and the trunk proper were copper end caps, cases with thick glass windows through which I could see the gears, chains, rods and valves of some kind of mechanical device working away. Both cases were cold to the touch, colder than the surrounding room even, and reminded me much of the equipment recently installed around me.

Fascinated, and wanting to obtain a better look at this strange equipment, I began disassembling the remaining portions of the crate, first loosening each side, then removing the spring before completely removing the panel. Taking care not to damage the trunk, I was able to have the entity of the shipping crate removed, save for the bottom on which it rested, in just under fifteen minutes. The process revealed the entirety of the trunk, which was much like what I had already seen save for some extremely interesting details. On either side, and on both ends, were rounded protrusions which at first seemed to be made of the same ebony wood as the rest, but on closer inspections showed to be lumps of smoky glass or perhaps quartz. Furthermore, several of the rivets on the blackened ring of metal that served to hold these objects in place were not rivets at all, but rather small hidden apertures that appeared to allow for the extrusion or connection of some sort of pipe or hose. Why it would be necessary to conceal such things, and what purpose they served, I could not discern. Nor could I determine how the trunk opened, for while there was a slight but apparent line where the upper and lower portions of the trunk met, there were no hinges and no lock that I could locate.

Stepping back to obtain a new perspective on the object that lay before me, I became aware of a strange whirring sound emanating from the crate, which had not been present before. The noise grew louder, reaching a crescendo that culminated in what was clearly a set of bolts being thrown back. As this sound reverberated through the room it was joined by a hissing noise, and I watched as the upper half of the crate rose slightly and then jerked sideways. As it did so a thick soupy fog, not unlike that given off by dry ice, began to roil out, accumulating around the base of the crate before creeping across the floor. Startled, I stepped back as the fog flowed toward me, but any trepidation on my part was overcome by an intense curiosity as to the contents of the now fully opened crate.

As I cautiously moved forward, the fog that now engulfed the entire floor cut at my ankles with claws made of ice, and each step toward the crate was noticeably colder. By the time I reached the trunk I had tucked my hands underneath my arms, and was noticeably shivering as the fog swirled around me. My forward progression reversed itself as I leaped back, startled as something familiar but wholly unexpected rose up out of the trunk and gripped the side. It was a man's hand, clad in a fine black leather glove, and as I watched, the hand was joined by its partner, and up out of the fog-laden sepulcher climbed the unmistakable form of a man.

He was of less than average height, and well built, with neatly kept iron-grey hair and matching beard. His eyes were dark, and his skin had that rustic olive complexion so common amongst those of Celtiberian origin, though in places it held a paler color and I thought immediately that he must be in the early stages of vitiligo. His aquiline nose hinted at a touch of Moorish ancestry, and held a pair of antique pince-nez glasses. He was well dressed, wearing a suit of grey silk with a white shirt and highly polished leather shoes. If I had met him on the street I would have thought him the most respectable of gentlemen. But as he made his way out of the coffin, for now I could see that it could be nothing else, I could not see the gentleman, but only a figure of undying horror pulled from my more salacious readings, Lord Ruthven from Polidori's *The Vampyre*. How ironic that I should draw such a connection in that moment of stress, and how tragic that in that moment I did not act, but instead, like Polidori's oath-bound protagonist, I kept my word, though it damned me, and welcomed this creature into my home.

It spoke English with a genteel and soft-spoken manner that betrayed a kind of aristocratic education. "You must be Dr. Hartwell. I was told by Peaslee that I would be your guest. That you and I shared a mutual interest. In life and perhaps—ummm—in death as well. Like yourself, I am a physician, trained in the finest academies of Madrid and Valencia, and most recently a resident of Barcelona. My name is Dr. Rafael Carlos Garcia Muñoz."

Unbidden, he reached out and took my hand, grasping it with his own, while at the same time pulling me forward and clasping the other arm around me in a typical European type of greeting. Later, apologizing, I would say that it was the sudden shock of his appearance, that I was unprepared for such a dramatic entrance. That the theatrics of the moment combined with the overwhelming odors of camphor, sandalwood and other exotic aromatics were the preferable explanation for my negative reaction to the embrace of Dr. Muñoz. It would not do for me to tell the truth, to let him know that I, a trained physician, one who has dabbled in the forbidden science of reanimation, was so horrified, no, terrified, by his grip that I almost immediately fell into unconsciousness. But that was the truth. It was not the drama of the moment nor the weird aromas that drove me to the floor, but rather the enfolding act itself, for as we embraced I was provided proof that reanimation was more than just a dream, that full restoration of all faculties was not only possible, but had already been achieved. For in that instant we touched, I discovered that Dr. Rafael Muñoz was cold, bitterly cold, and colder than any live man had a right to be. That my overwhelmed, prosaic brain allowed me a brief moment of oblivion was perhaps the most merciful of all things.

Chapter 8.

The Facts in the Case of Dr. Rafael Muñoz

It was in late 1911 that I first met Dr. Rafael Carlos Garcia Muñoz, and though my initial reaction was a deep-seated revulsion, that feeling faded rapidly, the result mostly of his cordial and most pleasant manner. He was an animated conversationalist, expounding fervently on any subject that caught his fancy, including his current unfortunate medical condition, which he masked with exotic spices and perfumes. The origin of that condition was also a frequent topic of discussion, for he had been unable to successfully reproduce the exact manner in which it had come about, but still believed that if he could determine a cause, some resolution was possible.

A child of privilege, he and his constant companion Esteban Torres had graduated from the prestigious *Universitat de Valencia* with honors in 1878, and the two set up a medical practice in Barcelona, which thrived, making both quite comfortable. Indeed, after twenty-five years, the two gentlemen, both confirmed bachelors, retired from service to lecture and pursue certain avenues of research in disease prevention. Their course of research and the politics of the Spanish Empire led them in 1903 to set up a small facility on an island off the coast of the African colony of Guinea. A mountainous outcropping, Fernando Po was ruled by a smattering of Europeans, and populated by a mixture of emancipated black Cubans and mestizos, and the dominant Bubi tribe, as well as a sprinkling of Nigerians, Cameroons,

Chinese and Indians. Most of the population lived in the main city of Port Clarence which was surrounded by plantations of palms and cocoa. The interior of the island was a mountainous jungle rumored to be full of strange animals and a lost city.

Muñoz and Torres operated a rough clinic and laboratory serving the outlying plantations and the port as well. Together the two men made great advances in understanding the pathology and treatment of tropical diseases, as well as several social ailments common to the crews of ocean-going traders. They were aided in their venture by a capable young German by the name of Englehorn. While in port, the young seaman had been unfortunate enough to contract yellow fever and his captain had abandoned him on the docks where he was found and nursed back to health by the two doctors. Englehorn's ability to handle boats was matched by his aptitude for languages, and both skills served the clinic and its patients well. By early 1905 the reputation of the trio began to bring patients not only from the island, but from the mainland as well. But to hear Muñoz tell it, it is the nature of all things to end, and it was on a fateful January evening that the first portents of the coming disaster were to make their presence known.

The dry season had been drier than usual, and the wet season rains were months away. Reports from the mainland of fires on the farms and grasslands, and even in the jungle, were common. On occasion the wind coming across the sea brought a sickly sweet smell and traces of ash would fall from the sky. The islanders—regardless of caste—grew restless and knew that tragedy was in the wind. So it came as no surprise one May evening that when the sun set in the west, it only served to reveal a ruddy glow coming from the distant mainland. Wireless dispatches soon confirmed the worst of fears; an inferno was rampaging across the mainland, spreading through grasslands, farms, villages and even into the deep jungle. Fueled by the dry conditions and unhampered by any attempts to control it, the fire had driven thousands of refugees to the coast.

The next day as the morning winds brought the heat and the stench of smoke to Fernando Po the residents awoke to find themselves staring at a most terrifying sight. Fed by the fire, great black clouds of ash were slowly creeping across the sky toward the small island. Lightning flashed within these unnaturally dark formations, causing the more superstitious to panic, and the more practical to gather up children and livestock. Perhaps most damnable was the slow pace at which the storm came towards them, like a cat stalking a terrified bird; the time only served to magnify the fear that ran rampant through the port. Long-simmering disagreements boiled over into heated arguments and soon the clinic was overwhelmed with injuries inflicted by domestic squabbles, bar fights and the like. When the storm finally came, a hot windy rain full of grey ash and soot, it was anticlimactic. The good people of the island did more harm than the storm itself, and those who had kept their heads were more than relieved. But this was only the first portent of things to come.

That evening, as the sun set and the rains washed the last of the ash from the clearing sky, the population of the small island was witness to the formation of yet another massive cloud roiling over from the mainland. Unlike the previous storm, this one moved quickly and seemed to spawn strange curvilinear formations, like tentacles or tendrils that would reach out and then collapse back into the main body. There was a noise as well, a high-pitched hum like that of a mosquito but infinitely louder. As the strange cloud moved closer, it was apparent that this was no natural atmospheric phenomenon, and once more people began retreating into the safety of their homes.

The sound of the storm rolling across the island was unusual. There was no wind to speak of, but the high-pitched whining hum had grown louder and was joined by a strange periodic squealing, as well as the sound of debris smashing through the upper branches of trees and thudding and skittering onto roofs. To Muñoz it sounded as if small coconuts were falling from the sky. Driven by an unquenchable curiosity, Muñoz, Torres, and their young companion went to the main door of their clinic and ever so slowly and carefully cracked it open.

There was no storm. The sky was blotted out, and the air was full of things, black things the size of a man's fist, swarming like locusts. It took a moment for the three men to realize what they were looking at, but as one of the flying, furry things careened past them, slamming against the wall, they all were made quite aware of what had come for them. Either threatened by the fire directly or by the sudden loss of food, the nocturnal predators that had once dwelt in the caves that dotted the mainland had been driven out, and swarmed to the nearest unaffected areas such as the coastal islands in search of new homes and food. Bats numbering in the hundreds of thousands had invaded Fernando Po.

Slamming the door shut, Muñoz and Torres slumped into chairs, and after a brief moment of silence began talking about abandoning the clinic and fleeing the island. Young Englehorn protested, suggesting that they should stay and help fight the invaders, but Torres shook his head no. The island, he said, was going to be ravaged by a disease which it was already too late to do anything about. Bats were the primary carriers of rabies and the sudden influx of this many of the small predators onto the island made an outbreak probable. Even if people could be persuaded to avoid contact with the bats, the dogs, cats, livestock and wild animals were going to become infected. Transmission to humans on a large scale was inevitable. The epidemic would overwhelm the cities and villages; only remote outposts would remain unscathed, and only then if ruthless vigilance against possible carriers was enforced.

That night, cowering behind the shuttered windows and bolted doors, the three formulated a plan to leave the island. They would steal a boat, something small enough for them to handle alone, stock it with provisions and then sail north hugging the coast to the Canary Islands and then catch a freighter back to Spain. It was a beautifully optimistic plan.

The morning came without incident, and although they were tired the plan was put into action. Englehorn went down to the harbor to identify likely candidates, while Muñoz packed up supplies and Torres went to various shops to buy necessities. By mid-morning Torres had returned to find Muñoz completely swamped by patients, all of whom were suffering from bat bites or scrapes. Driven by their Hippocratic Oath, the two doctors labored through the day and into the night, treating more than a hundred patients, a great number of whom were bitten by bats and were suffering from fever, nausea and body aches. This was of particular concern as these were symptoms of rabies, but the normal incubation for that disease was two to twelve weeks. The development of symptoms in less than twelve hours was unprecedented and worrisome. The three agreed that if they were to leave, it should be before dawn, and Englehorn began ferrying supplies down to the harbor while the two doctors tried for some well-deserved rest.

It was just after four o'clock in the morning when Englehorn woke the two doctors and the three men stole into the streets of the town. The moon was full and bright, allowing them some light by which to find their way across the dozens of city blocks that separated them from the waterfront. Though both doctors were in their fifties they moved quickly, hugging the walls, ducking in and out of doorways, dashing across streets, all in a desperate attempt to avoid being seen. The reason for this secrecy was not clear, but since the influx of infected patients, the doctors had developed an unnatural fear of the residents of Port Clarence, and they felt the less contact they had, the better. Sadly, to their horror, they had good reason for such fears.

Skulking across the next street, the intrepid trio witnessed the most puzzling of sights. There in the middle of the road, just yards from the intersection, was a congregation of five men huddled together over a pile of cloth bags. The men were working vigorously, tearing at the contents of the bags with a manic fervor that made Muñoz uncomfortable. Whatever was in the bags was apparently edible, for the men were taking great wet globs of the stuff and greedily stuffing it into their mouths.

Englehorn motioned for them to be quiet, and together, shepherded by the young sailor, they dashed across the intersection towards the waiting shadows on the other side. The crossing brought them even closer to the huddled men and their feast, and Muñoz paused as he came to understand what it was that was happening in the streets of the fever-wracked town. The bags weren't bags at all. Englehorn grabbed him by his shirt and dragged him back into motion.

In the safety of the shadows Muñoz collapsed and tried to stammer out what he thought he saw. "Those men, they were eating, they were eating another..." But Englehorn forcefully cut him off.

"It was a dog," he said. "They were eating a dog." The doctor was forced to his feet. "Pray it was a dog."

Muñoz ran, for he knew that it wasn't a dog. The shapes that they had mistaken for cloth bags were a shirt and a pair of pants, and the dripping chunk that one of the men had ripped from the immobile shape had passed into the light of the moon long enough for Muñoz to see the four fingers and thumb of a disembodied hand, before it was carried upward and shoved into the hungry mouth of the man who had torn it free.

A block further and the three men stopped to rest in the shelter of a recessed doorway. At first no one spoke, but finally Torres broke the silence and whispered forth his concerns. The basis for his worry was the rapid onset of symptoms, which suggested that the infection was not rabies, but rather something else, closely related, that engendered a similar set of reactions. There were references, he said, in the ancient medical texts, particularly Ibn Sina's *Al-Qanun fi al-Tibb*, of whole towns succumbing to plagues of devouring violence that could only be stopped by beheading the infected. Such outbreaks were rare and the ancient authorities often resorted to the wholesale burning of villages, with villagers imprisoned within, to bring the outbreak to an end. What was happening in Port Clarence could be the beginning of just such an event. If such a disease had come to Fernando Po, then destruction by fire of the town and all of its inhabitants might be the only way to bring an end to it.

With such a suggestion Muñoz felt compelled to get out of the town as soon as possible, and without taking proper precautions stepped out of the doorway and into the street. There was a man waiting for him; at least he used to be a man. Whatever disease had infected him had transformed him into a simian beast, stumbling down the street, drooling incessantly. He fell upon Muñoz like a wolf, tearing at him with claw-like hands and knocking him to the ground. There was a stench about him, not unlike sour milk or strong cheese, and his flesh was cold. With Muñoz pinned to the ground, the thing thrust its face toward his throat, mouth and teeth gnashing violently, clearly intent on ripping the poor doctor's throat open. Muñoz felt the cold wretched mouth close down on his neck, felt the teeth grasp the flesh, and felt the canines pinch then pierce the skin. There was a brief moment of fear-mitigated pain, and then it was gone. Muñoz felt nothing. Torres and Englehorn had pulled the thing off of him, and as Torres helped Muñoz to his feet, the young sailor was busy kicking the infected attacker in the head.

Someone was screaming, and by the time Muñoz realized that the horrible sound was coming from him, it was too late. As Muñoz grew silent, and Englehorn finished smashing in the skull of his attacker, the town grew suddenly quiet, as if in anticipation of a coming storm. The three men stood there, enthralled by the silence, hypnotized by it, and then it was gone. From every side street monstrous shapes shambled into view, moaning and screaming, hobbling toward their position slowly but inevitably. Shocked by the dozens of things that suddenly lurched toward them, Muñoz, Torres and Englehorn turned and ran as fast as they could, knowing that the harbor was just a few short blocks away.

As they ran, the infected poured toward them. Thankfully the transformed citizens of Port Clarence were relatively slow-moving, and dodging them was surprisingly easy. But as each individual was avoided, it merely fell in behind them, joining the shambling mob that was relentlessly trailing them.

Muñoz cast a glance backwards, and seeing the horde of villagers, many of whom he knew as either patients or neighbors, loping after him with empty black eyes, greedy hands and gnashing teeth, tears of compassion and regret came to his eyes.

Coming to the waterfront, they rounded the corner, following Englehorn down the shell rock road that bordered the small bay. The tide was in, and by the light of the moon Muñoz could see the small ship that Englehorn had selected for the trip. It wasn't much to look at, and it had seen better days, but the seaman had assured them that it was more than up to the task. All eyes must have been on the two-mast sloop, for without any warning the desperate trio plowed headlong into a large foreboding shape that had somehow blocked their path. Knocked to the ground, the two doctors and their assistant scrambled to regain their footing, fully prepared to defend themselves against the impending attack.

It came as quite a surprise when the oversized shape took a few puffs from a pipe and in the most genteel of voices inquired, "What's all this running about in the dark? A man could get himself hurt doing that." As one, the three men let out a sigh of relief. The man who had blocked their way was a well known Dane by the name of Larsen who was universally referred to as Bull, both for his size and the manner in which he captained his steam freighter *Adventura*. Under normal circumstances, such an encounter would have been something to avoid, but given the mob of fever crazed cannibals pursuing them, Bull was the perfect individual to run into.

Between attempts to catch their breath, the three tried to explain the situation to the incredulous Dane, but there is nothing like actually seeing a horde of bloodthirsty monsters rush around the corner to drive home the gravity of the issue. Even Bull was taken aback by the appearance of the ravenous things, and after selecting a particularly heavy boat hook, he herded the three men onward and followed closely behind. Putting some distance between themselves and the pursuing throng, Englehorn paused at the site of his hidden cache of supplies.

Bull grabbed a large rucksack at random and kept moving. "Grab what you can carry, men. *Adventura* was set to leave at dawn, and she should have a fine head of steam by now. We'll put some distance between us and this mob." Englehorn, Torres and Muñoz followed suit, though Muñoz was careful to grab the bag full of medical supplies. Less than a hundred yards further and the team was running up the gangplank that led to Larsen's ship.

Once they were all onboard, Bull and Englehorn pulled the walkway up, effectively blocking any easy way of access from the land to the boat. As the degenerate hordes made their way onto the dock below, Bull violently rang a brass bell located near the door to the wheel cabin. As he did so, the crew of the *Adventura* crawled onto the deck like ants out of a rotten tree. Bull shouted orders which were obeyed without question or hesitation, or nearly so. One mate, ordered to cut the dock lines rather than untie them, caught sight of the things that were clamoring about below and froze, out of either fear or confusion. Either way, Bull rapped him swiftly against the back of the head and told him that unless he moved he would be joining the dock-side rabble. In seconds the bow lines were cut and the stunned man, whom Bull called Allnut, was coiling the remaining rope. Muñoz staggered as the ship lurched forward and the bow swung out away from the berth. The stern slammed into a piling hard, causing the dock to split and splinter, tossing the monstrous horde into the water and against the hull of the ship. Several unfortunates, caught between the remaining piling and the boat itself, were screaming in agony as the stern of the *Adventura* ratcheted forward and crushed the men, popping their heads like grapes.

When Allnut finished, he and Bull conferred briefly, casting glances toward the two doctors as they did so. After a moment or two of consideration, Allnut nodded to his captain and then shambled down the rail to where the three men were trying to stay out of the way. He addressed Englehorn first, "Captain's not fond of Germans, and I can't say that I am either." His accent revealed him as a Brit. He pulled a fat greasy cigar out of a shirt pocket. "But given that we have little choice in the matter, he says that you can bunk up with the crew, and if you work out there may be a space for you." A quick flip of a match and he lit the cigar and took a long drag. "Doctors, we have an empty hold you can use as a cabin; it's not much, but considering the alternative." He cast a glance over at the mob milling around on the dock.

Torres nodded his understanding. "We are appreciative of the situation sir, and you can relay our thanks to Captain Larsen. If we could ask, what is our destination?"

Allnut turned to stare at Port Clarence. The sun had broken to the east, and the dawn revealed a city devastated. Smoke billowed from four different fires, and crowds of the infected dotted the dock and the shoreline. Somewhere a church bell rang. "Not that it makes a difference, but we're loaded with cocoa, and headed for ad-Dar al-Bay."

Englehorn asked, "Where?"

The gruff sailor adjusted the handkerchief that he wore around his neck and waved for them to follow him. "Ad-Dar al-Bay," he repeated. "It's a city in Morocco; you might know it as Casablanca." With that the mate led them below deck and to their quarters.

Once Englehorn and Allnut had departed, the two doctors made it their first priority to clean and suture Muñoz's wounded neck. Torres treated the area with alcohol as a preventative for infection, and then while Muñoz bit down on a leather belt, closed up the wound with some silk thread from his medical kit. After they were done, the two men stripped and tossed all their clothes out the porthole. They scrubbed themselves as best they could with rubbing alcohol, and then changed into clean clothes from one of the packs. Muñoz had lost a significant amount of blood and was extremely tired. Torres forced him to drink several glasses of water before injecting him with a sedative, a new drug at the time from Bayer called Luminal. After that Muñoz fell into a deep sleep.

When Muñoz next regained consciousness, it was evening and he was ravenously hungry. Thankfully Englehorn had been kind enough to bring the doctors an evening meal, a stew of some kind, salty with a meat that was tough and reminded Muñoz of both chicken and crab. Englehorn said one of the mates had shot a crocodile and the ship's cook was busy smoking the flesh, but the organs had been turned into the stew.

The men asked their young friend about the ship, which the sailor was happy to report seemed well run and amicable. The captain was a tough man, who didn't tolerate laziness or drinking. Men under his command were expected to work for their pay, but the wage was fair and the crew seemed to at least respect the man. Allnut was the first mate, but he spent most of his time in the engine room working on various pieces of equipment. Englehorn had been assigned the duties of cabin boy, cleaning up after the captain and crew, and running menial errands for whoever needed them. That he was more than qualified for the position, and was capable of much more, made no difference to Bull, and the captain made it clear that the young man was not to take on any jobs other than those he was assigned.

As for their former home, ships and soldiers had been dispatched from the mainland, and there were radio reports of intense fighting and shelling.

A blockade had been set up, effectively placing the island under quarantine. With this news all three agreed that they had made the right decision, but secretly Muñoz knew that Torres had doubts, that the *Adventura* could be a plague ship, and that the most likely carrier on the entire boat was Muñoz himself. Determined to protect the rest of the crew, as well as the next port of call from infection, Torres decided to quarantine Muñoz and keep close tabs on the rest of the ship.

Over the next several days Muñoz's wound healed nicely, but he began to ache at his joints and he had a low fever. Fearing that he might succumb to the virulent frenzy that swept through Port Clarence, Torres kept his partner sedated using the Luminal liberally. The rest of the crew showed no sign of medical problems, save for those normally associated with running a ship, and Torres soon ingratiated himself with the men by tending to their various wounds and injuries as best he could. Though the crew had grown comfortable with their two passengers, the captain had concerns and Muñoz was unfortunate enough to overhear a conversation between Torres and Allnut that warned the doctor that if Muñoz began to exhibit any signs of carrying the disease, he would put the two men in a lifeboat and set them adrift. Torres assured Allnut that Muñoz's symptoms weren't a sign of infection, but rather the result of an uncontrolled case of malaria. The lie seemed to satisfy the gruff first mate, but Muñoz knew the truth: the Luminal may have slowed its progress, but there was no doubt he was infected.

It was under these conditions that the two doctors hit upon an idea as to how to cure Muñoz. Using the Luminal, Muñoz would be placed in a deep state of unconsciousness, and then he would be alternatively immersed in hot and cold water for extended periods. It was hoped that the unconscious state would protect the brain from pain, while the hot and cold baths would act to kill whatever pathogen caused the disease, much like the process of pasteurization. It was a risky procedure, but one Torres thought he could handle on his own, using the equipment at hand.

What happened to Muñoz following the injection, Muñoz himself could not say, but Torres recorded the treatment in detail in his journal. After assuring himself that the subject was unconscious and failed to react to stimuli, Torres immersed the patient into a bath of seawater. Though not anywhere near freezing, the seawater was cold enough to slowly drop body temperature. After an hour, Muñoz's body began to show the early signs of hypothermia, but Torres did nothing and let the body drop even colder, well below what was normally considered safe. Then he pulled the body from the tub and slid it into another tub, this one filled with water at extremely high temperatures, near boiling. While immersed in this bath, Muñoz's head was wrapped with cool wet towels. After twenty minutes in the hot bath, Muñoz's body temperature began to rise above a safe level, and Torres plunged him back into the cold water tub. This alternating process of cold and hot water treatments was repeated four times in about five hours. Afterwards, Torres wrapped the body in moist bandages and made sure the man remained unconscious for another twenty hours.

The next day, Muñoz awoke feeling tired but relatively pain-free. He had no fever and it appeared that the treatment, as radical as it was, had been successful. The only issue was a lingering odor of spoiled milk, which seemed to come directly from his skin. Torres theorized that the moist bandages had contributed to a dermal yeast infection. Regardless, there was no trace of infection, and Muñoz was soon up on deck and taking in the sea air.

A day later they were in Casablanca. There was some concern amongst authorities that they had come from Port Clarence. Apparently the entire city had been burned to the ground with all inhabitants lost. Captain Larsen eased these concerns with a forged log book showing that they had left a week earlier than the outbreak, and a hefty bribe to the port master. Young Englehorn had performed his duties with distinction and was offered a permanent berth on the *Adventura* which he happily accepted. Allnut, the gruff first mate, made arrangements for the two doctors on a freighter heading to Spain, at Captain Larsen's expense. The two doctors spent one last night with the *Adventura* and then transferred their meager belongings to the *Susan B. Jennings*. Muñoz never saw Englehorn, Captain Bull Larsen, or Allnut ever again.

The trip to Spain was uneventful, though the doctors spent considerable funds preparing for their sudden return to Barcelona. Winter still gripped the region, and the two doctors had little in the way of protective clothing. Although, oddly, Muñoz seemed not to be bothered by the chilly breezes that blew across the Mediterranean Sea. Indeed, if anything, he was more comfortable at temperatures that would make other men shiver. This strange adaptation to a cooler climate, coupled with the milky odor, were the only discernable after-effects of the infection and subsequent treatment. Such aberrations seemed a small price to pay for survival.

It was not until March of 1905 that the true nature of Muñoz's transformation began to become clear. That was the day that Muñoz awoke and had the greatest of difficulty speaking. It could be done, but only with intense concentration, and the result was a muted, whispering lilt that was at best a parody of his previous voice. To Torres's surprise, the cause was rudimentary: Muñoz's lungs were no longer functioning in any appreciable manner; indeed, the volume of air moving in and out of Muñoz's mouth was fully less than a tenth that of a normal man. A full examination revealed a similar situation with his heart and circulation. All of the man's vital signs were severely depressed, and were it not for the fact that he was moving and talking, Torres would have considered the man near death.

Both doctors agreed that examination of the metabolic processes that allowed Muñoz to function without significant respiration or cardiac activity was needed, and so the two embarked on a battery of examinations and analyses that put their medical and scientific skills to the ultimate test. In the end it came down to the odor that still originated from Muñoz. The stench of spoiled milk had never faded and was a clue to the strange transformation that had altered his physiology. For Muñoz's metabolism had suffered a radical change; instead of functioning in a primarily aerobic manner, the tissues of his body had become anaerobic, not unlike yeast cultures. This was the source of the sour odor that came from Muñoz, and also explained his comfort at cooler temperatures.

It was an amazing discovery, but it was not without its negative connotations. His immune system had slowed as well, and as a result, bacterial colonies had begun to thrive. The cold was keeping these things from overwhelming him, but routine cleansings of the intestinal tract and the abdominal cavity were going to be required to keep things in check. Additionally, certain specialized cells seemed to have died out altogether, including sweat glands, hair follicles and the cuticles of his fingers and toes. It seemed unavoidable; the bat-borne virus had infected Dr. Rafael Carlos Garcia Muñoz and radically altered the metabolism of his body. Only Torres's treatment had protected the brain, preventing Muñoz from suffering damage from the extreme fever, and becoming a mindless cannibal like those that had ravaged Port Clarence.

Such a finding was astounding, and the two researchers spent several marathon days carrying out experiments and documenting their results without sleep. Thus when Torres collapsed and Muñoz was forced to carry the poor man to his bed, it did not immediately cause concern. But a day later when

Torres began to complain of joint pain and a fever, Muñoz became suspicious. By that afternoon Muñoz had confirmed that Torres had somehow contracted the fever and was now manifesting symptoms. He broke the news as gently as he could to his oldest and dearest friend, and the two spent some time commiserating and deciding on a course of action.

It was agreed that Muñoz would repeat the treatment of Luminal combined with cold and hot water immersions. The procedure would be significantly easier as cold water and ice were readily available. Together they outlined the procedure, prepared the syringe, and baths, and scheduled when the transfers would occur. No detail of the procedure was left to chance, and the notes that Torres had made were consulted frequently. Despite such preparations, when the time came neither man was fully prepared to carry out the procedure, and Muñoz's hand shook as he injected his friend with a dose of Luminal.

Over the next five hours Muñoz labored over the body of his friend, transferring it from cold water bath to hot water both and then back again. Over and over again Muñoz dragged his friend from one extreme to another, always careful to follow the schedule the two had laid out. Time crawled slowly, and on more than one occasion Muñoz despaired that his friend might not respond to the treatment, but always he followed the directions and made sure the procedure was completed. Afterwards, with his friend wrapped in bandages and left in his bed, Muñoz collapsed in exhaustion, disturbed only by the fear that Torres would not survive the treatment.

It was twenty hours that Muñoz had to wait, twenty long impatient hours in which Muñoz could do nothing for his friend but watch and wait. He slept for the first half, and then prepared and ate a modest meal. With five hours to go, it dawned on Muñoz that Torres would be famished when he awoke, that they should celebrate, that he should prepare a feast. So the remaining hours were spent gathering the ingredients and combining them in the most spectacular of ways. He made ropa viejo, picadillo, and arroz con pollo with a black bean sauce. He prepared madeira and bought an exquisitely delicate flan. He brought out the fine silver, the best crystal, and plates they only used for special occasions, matched with silk linens. With an hour left he lit the candles and left to awaken his friend, carrying with him a plate of bread, cheese and a large knife.

It had been nearly twenty hours, and Torres had yet to show any sign of awakening. Even as Muñoz unwrapped the bandages, his friend lay still and silent, and Muñoz began to fear the worst. His fear grew as the bandages parted, revealing the grey, still flesh of the body below. Tears filled his eyes as the stiffness in the limbs hinted at the rigor so commonly associated with death. In despair, Muñoz collapsed at the side of the bed and wept. So deep was his sadness that it was only when Torres sat fully upright that Muñoz noticed that his friend was moving.

Tears of anguish turned to tears of joy, and with unbridled zeal Muñoz embraced Torres, cradling the man's head against his own. But for all of Muñoz's elation, for all of his happiness, for all his joy, Torres sat as still as stone, and as silent as the night ocean. He said nothing and his breast did not rise, for he did not breathe. Slowly Muñoz ceased his uncontrolled outburst, and came to realize that the body of his friend was warmer than it should have been; in fact it was more than warm, it was hot, sweltering, feverish.

With a start Muñoz drew back. The doctor looked into the face of his friend, and he saw the eyes, those dark, hollow empty eyes. All trace of his friend was gone, forced out by the infection that brought only rage and pain. In a last desperate gesture Muñoz reached out and placed his hand ever so gently against Torres's cheek. It rested there for a moment, and for a second there was a glint of something that might have been recognition. Torres reached out and placed a hand on Muñoz's wrist. A smile broke on Muñoz's face as hope gave way to belief and then once more a hint of joy. It was just as that joy began to blossom that Torres lunged forward, pushing Muñoz to the floor.

Torres rose up off the bed, and as he did so his jaws opened wide in a great maw of gnashing, ravaging teeth and blood and spittle. He roared as he came up off the bed. Like a great beast hungering for prey, Torres slavered forward, forcing Muñoz to scramble back across the floor until he was pinned against the dresser. Torres—or what was once Torres—stalked toward the cowering Muñoz, slowly and methodically. It gave Muñoz more time, and as he pulled back, the tray of bread and cheese tumbled down off the dresser and onto the floor. With it came the knife; the steel blade shone like a star as it lay there on the floor, calling out to him. With a swift fluid motion the blade was in his hand and a moment later he was on his feet. Torres lunged, but Muñoz slipped to the side, letting the thing that was once his friend slam into the dresser and the wall as well. Unaffected, the creature spun around and searched the room for its prey. There was a flash of brilliant steel, a lightning strike that cut across the thing's throat, leaving a trail of crimson in its wake. Blood erupted from a gash in the Torres-thing's neck and flowed like a torrent across its chest. Torres staggered back and Muñoz took the opportunity to strike again. A second gash, a third, and Torres collapsed backwards onto the dresser.

Hours later, as Muñoz fed pieces of the body into the flames, there were tears in his eyes. His friend of forty years was dead, killed by his own hand, and as much as he would want to, there was no time to mourn. The body was infectious, it had to be destroyed, and the rest of the house had to be cleaned as well. Blood coated the floor of the bedroom, and it took hours to mop up and feed the rags into the flames. But it was the last piece that Muñoz held onto that brought the grieving doctor to his knees. He held it at a distance, the thing that he had hacked off of the body of his friend, and with care he said his goodbyes and tossed the severed head into the flames. He watched for a moment, to assure himself that it was well into the blaze, and then despite all of his reservations he walked away, unable to watch as the still undead head of his friend mouthed a silent, raging scream as the fire consumed the last traces of Dr. Esteban Torres.

CHAPTER 9.

THE MISKATONIC VALLEY MEDICAL SOCIETY

With the arrival of Dr. Muñoz I was faced with a most uncomfortable dilemma. The practice that I shared with Dr. Wilson still occupied the offices that were essentially located just upstairs of Muñoz's refrigerated quarters, and it was unlikely that I would be able to keep his presence secret for very long. Thankfully, the bitter cold winter allowed Muñoz to leave the basement apartment and thus avoid raising any suspicions concerning his condition. I introduced him as a distant maternal uncle, and he took to this role with some fervor and soon, even in private, Muñoz would refer to me as his "brilliant nephew".

Those first few months, we devoted ourselves to familiarizing him with the customs and fashions of Arkham. To this end we attended many social and academic events, which Muñoz thrilled at, and soon we were regular attendees at the weekly Miskatonic Valley Medical Society Lectures. At these semi-formal affairs, visiting physicians and researchers would give perfunctory talks on various aspects of clinical or experimental facets of medicine or surgery. Afterwards, the society would host a reception in honor of the speaker, complete with substantial quantities of food and drink. It was at these social gatherings that I introduced Muñoz to the medical practitioners of Arkham, Bolton and Kingsport, and all the outlying communities, including Innsmouth, Aylesbury, and the little hamlets that dotted the countryside such as Misty Valley, Witches Hollow, and Martin's Beach. It was here as well that I pointed out to Muñoz the two men responsible for the death of my parents and other atrocities, all committed in the name of reanimation, the dreaded Herbert West and Daniel Cain, who attended on occasion.

Despite the periodic presence of those I considered my foes, I generally enjoyed these lectures and soirees, and made a point of complementing the organizers, Doctors Alfred Morris and Evan Beaumont, half-brothers who had opened up a practice in Kingsport catering to the summer tourists and more affluent members of the sleepy seaside town. Yet while I enjoyed these events, Muñoz bloomed, often holding court on a chilly porch or veranda, entertaining the younger set with his tales of European cities and exotic women with even more exotic afflictions, both real and imagined. It wasn't long before he had a regular following which included many of the area's rising stars, including Paul Rigas, Henryk Savaard, and Richard Cardigan. While most of this clique was welcome, one was particularly annoying, but thankfully only an occasional attendee. Francis Flegg was a mere medical student who would often accompany his mentor, the surgeon Maurice Xavier. Whether Xavier had invited Flegg or the overeager youth had simply invited himself was never clear, but it was only out of respect for Xavier that young Flegg's presence was tolerated, for he was perhaps one of the most sycophantic I had ever had the displeasure to encounter.

Now, one would think that such social gatherings would have little to do with the work that Muñoz and I planned on doing. Circumstance however conspired to bring our studies in reanimation crashing into the world of the Miskatonic Valley Medical Society, forever changing the face of medicine as we know it.

It was late December, the last meeting before the holidays, and Muñoz and I had spent the better part of the evening at an upper class home delivering a bouncing baby boy whom the proud parents named Edward Derby Upton. As a result, we were late to the lecture, and entered the Miskatonic Club with the reception well underway. The guest speaker was a Frenchman rumored to be in line for a Nobel Prize, Dr. Alexis Carrel. Carrel was a surgeon noted for his achievements in vascular surgery and the grafting of tissues, so it came as some surprise to both Muñoz and myself that the subject of conversation in the room was in no way related to Carrel's acknowledged specialty. Instead he was speaking about cellular senescence, immortal cell cultures, and even the artificial reactivation of long-dead tissues. By all that

I held dear, Carrel was talking about reanimation.

He was surrounded by a small group, including Xavier, Darrow, Clapham-Lee, Armwright, Cardigan, and Rigas, amongst others. This crowd was laughing, speaking jovially and clearly being entertained by whatever was occurring in their midst. Intrigued, Muñoz and I worked our way over and infiltrated the gathering. In the center next to Carrel, and holding his attention, were Doctors West and Cain. Between the two of them they were holding a large glass specimen case which contained a young chicken. The beast was frantically trying to get out of the case. It was enraged, and repeatedly bashed itself into the glass walls, tried to peck through the glass, and leapt at any sudden movement. It was behavior I had seen before, in the rats that I had subjected to experiments in reanimation. West and Cain were showing off a reanimated chicken, and by all of its behavior it was yet again a vile bloodthirsty revenant.

While Carrel and the younger generation were transfixed by the monstrosity, the older, more genteel doctors were horrified, disgusted by what had been done to a living creature in the name of science. There were cautious furtive glances followed by disapproving scowls and whispered statements of contempt. The little clique of young professionals was so enthralled by the horrid little creation, that they were oblivious to the machinations and the wave of rebuke that was mounting in the rarified pools of senior fellows and department chiefs. Only Muñoz and I seemed cognizant of what was happening and were able to distance ourselves from the crowd of gawkers and their morbid entertainment.

We sidled over to a gathering of the more senior physicians of the area, including Dr. Waldron, the University doctor, and the retired Arthur Hillstrom, from whom I had inherited many of my patients. Both not only served as trustees for the medical association, but also on the review board of St. Mary's Hospital. We arrived just in time to overhear these two distinguished gentlemen finish a most interesting conversation.

"The truth is," said Waldron, "we've let this morbid little group get out of hand. It is long past time that we dealt with it."

Hillstrom nodded in agreement. "It won't take us long. There's more than enough evidence, and with the proper incentives we can purge this festering cancer from our beautiful town. I'm thankful that Carrel's visit was able to flush them all out into the open."

What they had been talking about was not clear at the time, but within weeks it was made plain. A sudden influx of new patients revealed that Savaard's office had suddenly closed. Xavier had been told his services were no longer needed at the teaching hospital. Darrow's grant extension was revoked. Rigas was threatened with revocation of his license if he didn't leave Massachusetts. By February of 1912 nearly every doctor who had formed any sort of friendship or relationship with West and Cain had been forced out, made to relocate out of state. Only Armwright and the despicable originators of the reanimation process remained in the area. I can only assume that Chester Armwright's family connections served to protect him.

With the influx of new patients, the practice of Hartwell and Wilson had no choice but to expand. We weren't the only practice in Arkham, but certainly we were one of the most successful. Muñoz began seeing patients, mostly Spanish and Portuguese immigrants and Negroes at first, but as time went on any illusions we had concerning the need for separating our clients soon went to the wayside. Any clients who objected were welcome to obtain services elsewhere. As for West and Cain, there was no protection for them at all. Their privileges at the hospital were revoked, but they remained in practice serving the poor and ignorant folk of Bolton as they saw fit, experimenting on what specimens they could. Hillstrom made it clear that the two were not welcome in Arkham and that, were they to ignore his warning, certain facts would be made available to the authorities both locally and in Bolton. That Hillstrom made regular visits to the offices of Hartwell, Wilson and Muñoz, and would on occasion spend an inordinate amount of time staring at the little Spanish doctor, who seemed so polite, but whose hands were too cold, worried me at first. In the end it came to nothing and whatever Hillstrom suspected, he took to the grave when he died in March of 1912. That his regular physician was out of town, and that it was I who came to Hillstrom's bed has no relevance to this tale. Nor will I reveal what he told me as he lay there dying, but he knew enough to beg me for his life.

And I knew enough to let him die.

And stay that way.

Chapter 10.

The Disaster and the Detective

The end of March and then April came, and Muñoz and I found ourselves immersed in efforts to do just what Peaslee had suggested so many years ago: develop a vaccine against death. Indeed, preliminary trials with rats proved quite successful, with our test subjects showing significant resistance, if not immunity, to a variety of traumas, poisons, and other fatal conditions. It seemed apparent that we would have no choice but to begin clinical trials, trials that would use the citizens of Arkham themselves as test subjects. We laughed maniacally at our devious plot, for it sounded so much like something that West and Cain would conceive of, and the macabre humor of it all was not lost on us.

If only we could have maintained that sense of humor in the days that were to come.

A letter from Peaslee arrived toward the end of the first week of April, postmarked Southampton. He detailed some of his exploits in the Congo with Lord Jermyn, spoke wildly about some incredible archeological find, and hinted at amazing still-extant paleontological bridges. The whole matter was lost on me and I became much more interested in his return to the British Isles in March. There was a visit to Belfast and discussion of a young man named John Coffey. As usual there were a number of photographs, including one of Peaslee and Coffey standing on what appeared to be the deck of an ocean-going passenger liner of some sort, identified only as *Harland and Wolff, Belfast*. As usual, I forwarded the details of his adventures off to the paper, but kept the more personal pages, those directed toward Dr. Muñoz and me, providing us with instructions and direction, private. Of these there were several, including that he would be sending several crates of valuables to us via ocean liner, and the requirement that we draw up orders of payment for Mr. Coffey's father. The young man had apparently made some impression on Peaslee, rendering to him services he would not disclose.

It was on Monday, April 15, 1912, that the horror that had occurred the night previous was made public. The ocean liner *RMS Titanic* had struck an iceberg, causing the great ship to take on water and sink. Of the more than 2000 passengers and crew, only a sparse 675 were reported to be saved, though later this number was revised upwards of 700. From that day on the papers were filled with news of the disaster. Much was made of the survival of J. P. Morgan, who had been scheduled to be on board the ship, but had cancelled his travel because of other business. The paper ran a photograph of Morgan talking about the disaster with his advisors. Much also was made of the young seaman who had abandoned his post on the *Titanic* and jumped ship in Queenstown. The young man claimed that he had a sudden premonition of disaster, and that he had no choice but to forego his duties.

While such interviews and revelations sold newspapers, I and Muñoz were so involved with our own work that we had little time to trouble ourselves with such things, even if they were disasters of international proportions. The only thing that took time from our project were our patients, and a second communication from Peaslee. Unlike his previous missives, this was a Western Union telegram, and was relatively simple in content. Apparently, the crates of valuables that Peaslee had shipped to us had been aboard the *Titanic*, and had been swallowed by the hungry sea. Fortunately, Peaslee had taken out a significant insurance policy on the shipment and now sought to recoup his investment. I was astounded to find that Peaslee had significantly overinsured the cargo, using an American company rather than a British one. The contents of the shipment were lost on me, mostly antiquities and the like gathered from his travels, but all confirmed and documented by the company's European agents. When the insurance check came, it would place in Peaslee's account more than a million dollars.

It was towards the end of April that the first significant steps in the trial of our new vaccine were made, and while such movement was made purely through circumstance, it was a complete success. Though, as I shall reveal, the success was tempered by a revelation of a greater horror, one that seemed to keep intruding into our lives in the most unobtrusive but repugnant of manners.

Early in the day I received an urgent telephone call from Wendell Atlee, one of my patients, and the proprietor of the Hotel Miskatonic, a rooming house on the far side of the University. One of his female guests had fallen and although the injuries did not seem to warrant a trip to the hospital, Atlee hoped that I would see the young lady just to make sure. I readily agreed, and assured Atlee that I would extend her all courtesies. Atlee thanked me profusely, adding that the couple spoke English well despite the fact that they were Chinese.

It wasn't long before a taxi cab pulled up in front of the house and released a dapper man who dashed around the car to extract his wife from the other side. He stood about five and a half feet tall, and was dressed in a cream on cream suit, with a cream bowler. As he helped his wife down the walkway, I could see that the two had a significant disparity in age. I placed the husband in his late thirties, but his wife could not be more than twenty-five.

Leaving the office, I met them halfway with an offer to aid in her transport. "I am Dr. Hartwell; would you be offended if I offered to help you carry your wife into the office?"

The husband, who was heavier than a man of his age should be, bobbed his head in quick agreement and said in perfect, if slightly accented, English, "Propriety is like the speed limit, in emergency it may be ignored."

I chuckled as I slipped my shoulder under the young lady's arm and the two of us maneuvered her through the empty front and into one of the examination rooms. As we deposited her on the table, her husband said to me, "Thank you so much," bowing as he did so. It was then that I noticed the holster and gun hidden under his coat. The man caught my look and quickly buttoned his jacket. "You will forgive me, I am Officer Chan of the Honolulu Police Department, and this is my wife Jinghua. She stumbled on the stairs in Mr. Atlee's rooming house this morning; I think she may have injured her ankle."

The young woman smiled and stared at her husband lovingly. When she spoke, her voice was melodious and soothing. "You will forgive my new husband, for he is being disingenuous. He is more concerned over the fact that I felt somewhat ill this morning, and that this led me to lose my balance and my footing. He is foolish, but I love him."

I leaned Jinghua back onto the table and began a standard examination, which included her ankle, but also her neck and pelvic region. "Arkham seems an odd place for a honeymoon. It is very far from the Territory of Hawaii, and I am sure quite different."

Officer Chan bobbed his agreement. "We had intended to spend it on a cruise to Europe. Sadly, recent tragic events have forced happy couple to trade Old England for New England."

Apparently a puzzled look crossed my face, betraying the fact that I hadn't grasped his meaning. Fortunately his wife provided an explanation. "We had tickets to travel from New York on the *Titanic*'s return voyage. They were a gift from my father. I assure you, Doctor, we are citizens of the United States. Do you wish to examine our resident permits?"

I shook my head. "Madame, while I appreciate your compliance with the Geary Act, your national status makes no difference. Though I have to say that undertaking such a voyage seems a bold act given the sentiment that some in this country have been filled with," I remarked.

"Father is not without certain influences, and he and Mother place a high value on travel. Many years ago my father had quite an exploit, traversing through China. It is how he and my mother met and fell in love, but it also opened Father's eyes to what he calls 'globalization'. My family has trade interests on both sides of the Pacific, and on many of the islands in between. We are headquartered in San Francisco, where my parents live. My sister and I look after our assets in Hawaii, where I met my husband." She smiled at her doting husband, who seemed embarrassed by his wife's discourse. "The laws of your country may be oppressive, Dr. Hartwell, and based on irrational fears, but I assure you that compared to the political and economic climate in our homeland, they are quite tolerable. In China, you and I would not even be able to have this conversation."

I fumbled on the table for a stethoscope. "You've been married for about six weeks now. Is this the first time you've felt sick or dizzy?"

Suddenly the erstwhile policeman showed his colors. Rising, he gestured with his hat in hand as he talked. "Excuse please. How you know we have been married for six weeks?"

I stood up, removing the stethoscope from Jinghua's abdomen. "Simple deduction really, based on the medical information available to me. Since your wife is experiencing symptoms of what we commonly refer to as morning sickness, and those usually appear about six weeks after conception, I concluded that you had been married approximately six weeks ago."

I didn't think it was possible, but the man suddenly turned pale. "Conception, you mean Jinghua is pregnant?"

The young woman on the table began to giggle. "That is exactly what he means. For a man who wants to be a detective, you have certainly been oblivious these last few days." And with that, Officer Chan neatly passed out, falling like a tree onto the floor with a tremendous reverberating thud.

I was to his side in seconds, and soon had him on his back. His skin was clammy, and his breathing shallow and labored. As I placed the stethoscope to his chest I saw Muñoz coming through the door. "Help me get him into the other room." I caught a glimpse of his wife's panicked face. "Not to worry, Mrs. Chan, a simple fainting spell. We'll have him up and about in a few minutes. You just lie back and try to relax."

As Muñoz and I moved out into the hallway I whispered to my colleague, "Take him into the house. This may become unpleasant and I don't want her to hear it."

With all possible swiftness we deposited our charge onto the parlor settee, and while I took his jacket, holster, shirt and tie, Muñoz ran for my medical bag. I checked his neck and wrist for a pulse, and found none. With little choice, I began using the Holger Nielson modification of the Silvester Method of artificial respiration, lifting the arms behind the back, and then pushing them back down to drive air into the lungs.

Soon after I began, Muñoz dashed back in and began to unpack my kit. Within seconds Muñoz had injected our patient with a proper dosage of epinephrine. As he finished, he touched me, indicating that I should cease artificial respiration to see if the injection had the desired effect. We paused and waited, but seeing no response, I once more began treatment, frustrated that the normal treatment had had no favorable result. Muñoz prepared another syringe and administered another, more potent dose. Once more we paused and once more I reinitiated the resuscitation attempts. Without a word Muñoz leapt from my side and disappeared from the parlor.

He was not gone long, and what he carried with him made me rise up in opposition, for in a large glass syringe my colleague carried a dose of the chemo-luminescent reagent that we had recently developed to begin testing on human subjects, and from the way he held it, there was no mistaking his intention.

"Rafael, you can't do this. He's a stranger, his wife is right down the hall, he's a policeman. What if it doesn't work? What if something goes wrong?"

Muñoz never took his eyes off the man lying on the settee. "As of right now, Stuart, he is dead; with the reagent, he may have a chance. Or, would you rather tell his young pregnant wife that her husband has died?"

I lowered my head, in shame as much as in frustration. I was caught in a trap of my own creation. Were I to do nothing, I would always regret never trying, but the risks of actually using the formula, and it failing, weighed on my mind as well. The only glimmer of hope was that the years of research that I had carried out alone had been sufficiently refined by Muñoz and me over the past months. Did I have faith enough in my own work to test it? I closed my eyes, took a deep breath, and then reached out for the syringe. "I'll do it, please."

Rafael Muñoz lifted our patient's head and shoulders, providing me access to the soft spot where the skull met the spinal column. Carefully, but swiftly, I pierced the skin and slid the needle into the brain. Once I had reached a sufficient depth, I placed my thumb on the plunger and slowly injected our reagent into Officer Chan's body. I removed the needle swiftly, and as I finished Muñoz lowered his head back onto a pillow.

I stood there for a moment, unsure of what to do, but then remembered the gun that I had removed from Chan's possession. The gun was heavy and cold, but I took some comfort in holding it. I remembered what had happened before, to Dr. Halsey, and to James Robinson, and I had no desire to be a victim, nor to let anyone else suffer, at the hands of my own monstrous creation. Should Chan become uncontrollably violent I would not hesitate to shoot him.

As I expected, Chan awoke in agony, screaming like an animal, thrashing about on the settee. I stepped back and brought the gun between the two of us, but to my surprise Muñoz stepped in between, "Easy, Stuart. We have seen such seizures before, in the rats, no? They always come back like this. Give him a moment."

I lowered the gun, and Muñoz went to his side. My partner had been right; already I could tell that our subject wasn't entering a frenzied state at all, but rather one of panicked confusion. He was hyperventilating and scared, but I saw a glimmer of recognition and reason in his eyes. I placed the gun on the table and knelt by his side. "Relax, Mr. Chan. You had a minor heart attack, but you are through the worst of it." His eyes darted back and forth. "Your wife is fine," I told him, "just a little worried about you.

This is my colleague, Dr. Muñoz. He helped save you. Don't worry, you are safe and in good hands."

It took a few moments for Chan to relax, after which I went and got his wife. I told her that her husband had suffered a mild heart attack, but that was all. There was little else that could be done for him save initial rest, followed by a course of regularly increasing exercises to aid in the strengthening of the heart muscle. I advised him to avoid smoking and drinking, although an occasional pipe or drink would not be injurious. It wasn't until my medical advice ran out that I realized what we had done, and what we still had to do. After a brief conversation with Dr. Muñoz, we broached the subject of both Chans spending the night at the house, under the pretense that we would like to keep Mr. Chan under observation. Of course technically this was true, but the reason had little to do with his heart attack, and more to do with his ongoing reaction to our reanimating treatment. Thankfully, the Chans readily agreed, and it took little effort to have one of Atlee's bell boys bring their luggage over from the hotel.

That night I made a simple dinner of spring vegetables, baby potatoes, and roasted chicken. Afterwards, we spent the evening lounging in the parlor, the men playing cards and talking world affairs, and Jinghua composing a letter to her father in San Francisco. About nine in the evening, Jinghua apologized but said she was tired and needed to retire for the night. She asked if it would be any trouble to include her letter in the morning's mail. I looked at the envelope briefly to ascertain that it had been properly addressed and sealed. As I did so, I was met with a slight shock, as to the addressee, but I quickly recovered, telling her that it was no trouble at all, and wishing her a good evening.

It was only after she was well up the stairs, and out of earshot, that Mr. Chan spoke. "Does the identity of Jinghua's father bother you, Dr. Hartwell? Or, perhaps it is his occupation that concerns you?"

I sat down slowly. "I'm sorry, what did you say?"

It was Chan's turn to rise. "Jinghua's father is Kin Fo, president of the Pan-Oceanic Banking and Insurance Corporation. The same company that insured cargo on the now sunken *Titanic* cruise liner, cargo owned by your neighbor Nathaniel Peaslee, in whose behalf you filed a claim of insurance." There was a glimmer in his eye, like a cat stalking its prey.

I jumped from my seat, followed by Muñoz. "Just what are you playing at, Chan? If you've come here under false pretenses, taken advantage of my hospitality—"

He lifted his hand in a calming motion. "Please, doctors, no ruse was planned or intended; we are victims of curious coincidence, nothing more. Earlier this evening you demonstrated an impressive ability to deduce the date of my marriage from my wife's pregnancy. I merely return the favor. I am not unfamiliar with the sensational newspaper stories of Peaslee and his strange loss of personality, which occasionally mention you, Dr. Hartwell as his physician."

"But how did you know about the insurance?" I begged.

He bobbed his head in that strange parrot-like manner. "As son-in-law to venerable Kin Fo, I also am familiar with various forms and documents of insurance company, many of which sit partially completed on the desk in the corner, along with correspondence and photographs of Peaslee. Would seem a simple deduction that you are still handling some of his affairs while he travels in Europe."

I settled back into my chair, while Muñoz crossed the room to pour us both a drink. Chan casually sat back down as well.

"Still, I am puzzled by one detail of Peaslee's correspondence."

Muñoz handed me a drink and joined us. "What would that be, Mr. Chan?"

Chan rose and quickly crossed the room to the desk where he selected a photograph and brought it back to us. I recognized it as he laid it down on the table. "Photograph is of Peaslee and of a young man on the deck of a ship that is likely the doomed *Titanic* still being constructed at shipyards in Belfast."

I recalled the writing on the back of the photo, *Harland and Wolff, Belfast*. "Perhaps he inspected the ship prior to deciding to use it for his cargo, nothing unusual about that."

Once more that strange little bob. "Perhaps, but Peaslee is not the most interesting person in photograph, young man more interesting, and currently quite famous, or infamous."

We peered closer, but I didn't recognize the man from anywhere in particular. To our embarrassment, Chan soon enlightened us. "Young man is John Coffey, seaman who is currently subject of much scrutiny by the press, legal authorities and insurance companies."

I sat back. "What did Coffey do, kill someone?"

"John Coffey seaman, suddenly overcome with sense of dreadful foreboding, had a great premonition of impending disaster so strong that he abandoned his post and stowed away on a mail boat heading back to Queenstown." Chan paused. "The ship Coffey abandoned was the cruise liner *Titanic*, on which your patient Peaslee consigned much valuable cargo, with much more insurance. What were both Peaslee and Coffey doing on board *Titanic* before her completion, and why was Coffey so desperate to get off? These are questions that puzzle Chan."

Chan rose from the table and walked daintily to the door. "Truth is like delicate shell on a rocky beach: hard to find, but worth the time looking for." He took the stairs, and without looking back wished us a good night.

Muñoz and I were stunned; this apparently simple policeman had deduced something horrifying about our absent benefactor, something that neither of us had even thought of. Could it be true? Did Peaslee consign cargo on board the *Titanic*, insure it, and then through Coffey, somehow engineer the disaster? It seemed incredible, but I was reminded of my own suspicions regarding Peaslee's activities near Sicily, and the subsequent earthquake. Could he really have done it? I knew him to be inhumanly unemotional, but this seemed too much. Were thousands of lives traded for millions of dollars?

I said nothing of my suspicions the next morning, and neither did Chan or his wife. After a lovely breakfast the two bade me good day, as they were heading for New York where they would be staying for several weeks. I suggested that they both follow up with Dr. Vollmer, whom I knew from University, and trusted implicitly.

Mrs. Chan bowed in thanks while her husband presented us with a small token of his appreciation. It was a small book, bound in red leather with gold stamping. I flipped it open to reveal the title *The Quotations of Kin Fo* compiled by H. Chertok and M. Torge, and published by Golden Goblin Press in 1907. "Jinghua's father is a most remarkable man. You may know of the biography of his early life, *Tribulations of Chinaman in China*. This is his fifth book, a collection of Confucian aphorisms. I have studied it for years, and it has brought me much wisdom. Perhaps it can do the same for you?"

I thanked the man for his gift and bade him farewell. As their taxi pulled away, Muñoz joined me as I came back into the house. "What do you think?" I asked him. "Our first success or simply a delayed failure?"

"How can we know such things, my friend? He is a faceless man, one of the masses, and we shall never hear from him again. If he died tomorrow, or lived a hundred years, or a thousand, how would we ever know? What happens to Officer Chan in the future will always remain unknown to us."

Such musings brought on a melancholy, and that afternoon I pored through the stacks of newspaper back issues that had accumulated in the days since the accident, scouring the articles for all possible information on the sinking of the *Titanic*. It did not take me long to find the evidence I needed to condemn Peaslee and myself through association, for it was just days after the accident that a British photographer rudely snapped a photograph of J. P. Morgan and his retinue of advisors. Morgan, who had been booked on the *Titanic*, had cancelled at the last minute, citing issues of business that needed to be attended to. The majority of the photo was of the camera-shy Morgan sneering and raising his cane in the general direction of the reporter. I am sure that few people in the world could identify the man behind and to the left of Morgan, but I could. The image is blurry, slightly out of focus, but I am positive that one of the men walking with Morgan was none other than the inhuman thing that masqueraded as Professor Nathaniel Wingate Peaslee.

Chapter 11.
A Visit to Dunwich

The road that follows the Miskatonic River west out of Arkham, past Billington's Woods and into the wilds of central and northern Massachusetts, is not one I am particularly fond of, and my adventures along the route have never taken me beyond the turn off for Misty Valley, where I and my friends spent many fall days hunting small game and fishing the wider, slower expanses of the river. Yet it was without trepidation that I abandoned the hustle and bustle of Arkham and with a minimal amount of baggage boarded the bus that ran the length of that desolate winding road to the distant town of Aylesbury.

The events of April wore heavily upon my mind, and after some discussion with Muñoz and Wilson, I decided that a brief holiday was in order, a week out of the city; in the wilds seemed appropriate. It had been many years since I had spent time with friends in the country, and though I had not seen him in years, William Houghton, whose practice was in the sleepy little town of Aylesbury, seemed eager to have me out to his family's hunting cabin in the nearby Round Mountains. The morning air was chilled that last Monday in April, but I boarded the bus with a great sense of relief and the expectation that a rest would do much to relieve me of my troubles, or at least lessen them.

The old bus that served the meager travelers along the rural route made only a single round trip each day, and supplemented its fares by carrying mail and other non-perishables back and forth between the two destinations. It was also not unknown for the driver to pick up packets and individuals from many of the farms or isolated communities along the road such as Dean's Corners or Dunwich. Indeed, within an hour of leaving the outskirts of Arkham we came upon a rugged-looking man carrying a bird gun over one shoulder, and a covey of freshly shot doves over the other. Without any sign or negotiation the bus slowed to a near stop, and the man with a practiced hop and jump swung himself onto the driver's side running board. He did not attempt to open a door or take a seat but rather stood there for a good three or four miles conversing with the driver about the weather, local gossip, and the like. As we came to a crossroad the driver gave the local a small package wrapped in oilskin which the man tucked into his coveralls. Then without a word, the hunter hooked his string of doves to the side of the car and, in a move that I thought was too daring for one of his age, jumped from the moving car onto the road and dashed into the wood. The dark, thick trees swallowed him up like a blanket, and in seconds I had lost all sight of him.

Hours later, as noon approached, the driver steered the clunky vehicle to a spot on the side of the road that had been covered with gravel. There was a clearing with several rough tables and benches beneath a spreading oak. It was an idyllic setting, including the dirt path that led up a hill to a quaint farmhouse. In the distance I could hear the faint sounds of the river rushing by. The driver shut the engine off, and announced a thirty-minute rest for lunch and whatnot. Several of the men traveling with me sprinted for the woods, while the two women strolled slowly off in the opposite direction. I wandered over to the table and removed from my satchel a small thermos of tea, and a cheese and mustard sandwich wrapped in wax paper. As I settled into my lunch I became aware of why the driver had stopped in this particular location.

From the farmhouse, making her way down the hill, came a young woman of not more than twenty-five, who was followed by a girl of perhaps ten. The woman carried a large pot from which a thick steam emanated, while the girl carried two gallon pails, one in each hand. The spring breeze caught them from behind and carried the aroma of the pot to me, and I thrilled at the smell of stewed vegetables, cloves and what I thought would likely be rabbit. As the pair came closer the driver rose from the table and greeted his wife and daughter.

A bowl of stew and a cup of fresh milk were a quarter, a bargain by

Arkham standards, and as the passengers wandered back to the tables I was soon surrounded by the sounds and smells of a half dozen bowls of stew being devoured hungrily. Overcome, I dug deep into my pocket for a quarter and gladly handed it over. The stew was rich and thick, with chunks of potatoes, carrots, onions, celery and tomato as well as ample chunks of rabbit. The milk was warm and soothing and brought back memories of my mother's kitchen, while the gamy texture of the meat reminded me of my father's butcher shop.

I was roused from my daydream by a sudden clatter and then the wailing cry of a child in pain, followed by the concerned cries of her mother. The young girl had stumbled on the path and fallen on the handle hinge of one of her buckets. Blood was gushing down her leg, turning her sock a vibrant red. Always prepared, I dashed over, introduced myself as a doctor, and pried the girl's hands away from her knee. There was a deep puncture wound that looked worse than it actually was. It needed one or two stitches at the most, as well as something to prevent infection. I sent her father scurrying to the bus to fetch my medical bag.

When he returned, I knew immediately that something was amiss. Inside my suitcase I had not noticed it, but now as I held it in my hand my medical bag felt oddly heavy. Something had been added, and I had a dread suspicion that I not only knew who had added it but what it was as well. Undeterred, I undid the clasp and opened it up. My suspicions were confirmed, and I took the offending item, which was wrapped in a felt cloth and paper, and deftly slipped it into my pocket. Then I cleaned the wound with alcohol; the girl jumped but her father steadied her. I applied a mild topical anesthetic and then, using a needle and some silk, quickly stitched the girl up. The whole incident took no more than ten minutes, and once some pleasantries were exchanged we were all back on the road.

The rest of the trip went by without incident. The two ladies and two men left the bus at Dean's Corners, leaving just myself and one other as passengers for the last leg of our journey. Under these somewhat private conditions I carefully took the item from my medical bag that I had slipped into my pocket out for review. Inside the protective felt cloth I found a small vial of glowing green fluid and a note written in Muñoz's distinctive handwriting:

Stuart,

Hopefully you will not need this, but it never hurts to be prepared

M

I sighed and replaced the small offensive thing in my medical bag. I had no desire to even contemplate such things over my holiday.

It was after three o'clock, a quarter hour behind schedule, when we rolled into Aylesbury, and I could see my friend Houghton waiting for me in his car. I quickly gathered up my things and was hurrying through the door when the driver reached over and grabbed me by my sleeve. He thanked me for what I had done for his daughter, in his own way; his language revealed him to be uneducated, but his thanks was sincere. I proffered that I was only doing what any doctor would have done, but he was having none of it. He reached beneath the seat and brought forth another one of those odd wrapped packages and handed it to me. It was hard and heavy, and the weight shifted as I tucked it into my coat pocket; a bottle of liquid of some sort. I thanked him and went to join Houghton.

William Houghton had aged little since I had seen him at Miskatonic, and as we drove back on to the road that I had just come in on, it was as if the years since University had never happened. As we trundled past the last outpost of Aylesbury Houghton turned the conversation to the furtive exchange at the bus. "What did young Corey give you?"

"Not a clue," I responded, digging into my coat and extracting the cloth-wrapped package. It was a clear glass pint bottle containing a clear liquid, which for all I knew could have been water. I unscrewed the top and took a whiff; my senses reacted violently as the aroma burned through my sinuses and into my throat. My eyes were watering and soon I was coughing almost uncontrollably.

Houghton laughed. "Dunwich Wood Goat, Corey's specialty. His family has been brewing that since before the Revolution. Seems you've made a friend; he doesn't hand that stuff out to just anyone."

I twisted the cap back on and tucked it away. "I would hate to see what he gives out to people he doesn't like."

"More often than not, that would be a back full of bird shot. Dunwich is a wild area, Stuart, filled with wild characters and no real law. Nearest sheriff is in Aylesbury, only real authority is Squire Whateley, but he's not much when it comes to keeping folks in line. More than one man has been the victim of a country mob out this way."

I stared at him with a sense of incredulity. "Hell of a place for a cabin, Will. If I wanted to mingle with a town full of ignorant hicks, I could have gone to Innsmouth."

"Careful, Stuart," he shot back. "The people of Dunwich aren't ignorant, far from it. There's some in these parts that could teach our professors back at MU a thing or two, if they were so inclined. Problem is they simply aren't that inclined. They're a self-reliant bunch that prefers to keep to themselves. They have their own ways, and they aren't particularly fond of outsiders, especially those from Arkham."

"I've always wondered about that."

"The early history of Dunwich, or New Dunnich, is pretty poorly documented. Everything I've ever read suggests that the founders were an early group of freethinkers living amongst the rest of the more traditional Arkhamites. As the fires of the witch hunt were getting started, the group realized that such things didn't bode well for them, and a slow exodus from Arkham began, some of which ended up settling in what would become Dunwich. There are a whole slew of variations on that theme, some of which talk about a divine vision, others mention a supply of lost gold. There's even a rumor that the notorious witch Goody Watkins was the leader of the exodus. All of this is humorous when you consider that not long after, when John and Prudence Doten of Duxbury produced a significantly disfigured child, the High Sheriff was so repulsed he charged them with witchcraft and burned them alive."

"What happened to the child?"

"No one knows. There's no record of it ever being killed or dying or anything like that. There's a sermon given by a Reverend Hoadley at their execution, condemning the demon offspring of the Dotens to the dark of the wood, but beyond that nothing else is ever mentioned."

The countryside crawled past; ramshackle farmhouses and barns surrounded by overgrown fields with a few sickly-looking cattle dominated my view. There were people, drab women and children mostly, an occasional man. Someone in Dunwich must have cornered the market on grey cloth, for that was the dominant color for pants, shirts and dresses. Even overalls, normally universally blue, were nothing more than faded gray. As we pulled into what passed as the village center of Dunwich, I was not surprised to discover that the buildings all suffered from the same affliction. Some of the structures still bore remnants of paint, peeling and flaking off, but underneath was that same monotonous sickly grey.

We stopped at Osborne's General Store for some supplies, and inside I was confronted by more of the same drab grayness that permeated the exterior. Two men were playing checkers on the head of an old barrel, while another sat rocking in an old chair. The proprietor, distinguishable by his apron, greeted Will and acknowledged my presence with a nod. Will rambled through some pleasantries and then started listing off the things he needed, which the shopkeeper began gathering from the dusty shelves around the shop.

While our order was put together Will paid his regards to the men playing checkers, two septuagenarians who were apparently relatives, brothers or maybe cousins. Given what I knew about the habits of Dunwich families, they could have been both.

"Yer otta be carfuwl ouat thar in them wuds, Doc," said one of them, flashing a mouthful of missing teeth and a tongue missing a good chunk out of it. "Ol Whateley, he's all rild up, and his albinny darwter too. She's inna right awfool state."

Osborne stepped into the conversation. "Don't you be minding them two, Doc Houghton. The mountains have been trembling somewhat for the last week, and its nothing we ain't use to out here. Noah's just a little bit more excitable than most folks; sees the rumblings as evidence of spiritual forces. That's what the folks in 1663 and 1755 thought, and that branch of the Whateleys ain't progressed much since them times."

"Progressed!" scoffed one of the brothers. "Iffin you awsk me they dun gone in te opposite direction. Noah's crazier than his father Ezekiel ever was. Sure the man had some right odd notions abaout things. But he kept em to himself. Noah goes around talkin abaout spirits, things invisible in the air and the earth. It ain't normal. And its only gotten worse since his wife Vesta died, what 12 years gone by now. That girl Lavinia ain't right in the head neither, she got no proper schooling ta boot. Spends her days wandering the hills and fields chasin after things that only she and her darn fool father can see."

The other one nodded. "Been ouat te Sentnal Hill evry night fer a week. Settin fires biggun enuff to see fer a good ways. Burnin sumthin gawd awful by the smell offit."

"That there is the smell of goat burning," the old man in the rocking chair croaked. "Noah's been making sacrifices like the Philistines done in the old days. Says that the end days is near and we should all be making ourselves ready for the return of angels and spirits to the earth."

Osborne finished packing our boxes and hustled us out the door. "Fellers, Old Whateley ain't nothing to worry yourselves about. He stays mostly on his own farm down there in the glen, and up on Sentinel Hill, and in the fields between. You stay out of there, ye ain't gonna run into him. Iffin ye do, and you'll recognize him cause of that crazy old Indian blanket he wears, just walk away fast as you can. He ain't one to go looking fer trouble. Same goes for Lavinia, you'll know her cause she's an albino, all white skin and hair with pink eyes. She's tetched in the head, but she don't mean no harm. But you both take my advice and be leavin them Whateleys and their lands well alone."

Will thanked the man, shaking his hand in a gregarious country manner, and assuring him that we would stay well clear of the Whateleys. It was another hour to the cabin, and as we traveled the woods grew wilder, thicker, and the road slowly devolved into little more than an overgrown path. As we unloaded the car, the last rays of the sun winked out behind the hills and mountains. Will lit three kerosene lamps, and built a fire in the modest fireplace. Dinner was a simple stew of salted meat and fresh vegetables. Exhausted from my journey, I retired early, looking forward to the peace that a few days in the country would bring.

The next morning, I spent a few minutes unpacking my bags and organizing the closet and dresser. For a brief moment I was unsure what to do with the bottle of moonshine, but after mulling it over, it joined my medical bag in a small trunk at the foot of the bed. Over coffee and cheese omelets Will and I discussed plans for the day, eventually agreeing to hike down to the nearby brook and spend the day fishing, and hoping for enough of a catch to make a meal or two.

The trip down to the stream, one of the many that formed the headwaters of the Miskatonic, sounded easier than it actually was. Like the road to the cabin, the path to the brook had not been in regular use, and was overgrown with limbs, saplings and brambles. More than once we had to detour around an overgrown bush or fallen tree, only to have severe difficulty in once more finding the trail. Not to say that I did not enjoy the walk; songbirds provided fine accompaniment, and both Will and I thrilled when a large buck snorted and bounded away from us. Tracks were plentiful on the trail, and after examining a particular large set Will checked his pistol and ominously said, "Wild dog." As we came closer to the brook, made obvious by the sound of rapids, the trail grew steeper, and we were forced to use the occasional bush or sapling as tethers to keep from sliding down the slope. Inevitably, we reached the point where the slope took a drastic incline, and we had no choice but to slide down the four-foot bank on to the pebbled plain below.

As we sat there on the hard, cold, wet carpet of stones, our backsides painted with mud, we were greeted by twittering laughter which although I could not see it, I knew belonged to a young woman. Looking around, I was stunned to find a figure wrapped in an oilskin cloak standing on the ledge of a stone bridge that spanned the brook, not more than fifty yards away. On the far side of the bridge a rough-hewn stairway led down past the bank. Under other circumstances I might have been upset, but observing the state that Will and I were both in, we slowly began to chuckle, and then both of us let out a raucous guffaw. Our watcher on the bridge joined in, and soon the little stream-worn valley was echoing with our combined laughter.

Wandering slowly toward the bridge, Will called out "Do you happen to know a good spot for fishing this brook?"

The figure was suddenly quiet and still. With her cloak on her features were invisible to us, and it seemed odd that she waited so long to respond. "My pa and I always have the best luck about a mile downstream from here. Where the river turns and forms a still pond underneath a stand of birch."

Will paused and strained to see to whom he was speaking. "You said that's a mile downstream?"

The figure climbed backwards off the ledge. "Maybe a mile and a half. It's a large pool underneath a stand of birch. You can't miss it. I caught myself a four-pound catfish there just yesterday." And then without another word the featureless young woman was gone. We could hear her as she tramped down the bridge and into the woods, and realized that the worn footpath she was traveling on was mere feet from the rugged route we had come through.

The wide shallow brook was easier to walk along than the path from the cabin, and side by side we two set off for the deep pool under the birch stand, all the while jabbering to each other about the things we had done since college. It was a refreshing change of pace, to not have to talk about

Peaslee or reanimation, and soon both of us were so engrossed in our conversation that we were oblivious to the passage of time or distance. It was only when my stomach began sending out waves of hunger pangs that I glanced at my pocket watch and discovered we had been walking for nearly an hour.

Realizing we had been made the butt of a joke, we turned round and plodded our way back. Driven perhaps by hunger, frustration or embarrassment, our return pace was quicker and we soon were back at the stone bridge. This time we ascended those rough-hewn stairs, though covered as they were with moss and detritus the climb was only marginally easier than our previous slide down the bank. On the path our pace, unhindered by river rock and other debris, quickened further, and soon we were within sight of Will's cabin.

It was plain to both of us that things were not as we left them, and upon entering the edifice our worst fears were confirmed. The rooms had been ransacked, and anything of perceivable value had been taken. The kitchen was in shambles, with the vast majority of dry goods left behind, but the meats, cheeses and the like missing, as was the cooking oil. After the initial shock wore off, Will and I began trying to make a list of things that were missing, and soon we had both wandered into our separate bedrooms to examine what remained of our personal belongings. My good winter coat was gone, as was a pair of long underwear, and my extra thick socks. My toiletry kit had been rifled, but apparently nothing in it was of any interest. With great reluctance I opened the trunk at the foot of the bed where I had deposited my medical kit. With a sigh of relief I found my kit intact with everything present. It was only after a brief moment that I furtively began searching through the case and then the trunk itself. For while my kit was intact, two things were missing. Of the missing jar of moonshine that I had been given as a gift for my act of medical kindness, I could not care less; but it was that other item that was missing, the thing that Muñoz had surreptitiously added to my supplies, that made me quake with worry and fear. Whoever had been in the cabin had taken something I had to get back, something more powerful, more dangerous than the missing shotgun Will was complaining about. Missing was that glowing green vial of reanimation fluid that Muñoz had so thoughtfully added to my medical bag.

We spent the afternoon cleaning up the mess that was left us and restoring a sense of order to the cabin that was our temporary abode. Thankfully, there were enough foodstuffs left to us to create a few meager meals, though we both agreed that another trip to Osborne's Store was going to be needed. So after a brief discussion of needed supplies it was agreed that we would set out on foot the next morning, hiking down to the town and then back. Although perhaps not the easiest way—we could have driven down—Will assured me that there was a footpath that led to town, and I hoped that the walk would serve to further clear my head of the madness that seemed to have crept in over the years.

Sadly, such simple delights were not to be had. Long after the sun went down, and an hour or so after Will and I had moved into the cabin, we heard the distinct sound of footsteps on the path leading to the cabin, accompanied by the heavy labored breathing and lumbering gait of some sort of beast of burden. We exchanged confused glances as the sounds came closer, changing in tone as they reached the stone walkway, and then again as someone mounted the wooden porch. When the door was quickly rapped twice we were both already on our way to answer it.

The man standing outside in the dark was a stranger to us, but the figure in the cloak standing behind him with the calf was the same one we saw on the bridge earlier in the day. Even more recognizable were the contents of the crates that were being laid out on the ground, for they were none other than the missing supplies that had been burgled earlier in the day.

Reluctantly, the stranger stepped forward into the light, revealing an older man with a round head surmounted with a grizzled grey beard and fringe with wild eyes. Around his shoulders he was wearing an old Indian blanket decorated with odd geometric designs and strange angular figures that I could not place as man, beast, or fowl. When he spoke his voice was a throaty whine. "I have come to apologize for my daughter," he said, glancing over his shoulder at the figure with the calf. "She ain't accustomed to strangers in these parts, and with all the excitement of late she seems to have forgotten that she shouldn't take what doesn't belong to her." Suddenly the young woman was standing beside her father with an armful of our supplies. The firelight revealed what we had not seen earlier in the day: alabaster skin, chalk hair and eyes with cherry-colored pupils, she was a textbook case of albinism. That was all that was needed to reveal the identities of the pair before us, Noah Whateley and his simple daughter Lavinia, the two individuals we had been warned to steer clear of.

Without a word of invitation the two moved through the door and began unloading a crate on the rough wooden table that occupied the majority of the front room. Like me, Will was flabbergasted, and as the pair walked back and forth bringing in crate after crate of dry goods and gear, we two stood in stunned silence. Not that we had much choice, for the two strangers were constantly jabbering to themselves in a strange patois of which I could only comprehend a few words, most of which were apologies and supplications of one form or another. After a half dozen trips the calf was unburdened and the table was cluttered with what appeared to be the vast majority of our missing materials, though one or two things were noticeably missing. I was about to say something when the old man reached beneath his blanket and pulled out an empty bottle.

"Lavinia, like her mother, has a taste for spirits. I'll see if I can obtain you another bottle." The young girl hung her head in shame.

I shook my head. "There's no need, but there was another bottle, much smaller, that I would like back."

The old man turned to his daughter who seemed to crawl deep inside her cloak. "Sorry, Pa," she said. "I drank that one as well. It had such an awful taste. I fell into such a terrible fit, and when I was done, the bottle was broken."

I dipped my head and rubbed the space between my now closed eyes. "How do you feel now?'

"Just as right as rain, mister, I sure am sorry that I did what I did. I was just excited about going to the congregation, and lost my wits for a moment. Pa says I shouldn't steal no matter what, I hope I ain't done no harm."

I paused, trying to think of something to say, for unwittingly this young lady had become a participant in my study of the effects of the reagent on the living. At least now I knew that the solution taken in extreme doses was not a poison. "No, Lavinia, you've done no harm, none at all."

The old man shuffled back into the darkness. "Come on, girl, time we got on up to the hill. Folks there'll be awaiting for us before the sacred rites begin."

Will and I exchanged puzzled glances. "You'll be up on Sentinel Hill tonight then, praying?"

Noah Whateley whipped around and fervor filled his eyes. "Me and mine will be doing more than praying up there. There's too much praying in this world, people asking for things and not offering anything in return. Most folks have forgotten the old ways, what obeisance and sacrifice truly meant."

His voice was strained. "But we haven't, not us Whateleys, we still remember the real reason the Christ was born in a manger, and we will gladly give forth the same sacrifice. You would be wise to find your way back to the old ways, young sirs."

With that the old man and his albino daughter with the calf in tow wandered into the darkness and were swallowed up by the forest, leaving Will and me to stare in silence as their footsteps faded into the depths of the night.

Will turned to me and with a half-mocking tone suggested that we might follow them on up to Sentinel Hill and spy on their sacred rites. I shook my head. "That, I think, would be an extremely bad idea." Will chuckled and we went inside to put the newly returned supplies back in order.

That night we two retired at a little past eight in the evening. Having been up early and busy all day, I had no problem falling into a deep and restful slumber, that I wished I had never been awoken from, but that was not the case. It was well after midnight when I was roused from bed in a most unusual manner. At first I had thought it was a thunderclap of immense proportions that jolted me awake and onto the floor, but it soon became apparent that was not the case. The sound and accompanying vibration rolled through the house making picture frames shift, pottery clink and the glass in the windows shudder. Throwing on my pants and a shirt, I rushed into the main room to find Will doing the same thing.

"Earthquake?" I asked buttoning my pants.

My friend gave me a puzzled look. "They did say they've been having tremors."

It was then that we noticed the light seeping through the window. Not moonlight but an inky violet, unnatural pulsing radiance that seemed too weak to cast shadows, but seeped into corners and places where it had no right to go. Will casually picked up his rifle and we cautiously opened the door.

The eerie pulsating radiance that had been seeping through the window filled the clearing and cast queer shadows amongst the trees and underbrush. Its origin was apparently a cluster of roiling storm clouds that had gathered in the distance above Sentinel Hill. The pulsing light was something akin to heat lightning, but for the life of me I would have sworn that something was inside those clouds, something massive, titanic even, something that coiled and pulsated with unnatural life, and with each beat gave off a burst of that cold colored light, illuminating the clouds and casting the valley in a shade not known to men. Each wave of radiation, whether slight or intense, was accompanied by a proportional tremor, like a wave, that rolled down from the hill and into the valley, rattling not only our residence, but even the trees and shrubs themselves. I could not fathom how an atmospheric phenomenon, even one as abnormal as this, could generate such a response in the very Earth itself. Will recited a short prayer, and for a moment I wished that I had faith so that I could seek some comfort in it.

As my eyes adjusted to the weird light, I became aware of yet other lights. These were fires, huge bonfires that dotted the crown of Sentinel Hill, and by their flickering light I could see a dozen or so figures moving about on the crest. What they were doing I cannot rightly say, but their movements were animated, and seemed timed with the pulsating lights. Nor could I discern the presence of the Whateleys, but something in my gut told me that they were central to the chaos that was unfolding up on the small mountain. There were other lights too, balls of white light that seemed to circle the larger cloud like moths to a flame. There was a sound that came with them as they zoomed around, a high-pitched buzzing or whistling, perhaps one might have even called it a maniacal piping.

Entranced by the light show on the hill, and above it, I failed to notice the strange activity that was occurring around me, and only became aware of it when Will nudged me on the shoulder and gestured towards the edge of the forest. Even with such prompting it took me a moment to understand what I was supposed to see, but then my eyes beheld such strangeness, such an unnatural occurrence, that the experiments that had been performed in my own lab seemed tame by comparison. Above the woods, moving away from the hill were birds, great flocks of birds, so much so that for brief instances they blotted out the sky. They moved in silence, and I could make out owls, hawks, whippoorwills, doves, and even the occasional bat as they passed overhead, all in eerie silence. But it wasn't birds and bats alone. From the direction of the hill small game suddenly began traipsing out of the forest, squirrels, raccoons, opossums, porcupines, rabbits all paid us no heed as they scrambled past. Something large broke cover and startled both of us; a four-point buck bounded through the clearing. Will raised the rifle and tried to find a shot, but something stopped him from pulling the trigger, and he lowered the gun with tears coming from his eyes. There were larger things moving through the forest outside of our sight, boar, bear, maybe even wolves, but for all the novelty of this strange migration it paled in comparison to what was happening in the sky above Sentinel Hill.

There was a sudden explosion and the strange light turned a sickly green. My eyes hurt to look at it, but at the same time I found that I could not turn away. The cloud shrank, condensed, folded in on itself; it ceased being amorphous, and the swirling lights plunged inside. Where once had been a cloud, now was a near-perfect sphere, pulsing with sickly green radiation. Without sound or warning, the strange sphere suddenly split, and where there was one, there were now two. Then again, and again, splitting into a congeries of bubbles that seethed and crawled across the sky toward the figures that still pranced about on that loathsome hill. As the thing moved forward, some of the revelers noticed and began to run, and from the distant sound of their screams, they were in abject terror. Others fell to the ground and lay still, while one, who even from this distance was identifiable as Noah Whateley based on the stylized robes he wore, seemed to raise his arms up chanting a strange indecipherable hymn.

The bubble thing swarmed over the hill, engulfing its precipice, and laying waste to it like a great hand reaching down and clearing the earth. Rocks and trees were uprooted and flew through the air like a child's playthings, and in their path, those who had earlier fled were suddenly mowed down by the airborne debris. Even around our camp, Will and I ran for shelter as pebbles and dirt rained into our midst. When we turned back, the green glowing mass was suddenly a single sphere again, and shrinking fast, but as it grew smaller it grew brighter, and the brighter it grew, the worse it hurt to look at it. It shrank so fast, in seconds it was the size of a small house, then a man, then in the blink of an eye it was a street light, a lantern, a pinprick, and then in an instant it was gone. But only for an instant, for as it winked out, a massive amount of illumination seemed to explode, radiate out from the point it had once occupied, bathing the surrounding area in a brilliant if eerie light. As the explosive radiation struck me, there arose from my skin an intense amount of pain, and I quickly realized that in a matter of seconds I had received the equivalent of a severe case of sunburn. As William and I retreated into the house for cover I saw the plants around the cabin suddenly stiffen and their leaves wither as if in a state of extreme desiccation.

The radiating light faded quickly, and although our skin was tender we were not severely injured. We had been fortunate in that we had been able to retreat to a shelter, but I knew that there were others, those who had fled from the hill, and those still on it, who must have suffered more severe burns or even injuries from the flying debris. Houghton and I had a quick discussion and within moments we were loaded down with supplies and headed up the hill in search of the wounded.

About halfway up the hill we found our first victim. He was lodged under a large tree that had apparently come down on his legs, which were obviously broken. He wasn't moving, and I thought that either the impact had killed him, or he was unconscious. I was wrong on both suppositions. The man was dead, but it hadn't been the tree. His throat showed a clear straight cut; the trapped man had been murdered. And in our trek up the hill we learned he wasn't the only one. Of the eight additional bodies we found, six had died from either debris or exposure to the intense sickening radiation. The other two had been killed like the first, throats slit, death by exsanguination. With each discovery William became more nervous, and as we made our way up to the top of Sentinel Hill he clung to his rifle like a child to a comforting blanket.

I cannot fully describe the extreme devastation that I bore witness to on the hill, but I will say that never before or since have I seen such a thing. I have not been out to see for myself what they are calling the Dunwich Horror, but I can't imagine that it is in any manner worse than what I saw that day. The world had been destroyed on that low peak, the vegetation, all life was gone. The soil had turned to ash which the wind was rapidly stripping away, leaving nothing but barren rock behind. There remained the great megalithic erections that had stood for countless ages, still grey, somber and menacing but now covered here and there with ashen shadows that made me shiver, for the shape of some of those shadows was undeniably human, and hinted that those who had remained on the hill during the explosion had been incinerated, leaving only this eerie trace. Yet it was those other ashen shadows that bothered me even more. I know William saw them, for he too went strangely silent, and we trudged down back to the cabin and into town in silence.

We only spoke when we used the phone to call the sheriff in from Aylesbury. We spent the next day telling our tale to various officials, who cast doubt on our version, for by the time they reached the site, there were no bodies to be found, and Noah Whateley and his daughter Lavinia had been found safely ensconced in their farm home. The authorities admitted something had happened on the hill, a freak tornado perhaps, but I don't think they saw the ashen shadows on the standing stones, and neither of us ever mentioned them again. I speak of them now, only because it offers up some clue as to what happened then, and perhaps what has happened more recently.

There were, as I have said, the shadows of men, but some were undeniably the shadows of women, and there should be no reason for one to think that women would not have been present on the hill. But it was the other shadows that disturbed us, the ones that seemed to be grasping the images of men and women, embracing them in wanton ways that I chose not to describe. No man could cast such a shadow. I will admit that the six sets of appendages may have been the result of some sort of odd effect, like a double image on a photograph from a long exposure in which the subject moves. But the limbs that were captured in those negative images on the great rocks, they were thin, like pipes or rods, and the bodies were rounded ovals that seemed more like some kind of titanic beetle or crab than that of a human. But worst of all were the strange singular appendages that jutted out oddly from the shadowed things, appendages that linked the monstrous shadows to those of the more human shades, seemingly penetrating not only the bodies of the women but the men as well.

CHAPTER 12.

THE MYSTERIOUS DOCTOR C.

The State Police were kind enough to drive me back to Arkham, which I appreciated mostly because of the sudden cold that had unexpectedly seeped down from the north. By the time we arrived at my Crane Street home the chilly winds had dipped below forty degrees. Moreover, the weather forecast which I heard over the officer's radio suggested that such weather would be impacting the whole of New England for a week or so. Thus, I was not surprised when I saw my colleague Muñoz walking down Crane Street, enjoying the night air. As I exited the cruiser, Muñoz helped me with my bags, and soon we were inside the house, each of us relating events that had occurred over the last few days.

I was by all accounts still on vacation, and because of what we thought was going to be the beginning of a warming trend, Muñoz had no patients either. All appointments were in Wilson's capable hands. This created an interesting opportunity which Muñoz related to me and suggested we take advantage of. Over the months, Muñoz had isolated several ingredients which were crucial to the tests we were carrying out. One of these, a specially treated royal bee jelly, was difficult to come by, but we had secured a steady supply to meet our needs. The other ingredient, an enzyme isolated from the nervous tissue of crocodilians and other large reptiles, was more difficult to obtain, not because it was rarer, but rather because it was apparently in higher demand. We had located a supplier in the vicinity of El Mirada, Florida, but his entire production was spoken for by a researcher in a nearby city. Muñoz had contacted the man, and after exchanging letters and a telephone call, we had been invited down to meet with him, examine his research, and if we could resolve his particular problem, he should free up the supply of saurian enzyme.

It amazed me that I had not heard of this man before, particularly given that I knew most of those who had given themselves over to researches into reanimation or life extension, but Muñoz assured me that the man was genuine, and that his lack of notoriety was not the result of incompetence or quackery, but rather of self-imposed isolation. Apparently he had had some success with his studies, but as a result had suffered a condition that made it difficult, if not dangerous, to meet with the public. He was, however, the holder of several intellectual and physical properties which provided him significant income in lieu of actually seeing patients. If we were to see him, and successfully carry out the procedures he desired, not only would the saurian enzyme become more available, he would also transfer over the rights to one of his properties as a form of payment. After some discussion Muñoz and I both agreed that it was an opportunity neither of us could resist. There was, however, some concern over Muñoz's own medical requirements, for if the cold snap were to suddenly end, Muñoz would need immediate access to the cool air that helped to keep him in a semblance of life. Not surprisingly, Muñoz had come up with a solution to the problem. He had recently purchased an arctic survival suit several sizes too big, and modified the well-insulated outfit with pockets for ice. Thus, while such an outfit might appear strange, it would at least keep the man safe while he returned to Arkham.

The journey we undertook was comfortable and enjoyable. Muñoz genuinely seemed to love the open air and landscape that we passed through, and even the city streets, a change from the sleepy little village of Arkham, seemed to engage him. The house at which we arrived was a classic antiquarian structure, with architecture uncommon in the New England repertoire, and complemented with an attention to detail and design that was both subtle and enthralling. Situated on a large lot, the three-story house seemed too large for one man to occupy, and indeed around the edges, there was evidence that the upkeep of the property had become somewhat lax, with bushes overgrown, weeds invading the flower beds and paint peeling from the porch handrails. The stairs creaked as we ascended them, as did the doorknocker, indicating that it had not been used in some time. Still, mere moments after we sounded our presence the great door creaked open and our host was revealed to us.

To this point, I have not yet revealed the name of our mysterious colleague, his residence, or any other personal information, and it is my full intention not to do so, for reasons that will become apparent. So for the purpose of this document I will refer to him under the pseudonym of Dr. C. Dr. C was a small man, light of frame with long gangly limbs and fingers. His neck was fat and short and topped with an oval-shaped bald head that twitched back and forth. On either side of his head were small, nearly undeveloped ears. His eyes were large and spaced far apart above a broad flat nose, which itself was set above a nearly lipless slash of a mouth. When he spoke, he revealed two rows of tiny teeth, like neat little intermeshing nubs and a large active bright pink tongue. His English, although excellent and well mannered, was tinted with a French accent.

As the good doctor ushered us into his home we were immediately struck by an extreme change in climate. While the external clime had remained chilly, although comfortable for Muñoz, the interior of Dr. C's home was maintained in what I can only describe as tropical conditions, with high temperatures and equally high humidity. I immediately began to sweat profusely, but Muñoz's response was more violent, and a look of abject terror overtook his countenance. We had been there for less than a minute and Rafael, in fear for his life, was already retreating back outside, to the relative safety and comfort of the cold.

Oddly, he was stopped by Dr. C, who apologized and, throwing open a hallway door, ushered the two of us down into the darkness. After we traversed a short flight of stairs and passed through another door we found ourselves in a large rough-hewn stone chamber. The air was noticeably cooler; indeed the temperature was easily well below that outside, and I could tell Muñoz was relaxing. As the lights came on we soon came to understand how this had been accomplished, for there in one corner of the cellar, linked to a complex of pipes and ducts, was an immense mechanical apparatus that looked quite a bit like the heat engine that resided in my own basement. What Dr. C had done was to apply the same concept on a grander scale. Where our engine gathered heat from a single room and then shunted it away to other areas, this engine gathered small amounts of heat from a number of sources, and then warmed the entire house. The cellar, which was apparently built with access to a well, was frigidly cold because the well water was a primary source for this heat engine, and indeed while the water flowing up out of the well was cool, the water leaving the heat engine was frigid, nearly frozen, and this small amount of energy, harvested in vast quantities, was the source of the heat. So, ironically, the engine that maintained the threatening temperatures throughout the house also maintained a cool enough condition in the cellar for Muñoz to be comfortable. Indeed, the engine even produced ice that could be used to line Muñoz's coat and allow him freedom to move about the steamy home above. Once Muñoz had acquired sufficient amounts of ice for his suit, the two of us were soon touring Dr. C's home in relative comfort.

The first floor of the sprawling house was comprised of two main sections: the front rooms, including the parlor, library, dining room and conservatory, and those beyond the kitchen, which included three distinct vivariums. In these he raised a variety of exotic plants and animals, including pitcher plants, exotic lichens, weird deep sea clams and jellyfish, caimans, and a selection of freshwater eels, amongst others. These all radiated out from a single central laboratory comprised of gleaming steel cabinets, porcelain fixtures, dissection tables and an assortment of glass apparatus that in all truth reminded me a great deal of the facility that was located in my own household. It was in this setting that Dr. C explained that he had in recent years come to believe that the secret to extending the human life span was to be found in the anatomy and endocrine systems of the crocodilian species. He had over the years learned that these animals, although primitive in appearance, had in fact a highly developed immune system that was capable of not only fighting off disease and toxins, but of repairing damaged tissues at an accelerated rate, and even replacing entire organs as they approached their eventual senescence. In many ways what Dr. C spoke of reflected that we had heard from Alexis Carrel, albeit at a more advanced stage. As Dr. C lectured, Muñoz and I exchanged knowing glances and I knew that we agreed that we had found a kindred spirit who was perhaps, if not on the same path, then at least traveling nearby.

We spoke for about an hour or so, and then in a most agreeable mood Dr. C handed us both folders containing copies of his experiments, conclusions, theories and proposals, and left us alone to study them at our leisure. Muñoz retreated to the artificially cool cellar while I was shown to a room on the second floor. Even on the upper story the heat was tremendous, but Dr. C suggested that I adjust the temperature by plugging the duct work and partially opening the window and letting some of the cooler outside air in. It only took minutes for me to find a balance between the two and obtain a state that was neither too hot nor too cold.

It took several hours for me to digest all of Dr. C's research and theories, and by the end of it my brain was fairly swimming with possibilities. So full of ideas was I that on more than a single occasion I had to be reminded that it was improper to speak of work during dinner. Dr. C served lobster bisque followed by a tasty baked vegetable dish which he called Ratatouille de Ego, a recipe he learned from a woman named Antoinette who had been his mistress when he lived in France. Dessert was a banana pudding topped with nutmeg and a dash of cinnamon. After clearing the table, Dr. C joined us in the study for brandy and cigars. It was then that the three of us finally sat down and discussed Dr. C's research and proposal.

I will not bore the reader with the finer details of the theories and methods proposed by our host, but to understand what happened next some exposition must be made. Dr. C had long ago isolated certain hormones, compounds and specialty cells from the glands of various reptiles and other animals and had then concocted an elixir that had served to keep him preserved for an extended period of time. How long he had lived he would not say, but he implied that he was well over a century in age. As with all things, particularly living things, a new problem had developed. The rejuvenation elixir, which was remarkably similar to my own reagent, seemed to preferentially target organs that were most in need of repair, while other, seemingly less vital organs were not renewed at all. So while Dr. C's heart was in excellent condition, he had in the last year broken three ribs.

Not surprisingly, Dr. C had developed a possible treatment, including a procedure that would likely resolve the issue. His proposal required exposure to the elixir during an extended period of quiescence, most likely years, during which the elixir would completely rebuild him. He likened this to the metamorphosis of caterpillars into butterflies, or the estivation of some fish species during periods of extreme drought. Unfortunately, the human body was not designed for such prolonged periods of hibernation. Nor could Dr. C imagine the machinery necessary to administer the elixir over that extended period of time. What he could imagine is what he had seen in his own laboratory, individual crocodilians of such resilience that the impacts of drought and famine, even extending for years, could be tolerated. Likewise the glands of these animals seemed reasonably sturdy and open to transplant and manipulation, and indeed that is what he had done. In the laboratory facility in his home Dr. C had selectively merged the glands and tissues of a dozen creatures to create a single artificial construct that would function as an organic generator of his elixir. Similarly, he had created another such organ that would serve to aid in the storage and release of nutrients during the extended period of quiescence. Like some animals, he might emerge from his artificial hibernation on occasion to replenish food and water, only to return to a state of torpor once his needs were satisfied.

It was a magnificent, beautiful, terrifying and horrifying plan, and I was as much for it as I was opposed to it. In the end, after much deliberation, I had no choice but to reject any possibility of my being involved with such a procedure. It was simply too risky, and I was not willing to take such risks with a patient that seemed in no imminent danger. I suggested that we delay the procedure until animal experiments were complete and successful. Not surprisingly, Dr. C refused to follow this more conservative path of treatment, as he was dead set on beginning the process as quickly as possible, with the understanding that it might take years to accumulate sufficient nutrient reserves to initiate the torpor he wanted to enter. What was surprising was Muñoz's reaction, for instead of siding with me, he sided with Dr. C, suggesting that whatever risk existed was best understood and borne fully by the very man who had developed the procedure. It was an impasse and we argued late into the night. In the end, we left the study in total disagreement.

The next morning nothing had changed, and reluctantly I found myself traveling back to Arkham alone. Over the next few days I packed up Dr. Rafael Muñoz's personal belongings and I crated up his strange coffin-like transportation. Workmen removed them to a truck which I hired to take them to Dr. C's residence. I sent several letters, at first merely professional, covering my progress on the reagent and making several suggestions for both Dr. C's and his own treatments, but neither they nor the later more personal letters were ever answered. That chilly May of 1912 was the last I ever saw of my friend Dr. Rafael Muñoz.

Chapter 13.
The Shadow Wanes

While I lamented the loss of my colleague and friend, the truth of the matter is that his departure marked the beginning of what can safely be said to be my own story. What I have told you up to now has merely been prelude. By the summer of 1912 my preliminary research was complete, my formula had been finalized, and I was ready to begin long-term clinical trials on human beings. Let me be clear, I consciously chose to use my patients as unwitting subjects of my experiments in reanimation using a reagent designed to be administered much as a vaccine would be, through a series of regular inoculations over the course of many years. My partner, fellow doctor Francis Wilson, had no knowledge of my intentions or of what I did over the next fifteen years. I alone am to blame for these macabre experiments, and for the events that they would lead to, the deaths of three men for which I am accused of murder.

It was June when I began treatments in earnest. As patients came in for regular appointments and treatments, I randomly exposed them to three different levels of treatment, and a fourth option, which was no treatment at all and provided a control group. As the vast majority of my patients were employees of Miskatonic University, the resulting study groups were primarily comprised of University faculty and staff. As much as I would like to protect my patients and maintain their privacy, the truth of the matter is that my files have already been riffled and those who were exposed have already been identified, and I will admit that my long-term patients, including Professors Henry Armitage and Laban Shrewsbury, were treated with the reagent. Additionally, Randolph Carter, and both Professor Henry Jones and his son, were exposed to the reagent, but as these three, amongst others, left my care, they did not receive a full regiment. To fully document who was treated and to what extent, I would have to consult my notes, which are currently held by the police. It may also be scientifically, and perhaps legally, relevant to discuss which individuals were members of my control group and therefore not treated. As with those exposed to the reagent, I would have to consult my notes to provide an accounting for this group, but as best memory serves me these individuals included Edward Derby, Zorad Hoag, and Franklin Scudder. All in all nearly one hundred and fifty people were in one way or another treated with my formula that summer, and I have no doubt, for my data leaves no room for doubt, that these treatments have had significant impacts on resistance to injury and disease, as well as longevity. I challenge anyone to review the collected data and dispute these conclusions.

Strangely, or perhaps unexpectedly, as I undertook my great experiment I found that it had been some time since I had dealt with the enmity that I had once felt for Herbert West and his aide. Indeed, while I still blamed the two for the death of my parents eight years earlier, the rage that had initially fueled my researches had waned, and for the first time in a long period of my life I seemed at peace. I dismantled Muñoz's refrigeration unit, and disposed of my extensive colony of experimental rats. I had no need for this equipment anymore. All of Arkham was my laboratory, and I reveled in the knowledge that if the formula worked as I hoped, the residents of Arkham would enjoy long lives free from the debilitations of disease and serious injury. It could lead to a golden age, a utopia of peace and serenity undreamed of save by the most idealistic of poets and philosophers.

What a fool I was, for somehow I had forgotten the lessons taught to me by my own experiments as well as those of Herbert West. I should have realized that one day, my lack of forethought would rise up, like forgotten Titans, and threaten everything I held dear.

Still, I was happy at the time, Wilson and I were enjoying our work, and without Muñoz, and the pressures of my rats, I became more open and outgoing, enjoying life as I had not since before I had become a doctor. It was inevitable that a creeping doom should cast its long-forgotten shadow over my life. In September I received a note from Peaslee, who was in Oslo of all places, recently returned from a disappointing trip to Spitzbergen. It was his intention to return to the United States as soon as possible. There were disturbing undercurrents in the politics of Europe and he had no desire to spend much more time there. His travels would bring him back in October to New York from where he would travel to some caverns in West Virginia. He was to spend several weeks in the area and then head west to visit with a man named Kirowan in Texas. Although not made explicit, there seemed to be a growing sense of ennui in Peaslee's writing. That his global travels had taken a physical toll I had no doubt, but the price seemed to be psychological, and there was some suggestion that he would be returning to Arkham within the next year.

The thought of Peaslee, or more precisely the thing that was pretending to be Peaslee, returning to Arkham made me sick. Yes, it was true that he had been responsible for helping me perfect my formula, and he had introduced me to Muñoz, but his presence, the thought of his presence, created in me such an anxiety that as the end of that lazy summer approached, something untoward happened. It was little more than a notion at first, but it then grew into a thought, and then an idea. Before long it was a plot and then a plan. Somehow or another, the hate that I had once felt for Herbert West had been transplanted to the Peaslee thing, and as the summer turned into the fall I sat down with pen and paper and carefully figured out how to kill the thing that called itself Professor Peaslee.

CHAPTER 14.

THE LAST TRANSLATION OF PR. PEASLEE

Once he returned to the United States, Peaslee's correspondence increased dramatically, and except for the two weeks that he was incommunicado in western Virginia, I was subjected to at least three letters per week detailing his travels around the country. These letters did not find their way to the newspapers, for I felt them to have no redeeming value beyond titillating the public. His travels, which crisscrossed the nation, were primarily by train or hired car, and were now focused on reading the most esoteric of volumes and communicating with the oddest of people. His focus had over the years moved steadily from the mainstream of culture to the branches of mysticism, and now finally to the fringes where the most disturbing and repudiated proponents of human thought were to be found.

He spent much time at the Sanbourne Institute in California, and even more at a settlement of Indians in the desert of Nevada. Funds were expended in the form of donations to gain access to various university libraries, but for little more than a day or so. A colleague of mine wrote to me concerning his visit, an event that had greatly disturbed the library curator. It seemed that Peaslee had met with a dean of New York's Hudson University and had some way or another persuaded him to allow him access to the University's collection of rare medieval manuscripts. What disturbed my friend the most was the manner in which the dean, normally a most strong-willed individual, seemed to be completely under Peaslee's influence. Indeed, following the visit the poor man remained in a kind of haze for days afterwards, and only recovered after the administration of several powerful stimulants. Curiously, and perhaps most disturbing, was that the dean had no recollection of the events of the week, or even of meeting with Peaslee at all.

Once word of the Hudson University incident began circulating, Peaslee found it more and more difficult to gain access to facilities, and by June of 1913 it was clear from his letters that he would soon be returning home to Arkham. In the middle of July I was asked to retain a pair of servants and a workman, and to make the house ready for his return. It was a relatively simple task and one that I took some delight in, for as I set about having the house made ready, I took time to formulate a plan for what can only be thought of as the murder of Professor Peaslee. I walked through the house and explored all the rooms. With the housekeeper and the maid I set schedules, routines and menus. With the handyman, a young engineering student by the name of Crawford Tillinghast, I created and prioritized a list of repairs and projects needed about the house and garden. Although I hadn't done it for quite some time, I made a trip to the bank and reviewed the investments and available funds. I was quite surprised at the balances and realized that Peaslee's investments had earned far more than he could possibly spend, and had accumulated a substantial savings. In the end I was in a magnificent position to plot, arrange and bring to fruition the death of Peaslee, and for that very reason, as his return became more imminent, I realized that it would be foolish to carry such an act out. For there was no more likely a suspect than I, and I had no desire to have my practice investigated by the authorities. So, as much as I would have liked, I had to put aside my desire to kill Peaslee.

The man himself sent word that he would be returning to Arkham in early August, and I arranged it so that I was personally available to meet him at the train station and transport him home. The years of travel had not been kind to Peaslee. He was thin, gauntly thin, and his eyes were sunken and heavy. His skin hung loosely in places like a second set of clothes. Despite this, he seemed rather energetic, though I was reminded that he had been subjected to a dose of the reagent that allowed for increased metabolic health. His demeanor was positive, and he greeted me with as much enthusiasm as he ever had. He had little baggage, and after loading it into the cab we drove home. He spoke at length about recent dreams that he had been having, strange dreams that brought back memories of his former life. He had visions of his classroom, and his students, as well as of the frustration he dealt with in writing his paper on seasonal patterns in economic trends. There were also discussions of his wife and family and memories of birthdays and holiday events.

I took these revelations with some skepticism, for although he spoke at length of these personal matters, they lacked any specific details, and were so generalized that they could have been memories of nearly anyone's life. He persisted in relating the existence of such memories to whomever would listen, and over the course of several weeks the story had expanded to include some details, but only of the most superficial kind. For example, he suddenly had memories of the names of former students, but could not describe any of them. Likewise he knew that one of his sons collected insects, but couldn't tell you which child that was. To me it took on the appearance that he was laying the groundwork for something, much as a writer will provide foreshadowing of major plot twists. The whole thing grated on me, and in late August I asked that he refer any future medical needs to Dr. Wilson. As for our so-called business relationship, I asked to be removed of my responsibilities. I fully expected him to threaten me with extortion over my experiments, but Peaslee simply slumped back in his chair. He seemed resigned to the thought that the days in which he could bully me into submission were long past.

The next month or so was quite difficult for me, as I did my best to ignore the man who had so greatly influenced my life over the last few years, and with whom I had finally broken, despite the fact that he lived just a few yards away. I kept tabs on the staff, and from them I learned of an odd device or machine that was being constructed. Peaslee had, over the course of several days, placed orders with craftsmen and manufacturers all over the world, and it was toward the middle of September that these orders were coming to fruition. What the device was, no one could say, and Peaslee had barred the housekeeper and maid from the room in which it had been assembled. The workman, whose knowledge of tools and parts was apparently needed at some point, described the mechanism as a confusion of metal rods and mirrors, some concave, some convex, assembled in a complex manner reminiscent of a weathervane or a whirligig. Peaslee was obsessed with the thing, apparently spending hours tinkering with its parts and perfecting the motions of its components. What it actually was, the workman would not hazard.

Peaslee redoubled his efforts to convince people that he was regaining some of his old memories, often suggesting that he was drifting in and out of different states of being in which he was at one point his new persona, and then once more his old self. I listened to these secondhand discourses with some amusement, as it was becoming more and more apparent, at least to me, that Peaslee was planning something untoward, and I shuddered at the things that I believed he had already done, and the loss of life that had resulted. Just a few days later, all of my suspicions were validated when the first chapter of the strange case of the man who forgot himself came to a crashing end.

For me, the events that led to the final closure began on Monday, September 22, 1913, for that was the day that I first saw the swarthy man that seemed to play such a crucial part in those final days. The high days of summer had passed, and now that the temperature was more tolerable I would spend my mornings between breakfast and my first patient lounging on the front veranda with my coffee and the morning edition of *The Arkham Advertiser*. I found such morning repasts to be invigorating. The sound of the city waking up, birds singing, bees buzzing, car engines humming in a mechanical drone, the soft regular step of the milkman, and the wind meandering through the streets and the trees brought a sense of much-desired normalcy to my day. But it was on that particular Monday that I noticed the dark sedan roll cautiously onto the street and crawl down the row like a cat, until it found a found a convenient place to park. Truth be said, that car to me was like an entity unto itself; with its dark windows and sleek look I did not think of it as a machine or as a possession of someone else that was operating it. No, for me that sedan was its own creature with its own will and motivations. It was only when the door opened and the swarthy man stepped out did it even dawn on me to think that there was an actual driver.

As I have said, he was a swarthy man, olive-skinned, lean with a foreign manner to his stance and walk. He was clean-shaven with round glasses perched below bushy eyebrows. Oddly, he wore no hat, nor did he even carry one. His hair was jet-black and neatly cut. As he walked he took out a pack of cigarettes, even from a distance I could tell they were Morleys, and he casually lit one before shaking the match out and letting it fall into the street. His steps, as I said, had a foreign manner to them, but he walked with purpose and determination to a rhythm that was in my mind not entirely benign. He walked as if he planned to hurt someone, as if there would soon be blood on his hands.

I leaned back into the shadows, hoping that my presence would remain unnoticed, but the movement revealed me and as those eyes turned to look at me a shudder traveled down my spine. His stride never broke as he looked me up and down with those deep black eyes that peered out from behind the curls of smoke rising from his cigarette. He took a long smooth drag before palming the smoke and reaching the curb. I stared back, mesmerized by his graceful movements and penetrating gaze. It was only after he reached the steps to Peaslee's home that he turned away, and in that moment I knew without a doubt that all the things that I had ever suspected Peaslee of doing, all those horrible things, all those dead people, I knew then that they were true, and I knew that Peaslee had brought that horror home with him to Arkham.

The swarthy man was ushered inside by Peaslee himself, and I saw no more of him that first day, though I knew that he was gone by noon, which was when the housekeeper and maid always began their days. Peaslee had long ago adjusted the schedule of the house to one of his own liking, and that included privacy in the morning hours, after which he would often consume a massive midday meal followed by a similar evening meal. Both the housekeeper and the maid would normally stay at least until eight in the evening. Not bound to this schedule was the workman who would begin his day much earlier, but had strict instructions not to enter the house in the morning or to create any significant disturbances prior to that. Thus the gardening and any of the light outdoor work was carried out in the early part of the day while other noisier work was delayed to the afternoon.

The pattern repeated itself on Tuesday and Wednesday, though on these days the visitor carried with him several large iron-clasped books with tattered covers and thick rough-cut pages. Large metallic characters that I did not recognize were inscribed on their covers, and consisted mainly of groupings of triangular shapes linked by lines. Intrigued, and knowing that whatever was going on between the two men was likely of a devious nature, I took some time Thursday morning, and when the strange swarthy man made his way from the car to the house I endeavored to copy the characters as best I could. I then met with a friend at the University who specialized in the study of Middle Eastern language and literature. I explained to him about the strange visitor and how I was concerned for the safety of my client. He was intrigued by the design of the characters and suggested that they were reminiscent of cuneiform writing that was amongst the earliest of known languages. While he couldn't promise me anything, he said he would try and figure out what the characters meant. I thanked him and hurried home. I had not expected to hear from my friend for several days or perhaps even weeks, but to my surprise it was on the morning of the next day that he surprised me by meeting me on the veranda while I was having coffee.

Dr. Angell was very excited over what he had found, but the details escaped me. As I tried to calm the young academician my gaze was drawn to the sleek black sedan as it crawled down the road and coasted to a stop in the location it had occupied every morning of this week. I must have been staring, because Angell turned to look at what had distracted me and saw for himself the swarthy man as he stalked across the road with his armful of books, the strange and intriguing symbol glinting in the morning sun. Angell stepped away from me, and even though I put a hand on his shoulder to stop him, he twisted away and with a leap down the stairs and a brisk pace he was soon on a course to intercept the man. Angell called out, asking the man if he could ask him a question. When the man did not respond, did not even break his queer stride, Angell tried again, this time in Latin. As the man reached the curb he turned and allowed Angell to approach him. Angell spoke to the man at length in Latin, though my own grasp of the language being poor I cannot tell you exactly what he said. After nearly a minute of this Angell paused in his monologue, obviously expecting an answer. He waited in silence for a response. The stranger looked the young teacher up and down and in silence turned to leave. Forgetting himself, Angell reached out and gently tried to persuade the man to stay. As soon as his hand touched the man there was a flurry of motion, and suddenly Angell was on the ground. I moved off the porch, but the man's violent stare and a single raised finger made it clear that I was not to interfere. As I raised both my hands in a gesture of peace, the angry dark man opened his mouth and in a clear and booming voice uttered a strange and violent phrase, "WARD AM NA TAK!" Then as if we weren't there at all he turned and went up the walkway to Peaslee's house where, as ever, he was ushered in by Peaslee himself.

I rushed to my friend's side and helped him up and onto the veranda. I brought him a drink and allowed Angell to compose himself before questioning him. The young man related how after I had left him with my copy of the glyphs he had almost immediately recognized them for what they were, and was quick to consult the works of master linguist Harley Warren. The figures seemed to be Nacaal, a kind of proto-Akkadian, the language of the ancient Sumerians. Nacaal had been the language of the gods, and was used in only the most sacred of institutions, religious texts, laws, ceremonies and the like. The symbols that I had provided seemed at first to be a Nacaalian version of the Sumerian Summa Izbu, literally the law books for the prophecy of monsters, an ancient codex which suggested that the appearance of certain human oddities and mythological creatures could be used to predict the future. This in itself, the discovery of a text purporting to be the Summa Izbu, as opposed to clay tablets, would have been a significant anthropological discovery, as would have been the sect that had maintained it. However, the more Angell delved the more he realized that the subtle differences between the Akkadian glyphs and the Nacaal were not merely the result of a drift in the style of form, but rather represented a true difference in words, phrase and meaning. The symbols on the book were not Summa Izbu, but rather Summa Ysgl, a phrase that Angell translated as a course in the prophecy of monsters, though this was not a literal translation. More literally, the Summa Ysgl would mean "A Future History of the Monsters of the Earth," although even this was difficult because the term Monsters of the Earth was never defined.

Angell cursed as he finished up his coffee. "If we were to obtain a copy of that book, Stuart, the recorded history of our world, everything we know about the ancient civilizations, might be changed forever."

Thankfully Angell had not yet developed my sense of foreboding when it came to dealing with Peaslee, and I viewed his optimism as refreshing, for while he looked to the book as potentially a fresh window that would illuminate the past of the human race, I feared it, for I thought that it might be something men should not have, a scrying glass that would forever doom our futures. Composed, Angell made to leave, but I stopped him before he reached the sidewalk.

"He said something to you, something I couldn't understand."

Angell nodded as he put his hat on and twisted it down over his ears. "I can't be sure, mind you, but I think it was Nacaal. It sounded about right though I have never heard it spoken before, but we have always assumed it would sound much like Arabic or Hebrew, and this fits the bill. It was a simple phrase, and if I were to guess it would probably be in a pidgin so that I would be sure to understand it. He made it clear that I was not to bother him in the future."

Frustrated by Angell's indirectness, I finally put the question to him directly, "What did he say?"

Angell turned away and started down the walkway, smiling as he did so. I thought he was going to leave me guessing, but after a few steps he turned round and with an odd tone to his voice he repeated those strange words. "Ward Am Na Tak means 'A slave should know his place'." And with that young Dr. Angell continued his meandering walk back to Miskatonic University.

The rest of the day went as normal. I saw patients and a quick glance out the window let me know that the dark man, whom in my mind I kept referring to as the Akkadian (although clearly this was a misnomer), was gone before the housekeeper and maid arrived at noon. Over dinner, I resigned myself to the fact that if I were to gain any more knowledge concerning what was going on in my neighbor's house, I was going to have to take a more active role. It was as this serendipitous thought rolled about in my head that a most curious thing occurred. As I have said, the housekeeper and maid were scheduled daily from noon till about eight in the evening, but for some odd reason I suddenly heard the voices of these two women walking past my house hours earlier than normal. Eavesdropping on their conversation, I soon learned that Peaslee had dismissed them for the evening. Realizing that events might be coming to a head, I finished my own dinner and quickly locked up the house and turned off all of the lights. Any casual observer would conclude that I had either retired early or gone out for the night.

It was just after ten when the great black sedan arrived and took up its perch on the street. The Akkadian crossed the street with that strange smooth gait that was so foreign in its cadence with the iron-clasped books tucked under his arm. It was hypnotic, the way he moved, and it was different than how he had done so during the day. The dark of night seemed to feed him somehow, lending him an air of mystery and weirdness. He walked like a man with a purpose; he walked with confidence and grace, as if the world were watching and as if the whole of existence depended on what he did next. It wasn't until the door opened up and the Akkadian slithered out of my view that I was finally able to take my eyes off of him. It was then that a seed of a plan began to take root and grow within my mind.

To tell the truth there was not much of a plan, but I was determined to learn what my nefarious neighbor and his strange foreign partner were up to. It had been many years since I had skulked about in the fields and woods outside of Herbert West's farmhouse, but those trips had served me well, and soon I was slinking out the side door and creeping through the gardens. I cursed silently at Tillinghast and his damned penchant for beds full of delicate flowers and soft soil, but I negotiated the treacherous lovelies without leaving any tell-tale signs of my presence. In mere moments I was secreted beneath the window which led to Peaslee's private study, the one from which the servants had been barred. With great care I slowly rose up until I could see through the window and into the room.

There were heavy curtains on the inside of the window, drawn tight but not tightly enough, for a small gap near the sill allowed me a limited but sufficient view of the room. Through the gap I could see that Peaslee and the Akkadian were going over the contents of several sheaves of paper that were covered in clusters of the symbols which Angell had identified for me as Naacal. They were not speaking English; I would say that the words had to them a Semitic sound, not unlike Hebrew, and certainly not unlike the words cursed at Angell when he accosted the Akkadian on the street. In all likelihood they were speaking Nacaal. What they were saying was unknown to me, but there seemed to be some disagreement over how what was written on the free sheaves compared to what was written in one of the iron-clasped books, the one that Angell had suggested was called the Summa Ysgl. Evidently Peaslee was unhappy with how certain things had been transcribed from one to the other. I wish I could say that the argument was one that had occurred between equals, but from what I could see it was plain that Peaslee was the dominant party and that the Akkadian was subservient, for soon the strange dark man was amending the contents of the book, albeit under Peaslee's close supervision.

The changes took more than an hour, and there seemed to me to be some pressing need to complete the task. More than once Peaslee paced about the room, several times coming dangerously close to the window; each time I shrank back, thinking he might casually part the curtains and catch me there spying on him. At just after midnight Peaslee finished reviewing the Akkadian's work and seemed to find it satisfactory. It was then that an even stranger argument began to ensue. In the study's fireplace the Akkadian quickly built a small but functional blaze and busied himself feeding the free sheaves of paper into it, and then stirring the flecks of burnt and burning paper into a fine unreadable ash. The disagreement seemed to concern a stack of manila envelopes that Peaslee produced from his desk drawer. The Akkadian seemed to have no desire to involve himself with these files, and indeed there apparently had been some breach of protocol, for suddenly the Akkadian was outraged and insistent. From the way he grabbed at the documents and motioned, it was clear that the man was intent on burning these as well. The heated discussion went on for a good two or three minutes when suddenly Peaslee snapped and in a firm bellowing voice repeated the same words that I had heard the Akkadian mutter the day before, "WARD AM NA TAK," a slave should know his place!

There was what appeared to be much supplication on the Akkadian's part, and some sort of arrangement concerning the envelopes was agreed upon, though what it was I could not say. The stack of files was placed on a side table and the moldy text that was the Summa Ysgl was placed on top of them. The desk top was cleared of whatever clutter remained and from off to the side somewhere the Akkadian produced a crate about two feet tall and a foot both deep and wide which he carefully set in the center of the desk. He deftly clipped free two pairs of latches and with some trepidation lifted the crate off of its base revealing the contents within.

It was every bit as odd as the handyman Tillinghast had said, and I could see why his description had referenced the whirligig, for indeed there was resemblance to that childhood plaything, but it was so much more complicated than that. There were rods jointed to rods with more joints and more rods yet. There were mirrors as well, convex, conical things that splayed light across the room, and deep concave bowls that seemed to swallow light into tiny pools of infinite darkness. With a simple flick of his finger the Akkadian put the tiniest of tertiary rods in motion, sending the convex mirror at its apex spinning, and showering the room in a prism of color that danced around the walls in a multitude of streaking stars.

What happened next I do not fully understand, for I did not see the Akkadian or Peaslee touch the device, but inexplicably the electric lights throughout the house suddenly went dark while the spinning rod accelerated to a point that the radiant streaks about the room seemed to cease being singular points but rather had become smears shifting from indigo at one end through the full range of the spectrum and then vanishing into the sharp burning red at the other. It was then that I heard that awful high-pitched whine, and the single smear of lights was suddenly joined by another set traveling perpendicular to the first. Somehow, without losing any of its own velocity, the spinning tertiary rod had enticed the secondary rod to which it was attached to begin moving as well. This spontaneous transfer of energy from one plane of movement to another was inexplicable to me, and I must admit that I stood outside that window with the lights spinning and dancing with a look of utter bewilderment upon my face.

My amazement was only to grow, for as I watched, the individual rods and mirrors of the contraption, without any outside influence, continued to spontaneously initiate their angular rotations, casting upon the walls of the room an unending spiraling dance of light like some fiendish psychosis-induced maelstrom of color. Through it all, that high-pitched screeching whine ate at my ears, devouring my nerves and seeping into my skull like an acid poured onto a metal plate.

While I watched this phantasmagorical light show unfold I seemed to transcend myself, time and space suddenly seemed to be meaningless and I seemed suddenly unbound from my body. As I floated free, I could see other forms floating about me. Some were pale, transparent, abstract geometries; others were clusters of repeating forms like bubbles, or stacks of dodecahedrons. There were other more bizarre forms, and a sensation that there was not only intelligence behind some of them, but also malevolence. Thankfully, I did not stay in this disembodied state long, for suddenly, as if I had been forced into a rushing torrent, I was returned to my flesh, and once more stared out through my own eyes. The light show had ended, and as I clung to the windowsill trying to recover some sense of balance I watched as the Akkadian carefully moved Peaslee's body from the chair to a small divan in the corner. He then with just as much care began to disassemble the strange conglomeration of rods and mirrors before packing them into the case. A quick glance at my watch told me that it was well after 2:00, and I suddenly had a sneaking suspicion that if I was ever going to do anything, it would have to be now.

With great care I dislodged myself from beneath the window, and quickly but quietly made my way to the front door. Surprisingly, the door was not locked, and I gently eased it open wide enough for me to slip in. I scanned the foyer for a weapon and found one in a walking stick tucked into the umbrella stand. The lights of the house were still off, but there was a fierce glow emanating from beneath the door to the study which based on the way it flickered, I took to be a candle. Softly I crept through the house toward the study door, from beyond which I could hear someone, whom I assumed was the Akkadian, moving about. From the flickering of the candle and the shadows it cast, I had some idea where the man was, and when he moved away from the door, I took a deep breath, firmly grabbed the knob, and in a single manic motion flung the door ajar and charged in, my makeshift club raised up and ready to strike. Caught by surprise, the Akkadian quickly latched the crate shut and clutched it to his chest as he maneuvered behind the desk. He was obviously startled, but frightened as well. I stalked toward the desk and he backed away toward the window beneath which I had been hiding. As I rounded the desk to reach him he countered, and soon he was backing out the door. He paused briefly and glanced at the prone form of Peaslee; I took advantage of the distraction and moved in closer, causing him to jump back. He shifted the weight of the box onto one arm, and with his free hand he grasped the binding of that horrid thick volume that was sitting on a side table and transferred it to on top of the crate. In the process he spilled the various files that had been of such contention onto the floor. He bent down at the knees in a desperate attempt to pick them up, but I raised the stick even higher and shook my head meaningfully. Understanding me completely, we two took the next few moments to slowly continue our little charade until the Akkadian had reached the front door and then was outside of it. As he stood there in the dark of the night, his eyes frantic but silent, I smiled evilly and without a word shut the door behind the horrid little man. The lock clicked into place and from the side window I watched as he trotted to his obsidian sedan and quickly drove off.

Returning to the study, I glanced at the clock and was surprised that the hour of 3:00 was rapidly approaching. I will not deny that I went in and stood over the prone and helpless form of Peaslee. Nor will I deny that I raised the walking stick above my head with full intent on striking Peaslee's unprotected skull. I did this three times before the courage to follow through left me and I staggered back away from the couch and slumped down against the table in emotional agony. I sat there with my eyes closed, my hands shaking, my heart pounding, unable to bring myself to kill the man—the monster that lay vulnerable before me. I sat there pitying myself for my own weakness when the scattered files, Peaslee's five manila envelopes, came to my attention. Each was addressed to a different person, and these were scattered over the globe. Knowing the horrors that had been inflicted by Peaslee on the world, I felt justified in opening each package and reading their contents. After determining that the contents of each packet were identical, I sat down and took the time to completely read the dozens of pages Peaslee had intended to post. It took me more than an hour to pore through them, during which I periodically checked to make sure that Peaslee was still alive but unconscious. Afterwards, I fretted for a moment and then with stoic determination tossed four sets into the fireplace and, after stirring the dying embers, made sure that the contents were irretrievably burned.

It was after five when I crept back to my own home. I showered, shaved and made myself coffee and breakfast before wandering out to the veranda around 6:15, just in time to find my partner Dr. Wilson scrambling down the sidewalk. Seeing me, he called out, telling me to grab my bag and the key to Peaslee's home. I did so and soon joined him as he trekked over to my neighbor's door. He had received a phone call just around 6:00 that had urged him to go and check on Peaslee. The voice, oddly foreign but of indeterminate origin, suggested that Peaslee had suffered a seizure of some kind and was in mortal danger. Police would later trace that call to a phone in Boston's North Station. That it was the Akkadian that had placed the call, I have no doubt, but inquiries by the police revealed that no one at the station could recall seeing anything out of the ordinary that morning.

Peaslee was where I left him on the divan, and yes, I have realized that I have confessed to the crime of breaking and entering as well as an assault, and possibly attempted murder, but I do not care, the truth must be revealed. Wilson checked Peaslee's vital signs and found his breathing shallow and peculiar. We discussed a course of action and Wilson and I agreed that a hypo-injection of stimulants would be called for. I returned to our offices and prepared the syringe, and only contemplated contaminating the mixture with a toxin briefly, before returning to the house and handing the needle to Wilson. The treatment seemed to work, for Peaslee's breathing became more regular almost immediately.

Briefly, I returned to the house, and with the help of our receptionist, proceeded to cancel all of our appointments for the day, and then quickly returned to Wilson's side. We moved Peaslee's unconscious body from the study to one of the bedrooms and made him as comfortable as possible. Fearing that the worst might occur, we agreed that others must be notified of Peaslee's condition and therefore called both the police and Alice, Peaslee's ex-wife. While the police said they would send over a representative,

Alice simply thanked us and asked to be kept informed for the sake of the children. Given the last few years, I couldn't fault her for her position.

The rest of the story is well known. At a little after eleven in the morning Peaslee began to thrash about, though not violently, and the strange emotionless mask that had for so long adorned his face for these many years seemed to melt away and relax, and in that moment the humanity that had once graced his form returned. A little after this, at approximately 11:30, he opened his mouth and there issued forth a curious conglomeration of syllables that none present could make heads or tails of, and at that moment no one thought to write them down. It was noon when the maid and housekeeper joined us, and soon after they let in Detective Sergeant Kohler. No sooner had we finished bringing the officer up to date than we were suddenly interrupted by a voice I had not heard in quite some time. Peaslee was speaking, and more than that, he was speaking words I myself had heard when I took one of his classes, for it was a passage from one of his many lectures that he was reciting. Kohler had the sense to write it down, and we later compared it to his notes. Without a doubt the old personality of Professor Peaslee had returned to us and picked up in his life exactly where he had left off those many years past, lecturing to his students on economic theory.

It took many months for Nathaniel Peaslee to come to terms with what had happened to him. I did what I could to help, but kept my distance as well, allowing Wilson to be his primary physician in concert with a psychoanalyst. Soon after this event I ceased to be his executor, and turned over control to one of his bankers. I could no longer stand to be in the room with Peaslee. He was pleasant enough, but his mere presence reminded me too much of the ease in which some monstrous thing had displaced him and usurped his being for so many years, for if it could happen to him why not anyone else, including me?

Of the things that had been written and left behind, of those strange files that were to be sent around the world, I shall make only this confession. I still have the copy I did not burn that day, and on occasion I still read them, and I must admit I have yet to comprehend them in their entirety. They are excerpts; key excerpts, of what Angell purported to be a translation of the Summa Ysgl, or as my friend had translated it, "The Future History of the Monsters of the Earth." In keeping with its title the text prophesies-key events that are to occur, though they have nothing to do with the appearance of monsters, at least not as we know them. Many are completely incomprehensible, except in retrospect, and others are seemingly minor developments that I cannot understand the significance of. Why these things were to be shared with a select group of obscure savants I cannot know, but I have learned one thing. The monsters that are referred to in the title, the monsters of the earth, have nothing to do with any chthonic deities or infernal demons; no, I think the term monster would be better translated as "oddities" at least in the eyes of the author. It is a book about the future written by those that consider the earth their rightful dominion, and the monsters of the earth are its current inhabitants, the species I myself belong to, humans.

CHAPTER 15.

DOCTOR GOGOL'S EXAMINATION

The year that followed Peaslee's recovery was, for me, a time of re-evaluation. For the first time in many years, I was able to focus solely on my medical practice and my experiments in death, without fear of interference or pressure from outside forces. I was no longer Peaslee's servant, and neither my colony of rats nor Muñoz were hiding in my basement. Oddly, the years had softened my resolve and the anger and desire for revenge against Herbert West and Daniel Cain were naught but cooling embers. I was free, and except for the responsibilities to my patients and my partner Dr. Wilson, I had no other concerns or projects beyond those I set for myself.

After much deliberation, I decided that I would stay focused on what I had come to think of as the great experiment, and I expanded my experimental design to include nearly all my patients. The components for my reagent had recently become readily available, and I assumed that the previous primary consumer, Dr. C, was no longer in need of them. Excluded from the inoculations was a small control group, and infants and children under the age of 16, primarily because I had no understanding of my reagent's impact on the developmental process, nor did I want to explore the possibilities of such results. Strangely, in late February of 1914, I received a letter that suggested that the effects of my reagent on human development might be profound.

It had been more than twenty months since I went to visit my friend and colleague Dr. William Houghton, at whose cabin in the Round Mountains around Dunwich we spent a strange and harrowing weekend, and in that time a most curious thing had developed. The news conveyed by William in a letter concerned Lavinia Whateley, the albino girl who had stolen and imbibed a vial of my reagent, and then was the victim of some strange and wholly unrelated events on Sentinel Hill. Apparently not long after, the girl showed signs of having become pregnant out of wedlock—sometime around our encounter with her—and in February of 1913 had given birth to a son whom she named Wilbur. Neither Lavinia nor her father would name her paramour, and there was some discussion of an incestuous relationship between the two. Other theories abounded, and William related how both he and I were occasionally mentioned as possible fathers to Lavinia's black brat, though no one ever took such talk seriously.

Such backwoods gossip served only to lay the basis for the real gist of Houghton's letter, for Wilbur Whateley was a precocious child, exhibiting developmental and behavioral traits well in advance of his peers. At a mere seven months old he was found to be walking unaided, and by eight months all traces of unsteadiness had vanished. Reliable witnesses reported seeing him on All Hallows' Eve, running after his mother up Sentinel Hill. Most recently, at the age of just eleven months, young Wilbur began to talk and showed no signs of the lisping habits so often associated with toddlers. Moreover, those who heard him speak swore on two matters: First, that the child, who had not yet turned a year of age, used complete and understandable sentences, simple sentences, local idioms really, most likely bantered about by his mother and grandfather, and no doubt parroted back, but the young child seemed gifted with some spark of genius, and seemed to understand the meaning of what he said completely.

The other thing that the villagers of Dunwich were willing to take an oath to was the child's precocious vocalizations, for while all agreed that Wilbur was a remarkably ugly child, his voice was hauntingly beautiful, and seemed to be produced by a process unassociated with his vocal cords. One local, who had once served aboard a trader that had plied the waters around Australia, suggested that the sound was not unlike that produced by an aboriginal wooden wind instrument called a dijibolou. This primitive instrument produced a kind of tedious droning, and could, like many wind instruments, be made to talk, or imitate the sounds of various words, though this took some skill. There were also comparisons to the throaty, cooing sounds produced by pigeons and other birds.

To my mind this sounded as if the reagent that Lavinia had ingested had had some impact on the neonatal development of the child, perhaps accelerating his post-partum growth and development to abnormal rates. Also given his strange vocalizations, I considered the possibility that there may have been teratological impacts to his organs as well. Fascinated, I wrote to Houghton and asked if he could arrange for me to examine the boy, and perhaps bring him into Arkham for an examination using the newly acquired fluoroscope at the hospital. Houghton wrote back in March with relatively bad news. Noah Whateley, Wilbur's grandfather, had scoffed at the idea of bringing the boy into Arkham for medical tests, going so far as to draw comparisons to the treatment of John Merrick, the Elephant Man, and accounts of the Frankenstein monsters.

Disappointed but undeterred, I chose to write to the Whateleys myself asking if I could come to Dunwich and examine the boy there. I posted my request in late March, and in April received a note back from Noah Whateley scrawled on what appeared to be a sheet of vellum torn out of an old black letter book. He apologized, but he could see no purpose in letting me examine Wilbur, for another doctor had already done that, and he saw no reason to subject either the boy or his family to a repeat of that experience, which had been somewhat traumatic for all involved.

I quickly wrote to Houghton, keen to find out who had seen the boy, and what conclusions he had drawn, and was surprised, in fact somewhat perturbed, when I received no response until June. Given the circumstances, the delay was understandable, and in a letter written later I apologized to Houghton for any ill thoughts I may have had toward him. Houghton had discovered the name of the man quite readily, Dr. Valentin Gogol, a native of Russia who had immigrated several years ago, and a recent graduate of the University medical school. Despite significant surgical skills, his aptitude with spoken English was rather poor and he had difficulty in finding a position. He had finally settled for a position as a state physician traveling amongst the backwoods of Massachussetts, seeing patients who didn't have access to regular medical care, people exactly like the Whateleys.

My interest in Wilbur's condition continued to grow, and within days I sent a letter to the state inquiring on how to reach Dr. Gogol. I did not have to wait long for a response. A brief note informed me that my quarry was no longer serving with the state, but had recently been sent to a hospital with which I had some familiarity. The Sefton Asylum was the location in which the Arkham Horror had been committed after being caught after the brutal murder of my own parents and others. At the mention of the asylum, there was a flood of emotion, and I must admit that I loathed the idea of visiting the place. Still, my desire to discuss Wilbur Whateley with Dr. Gogol and go over his notes and conclusions was foremost in my mind, and key to gaining a clue to the effect of my reagent on embryo development and maturation. Resolved, I decided to travel to the institution forthwith, and did not even take the time to check on Dr. Gogol's availability.

The trip to the asylum was short but pleasant, the weather being unseasonably mild, and I soon found myself in front of a robust receptionist who greeted me cheerfully as I came in to the notorious facility. I introduced myself and explained that I would like to consult with one of the hospital's physicians, Dr. Valentin Gogol. At this request, the smile that had graced the woman's face suddenly dimmed, and she solemnly asked me to repeat myself. Doing so generated no change in her demeanor, but she asked me to wait while she made inquiries. From my seat on a small couch I could do naught but observe that I had caused something of a furor. The receptionist made three separate phone calls, each time relaying my request to whomever was on the other end, but in a most unprofessional way that consisted of anxious whispers and furtive glances in my direction. Finally after several minutes of this she hung up the phone and announced that someone would be with me shortly.

The man who came to meet me was an aged fellow, balding and slightly heavyset, with a deep Boston Brahmin accent. He greeted me with a hearty handshake and introduced himself as C. E. Winchester, a psychiatrist who was working with Gogol. There was an air of superiority about him that reminded me of Muñoz, but while some might have taken it for aloofness, I recognized it as simply supreme self-confidence. In a rather direct manner he asked me why I wanted to see Gogol. Unprepared for such a question, I quickly fabricated a story as close to the truth as I could. I explained that I had for the last several years been studying Progeria and Werner's Syndrome, diseases that seemed to accelerate aging. Gogol had examined a young boy with an unusually rapid developmental process, and I had hoped to speak to him about his observations.

Winchester nodded. "We have all heard Gogol's stories about Wilbur Whateley, Dr. Hartwell. I am not sure that he will be much help to you, but I'll be glad to take you to him." With that enigmatic comment we were suddenly on our way into the wards of the hospital. Our walk was something of a tour of the facility, and although I cannot be certain, it would seem that we somehow or another made a circuitous path through the entire building, passing through every possible ward. Winchester gave a concise description of each section, and highlighted some of the more extreme cases of paranoia, amnesia, and dementia. I suspect that the brief visit that we paid to the Ward for the Criminally Insane was solely for the purpose of showing me the unnamed and unkempt thing that was kept there, for Winchester made it clear that he knew of my relationship to the thing that wandered aimlessly within that cell bound within a straightjacket, moaning and mouthing obscenely.

After a good twenty minutes of walking, we two finally came to the ward in which the least violent of patients were housed, a space that looked not unlike the common room in a private club; there were overstuffed chairs, a small library and even a phonograph. Were you to meet these patients on the street, you might not notice that they were disturbed, for they appeared quite normal in both dress and personal habits. Dr. Winchester pointed out a pair of men sitting at a table. "Gogol is playing cards with the Colonel; he's the one on the left."

I thanked Winchester and strode across the room to introduce myself. Gogol was a small dark man with dark wispy hair cut neatly and combed across the top of his round head. His eyes were deeply set but bulged out of their sockets. His lips were thin and pale. There was overall some queer resemblance to a frog, and I had to force myself to take the man seriously, particularly after he opened his mouth to speak, for his voice was raspy, almost gravelly, as if it was hissing out of a badly maintained phonograph.

"Dr. Gogol, I was wondering if I could speak with you about one of your patients?"

Gogol stood. "Excuse me, would you, Colonel?" He gestured towards a pair of chairs in the nearest corner that would provide a modicum of privacy, although I noticed that Winchester was discreetly watching us the whole time.

After we settled in he asked me what he could do for me. Building on the half-truth I had told Winchester, I made my request to Gogol. "I have been carrying out research on conditions associated with accelerated aging and degeneration, Progeria and Werner's Syndrome in particular. It has come to my attention that you recently examined a child who may be exhibiting some similar symptoms. I would like to discuss his condition with you and perhaps go over your notes."

A most puzzled look came over his face, and with great and deliberate care he lifted his left hand up and spread his fingers wide, flexing them open and closed. His eyes left mine and instead seemed to focus on the workings of his own hand. "I am sorry, Dr. Hartwell, but I am not sure of what child you are speaking."

I thought for a moment that the man was being deliberately obtuse. "In Dunwich, you examined the Whateley boy, Wilbur."

Gogol continued to flex his hand and fingers. "I am perpetually fascinated by the structure of the human hand, doctor. It is an amazing construct of bones, muscle tendons and flesh, and has not been reproduced amongst the invertebrates. One can think of the hand as the crowning achievement of mammalian evolution, far superior to the mollusk's tentacle or the crustacean's claw." His voice was distant, almost dream-like.

My frustration was growing. "Dr. Gogol, did you or did you not examine the boy Wilbur Whateley?"

Gogol's hand dropped limply to his lap and his gaze fixed mine in a most malicious manner. "You want to know about Wilbur Whateley, Dr. Hartwell. I'll tell you about Wilbur. The first thing you notice about Wilbur is that he has no chin, and that his eyes are an incredibly dark shade of violet. He smells like carrion, and when he speaks his voice bellows in a way that reminds me of whales singing. If you are a doctor, and you take the time to watch him, you will notice that he never blinks, ever. Nor does he breathe, though there is an odd rhythmic fluttering of his shirt tail. If you have the opportunity to actually examine him you will notice other things, things that should not be. His fingers bend backwards. He can roll his whole arm up like a length of rope. There are I suspect no bones in that hand, no bones in that arm. Perhaps no bones at all in his body."

I went to speak, but he interrupted me. "How is that possible? How is it that Wilbur Whateley can roll his arm up like a piece of rope or chain of sausages?" There was spittle leaking out of his lips as he spoke and his eyes grew wild. "What kind of man is he to have hands that look like ours, but aren't ours?" He rose up out of his chair shaking.

Dr. Winchester was suddenly there. "It's all right, Valentin, calm down. Dr. Hartwell, would you wait by the door for me?"

It was as I walked away that I realized my mistake, for Dr. Valentin Gogol was not employed by the Sefton Asylum; he was a patient. He had been driven mad by his examination of the child Wilbur Whateley, a child that was likely the product of my own reanimation reagent being ingested by his mother, and having a horrifying teratological effect on her fetus, a child that now only appeared human, but was more akin to the boneless creatures of the sea. A creature, no a monster that I had created. Wilbur Whateley's condition was my fault, as was Gogol's nervous condition.

It was a moment later, as Winchester was ushering me away, that Gogol called out to me and sent me fleeing from the asylum in abject horror. I am sure Winchester did not understand, for Gogol had shouted out a simple rhetorical question, one not so dissimilar to questions asked by students of medicine or theology or philosophy all over the world.

"What kind of God?" called out Gogol, "What kind of God, what kind of creator would make our hands, such beautiful hands, and then mock them with those possessed by Wilbur Whateley?"

To this day I do not know. If Wilbur Whateley was my creation, then what kind of creator, what kind of God am I?

CHAPTER 16.

THE ATROCITIES OF WAR

It was in June of 1914 that the spark of Archduke Ferdinand's assassination lit the powder keg of war in Europe. By the end of August the Great War had come upon the world, and although the United States was slow to enter, the people of New England were not. Throughout Arkham, it was not uncommon for me to learn that one of my patients had bid farewell to his family and then made the trip north to Canada to volunteer for military service. By November, the *Advertiser* estimated that five percent of all the able-bodied men of Arkham had left for the war. There was in those days a great feeling that the men of New England must rise up in aid of their ancestral homes of Great Britain and Europe.

So it came as no surprise when a representative of the Canadian forces came to the August meeting of the Miskatonic Valley Medical Society to discuss the recruitment of qualified medical professionals to the cause. West and his partner were there, as were others, and it seemed obvious that the war would create certain possibilities for those carrying out less than reputable lines of research; and even though I had somewhat abandoned that direction of study, the opportunity which presented itself was intriguing. I will admit that my first and foremost goal was to serve and aid the war effort, but if in doing that I was also able to forward the cause of medical science, so much the better.

It took several weeks to tidy up my affairs and bring Wilson up to speed on my patients. Knowing that Wilson was going to be alone in our office with what amounted to unfettered access to my home, I took the precaution of thoroughly sealing up my secret laboratory so that only the most detailed of inspections would reveal it. Additionally, I drew up documents dealing with the disposition of my estate were I to be killed or incapacitated while overseas. In this I made it clear that the notes and documents which detailed my methods and formula for the reagent, which I had placed in my safety deposit box, were not to be turned over to Wilson, but rather to the individual I thought could most benefit from them, Dr. Herbert West. However, knowing something of the whims of war, I included a clause that delayed distribution of these papers until seven years after I had been declared missing, or in the case of my apparent death, a four-year delay. Given all of these tasks, I did not leave Arkham until the fall of 1914, and did not arrive in England until the spring of 1915.

I will not bore you with a detailed record of my service, but I feel obliged to expound on one event that so impacted me that my experiments in reanimation and life extension were forever altered. It was the summer of 1916, and I found myself attached to a small unit of Americans at Fort Souville near the French town of Verdun. A vast network of tunnels and trenches served both the Germans and the French who had been battling in the area since late February. The frigid winter had given way to a wet spring, and by June the war-torn landscape had become unbearably humid. By the first week of July my infirmary was treating not only bullet and artillery wounds, but also a particularly infectious species of fungus. The creeping grey nodules seemed particularly fond of open wounds, and despite my best efforts to eradicate it, the troops were constantly scraping growths of the stuff off of their equipment, clothing, and bandages.

In my efforts as a doctor I was assisted by two other Americans, soldiers who had for one reason or another been reassigned away from the front. The first of these was a downed pilot, Casey Lee, a dull young man who seemed eager to play the hero. The fact that his return to an airfield had been delayed by the vagaries of war seemed to perturb him to the extreme, and to be honest such an attitude did nothing to help either me or the wounded. The second man was almost completely the opposite. In his early twenties, older than Casey by a good five years, Nick was a dashing young man from a small town in upstate New York called Sycamore Springs. Where Casey was inattentive, Nick was observant; where Casey was brash, Nick was modest. Never in the world could I have seen two more opposing personalities, and

I cannot understand why they quickly became inseparable friends. This in itself created problems for me. With Casey always intruding, and Nick acting almost as a kind of camp policeman, my ability to carry out any kind of rigorous experiments on casualties was extremely curtailed. Only when the workload became especially heavy, and my two assistants were forced to leave me alone, was I able to experiment in the administration of my reagent, though admittedly, I was able to carry out some prophylactic work on troops who came to me for minor issues, such as bad teeth and the occasional delousing. All in all, I had inoculated approximately one hundred of the soldiers in the American unit.

It was in the early hours of the tenth that we began to suspect things were about to turn for the worse. The Germans were pulling back from their positions, quietly abandoning the most forward of their trenches. This act was a common prelude to artillery barrages that were meant to soften the French front before a push forward by the German infantry. On edge, we made preparations to receive the wounded that were sure to soon be flowing into our midst. If only it had been artillery that the Germans had used, perhaps things would have been much different.

It was just after dawn when the first distant thuds of cannon were heard echoing across the landscape. They came in rapid succession: Thud! Thud! Thud! What followed was that awful high-pitched, slow whistling that chilled you down to your bones and made your teeth ache. We waited with bated breath for the impact thump and the nearly instantaneous after-explosion, but when the deadened sound of the shells hitting the soft ground came, there was a moment of still silence instead of the expected cacophony of deadly metallic shards. We looked at each other with questioning eyes, afraid to say anything for fear of being made the fool, even just for an instant. Then the hissing sound began creeping across the no man's land, and soldiers were screaming in French, and we knew that what had been launched was so much worse than mortar shells.

Green cross gas was so named for the color and symbol that decorated the shells that it was carried in, but I knew it by its true name: trichloromethyl chloroformate, or more commonly diphosgene. Odorless and invisible, you could only tell where it was by how the light seemed to waver slightly, for diphosgene was denser than air and clung to the earth like a blanket of death. More thuds and more screaming shells came down, this time closer to the French side. Soon the right range would be found and the shells would be falling amongst our troops, seeping down into the trenches and fortifications. Military historians will tell you that the shelling went on for hours, and in the end approximately 60,000 shells would have been expended. They will also tell you that the effort was of limited success, for by this time the French had been equipped with the new M2 gas masks which negated the effects of the gas. They will tell you this, because that is what officially happened. I will tell you what I know to be the truth.

The German bombardment of the French positions was an overwhelming success. The gas masks that were supposed to protect the troops were only effective if they were properly worn, and based on my observations less than a third of the troops were able to carry out this simple task. With the majority of the French unprotected to some degree or other, the gas inflicted its damage, driving soldiers into a gasping retreat. Even those whose masks were properly functioning fled the lines, either out of a need to help those afflicted, or from simple fear that at any moment their masks would fail and they too would fall victim to the invisible poison. Some grew so fearful that they blamed the masks themselves and tore them off, leaving a surreal trail of goggled head gear strewn across the battlefield. This is not to say that all the French retreated in panic, but as the bombardment of the lines raged on, the remaining troops were so few that their effectiveness, their ability to mount a defense, was reduced to a deplorable state, which I suppose was the whole point of the attack in the first place.

While the trenches emptied of infantry, and the heavy equipment was pulled further back, Fort Souville came under a barrage of German artillery. Shells whistled through the air, laying waste to the landscape, the fortifications and men who occupied them. Strangely, as the shelling stretched into the night and then the next day, and the next night, it became clear that the effectiveness of the German artillery was somewhat lacking. The vast majority of shells fell well short of their target, or to either side. True, there were shells that impacted on the walls of the fort, and even within its defenses, but these caused minimal damage; some even failed to explode. By dawn on the twelfth, those of us who were still taking refuge within the fort were equally as amused as we were frightened. It was as if somehow the odds had been tilted in favor of those defending Fort Souville, and against any attempt by the Huns to dislodge us. The mood in the bunkers was so calm that many of the men were playing cards or chess. Nick, the dashing young man from New York, dozed through most of the barrage and suggested that it was the best sleep he had had in weeks.

An hour after dawn the rate of fire picked up, and the men became nervous. Helmets were inspected and adjusted, guns were cleaned and reloaded, ammunition stores were dusted off and restocked. For my part, I prepared as best I could for the influx of casualties that were sure to soon be flowing into my surgery. The bombardment was ending; the increase in activity was an attempt to soften up whatever forces remained before the assault by German artillery was replaced with German infantry. It was all down to timing now. Once the shelling ended, could the invaders overtake the fortifications before the defenders could reset their defenses? I looked around at the men with whom I had been serving and I knew that today might be their last day. There were barely three hundred men in the fort, and we likely faced an onslaught of thousands. That I had exposed a hundred of them to my reagent seemed too little of an advantage to make a difference. All around me men were whispering short prayers, and again I wished that I could find solace in such acts.

Then without any real notice, the whistling sound of shells that had filled the air for the last two days suddenly ceased. The distant sound of artillery had grown silent, and in its place was the unmistakable sound of men by the thousands marching across the fields that formed the vast no man's land between the two opposing forces. This sound was quickly rejoined by that of my own troops scrambling up stairs and ladders, carrying machine guns and ammunition into the fortified positions along the top of the wall. Those first few to the top, armed with rifles and pistols, found themselves in the unenviable position of having to defend those who followed from the weapons fire of the assaulting forces, without the support of the yet to be installed heavy machine guns and grenades. Soon after the scramble had begun, the first of the casualties made it back to me, and I knew that the battle had truly begun.

The first of the injured to arrive presented the most common of war wounds, and I was soon patching up hands and shoulders that had forgotten to move out of the way of the bullets of the enemy. The enemy forces were still too far away to inflict serious injuries; their shots at this distance were meant to hamper the installation of our defenses so that we could be overrun, not to kill or maim, but with each passing minute they trudged forward and soon the forces would engage, the feints would end, and the battle would be to the death. There was no doubt in my mind of the outcome.

Sheltered as best I could be in the depths of the fort, I was not witness to it, but somehow the remaining French and American troops were able to install their guns and begin a full-fledged defense. The single shot retorts of rifles and pistols were suddenly replaced by the horrible droning of machine guns, and the tinkling fall of wasted shells. A minute or so of this and I was shocked to hear the strangest of sounds, for within the walls of our position a sudden and unexpected roar of excitement rose up. Distracted, I dashed to the wall and climbed the ladder to a small break in the upper wall through which I could see the fields of war below. Suddenly my death was not so assured and I, like all the others around me, saw more than just a glimmer of hope.

The enemy had reached our trenches, but the thousands of shells they had rained down upon these dirt fortifications had made them all but impassable. The thousands of troops streaming across the land were suddenly forced into a choke point maybe a hundred yards wide and nearly dead center in front of the fort itself. As the enemy troops forced their way through the gap, they found themselves at the mercy of two machine guns and supporting riflemen. The Germans were being cut down by the dozens each minute. I smiled, not out of joy for the death of so many of the enemy, but rather out of pride, for the soldiers who were manning those guns were the men of my own unit, American soldiers whom I had treated and worked with for so many months now. I was proud of them, for they had given me a taste of what they had given the world: hope.

Then, in an instant that seemed to last longer than it had any right to, things suddenly changed. There was a pause in the rattling scream of the machine gun to my left, and I saw the men scrambling to wrench a miss-fed tangle of ammunition out of the smoking weapon. The other gun sped up, trying to compensate for the temporary loss, spraying metallic death across the front of the oncoming enemy. In an instant three German troops slipped past the now-deficient crossfire, and into one of the cross trenches that still remained. A tick of the clock later, all three rose up out of the trench, and in a coordinated effort fired at the still-incapacitated machine gun. The gunner, a Texan named Rick Williams, and his assistant, a boy called Hammond, tumbled backwards out of the tower nest and plummeted down the side of the wall to the ground below.

There was no time to mourn their passing. Instead there was yet another mad dash by brave men to occupy that position and get that gun going again. Three more men were shot from the wall trying to make it to the tower before Nick found his way into the position. The gun cleared in an instant and soon was chattering away once more. As the gun kept them pinned, a pair of hand grenades were lobbed into the occupied trenches and the trio of enemy snipers were silenced.

The wholesale slaughter of enemy troops at the single pathway through the trenches resumed, and this time each team was fortified by a second set of guns as well. However, in the minutes that the crossfire had failed, the enemy had been able to scatter even more soldiers into the cratered trenches. Sudden desperate communications ricocheted like bullets. One observer had estimated that in the confusion, two hundred men had slipped over the top of one crater and were now likely winding their way through the labyrinth of trenches. Dismayed, I retreated to the infirmary and did what I could for the wounded as they trickled in.

Not long after my return, the broken bodies of the unfortunate gunners Williams and Hammond were brought in. Having personally witnessed the event that wounded them, I waved the orderlies off, directing them to consign their charges to the area set aside for the deceased. I was unprepared for their adamant refusal and assertion that both men were still alive. I was even less prepared when Williams rolled his head over and stared at me with weeping eyes and begged me for help. Stunned, I directed the two to the central tables and chased the two orderlies out.

Williams had taken a shot to the right shoulder that had shattered several bones before leaving through a much larger hole in his back. The fall and subsequent impact had dislocated his hip and, as far as I could tell from the near 180-degree rotation, broken his neck. Under normal circumstances such a condition would have resulted in his death, but despite his injuries he was quite alive, and talkative. It took me a moment, and a consultation with my notebook, but I realized that Williams was indeed one of the many I had inoculated with my reagent. Here was my first true example of its ability to prevent fatalities even in the face of major physical trauma.

Hammond, who was also an experimental subject, had suffered a more serious wound. Apparently, Williams had cushioned Hammond's fall, for there were no impact injuries from the fall to the younger man. Unfortunately, Hammond had been shot in the face, and although he maintained some semblance of life, the gaping hole in the back of his head and the missing brain matter made me wonder if the boy would ever recover any semblance of consciousness. As it was, he apparently could do little more than kick against the restraints and claw at the air.

I turned back to Williams and examined the shoulder wound from both sides. Amazingly, though the wound was only minutes old, it already showed signs of scabbing over and healing, though not in a manner consistent with normal anatomy. Indeed, it was as if a cancerous mass of flesh and bone was desperate to fill the hole, regardless of the actual anatomical need. Distressed by the uncontrolled and rampant growths of bone, muscle and skin, I did what I could to guide the tissues into their proper paths and hoped for the best. Unable to do much more, I jerked his hip back into place and quickly built a crude brace to hold his neck upright. Within the quarter hour since he had been brought in, Williams was suddenly mobile enough to carry a gun and return to the line. I suggested he wait and recover, but nothing I said could dissuade him from returning to the battle that raged above. Indeed, I had little time to argue as more wounded suddenly poured into the infirmary begging for my help.

In an hour I was knee-deep in the blood and gore of war, and my casualty rate was surprisingly low, for indeed those whom I had subjected to my experiment in inoculations against death seemed superhuman in their stamina and ability to heal. Even those who had taken instantly fatal wounds showed some semblance of recovery, though like Hammond those who had suffered traumatic brain injuries seemed unable to properly function as a conscious human being. These poor individuals soon became problematic. Though undeterred by their wounds, they were not sufficiently functional to obey directions; thus I found myself forced to come up with creative ways in which to restrain them, including lashing them to stretchers, timbers or any other large object that would keep them from wandering about. A good number of victims showed violent tendencies, constant attempts to scratch, rend, or bite, and reminded me of the revenant rats from my early experiments. For these individuals I quickly devised a set of restraints and a bit that would keep them in check.

The day turned into night, and then into day again. The battle raged on, with the Germans throwing their forces against our fortification in a desperate but nearly futile attempt to defeat my unit of undying soldiers. I say "nearly futile" because as the conflict raged on, it soon became apparent that although my experimental subjects may have been resistant to injury, they were not immune, and slowly, the number of those who had suffered traumatic brain injuries was growing. It was a matter of slow attrition really, and as one by one my experiments joined the ranks of the uncontrollable, the diminishing ranks of those retaining their faculties faced an ever more daunting task. As our numbers waned, the fall of our position became inevitable.

I will not defend what I did next. Decisions made during the madness of war often appear perfectly logical; it is only in retrospect that their nature as heroic or cowardly can truly be evaluated. My actions seemed to me a logical manner in which I might turn the tide of the battle; it was only afterwards that I realized the horror of what I had done. The inspirations for my acts are a mystery; the idea came upon me and I acted on it. It was as simple as that. Grabbing my medical bag with my supply of syringes and reagent, I quickly prepared twenty double-strength dosages of the formula. Then with great care, I used a length of rope to lash twenty of the more violent cases together. With some effort, for although they did not resist, nor did they help, I led my small cadre up the walls of our position and to a point directly above the main gate of our base. There, sheltered by a pile of sandbags, I injected each of them with one of the prepared syringes, and with several swift slices of my knife to their bonds, sent them one by one over the edge of the wall.

Such actions must have confused our enemy, for each one fell to the ground below without coming under fire. I cowered there for a moment, and smiled viciously as I made out the sounds of those twenty things scrabbling to their feet and breaking loose from their restraints. There was an animal sound of movement, not unlike that which I had heard so many times from my rats. They wandered away, slowly at first, but then they stopped, seemed to focus on something, and then scrambled off as fast as they could, an angry, breathy growl trailing in their wake. This was followed by a sudden, almost incredulous pause in gunfire, both from our defensive positions and from the attackers. Then there was screaming, the gunfire became frantic, and I dared to raise my head above the wall to see what I had wrought.

The twenty were wading through the attackers like reapers through wheat, leaving a trail of carnage in their wake. Limbs were torn from bodies, heads were shattered like clay pots, and blood ran like ink over the pages of the landscape. Bolstered by the reagent overdose, my patients shrugged off wounds from bullets and bayonets alike. Indeed, for a dozen or more the dosage I gave them was apparently too high, for as they cut their way through the enemy, and the enemy cut them, I could see the green luminescent fluid leaking from their wounds. I was sadistically gleeful at my success, for I knew that it was I who had turned the tide of this battle. The enemy was not yet routed, but our victory was assured. So blinded was I by my apparent success that I nearly failed to see the horror as it crept up out of the abattoir I myself had created.

As I have said, several of the twenty were leaking reagent from their wounds, and this must have been sufficient to infiltrate the bodies of some of the dead they were leaving in their wake. As I watched, some of the more intact of the German soldiers were shuddering, convulsing and rising up to live again. Within minutes the number of resurrected things battling across the war-torn landscape had doubled. Thankfully, the newly inoculated seemed to have no particular memories of their allegiances, and indiscriminately tore into whatever caught their attention, at least at first. It took some time, but they seemed to learn that battling against each other was ineffectual, and soon focused their attention only on the more vulnerable living.

The dead tore through those German troops in minutes, and it was only when they reached the choke point through which the Germans were pouring that they were suddenly stopped. Some bright Hun officer must have realized what was happening and after pulling back what forces he could, he let loose with grenades and explosives and closed off the gap completely. As the smoke cleared, I watched as the undead slaughtered those trapped on the wrong side of the gap, and German snipers took up positions on top of the rubble. Mercifully, the first acts of these marksmen were to put the still-living soldiers out of their misery. Afterwards, the long-range weapons were turned on the shambling hulks of my creation.

Suddenly besieged by gunfire and with no one to conveniently attack, the monstrosities slowly worked their way back to our position. Shambling and stumbling they came toward our walls, grey lifeless things with twisted broken bodies and gnashing teeth. Still draped in uniforms that marked their allegiance, our own snipers proceeded to take shots at those still identifiable as German, though I had realized that such distinctions were at this point likely moot. It took several shots, but eventually the horrified gunmen learned that the only sure way of putting one of the things down was a headshot that destroyed a significant portion of the brain.

With the German infantry too far to threaten us, the soldiers remaining in the fort soon lined the wall to jeer at the horrid actors that milled about looking for a way in. It took a few moments, but soon my comrades realized that all sixteen of the things wandering around were Americans. As this dawned on my compatriots, I quietly tried to slink back to the infirmary and distance myself from any possible association with these things and the horrid atrocities they had committed. Imagine my surprise when a strong arm suddenly wrapped itself around me.

"Well, Dr. Hartwell," it was the righteous Nick who was now gripping me tightly, "perhaps you should do some explaining."

There was no trial. The French Commander, and Nick Charles, who assumed command of the American forces at Fort Souville, forced me to confess everything, and I think perhaps they would have liked to have thought me mad. But in the killing fields outside the fortifications wandered things that could not be denied, and in the infirmary were the men who had been wounded, mortally wounded, who had become misshapen mockeries as the reagent tried to keep their bodies alive. There was no denying what I had done, and there was no denying that my actions had turned the tide of the battle. For that my life was spared.

Do not misunderstand me, I was punished. It was I who was sent outside the gates with a pistol to dispatch the sixteen things that were once men and now were monsters both less than and more than human. It was I who was beaten by Nick Charles when he learned that like many others he too had received a dose of my reagent. He forced me to lie there and watch as he burned my notes and remaining reagent, and he cursed me as a new Frankenstein. As word and exaggeration of my deeds spread, I became ostracized, and soon my only companions were those eight soldiers who had suffered the most severe reactions to my reagent, but had maintained some semblance of rationality. These disfigured wounded would never rejoin society, for how could one explain the absence of a lower jaw, the back of one's head, or a gaping hole in the chest?

I lived with these poor creatures, my creations, and they lived with me, and we cursed each other. It was inevitable really. There was so much vehemence that it finally erupted in flames. After nearly a week, my companions turned despondent and wandered out of the infirmary, and in full view of everyone, slowly went about building a rather large mass of wood and cloth from scraps scattered about the place. Then without a word they set fire to it. The flames burned bright and licked at the night. Everyone came out to watch, fascinated with morbid curiosity. Then, still as silent as the grave, the eight men, who were now something else, doused themselves with kerosene and walked into the consuming flames.

I tried to turn away, but Nick Charles, that damned righteous Nick Charles, appeared out of nowhere and held me fast. Greasy smoke filled the fort as those burning shapes staggered around in horrid silence. Charles held me and made me watch. A few men grabbed blankets and buckets, but they froze in their tracks when Charles cried out, "LET THEM BURN!"

It was then that the morality of my actions finally took hold. As I have said, I am not a spiritual or godly man, but there must be an innate standard of right and wrong, of good and evil, and if anyone was to judge me, why shouldn't it be Nick Charles?

"Is this what you wanted, Doctor?" he whispered from behind me as the living finally succumbed to the cleansing flames. "Those men couldn't live with what you had done to them, they thought death was better. Would you trade humanity for immortality?"

I fell to the ground, for I knew that the answer could only be no.

CHAPTER 17.
THE PLAGUE ANGEL

In the spring of 1918, forty-two months after I had left, I returned to Arkham, weary of war and of my pursuits of perfecting the process of reanimation. My home was like an old and trusted friend, warm and inviting. Wilson had maintained our practice, and I was pleased to discover that he had even expanded it, taking on an association with Dr. David Schiff of Kingsport, who needed some relief from his workload as he entered his seventieth year. Schiff's practice was smaller than ours in Arkham, proportional to the differences in the size of the towns, though Schiff was the only professional in that sleepy seaside village. There was something about the pace in Kingsport that was appealing, and when in April Dr. Schiff announced that he would prefer not to return from his next winter trip to Deland, Florida, Wilson and I agreed to take on his practice full time.

The arrangement was rather elegant; Wilson purchased Schiff's home and office, a four-bedroom affair that sat behind the attached street front offices. His wife Mary moved into this home, and Wilson became the primary physician in Kingsport, while I would visit weekly and assist on more difficult cases. I hired Miss Soames, a woman who could function as both a receptionist and a housekeeper to help me in Arkham. Her son had been Dr. Halsey's houseboy all those years ago. Though we resisted it, we also hired a young man fresh out of his residency, Dr. Randolph White, to help both of us, with the full understanding that he would travel to either location depending on the needs of the day.

As for my studies and the secret lab beneath my house, I resigned myself to the fact that I would never again pursue such things. I made sure that my notes and samples were secure, and changed the sheets that covered the equipment. The war and my experiences in it had taught me that there were worse things than death. Who was I to play God and decide who should live and who should die? As for the motivating force behind my research, the vengeance I sought on West and Cain, I left that behind as well. The war it seemed had changed me forever, and I was content never to unlock that door again.

No sooner had we settled into a routine, one that I must say was quite enjoyable, than our tiny little practice was made aware of a growing medical threat. One June evening, Wilson, White and I were summoned to one of the lecture halls at the University. The subject was not revealed, but the urgency of the matter was made plain. As we arrived, the situation became most curious, for it seemed as if every medical professional in the area had been summoned. Moreover, campus security was furiously checking to make sure that everyone who was attending was actually invited. I had not seen such a mobilization of the medical community since those dark days during the typhoid plague of 1905. As I realized this, a cold wave of fear passed through me and I noted that others were showing signs of anxiety as well.

Once we had settled into our seats, the Dean of Medicine spoke briefly, thanked us for coming, and then quickly introduced a young doctor and military officer of the Public Health Service, who brought a message from the U.S. Surgeon General. His name was Ambrose Dexter, and despite his youth, he spoke with the voice of authority on a grave matter.

"As medical professionals you are no doubt aware of the recent reports of an epidemic of influenza ravaging Western Europe. The newspapers have dubbed this the Spanish Flu, but this is a misnomer. It is true that the Spanish newspapers are reporting extensively on the deaths attributed to the disease, and these seem to be more prevalent than in other countries. However, agents in service to the United States suggest that the epidemic is rampant throughout Europe, and may be devastating the Central Powers, and that the lack of press coverage of the epidemic in these countries is a result of wartime censorship."

A murmur of protestation erupted through the crowd, which Dexter quickly quelled by raising his voice. "I am here today to inform you of what is known about this disease, and what can be done to prevent it." He paused for effect. "As I have said, the term Spanish Flu is a misnomer, but the Public Health Service in cooperation with the Armed Services is asking that you continue to refer to it in that manner. Any information I provide you here will be denied."

He took a quick drink of water before proceeding. "In early March of this year, a company cook at Fort Riley, Kansas, reported to the infirmary with the symptoms of the common cold. He was isolated immediately and eventually developed full-fledged symptoms of influenza. Despite precautions and quarantines, the disease spread, and within a month, more than a thousand soldiers were stricken. Of these, approximately fifty cases, five percent, proved to be fatal." Another wave of murmuring crashed through the room. "Doctors with the Service and the Army have been tracking the progress of the outbreak, and we have confirmed cases in London, Berlin and Paris and throughout the United States. The bottom line here, doctors, is that this outbreak of influenza is not a Spanish problem, not even a European problem, but rather a global one, that appears to have originated right here in the United States of America."

The rest of the evening was spent going over details of the disease's transmission, progression, and mortality. Unlike previous strains of influenza, which tended to kill both the very young and elderly, initial results from the Spanish Flu also showed a high mortality rate amongst adults twenty-five to thirty-five years of age. Why this was the case Dexter could not tell us, but he assured us that government doctors were organizing and researching the problem, as well as searching for effective treatments. Dexter's team was stationed in Boston, and was operating throughout New England, setting up facilities where they could, primarily at hospitals and universities in major metropolitan areas. However, there were some who suggested that the smaller towns and rural areas might, by their being small and remote, be able to control the outbreak more effectively, particularly through implementation of quarantine measures. By midnight, under Dexter's guidance, and with the cooperation of the state police, we had devised a plan by which Arkham and the surrounding communities could be effectively quarantined. Certain things, including fuels, food, water and sundry medical supplies, would have to be stockpiled, but otherwise our plan to close off roads and rails, as well as the river, was sound, and quickly implementable. When we finally left, despite the seriousness of the situation, there was an air of accomplishment and satisfaction amongst the gathered physicians. Presented with a threat for which we had been trained, we had come up with plans to prevent and combat it. We had no way of knowing that Spanish influenza was unlike any other threat we had ever faced, and that our own haughty pride was to prove almost entirely ineffective against it.

It was too late to return to Kingsport, so after we dropped White off at his boarding house, Wilson and I returned to my home on Crane Street and I put my long-time friend up for the evening. We woke early and he left after a quick breakfast. He had a full schedule in Kingsport, and additionally had to plan for his wife's thirty-third birthday for which they were traveling to New York to visit family. During his time away, the first week in July, Dr. White would be working with patients in Kingsport, and I would be alone in Arkham. It would be a difficult few days, but Mary was a devoted wife, and excellent assistant. I not only considered her my partner's wife, but a valued member of our practice and a dear personal friend.

I wish I could have done more to save her.

Late June brought to Arkham an oppressive heat and near daily torrential rains that brought no relief and turned the evenings sultry and made nights stifling. With some reluctance, but also a secret kind of satisfaction, I found myself unlocking the doors to my secret laboratory and reassembling the core of Muñoz's cooling apparatus, which allowed me to drop the temperature a few degrees. I spent my nights in the cool comfort of my basement, smug in my own ingenuity, while the oppressive days stretched to July. With Wilson and his wife gone, I had expected, feared even, that there would be a sudden influx of patients, but instead the heat seemed to create a lull, and both White and I found our steamy afternoons almost entirely free.

A strange lethargy had come over Arkham; the streets were nearly empty and shops posted new hours, often closing by noon. Children seemed to purposefully avoid the sun and instead haunt the shadowy places, lounging in the shade of buildings and old oaks. In addition to the ennui, the heat brought decadence; a breakdown in formality, spawned I suppose by necessity. Men shucked their woolen suits and pressed shirts and went about in thin undershirts and swim trunks. Women, who could be spied through the open windows, followed suit, and often wore little more than silk slips or cotton nightgowns. Whether it was the heat, the humidity, the lethargy, or the decadence, the inevitable finally came to pass. Toward the end of that first week in July I was called to the home of Henry Armitage, the head librarian for the University. His visiting grandson was running a fever and coughing up thick gobs of stringy mucus. Spanish influenza had come to Arkham.

I reported my case to Dr. Dexter, who confirmed that four other cases had appeared in the area surrounding Arkham. A frantic conference was held at Miskatonic, and that evening the order went out to the state police. By the afternoon of the next day the roads in and out of Arkham were closed, including those to Bolton, Kingsport and Innsmouth. Early that afternoon, I was alone at the rail station as a train with a single passenger car pulled in and disgorged its sparse human cargo, including Wilson and his wife Mary. As we handled their luggage, I watched as the authorities posted signs and locked the station down, effectively isolating Arkham from the rest of the world.

Once Wilson and Mary had settled into my spare rooms, we called White to check on his situation. The quarantine seemed to be working as no cases had been reported in Kingsport. As required by our plan, the fishing fleet was remaining at sea, transferring its catch to barges with minimal contact between crews. The barges themselves were also attempting to remain isolated as they moved the catch to secure docks in Kingsport and Arkham. White had even held a meeting with several of the less reputable members of the community, asking and gaining their cooperation in the way certain contraband was moved from offshore into Kingsport and up the river. Mary fretted over having such people in her home, but White assured her that they had come and gone with certain measures of discretion.

That evening Miss Soames prepared a summer salad and steamed some fresh clams. Mary made some lemonade and after supper we lounged about the parlor. Wilson and I talked shop, while Mary spent her time reading a new volume of poetry by one of our patients, Randolph Carter, entitled *Pugmire and Other Observations.* She found the volume amusing and insightful, but also frustrating and at times despondent, and recited several pieces to us, a few lines of which I still remember.

In a red decade, far afield, my love for you did falter and wane
In the green year, with you near, my heart once more did flame
The yellow month stole that and more, and with tears my cheek did stain
In black weeks I hold you still with only voracious flies to blame

As the evening progressed, Wilson and I seemed energized by the conversation, and I broke out a bottle of Muñoz's Madeira that he had left behind. As I did so, Mary noted that she was suddenly feeling tired. Whether this was true or she simply disapproved of the wine, she retired for the night and left us to our conversation. Fueled by the thick, hearty wine, the two of us jabbered back and forth on a variety of subjects well past midnight. Slightly intoxicated, when I finally crawled into bed I quickly drifted off, unbothered by the pervasive and uncomfortable heat.

I slept late, and was honestly surprised when I finally wandered down the stairs and learned that Mary had not already prepared breakfast. I had thought that I had heard someone fumbling about downstairs, and attributed such noises to Wilson or Mary, which was apparently incorrect. However, even if Mary hadn't been to the kitchen, I was still puzzled as to why Miss Soames had not yet appeared and undertaken the task. As I entered the kitchen my puzzlement grew, as upon the sideboard were fresh eggs, several apples, butter, a fish and some beef kidneys, evidence that Soames had at least been here briefly.

My confusion was broken by the sound of Wilson calling me, an odd occurrence, made more so by the direction it originated from. Growing even more perplexed, I all but ran through the house and into the office. Wilson was in the exam room gathering supplies, the most awful look on his face. His hair was unkempt and his eyes had a wild frantic cast. He paused, and when he spoke his voice was broken with what could only be fear. "Mary has a fever."

Never have I seen a man more frightened or frantic. He had been up before dawn, and had as required by the plan applied a large X of yellow paint on the walkways to both entrances. Soames had also followed procedure and upon seeing the marks had deposited the groceries on the porch, knocked once and then quickly left. If she continued to follow the rules, she would monitor herself for signs of infection for the next twenty-four hours. If she remained uninfected, she would continue to deliver supplies on a daily basis.

Our more immediate concern was Mary, making sure that her condition did not worsen, and that the infection was not passed to Wilson or me. We gathered bottles of rubbing alcohol and Halsted surgical gloves, as well as masks and other supplies. More importantly, we established a protocol for how we would attend to both Mary and ourselves. Assuming Wilson had suffered a greater exposure than I, he would remain with his wife on the second floor, while I would remain on the first. Just as Soames had remained out of physical contact with us, so would I remain out of contact with the Wilsons. I would leave meals and supplies on the stairs for Wilson to retrieve. Likewise, Wilson would leave soiled dishes, linens and refuse in the same area. I would be responsible for the cooking, as well as the cleaning, disinfecting and if necessary incinerating whatever came down the stairs. Wilson apologized in advance for putting me in this position and warned me to be extremely cautious in my handling of contaminated materials. As he retreated upstairs, I saw tears well up in his eyes.

I could not bring myself to tell Wilson that it was highly unlikely that I was susceptible to infection. Indeed, since Peaslee had injected me with his version of the reanimation reagent, I had not experienced a single day's illness or even the remote symptoms of a cold or any other kind of infection. Even in the trenches of France, while those about me succumbed to various maladies, I had remained disease-free. Given such a state, it dawned on me that I might be the perfect physician for ministering to those infected by the outbreak, as long as I did not act as a carrier. With this in mind, and with some fervor, I descended into my secret laboratory and began to work.

It took me a good hour to ready the lab, and another hour after that to create a nutritive broth and then inoculate it with macerated tissue extracted from the beef kidneys left by Miss Soames. I left the concoction to incubate and went back up the stairs to prepare lunch. Wilson left word that Mary was feeling somewhat better, and I was comforted by the idea that she might already be past the worst of it. Afterwards I went back down to the lab and continued to clean up the clutter that had accumulated from years of neglect. It felt good to be back at work again and I took some sense of satisfaction as the lab took shape and returned to a usable state. After the evening meal, I retreated back down into the basement, this time taking down soiled material from the Wilsons. I ran a swab over the sheets and plates and then inoculated a tube of the cell culture I had prepared earlier. I then repeated the process, this time running the swab over my own skin. I returned the vials to the incubator and retired to a chair in the parlor.

The next morning Wilson informed me that Mary's condition had worsened, her fever was spiking and she was having trouble breathing. In addition to food and tea I sent up a small bag of eucalyptus leaves that should have helped to alleviate some of her congestion. In the lab I used a microscope to check on the two vials of cells I had inoculated the day before. The cells exposed to the swab from Mary's sheets were all damaged, exploded from the inside, a telltale sign of viral infection. The cells that had been exposed to the swab from my own skin remained intact, indicating that I was infection-free.

That afternoon, between administering to the needs of Wilson and his wife, I called Dexter and made discreet inquiries concerning the progression of the plague. Dexter obliged me by listing off names and addresses both in my own neighborhood and throughout Arkham. Afterwards I went into the office and packed a large valise with what medical supplies I could spare. That night, after I was sure that my partner was soundly asleep, I left the house with my bag and crept through the streets of Arkham. I made my way to six of the houses on Dexter's list, where I followed my Hippocratic oath and in my own way did what I could for those poor unfortunates.

It took me hours, and it was nearly dawn before I found my way home. I snuck in the back door, careful not to make a sound. The house was still dark and I was sure I had some time before the Wilsons woke up. My night on the town had left me somewhat rank and I desperately needed to bathe and change. There were facilities and clothes in Muñoz's old quarters, and I went down for a quick shower.

As I emerged from the bathroom only half-dressed, he was waiting for me. Francis Wilson was standing there waiting for me. He swung at me, his fist caught me in the chin, and I fell to the floor. "Get up, Stuart!" I sat there dumbfounded. "I said get up, you bastard." There was a sorrow in his voice and his eyes. "I need you to get up and get down to your lab and do whatever it is you do down there."

I was still stunned but managed to stutter out a single word. "What?"

He looked at me with tears in his eyes. "Mary is upstairs dying. I can't break her fever. I've tried everything that I know, Stuart, and nothing has worked. She's going to die. Unless you go downstairs to your secret laboratory and whip up a batch of your reagent to save her."

My mind reeled, but the look on Wilson's face gave me no time to think about what had just happened. I stumbled to my feet and placed a hand on Wilson's shoulder. "Bring her down." He smiled through the tears and dashed out. I grabbed a shirt and threw the switch on Muñoz's cooling apparatus to high before running down to the lab.

It was a half hour before Wilson joined me. He came down meek and quiet, and asked what he could do to help. I asked how Mary was and he told me that her fever was still high, though the cool air was helping.

I nodded and handed a beaker of chemicals to Wilson to continue mixing. "How long have you known?"

He refused to look at me. "About the lab? Almost as soon as we started to work together, I knew that there was something you were working on, something you wanted to keep hidden. But I didn't care. You were a good man. I could see that. Whatever you were doing down here, you seemed to honestly care about your patients. So I ignored it and let you keep your little secret, whatever it was." He paused and chuckled, just a little. "It was Mary who found the entrance, by accident of course, while you were in France. She was always a little too curious. She didn't even bother to tell me until she had finished reading your notebooks. At first I thought she was mad, and then after I read them myself, I thought that you were. But there were too many coincidences, too many referenced events that could be documented. Then of course there was the farmhouse. You, my friend, are meticulous, but West and Cain were terribly sloppy. The proof that you weren't insane, the evidence for reanimation, I found it in their basement."

I nodded. "So why the charade after I came back?"

"Well, Mary and I discussed it at length. For some time we hoped that you wouldn't return from the war, it would have made things simpler. Then after we tried to make our own batch of reagent we realized we needed you. Your notes aren't quite good enough to follow. Every subject we tested ended up becoming...well, what was the term you used, "revenant"? We needed you to come back and show us how to make the mix properly. Except..."

"You hadn't counted on me not being interested anymore."

"Yes, that was bothersome. But the influenza outbreak presented an opportunity that we could leverage. Mary would fake being sick and I would beg you to save her, and in the process you would show me how to make the reagent properly."

Now it was my turn to laugh. "Except Mary really did get sick and she really is dying." Wilson nodded. "What was the plan? What were you two going to do with it? I mean besides the obvious?"

Wilson stared at me incredulously. "You mean besides living forever? We could be rich, Stuart. People would pay a fortune for your reagent. There would be enough, more than enough, for all of us."

I nodded angrily and continued to work. "Well, now you've seen how it's done, I am sure that you'll be able to reproduce it."

I showed him the beaker of glowing green fluid. He smiled and whispered an earnest "Thank you."

I grabbed him by the shoulder. "I've never administered it to someone who was truly sick before. My experiments have always been on the healthy, injured, or already dead. There's no telling how she'll react." I could tell he wasn't listening. "Bring her down here and we'll start her on a regimen."

When he returned carrying his wife in his arms, I could tell things had gone from bad to worse. Her breathing was shallow and labored, her pulse was weak, and her skin showed signs of dehydration. Her response to stimuli was varied and poor. Wilson was correct, Mary was succumbing to the disease and had little time left. We laid her on the table and I prepared a series of five syringes with the reagent.

We administered the first syringe, a small dosage into her femoral artery, and watched for some sort of reaction. Her symptoms improved slightly, her pulse increased as did her breathing, but she remained unconscious, and her temperature actually increased by almost half a degree. After an hour those improvements faded and I suggested that we administer the second dosage. Wilson concurred, and this time I inserted the needle into one of the veins in her arm.

As before, Mary's symptoms improved, but once again her fever rose as well. Concerned, I ordered Wilson to soak towels in cold water and drape her with them in the hopes of bringing her temperature down. The towels worked to an extent, but after some time Mary's breathing became labored and her pulse unsteady. Wilson was pacing back and forth frantically, and I was becoming frustrated as well. I was just about to suggest a third dosage when Mary suddenly gasped and then ceased moving. I rushed to check her pulse, and found nothing. Her heart had stopped. Despite my efforts to inoculate her against death, Mary Wilson had succumbed to the virus that had ravaged her.

"I'm sorry." I said solemnly, whether it was to Wilson or Mary I wasn't sure. "Truly sorry."

For the second time that day Wilson hit me and knocked me to the floor. I watched as he grabbed at the remaining three syringes and finally fumbled the fifth dose into his hand. I screamed at him to stop but he ignored me, and in his grief he madly lifted up his wife's head and plunged the needle into the soft spot between her skull and neck. After the injection he dropped the syringe, letting it shatter against the floor. He cradled her body and I could hear him whispering like a child, "Please...please...please," over and over again.

Rising from the floor, I staggered forward. "Wilson, we need to strap her down."

He just sat there, oblivious to what I had said. "We need to strap her down. Sometimes when they come back, they aren't entirely right." I took a few steps forward.

Wilson stared up at me blankly and managed to sob out the words "What did you say?" Just as he finished, Mary returned from the dead.

She returned screaming and rose up from the table, throwing Wilson across the room in the process. He hit the wall with a sickening thud and slid to the floor, leaving a thin trail of blood behind. Mary's awakening seizure flipped her off the table and onto the floor. She clawed her way up like an enraged animal, her jaw clenched, spittle flying as she panted. She scanned the room, her head jerking from side to side. There was no humanity in her eyes as they locked onto mine, no recognition. She opened her mouth wider and roared.

I grabbed a beaker and threw it at her in a futile gesture of defiance. Strangely enough it worked, perhaps too well, for after a moment of being startled, the thing that was once Mary turned and ran up the stairs. I could hear her tearing through the house, breaking glass and knocking over furniture. There was a sudden loud crash and I knew that Mary was now free to roam the streets of Arkham.

I staggered over to where Wilson lay motionless against the wall. He wasn't breathing, and it was clear from the way his head was lolling that his neck was broken. I picked him up and carried him over to the table. It took me less than a minute to strap him down. The fourth syringe was still intact, and I lifted up Wilson's head and once more plunged a syringe into the base of a man's skull.

I left him there in my secret laboratory and went off in search of his reanimated wife. The sun had set, but even in the evening darkness her trail was easy to follow. This was the second time I had stalked such a creature through the streets of Arkham and I had no intention of letting this thing, which I had created, repeat the atrocities that had occurred so many years ago.

I tracked her through the streets of Arkham, down alleyways and across rooftops. I caught up to her as she crossed the Miskatonic; she was running like an ape and grunting. Carefully I took out my revolver, took aim, and fired. She shrieked like a cat and tumbled to the edge of the bridge. I took a deep breath and fired again, aiming for her head. The bullet exploded her jaw, scattering flesh and bone across the bridge. A mist of blood filled the air and drifted across the lamplight, giving the night a crimson cast. Mary gurgled out one last roar before she leapt off the bridge and into the river. I fired wildly, and I think that I hit her; I just didn't know if it was enough. The black river flowed eastward into the night, and whatever Mary Wilson had become, it was swallowed up and lost in the dark waters.

By the time I got home Wilson had returned, and I did what I could to repair his neck, but he would never stand straight again, and would ever after walk with a limp. We waited a day to call the police, and stuck to as much of the truth as possible. Mary Wilson, suffering from fever-induced dementia, escaped from our care and ran screaming into the night. I gave chase but lost her when she jumped into the Miskatonic. The officer who interviewed us seemed to accept everything we told him and even commented that he had seen worse things in the last month, far worse things.

In August a rogue tropical storm moved up the coast and battered Massachussetts for a day. When it finally moved off, it took the doldrums that sat over Arkham with it, and apparently the plague as well. By September, the city had returned to normal, and the only mention of the Spanish Flu was in the papers of far-off cities. Wilson returned to Kingsport, but he was never the same, and I fielded calls from concerned patients throughout September and October. In early November I finally suggested that he and I part ways: instead, Wilson signed documents turning the practice over. White readily agreed to assume Wilson's place. The last I heard, Wilson had moved south to a small town in New Jersey and was working as a company doctor for a paper company.

I wish that had been the end of it, but in early December Ambrose Dexter walked into my office bearing dark news. New cases of the plague had appeared in the last few weeks, first in London, then France and then in Northern Africa. The source of the new, and even more deadly, outbreak was unclear, and no pattern in its behavior could be discerned. Officials in the Congo, warned by agents to the north of the spreading disease, had in late November instituted a policy of inspecting cargo ships before allowing them to move upriver. It was a prudent act, and aboard one such vessel they found the most horrifying of things. It was a woman, albeit one who had suffered considerably and been deformed by some undocumented trauma. A local doctor, inspired by the case of Mary Mallon—Typhoid Mary—gave her the name Spanish Mary, for it soon became evident that she was a carrier of the new virulent strain of Spanish influenza. Where she had come from and how long she had been onboard the ship, the captain and crew could not or would not tell. In an act both prudent and horrific, the terrified Colonial Governor confined Spanish Mary and the crew to their vessel, towed it several miles offshore and burned it to the waterline, allowing the fire and sharks to deal with the bodies and survivors.

The route of the ship had been traced back through Northern Africa, to several ports along the Spanish Main and France. Before that she was in London where she dropped a load of salted cod that she had picked up in New England. Officially, the *Yellow Star* had never been further south than Maine, but inquiries made of certain disreputable businessmen suggested that the ship made frequent runs from Canada to ports along the Massachusetts coast, carrying rum and other contraband.

What Dexter wanted to know was, given her condition, did I think it was it possible that Mary Wilson had not only survived her fall into the Miskatonic, but somehow managed to make her way down to Kingsport, onto a ship and then remain hidden, circumnavigating the Atlantic Ocean? Could Mary Wilson be Spanish Mary?

Of course I refuted such a possibility; given the extent to which the disease had ravaged her body and mind, there was simply no way a normal woman could have survived weeks in such a manner. Wasn't it more likely that the ship had picked her up somewhere in England and then spread the disease to Europe and then Africa?

Dexter nodded and agreed that no normal woman could have survived such a journey, and that such a suggestion bordered on madness. He thanked me for my time, stood up and made for the door. He paused dramatically as the door swung open and turned back. There was seriousness to his expression and as he spoke, the tone of his voice contained an accusatory note. "The thing is, Dr. Hartwell, Spanish Mary, she wasn't a normal woman. The soldiers who were in charge of burning the *Yellow Star*, they took pity on their captives. After setting the fire, they took up positions on the upper deck of their cutter and shot all six members of the crew and Spanish Mary through the chest. They were good soldiers, well-trained, expert marksmen. All six crewmen died before the flames spread to their bodies. The woman, however, Spanish Mary, she continued to thrash about even after they had shot her. According to the commander, they put four shots into her with no effect. Even after the flames reached her and her clothing, hair and skin had burst into flames, she still continued to scream and flail against the chains that bound her." He paused and watched me for a reaction. "As you say, no normal woman could have survived such conditions. But it appears that Spanish Mary was no normal woman. I've seen many things since this plague started, Dr. Hartwell, many horrible things. Diseases can do strange, terrible, even wondrous things, but I have to wonder what it was that made this woman into what she was, Doctor. Is there anything in your experience that could do such a thing?"

I sat there in silence for a minute, maybe more, and then with a firm resolve I lied. "No, not in my experience. I know of nothing that could do such a thing."

He smiled, and suddenly Dr. Dexter had become predatory. He raised his hand to his forehead and gave me a funny little salute. "Be seeing you," he said, and then marched out the door.

That day my world changed. Somehow, despite my desire to cease my studies in reanimation, the past had returned and ensnared me in its horror. I had tried to leave such things behind, tried and failed. I had set out to wreak vengeance on the monsters that had killed my parents, and in the process I had become a monster myself. I, in my inability to stop Mary Wilson, was responsible for creating a creature that spread a plague around the world, killing nearly everything in its path. It has been nearly a decade since the outbreak ended, and even now I suffer from the knowledge of what I have done. West and Cain had killed, or had been responsible for killing, dozens; I was responsible for the deaths of hundreds of millions. And try as I might I could find no one to blame but myself.

CHAPTER 18.

THE THING IN THE ROAD

My resolve to cease experimenting shattered, and the blood of millions on my hands, I resumed my studies in early 1919 and once more began a program to inoculate the citizens of Arkham against death. Given what I had done, I rationalized that the world population was now significantly smaller than it had been before; it seemed only logical that I should help protect whatever remained. I held to this philosophy through 1919 and 1920, and even after a January 1921 report suggested that the epidemic had ceased. The report suggested that the virus had followed a natural progression, and burned itself out. Such a conclusion gave me little comfort, and I wondered if perhaps the real reason for the plague's demise was related to the destruction of the thing that I myself had created. Regardless, I knew that one way or another I had to atone for my deeds.

That my actions would haunt me for years became apparent in early February, on a cold winter's night as I slept comfortably in my home, without any idea of what plans had recently been set in motion, or that I was to be involved in them. The telephone is a wondrous device, and is a boon for physicians and other professionals who may be needed at any time of the day. It is also a detriment, for it can be used to spread gossip faster than common sense should allow, and even harass individuals in an anonymous and most vicious of manners. But these thoughts were far from my mind when the phone rang that fateful night and I, thinking only as a physician, answered it.

The voice on the phone was strange, throaty, and it spoke to me of things that I thought only I would know. It threatened and made it clear that were I not to do exactly as I was told, my life, my hidden life, would be exposed for all to see, but if I were to follow directions, my secrets would remain unpublished. Given little choice, I conceded and carefully took down notes on what exactly I was to do.

Well after midnight I found myself in front of a warehouse on the waterfront and, as directed, I rapped on the door thrice. The gate opened and without hesitation I entered the dimly lit building. Inside I could see little, but beneath a single, dangling bulb stood an imposing military figure carrying an immense black case; behind him was a large truck decorated with a stylized fish. In the shadows of the warehouse I could detect the movement and labored breathing of a large number of men. They shifted uneasily back and forth, and from the thick, long coats they wore I took them to be seamen of one sort or another.

"Thank you for coming, Dr. Hartwell," said the imposing figure in the coat and cap. Even at a distance I recognized the style of uniform and insignia as that of a major in the Canadian service. "It has been many years since I last saw you; it seems that time has been good to you." I studied the features of the half-lit face and tried to place it, but despite being a particularly handsome man with shining, unwavering eyes I could find no trace of him in my memory. "I apologize," he continued, "time and the war have not been as kind to me as they have been to you, and the visage you see before you is not one you would recall. You would perhaps remember the name of Eric Moreland Clapham-Lee from your days at University?"

I nodded. "I recall the name; you were friends with West and Cain."

Clapham-Lee chuckled, but, strangely, stood perfectly still. "My friendship with Herbert West and his assistant Cain is long in the past, though I still suffer from its detriments. Indeed, the wrongs West committed against others and me are things I intend to resolve in the next few days. With your assistance, of course; after learning what they have done to you, I suspect that you would not object to extracting a modicum of vengeance from Doctors West and Cain."

"Would it matter if I did?"

Again that strange motionless chuckle and he answered honestly, "Not really."

Clapham-Lee ordered me into the truck and explained that over the course of the next day I was to serve as his driver and that we would be traveling to only two locations: one in Sefton early this morning, and another in Boston at midnight tomorrow. I glanced about at all the figures moving about in the shadows and wondered out loud why none of these men could be his driver.

There was a somber cast to his voice as he answered. "Unfortunately, owing to circumstances beyond our control, these men lack the coordination needed to properly operate a motor vehicle. You will serve as our driver, Hartwell, and in under twenty-four hours you can go back to living your so-called life."

I acquiesced and climbed into the driver's seat, while Clapham-Lee cautiously occupied the passenger's seat. We sat there for a moment and I felt as well as heard the men who had been hiding in the shadows shuffle across the floor and climb clumsily into the enclosed compartment in the back. One of the shadowy figures must have stayed behind, for no sooner had Clapham-Lee given the order to start the engine, than the warehouse door began to lift jerkily up into the rafters. When the door had risen sufficiently, the order to proceed was given and I pulled carefully out into the dark streets of Arkham.

Clapham-Lee's directions took us quickly out of the city proper and we drove south toward Boston. That Clapham-Lee's directions were curious and circuitous would be an understatement, for instead of proceeding down the paved thoroughfare, he instead took us using by-ways, farm roads, and side roads that more than doubled what should have been a relatively short journey. Even more curious was my master's strange behavior. In the dim light that entered the cab, I still could see only a little of his face, for he kept his collar turned up, his cap pulled down and his whole head turned away from me. He gave directions in short, quick barking orders that seemed to emanate not from his mouth but from his chest, which was hidden by the folds of his coat, and the immense black cloth bag he clung to with both hands.

At nearly four we turned back onto a main road, and it became all too apparent where we were heading. My shock of recognition must have been audible, for Clapham-Lee softly ordered me to relax as we pulled through the gates and onto the great drive that led to Sefton Asylum. "It will all be over soon," he cooed as he directed me to stop at a side door that I knew to be the receiving entrance.

He ordered me to keep the truck running, and strangely, despite my fears, I was inclined to obey without question. I watched in the mirror as five figures clambered out of the back of the truck and slowly staggered toward the entryway. A sixth man, a large repellent brute with a bluish tinge to his face, came forward and helped guide Clapham-Lee from the truck and along the flagstone path. It dawned on me then that Clapham-Lee, for all his bravado, might, as the result of some wartime accident, suffer from some measure of vision loss, or even complete blindness.

The body of silent men pounded demandingly on the door, and did so at regular intervals until finally they gained the attention of the attendants who, just as I had been trained to respond to calls in the middle of the night, did what they had been trained to do and opened the door to receive a new patient. After all, who in their right mind would attempt to break into an asylum for the criminally insane? There was a skirmish at the door, but whatever resistance was offered was quickly withdrawn and the company of seven men entered Sefton Asylum in silence.

I cannot personally speak of what happened inside those walls. I would learn later that a man with a military demeanor carrying an immense black bag had demanded that the cannibalistic thing that had terrorized Arkham sixteen years earlier be turned over to his custody. The men in charge flatly refused such a ridiculous demand. Apparently expecting such a response, the commanding figure raised his hand and precipitated a riotous attack that killed four and left the others beaten, bitten and fleeing for their lives. By the time help could be summoned, the intruders and the monster they had sought to liberate were gone.

For my part, I can only speak to what I personally saw. Seven men left the truck I was driving, and twenty minutes later, eight figures including Clapham-Lee returned. At the Major's direction we left the asylum at a brisk rate which continued as we moved further south. After nearly an hour on several rough roads, we carefully merged onto a paved by-way somewhere near Lynn. We drove until we came to a small farmhouse that had obviously been abandoned. As we rumbled down the track of frozen earth, the barn opened and Clapham-Lee directed me to drive inside. As the doors slid shut I caught the first hint of the sun rising up over a hill to the east. Inside the barn, my passengers once more disembarked, and Clapham-Lee suggested that I stay in the truck and get some sleep. The concept seemed repugnant to me and I balked at the suggestion. The Major was insistent, though, and in the strange sourceless voice he ordered me to stay seated and sleep. I seemed bound to do what this man told me, and I settled back and soon drifted off.

When I once more returned to consciousness night had fallen. Indeed, according to my watch I had slept for more than twenty hours. In the passenger seat was an apple, a bottle of milk and explicit instructions on how I should attend to certain bodily functions. I followed these instructions to the letter and then returned to consume the apple and the milk, standing outside of the truck as I had been instructed.

At a little before the eleventh hour Clapham-Lee appeared and ordered me back into the truck. I complied and soon after the hulking brute appeared and guided the Major to the passenger door where he fumbled with the handle before climbing inside. I immediately noticed that the Major's black bag was not present, but instead in his hand he clasped a piece of paper bearing my name, which he shoved clumsily in my direction. As I opened it, I noticed that Clapham-Lee's men were loading a large box, about two feet square and four feet long, into the truck. After they had finished, they climbed up through the door and closed it behind them. Clapham-Lee gestured crudely at the open barn door and without further urging I started the truck and drove back to the main road.

The piece of paper with my name also bore directions that led us into Boston, and then into one of the more venerable neighborhoods that bordered what appeared to be one of the older and more historical burying grounds that permeated the city. As directed by the note, I carefully pulled up in front of the given address and kept the motor running. My human cargo unloaded themselves and the curious wooden crate, and then as before the great blue-cast brute came forward to help Clapham-Lee. As the Major stumbled from the truck, he fumbled in his pocket and once more produced a note bearing my name. I snatched it from his waving hand and tore it open, desperate to read its contents and have this nightmare of servitude finished with.

The message was simple and clear. I was, as I had hoped, finished. My only remaining task was to return to Arkham and secrete the truck back into the warehouse. As the passenger door to the cab slammed shut I turned to watch in the mirror, to make sure that the two men were clear before I began moving. Clapham-Lee was clearly having more trouble than previously, and was leaning heavily on his servant for support. The icy conditions of the road and walkway may have had some influence on the situation, and with what happened next.

Leaving the street, the brute cautiously helped the Major onto the sidewalk before taking a single broad step himself. That step proved too great, and coupled with the ice, the brute slid forward, bowling into Clapham-Lee's legs and knocking the straight-laced Major to the ground. In the light of the streetlamp I watched as the Major landed firmly on his back, knocking his hat off and letting it bounce and then roll back into the street. It was not until the hat arced and wobbled that the horror of the scene was fully realized, for the hat as it came to a stop suddenly broke in two. It took me a moment to understand what I had seen, and to recognize what it meant. Mere seconds later I was speeding down the street, barreling through Boston and onto the road that led north back to Arkham, urged on by fear nearly untempered by any sense of control.

I followed directions explicitly and returned the truck to its warehouse, securing the door behind me before walking the few blocks back to my home. Never before had I been so grateful to be back in my own home and my own bed, and although my sleep was haunted by what I saw in the streetlight that fateful evening, I swore to myself that it had merely been a trick of the light. Even the next day when the papers reported that Dr. Herbert West had disappeared from his Boston address that was but a single number away from that given to me by Clapham-Lee, I maintained my denial of what my eyes had seen.

It was a year later, in the spring of 1922, that I finally succumbed to the truth. A member of the District Attorney's office in Arkham called me and asked me to act as a consultant on a case. Out of some sense of civic duty I agreed before I even knew what the case was. Had I known I was to aid in the evaluation of the mental health of Dr. Daniel Cain, I would have refused outright. Not only out of a need for my own self-preservation, but also out of my own feelings for the man. I had never made my enmity for West and Cain public, and this it seems was the problem.

Following West's disappearance, the Boston authorities had kept Cain in various states of incarceration for more than a year. At one point, just a few months earlier, he had been incarcerated in a mental hospital, and while there he had undergone several doses of drugs which had resulted in a long and rambling narrative spanning the highlights of West and Cain's medical experiments, including several confessions that served to incriminate the two doctors. Cain's lawyer had the document suppressed, as releasing it would violate medical privilege. The Boston authorities had no evidence of a crime, and had no desire to expend the funds to prove one had occurred. Cain was simply insane, and had been transferred to Arkham for treatment.

As I had once been familiar with Cain, we both attended Miskatonic, the District Attorney assumed that I would be more than capable of evaluating his current mental state, as compared to that of years ago. I attempted to dissuade them from using me for such a task, but was assured that based on my handling of the Peaslee case I was more than qualified for the task.

Cain's confession, a virtual autobiography of the horrors he and West had committed over the years, revealed too much of the past. It detailed their early experiments, their failure with Dr. Halsey and again with John Robinson and scores of other unnamed victims. But as I read on, a slow creeping horror reached out to drag me back to that night in Boston. For it was clear from Cain's writing that Major Clapham-Lee had died in the war. He had been decapitated and then both parts had been reanimated by West's perverse sensibilities. That the head and body of the Major had been destroyed in a volley of German artillery was never proven, and would seem now to be in doubt. For even though he had seen little in the attack that had shattered the basement wall and carried West away, he had seen enough: The body of a man dressed as a Canadian major, a body with no head, the same thing I had glimpsed in the lamplight on the street when my master had stumbled and fallen, allowing the false wax head to bounce away and into the street where the tires of the truck crushed it like a paper carton.

It took me weeks, but I managed to convince the authorities that Cain had made the whole story up, that it was a drug-induced hallucination, and that the man should be released. I could see no other way to resolve the situation. He came to see me afterwards, just once. I asked him what had really become of the wooden crate that had been delivered that terrible night, the one he claimed to have burned in the furnace. He shrugged, opened his mouth to speak, but never said a word.

I thought that would be the last of it, but a few weeks later the postman brought a thick envelope bearing Cain's name and a return address on the other side of Arkham. He has started his own practice amongst the poor and uneducated Italian and Polish immigrants who either don't know or don't care about the scandals of his past. The contents of the envelope, pages upon pages of handwritten notes, were a manuscript of sorts, a missing chapter from his confession in which Cain and West seem to actually do some good with their experiments. I suppose somehow or another Cain felt he owed me something. I just wished he would find it in his heart to leave me alone.

CHAPTER 19.

THE MASQUERADE IN EXILE

Note
The following document was recovered by Federal agents from the home of Dr. Stuart Hartwell while he was in custody for events that resulted in the apparent deaths of several of his patients. It was in an envelope bearing the return address of Dr. Daniel Cain and the handwriting matches that on file for Dr. Cain. It is included here as the contents have some bearing on the validity of Hartwell's confession.
—Hadrian Vargr, Special Agent in Charge

Much has been written of the Great War, and indeed I have set forth my own accounts of my exploits in the trenches with my constant companion and fellow Dr. Herbert West. But I have until now refrained from writing of one of our adventures out of respect for those who were involved. Yet, this day the paper brings notice of disaster in the Antarctic and with it the sure death of the polar explorer the Comte de Chagny. The report states that he died heirless, just short of his seventieth birthday, and that his title will transfer to his nephew Emille Belloq. No mention is made of his wife and son who vanished so many years ago at the height of the war. Strange how the papers have such short memories, but I suppose that the war did its best to wipe clean the memories of newsmen either through death or simple overload of information. Still, as I appear to be the last living participant in those strange events, I see no reason why I should not convey the tale, and let the truth be known.

Dr. Herbert West and I came to fight in the Great War in service to the Canadian forces not as soldiers but as medical personnel, and I must admit we did not volunteer wholly out of a willingness to serve our Hippocratic Oaths. No, our motives also included a desire, an unwholesome need, to have unfettered access to a supply of both the freshly dead and the dying. With such specimens and in such quantities we could further our experiments into the science of reanimation and perhaps, given our skills as researchers and some luck, we might have found the key to resolving the problem of death itself. If only we had realized the truth of how deluded we were. That war is no place for men of science, that war devours not just truth and innocence but rational thought as well. We came to the war hoping to find the cure to one of man's greatest flaws. Instead the war corrupted us and we inevitably sunk into depravity, finding dark joy in carrying out the most twisted and amoral procedures on the mortally wounded committed to our supposed medical care. None were safe from our predations, for we experimented on allies and enemies alike, of all ranks from the lowliest private to the most highly decorated officers. Even those who knew of our secret tests were not immune from our machinations. West and I hardly hesitated from experimenting on our commanding officer and colleague Major Eric Moreland Clapham-Lee when his plane crashed during a battle in Flanders in March of 1915.

This is not to say that West and I did no good upon the field of battle. I particularly remember the Battle of the Somme, which raged from July through November of 1916 near Belloy-en Santerre. This prolonged engagement brought me wounded from around the world, including a trio of Legionnaires. Though I could do nothing to save the poet Alan Seeger from his mortal wounds, I was able to do better by his comrades Randolph Carter and Etienne-Laurent de Marigny. After several weeks of care and with the capture of the Ancre River, conditions in the war-torn countryside and of my patients were sufficient to ship the two and others to Bayonne for recuperation. Both West and I had grown weary of the frontline, and when the opportunity came to rotate to a field hospital several miles back we eagerly volunteered.

The Chateau d'Erlette was a small manor whose master had volunteered it as a staging area for injured troops to be taken to for stabilization before being moved to more competent facilities further away. Our liaison was a young American with a pale appearance and wild hair named Helman

Carnby, who explained as he drove us to the house that his mistress was the wife of a well-respected member of the aristocracy who was serving overseas in some undisclosed capacity. The war had not been kind to the landscape. The roads had been turned into paired ruts of mud and filth bordered by running mounds of debris. The refuse of years of human conflict littered the barren frozen fields of fire. Denuded trees stood like reapers, skeletal sentinels watching over the few emaciated cattle that still roamed the once-lush farmlands. There was no other animal life to speak of, save for the two horses pulling the cart. The war, hunger and disease had taken their toll. What animals had survived the battles and the need to feed its soldiers had fled to less unhealthy places. Over all of this dismal landscape hung the vilest of stenches, an unhealthy blending of rot, gun smoke and the strange metallic scent of bitter deadly cold; a miasma that would have sickened weaker men, but one West and I had grown used to.

The chateau was built on a squalid grey hill overlooking fields of crop stubble and clods of frozen earth. The building itself was originally of medieval French architecture, all gothic arches and flying buttresses, but it had long since become a chimera of features including heaped renaissance ornaments and baroque symmetrical facades that had long ago cracked and fallen into disrepair. In the barren hellish countryside of war-torn France, the Chateau d'Erlette was just another horror to inflict on the already shell-shocked populace and the men who had come to make war on their land.

The interior of the house was as bleak as the exterior, lit by meager oil lamps that did little but turn the deep shadows a murky grey. Only the massive fireplace with a roaring fire provided any real light and heat. Without invitation both West and I gravitated toward the comforting blaze while Carnby went to fetch his mistress. It didn't take long before West was browsing through the various accoutrements of the room.

"Daniel, these books, this library, there are things here that not even Miskatonic has." I wandered over to where West was perusing the shelves that lined the walls. It was a fascinating collection of volumes highlighted by the most wonderfully dark titles, some of which puzzled me.

"West, I thought I had read all of the works of the Marquis de Sade, but these: *Los Reliques*, *La Cure de Prato*, and this *Tancrede*, I've never heard of these."

West nodded and pulled down a strange, green, leather-bound volume. "This is an original copy of *Cultes de Goules*, written in 1665 by the Comte d'Erlette. Most of these were burned during the revolution. I've been trying to see the University copy for years." Just then my colleague audibly gasped, and I watched as he carefully replaced the precious *Cultes de Goules* and lifted out another folio, this one heavily beaten and stained. "I thought this was a myth: *The Pretorius Commentary on the Journals of Victor Frankenstein.*" He clutched the book with two hands, unable to look away from the cover, like a bird caught in the gaze of a snake.

"If you prefer, Dr. West, you can study that volume while you are here." The voice was angelic, full of music and poetry, but controlled. There was a trace of an accent, something Scandinavian, but the diction was perfect. We two turned to face the source and did encounter such a vision that both of us were stunned into silence. Our hostess was an older woman of substance and grace. Her iron-grey hair and firm figure were accented by an air of self-assurance and pride. When she moved, she glided across the floor, and not a hair on her head fell out of place. Had it not been for my medically trained eye, I would have thought her in her mid-forties, but certain lines around the eyes and spots on her hands suggested that she might be into her fifth decade of life.

West stepped forward to greet the charming woman. "Lady d'Erlette, I presume. You honor us with your hospitality."

I went to make my own greeting, but was quickly silenced by our hostess. "I am sorry, Dr. West, but the House of d'Erlette is all but extinct, at least in France, put down by the crown and the people one too many times to survive. Though I hear there may be surviving members in the Americas. These lands are now held in trust by the family of my husband, the Comte de Chagny; you may address me as Lady de Chagny."

With these words I recognized her immediately. "Lady de Chagny, your talent and fame are second only to your still-radiant beauty. Your likeness still hangs in one of the halls at the Paris Opera. We are at your service."

She nodded almost imperceptibly. "You are too kind. I have prepared a meal. Afterwards we shall show you the patient wards."

She led us out of the hall and into a once-grand formal dining room, now fallen into disrepair. The table had not been polished in years, and the chairs were threadbare with signs of dry rot. But the meal that Carnby served to us, a simple roasted pig with winter vegetables, was welcome after so many months in the trenches eating nothing but rations. The meal was accompanied with a bottle of house champagne, an extra dry rose that reminded me of the days of my youth, when my parents would host lavish parties on New Year's Eve.

After the meal the Lady de Chagny and Carnby took us to the wards. I was taken aback when Carnby unlocked a heavy oak door revealing a poorly lit stairway made of stone leading down into the bowels of the house. As we proceeded by torchlight, our hostess explained that the house had been built over the top of an ancient and vast series of catacombs that were used for a variety of purposes, including as storage for the vineyards and a refuge in times of trouble. Under the current state of war she had ordered them converted to a ward for injured soldiers.

As she remarked on this last usage, we rounded a corner of the descending tunnel, passed through yet another door, and found ourselves viewing the most astounding of sights. The cavern before us was a large tunnel approximately thirty feet wide, twenty feet tall and stretching a good two hundred feet back. Light was provided by a series of ornate chandeliers hanging from hooks drilled into the ceiling, which illuminated what I can only describe as a makeshift hospital ward. Four rows of beds ran the length of the cavern, only a few of which were occupied by soldiers in various states of injury. Six women milled about tending to the wounded and discharging various other duties as if they were trained nurses in a city hospital. All in all it was a magnificent operation, though one could see the weaknesses that simply could not be overcome. There was a shortage of linens and of proper clothing. Many soldiers still were dressed in the tatters of their uniforms, which revealed them to be of a variety of nationalities, including French, British and Canadian. Actual medical supplies were lacking, and we could see that many of the patients were suffering from either infection or crippling pain.

Though such conditions would normally lead to a cacophony of screaming, such cries were absent, replaced instead by the sound of a viol playing the most mesmerizing of melodies. It was a tune so hypnotic that it calmed even the most seriously injured patients. As we moved into the cavern I glanced upwards, following a wrought iron ladder set into the wall beside the entrance. There above the passageway, hidden behind a curtain, was a small alcove that was apparently the source of the music. Light from within the room cast shadows on the curtain and revealed the musician as he gracefully played his instrument. Never had I heard such music before, and I wondered aloud about the identity of the composer. The Lady de Chagny smiled and casually informed us that the piece was written by the violist's father as part of an operatic masterpiece entitled *Don Juan Triumphant.*

Without hesitation West and I began evaluating the conditions of the patients and the abilities of the ward itself. From what we could gather the majority of the patients had come from a single skirmish that had begun not far from the vineyards. A running battle, the injured had been left where they fell, and the Lady de Chagny, unable to tolerate the screams of the wounded, organized the staff and pulled the survivors from the fields. There was some talk amongst the staff and amongst those who were rescued concerning the equal treatment of enemy soldiers, but that was quickly squelched. Carnby was brutal in his reprimands and stressed to the wounded and caretakers alike that the Lady herself was not French and that accidents of nationality should not come to bear in determining who received aid and who was left to die. That was not to say that tensions did not run high, and all arms had been confiscated from both factions. The only things left for them to fight with were their minds, their hands, several decks of cards and a chess set.

There were thirteen patients in the cavern, and while most were well on their way to recovering from minor wounds, some were not. Based on West's assessment there were two legs and one arm that needed to be amputated as soon as possible. Additionally, there were numerous bones that needed to be set, and several infections that needed to be drained. Sadly, there were three cases that West saw no hope in wasting any effort on trying to save, including a poor soul who still had a bullet rattling around in his skull. West, with Carnby's help, had these three moved to a different room, one with a strong door and medical restraints. I knew that West had identified them as potential subjects for his reanimation experiments.

In a similar room, we constructed a surgery. Sadly, the equipment and supplies available to us were simply inadequate. Some resources had been liberated from abandoned field hospitals, but the supply of sulfa drugs, painkillers, and proper bandages was woefully low. When he inquired about anesthesia, the matron in charge pointed to a small cask of brandy and then laughed. West cursed and then made sure that his patient had three shots of the liquor before downing one himself and cutting off two of the young man's gangrenous fingers.

"Just remember," lamented West, "this isn't Hell."

I gagged as the man I was holding down vomited under the pain of having his leg re-broken. "No," I said, "not Hell, but on a clear day I bet you can see it from here."

Working through the middle of December, West and I kept to a strict schedule of tending to the wounded. While such a routine left little time to strategize or experiment, West found a way to reorganize the makeshift staff and cavern, and created a small ward for the isolation of those patients that were beyond the hope of any normal medical practices. In this we were aided by Carnby, who we found to be an able assistant and particularly skilled in translating the languages of the soldiers that made up our patients. Born and raised in Oakland, California, Carnby was the minutes-older of twin brothers who had decided to dedicate their lives to the study of the occult. Helman Carnby had come to France several years ago to specifically visit and study the library at the Chateau d'Erlette. When the war broke out, he found himself unable to abandon the Lady de Chagny, and stayed on in her service, all the while studying the vast collection of grimoires and occult treatises.

We were also assisted by one of our patients named August Dewart. This young Briton, whose bald head, flat nose and beard reminded us of a goat, had a significant amount of medical training, and despite the loss of a leg, was extremely helpful as a medical and surgical assistant. Roaming around the ward on a pair of crutches, he made sure that everyone was talked to at least once a day.

As for our gracious hostess, we saw her often. Daily she would come down to the ward, climb the ladder to the curtained alcove and accompany her son's playing with her prodigious vocal talents. While such performances were beautiful to listen to, there was such an undercurrent of sadness and despair to the Lady de Chagny's voice and her son's viol, that others and I were often moved to tears when they performed. During this entire period it was rare for us to catch even a glimpse of the virtuoso, and when we did see him, he always wore a matching set of a full crimson mask and gloves such that no flesh was ever seen.

The impending holiday was apparently weighing heavily on the officers in charge of the front lines, for the number of new patients we received shrank to a mere trickle, and West and I found ourselves able to spend time in the laboratory and surgery that West had cobbled together. All three of our special patients had long since succumbed to their wounds, and all three had then been subjected to the reanimation reagent, though this was but the first stage in a new direction of research. Inspired by the Frankenstein journals and from several pieces of correspondence, we had taken it upon ourselves to pursue the possibility of using the reanimated as sources for the transplant of organs from one body to another. Our primary inspiration for this was letters from the New Zealand surgeon Harold Gillies, who had left the battlefields and was fumbling his way toward actually being able to carry out skin grafts and facial reconstruction in the British Isles. Similarly, we received some notes from Doctors Alexis Carrel and Charles Guthrie, who had pioneered vascular transplants, and were kindred spirits, and their current work was just as inspiring. Carrel's transplant work had won the Nobel Prize in 1912, and when he stopped in Arkham to lecture on the nature of cellular senescence, West and I were compelled to meet with him and demonstrate our reagent. Taking a small sample with him, Carrell began a most controversial experiment, in which he has for the decade since publicly sustained a culture of embryonic chicken cells using only a nutrient solution of his own devising. Similarly, Guthrie had also wandered down areas generally shunned by medical science. There was strong suspicion that the Nobel was awarded to Carrel over Guthrie not because he was the superior researcher, but rather because of Guthrie's rather unorthodox and successful experiments with transplanting canine heads. Photographs of his two-headed animals, while fascinating to the medical community, were considered blasphemous monstrosities by conservative and unenlightened old men who held the reins of power and money.

Yet it was from the genius of these men that we began to formulate our own plan to resolve the problem of organ transplant. Using our reagent to inhibit rejection, we experimented in the transfer of skin tissue from one patient to another, before moving on to the actual exchange of limbs and then finally organs. In the end we had no choice but to follow in Guthrie's footsteps and remove one of our patient's heads and then graft it to another body. Our experiments taught us much and soon we were discussing the possibility of transplanting limbs and organs from one of our reanimates to a living subject, and we both agreed that young Dewart would be our first patient.

We made shadowy arrangements to carry out the surgery as soon as possible, but even as we girded ourselves for the extended surgery, we were accosted in the hall by Carnby, who sent word that the Lady de Chagny wanted to see us immediately in the great hall. With young Dewart already prepared, we left him on the table unconscious but secured to the table, instruments waiting.

In the house above we were ushered into a magnificently apportioned study in which both the Lady de Chagny and her masked son awaited us. In her hand was our journal, the record of our experiments over the last several weeks. West started to protest, but I placed a hand on his shoulder and told him to wait.

Once we were seated, Carnby began to speak. "As you may be aware, my lady, when she was much younger, was the victim of a most obsessive admirer. It was only through the heroic efforts of her fiancé, then the Vicomte de Chagny, that she was able to escape his unwanted attentions. Sadly, while she and Raoul escaped with their lives, the Vicomte's brother was not as lucky. Raoul became the Comte, he and Christine were married, and soon after they welcomed a new life into the world." As Carnby continued, the Lady lowered her eyes. "It was plain at his birth that the child was not Raoul's, but rather that of Christine's unwelcome admirer. Devastated by this betrayal, her husband banished the Lady and her child from the de Chagny household, and forced her to reside here. This is where she and her son have lived for the last thirty-four years; it has become their home, the only one the young master has ever known. The Lady cannot imagine how her son will fare when he is forced from this place."

"For what cause would the young man be forced from this house?" begged West.

The Lady de Chagny rose and turned her back to us. "My husband is given to moods, Dr. West. I have over the last thirty years been able to assuage him, but I am not long for this world. My doctors tell me that I have a cancer growing inside me, that I have little time left. And while I go to my reward without regrets, I cannot allow my son to suffer the rage that will be inflicted upon him by the Comte once I am gone." She turned toward us, eyes pleading. "He must be prepared for life outside these walls. We have been watching you for these last few weeks, and we have read your notes on your experiments. We think it may be possible that such procedures could be directed toward other kinds of conditions, congenital conditions. If my son is to survive in the world, he must be acceptable to it, his deformities must be made less pronounced. He must appear more human."

West rose, and I could see that he was prepared to reject her request. I knew his mind, and he had no reason to pursue such noble obligations as they in no way served his secret ambition. So rather than let West speak, I quickly spoke for both of us. "Lady de Chagny, you have been most hospitable, and we have abused your trust. If it is within our power to help your son, then we shall do so."

I waited briefly for someone else to speak, but then the Lady de Chagny motioned and her enrobed son rose up and stepped toward us. "Zann, would you show these doctors why we need their services."

If the music that the man produced was hauntingly beautiful, then the musician himself was hauntingly tragic. The man that stood before me as his robe, mask and gloves fell away would terrify the common man on the street. Skeletally thin, with no sign of body fat and little muscle, the virtuoso's skin was yellow, translucent, almost parchment-like. He had no nose, only two large gapped slits that sat above a slashed, lipless mouth. His eyes were red on a yellow background, and deeply sunken. On top of his head there were only a few wisps of jet-black hair. Had I found this man in one of the trenches that I had so recently left, I would have thought him long dead from starvation and dehydration. That he resembled nothing so much as a walking skeleton does not do justice to the tragedy of the poor creature's condition.

I overheard West ask Carnby, "His name is Zann?"

Carnby shook his head. "No, no. Zann is a pet name; it means 'ornament', for the way he used to cling to his mother's leg as a child. His mother named him Erik, after his father."

I turned my attention back to my patient. "Erik." I forced myself to adopt the mildest of manners with this patient. "Erik, my name is Dr. Cain, Daniel Cain; I would, with your permission, like to examine you."

The man-monster hesitated and then spoke. His voice was deep, full of inner darkness and mystery. "Dr. Cain," each syllable was pronounced with intensity, "you will forgive me if I seem reticent. Since my birth I have been hidden from the world, a world that would fear and despise me, and a world that, given the opportunity, would kill me as it killed my father. I think therefore a moment of caution before exposing myself to anyone is prudent."

I took a step forward. "Erik, I find that position to be entirely logical, even admirable. But if you let me, I may be able to find a way to change that and make it so that you never have to live in fear again."

I spent the next three hours examining the poor creature. I poked and prodded, looked in his ears and his throat, took samples of his skin and his blood. I checked his reflexes, his heart rate, and blood pressure and flashed a light in his eyes and checked pupil response. What I found surprised me. Despite all of his physical deformities, Erik's nervous system and constitution were remarkable. His strength and speed were preternatural. His senses, particularly his hearing, were highly acute. Furthermore, Erik's ability to not only repeat but also perfectly mimic any sound using either his voice or his ever-present viol was simply uncanny. His instrument was like a part of him and he never set it down, and only paused in playing it when absolutely necessary. This made examining him both difficult but strangely enjoyable as well. The only person who seemed immune to Erik's monstrous charms was my colleague Herbert West.

It was then that the nagging thought that was scratching at the back of my skull burst out. I looked at my watch and cursed as I dashed out of the room. West and Carnby were on my heels, but sadly we were all too late. Poor Dewart, who had apparently awoken hours ago, had done what any man would have done. Unfortunately, in his attempts to free himself from the table restraints, the entire apparatus had upended and tumbled down on to the poor man. Apparently unable to obtain any leverage with only one leg, he had slowly been smothered.

As West and I attended to Dewart, Carnby ran off to inform the de Chagnys. In his absence we righted the table and repositioned Dewart, checking to make sure the straps were intact and tight. Then without an afterthought I lifted up the man's head and West plunged a syringe full of our green bioluminescent reagent into the base of his skull. Laying his head back down, I took up my pocket watch and my notebook and observed the progression of our patient as our reagent began to work. As always, the first reaction was an uncontrolled spasm of the entire musculature sending the body bucking wildly against the restraints. This was followed by a sudden period of calm in which the eyes and indeed all of the senses suddenly began to work again, sending the patient into frantic hysteria as previously silent inputs suddenly overwhelmed the brain with massive amounts of information. As he laid there, eyes dashing about, Carnby, Lady de Chagny and Erik walked into the room. The timing was unfortunate, for it was at this moment that Dewart entered into the next phase of the reanimation process, and it had absolutely nothing to do with the fact that Erik had forgotten to don his mask. Dewart's lungs began to work once more, and this, coupled with the sudden flood of sensory information to his brain, created an automatic response that we had seen time and time again. From Dewart's lips issued the most horrid of sounds, a cry of anguish so terrible, so soul-wrenching, that both Erik and his mother began to weep.

As Dewart collapsed into a heap of raving muscle, Erik turned to Carnby and spoke. "I thought you said he was dead?"

Carnby was either too stunned or too confused to answer. Either way, West looked at the trio with that curious half-cocked head that indicated he couldn't tell whether someone was joking or just being stupid. "He was dead!" shouted West as he straightened his coat and shirt. "I brought him back!"

Once we were settled, West and I began discussing options on how to deal with Erik's condition. Initially, we thought about transplanting Erik's head, but this direction was rejected, primarily because it did nothing to resolve the issue of Erik's face, but also because it relied heavily on the constitution of the donor body, and the suppression of various rejection processes. If we were unable to resolve the rejection problem, it would be unlikely that we could reverse the procedure. Therefore we focused instead on transplanting significant amounts of skin and vascular tissue, primarily from reanimated donors. However, since the procedure we envisioned would require significant surgery, we quickly but crudely began to assess prospective blood donors. We assessed all of the patients, Carnby and even Lady de Chagny. Several of the patients were compatible, as was Erik's mother. Once she learned she was compatible, it was made clear to us that she was going to be his primary blood donor.

Our agreed-upon plan was simple; after determining compatibility, we would systematically remove Erik's face and hands, and replace them with samples harvested from the reanimated. The rest of his body could be hidden by clothing. Unfortunately, the first part of the surgery would be the most experimental and the most painful. In order to confirm the compatibility of the reanimated donors, Erik would be subjected to three simultaneous transplants, one from each of the donors. These we would do on his lower back, and in rather large sections. It was our hope that all would be compatible, but the reality we faced was that the odds of rejection, even with the reagent acting as a suppressant, were extremely high.

We began the first stage of surgery early one morning in one of the many bedrooms in the chateau, by intoxicating Erik with liberal amounts of brandy until he passed out. Carnby helped us strap him down to a table, while the Lady de Chagny was set up in an adjacent bed. West commented on how poorly the Lady appeared, and she simply nodded and whispered that the strain of the last several weeks had made her extremely tired. West and I both knew that tiredness could not explain away the weight loss and unhealthy pallor she had adopted in the last few days, and I suspected that the disease that was ravaging her body was progressing rapidly.

Carefully, I removed four strips of skin from Erik's belly, while West went off to obtain replacement strips from our donors. Each donor was color-coded Blue, Red, Green, or White, so that there would be no mistake as to the origin of any successfully transplanted tissue. Carnby acted as a go-between, bringing each strip up from West's laboratory to me as it became available. I worked as fast as I could, suturing in tissue first from Blue, then Green, then Red, and finally White. As I tied off my last piece of silk I noticed that West had not yet returned from the catacombs to join me in evaluating the response of Erik's body to the transplanted tissue.

Leaving Carnby with explicit instructions, I dashed down into the catacombs and flew into West's lab. There I found West violently pinned to the wall by the patient designated Green but whom I immediately recognized as Dewart. The soldier's hand was wrapped around West's throat, dragging him up against the cavern rock. Grabbing a wooden chair, I smashed it against Dewart's remaining leg, sending the man to the floor and West sliding back to the ground.

Brandishing the leg of the now-shattered chair like a club, I helped West up while keeping an eye on his attacker who floundered, unable to right himself with only one leg. Having some experience with such uncontrollable patients, West and I proceeded to strap Dewart down to his bed, and then gag him as well. We checked on the remaining donors, who all appeared secure, and then returned to the surgery to monitor Erik's progress.

After a few moments it was clear that Erik's body was rejecting three of the samples. The flesh around the transplants had swelled up, become red and warm to the touch. Agglutination of the blood between the recipient and the donated tissue was apparent even with the reanimation agent acting to suppress rejection. Fearing a serious reaction, West crudely ripped through my sutures and threw the offending tissue into a waste bin. He cursed as he studied the last transplant area, which showed no signs of rejection. We had found a compatible donor; unfortunately our only compatible donor was August Dewart.

West ordered Carnby to follow him, and the young scholar soon returned pale and frightened. I had a sneaking suspicion of what he had seen, but the medical procedure we were endeavoring to undertake allowed no time to coddle the meek. I took the two strips of tissue that West had carved out of Dewart and quickly sewed them into the vacancies created by the earlier rejection. As I finished, West appeared with a third strip and that was quickly installed as well.

We waited an hour. The tension was high. Carnby knew something unseemly had just happened, but either didn't or couldn't understand exactly what that was. I could see he wanted to tell the Lady de Chagny something, but he remained silent. For our part, West and I periodically checked the transplant sites. While the original donation seemed to be well received, we both feared that the reanimated tissue would complicate the procedure. Fortunately for both of us, the treated tissue showed no signs of initiating an adverse reaction. Without hesitating, I began to work on removing the skin from Erik's head while West left to obtain the replacement tissue.

I began my incision on Erik's chest just below the neck, and then made cuts that traveled over each shoulder heading toward his back. Then, carefully and with Carnby's help, we lifted Erik and I connected both cuts at a spot just between his shoulders. I then sliced from the back up his neck and over the rear of the skull. With care I gripped both flaps and peeled the skin away from his body, much in the way that you would peel an orange, on occasion using my scalpel to slice through areas of difficult connecting tissue. Once I was over the shoulders and the crown of the skull, I had Carnby hold the body up as I pulled the now hoodlike mass of skin up and off of our patient. The resulting skinless apparition was monstrous to behold. Thankfully, Lady de Chagny had mercifully passed into unconsciousness before the bloody raw shape of her son's head was ripped out of his skin.

Moments later, West arrived with the replacement flesh, including the cartilaginous tissue we needed to construct a nose. I nodded, thankful that for once he had put medical care above experimentation. West had performed nearly the same cuts as I had, so once the nose tissue had been pinned in place it was only a matter of wrenching the new skin over the skull, centering the face into place and then trimming and suturing it at strategic places to take up slack. The whole procedure took less than an hour, after which we took a moment to admire our work. Erik's new face was not particularly handsome, but it was a vast improvement over his own. He was still bald, but at least now he had a nose, although this last feature was rather large and flat. Combined with the mustache and beard that had belonged to Dewart, Erik looked like nothing so much as an operatic Mephistopheles.

Making sure that Erik was fully unconscious so that we could begin the next stage of the procedure, we were suddenly interrupted by a great and violent wailing, the source of which was obviously deep in the catacombs. West and I, accompanied by Carnby, dashed down the stairs to find Dewart free from his bonds and flailing about the room. Skinless from the chest up, the creature was like some ghoulish revenant come back to seek revenge on his tormentors. Furniture was thrown about the room, glass shattered, instruments flew, and as we three moved in to subdue the monster I saw it grab a slightly phosphorescent syringe, and the vial of glowing fluid that lay beside it. West and I could do nothing to stop what happened next. The syringe flew across the room like a dagger, only to lodge in Carnby's right shoulder. The vial was thrown as well, shattering against the wall and spraying reagent across the other reanimates. Enraged and empowered either by the events or by overexposure to the reagent, the three patchwork soldiers ripped through their bonds and began to lurch violently toward us.

Knowing full well that a disaster had been set in motion, I grabbed Carnby and ordered us all back up the stairs. West furtively grabbed his medical bag and followed us. We could hear the creatures thrashing about the room as we stumbled frantically away. Hearing the screams, the few nurses that were on duty came rushing into the hall. I ordered them up the stairs as well, but they paused in confusion. It was then that the door to West's private lab burst open and the creatures began to stalk down the hall and into the ward. They were horrid visions of phosphorescent death, killing the other patients without pause or remorse. Worse were the traces of reagent that they carried with them, which seeped into the wounds of their victims, spreading the plague of arisen dead throughout the catacombs.

Overwhelmed, and with the nurses in tow, we reached the top of the stairs and slammed the door shut, bolted it, and then lodged a large masonry statue between it and the floor. The nurses fled out the front gate into the night. Carnby fled toward our surgery, while West and I immediately began to think about how to deal with an apparent rampant reanimation problem growing underneath our feet. Our ruminations were shattered when Carnby cried out that the Lady de Chagny was not breathing.

I sprang to her side and checked her vitals. She was cold, so very cold, with no heartbeat or pulse to be found. I cursed my eyes. The Lady de Chagny had not passed out at the sight of her son's surgery; she had succumbed to her cancer. I shook my head, indicating that she had been dead too long, and that there was nothing conventional that could be done to save her.

West and I exchanged knowing glances, which Carnby caught. Never before had I seen such a look of resigned terror on a man's face. Helman Carnby knew what we planned on doing and knew that there was nothing he could do to stop us. Resigned, he slunk out of the room and left us to our own devices. What we did next needed to be done; it is what the Lady de Chagny had asked us to do, and it is what she would have wanted us to do. Erik's surgery went well, and in the end the skin transplants on his face and hands healed quickly and his recovery was rapid. He suffered a bout of melancholy over the loss of his mother, but he had been prepared for that event and overcame that tragedy as well.

As for the things beneath the house, we only ever opened the door once and then only briefly to add one last victim of our reanimation reagent to those who roamed below. Only Carnby, West and I knew the truth of what had happened that night, and we all agreed to keep the truth from Erik, believing that the less he knew the better. We foolishly hoped that the catacombs would have contained their horrid secret, but it was not to be. As we tended to Erik in our snowbound fortress, the moaning that had leaked out from the great door slowly ceased. We all suspected the worst, but all of us refused to open the door and venture below. Our suspicions were confirmed when word reached us from the nearby village. War-crazed soldiers had pillaged the local towns, attacking and killing residents without mercy. Inevitably, one of these madmen was captured and hanged for his crimes. When the body with its broken neck refused to cease moving, there was talk of necromancy and the superstitious peasantry quickly consigned the undying thing to a raging bonfire.

The winter held horrors for those in the trenches as well. Reports of diseased soldiers carrying out ghoulish acts on both sides of the lines were rampant and added fuel to the vile rumors of the German Kadaververwertungsanstalt or corpse-rendering works. Likewise frequent were the reports that echoed those of the Angels of Mons, of a spectral lady in white with red gloves, who would roam the field of war singing the most beautiful of operatic arias. Many of the French officers, older men who had spent some part of their youth in Paris, swore they recognized not only the melodies and lyrics, but even the haunting voice. Troops seduced by her siren song and longing to embrace her ghostly beauty walked out into the no man's land between the trenches, and were never seen again.

In March the thaw was such that the four of us packed up what things we could and made our way to Paris by horse and cart. Carnby took what portions of the library he dared, and I know that West absconded with *The Pretorius Commentary on the Journals of Victor Frankenstein*. Erik took his viol, a tintype of his mother, as well as several volumes of music and librettos, but left the vast majority of his life behind. Once in Paris we met with the managers of the Paris Opera, and with the aid of letters from his mother he obtained a position in the orchestra under an assumed name. West and I returned to the front and served and experimented until the powers called an end to hostilities. Carnby took passage to the United States and returned to California to study with his brother. I heard that many years later, something untoward had occurred between the two and both were lost when their Oakland house caught fire.

Over the years, I corresponded with Erik. He was perhaps one of our greatest scientific achievements, and I longed to follow his progress. He quickly became something of a minor celebrity, renowned for his music, his baritone voice and wicked appearance, all of which allowed him to be cast in various productions concerning supernatural forces throughout 1918 and 1919. His last letter to me was dated from 1920, after his return from a tour of European capitals in which he performed as the Devil who travels to Tblisi in Georgia and challenges a young farm hand to a musical duel. Sadly, the tour had seemed to take a toll on the young man. He had lost his voice, and the skin on his hands and face seemed to have aged dramatically in just a few weeks. He wondered if, after all these years, he could be undergoing a rejection of the transplanted tissue. I wrote back suggesting a course of treatment and the possibility of my coming to examine him personally. I never heard from him again, and my inquiries at the opera house were ignored as well. Still, I treasure the review Erik had sent me from his London performance.

While some would suggest that the production currently on stage at the London Opera House caters to the less refined tastes of the populace, this critic finds the performance of Erich Zann to be a significant contribution to modern operatic endeavors. Zann's performance as the Devil is complemented not only by his physical appearance but also by his nearly divine singing. Moreover, his voice is complemented, perhaps even surpassed, by his technique in playing the viol. So magnificent is his bowing style that it is my humble opinion that those most magnificently delicate hands must have been a gift from God himself, or perhaps stolen from some fallen angel of music.

CHAPTER 20.

THE RETURN OF CAIN AND WEST

By late 1922 I had buried myself in my practice and my long-term experiment of inoculating a portion of my patients with the prophylactic version of the reagent. Any concerns I had about Daniel Cain who had begun a small and seedy practice across town had faded, and I was free to worry about the more mundane things in my life. My partnership with young Dr. Randolph White, who had replaced the traitorous Dr. Wilson, was stable and genial, and I visited his office in Kingsport a little more than weekly. I had full confidence that Dr. White had become and would remain a fine and upstanding community physician.

In the closing days of the year, young White called to inform me that one of our patients, the writer Randolph Carter, had suffered some kind of seizure during the Christmas holiday and was being moved from the meager facilities in Kingsport to St. Mary's in Arkham. As his physician, I was of course concerned for his well-being, but more importantly Carter was one of my many experimental subjects and as such he should have been resistant to physical trauma and disease. I could not help but wonder what had triggered his sudden illness.

At the hospital Carter seemed physically healthy. He responded to stimuli and his vital signs were adequate, though slightly suppressed. His mental state, however, was of greater concern, for he seemed not only distracted but nervous as well. He seemed overwhelmingly relieved that he had been transferred to Arkham and out of Kingsport. At the mere mention of that seaside town which he had apparently spent a few days in, his respiration and heart rate would suddenly increase, his skin would become clammy, and his limbs would become uncontrollably frenetic. I soon concluded that whatever had happened to the man was not physical in nature, but rather psychic. Something in Kingsport had affected Carter in a most horrendous fashion.

Knowing that Carter was a writer of weird and fantastic fiction, I suggested to the staff that a pen and notebook be placed by his bed. Given access to such tools, he might just find a way to exorcise whatever demons he had allowed to possess him. Oddly, my suggestion was met with some resistance. Several of the staff recalled Carter's tale "The Attic Window" that had appeared more than a year earlier in a magazine called *Whispers*, and the furor that it had generated amongst certain vocal critics who had called for its censorship. Thankfully these silly milksops were overruled by more senior hospital staff and Carter was allowed the tools of his trade.

This course of therapy seemed to accomplish its goal, for within a day the man had filled the notebook with the observations and occurrences that he had made and witnessed while in Kingsport and seemed much improved by the process. By the end of the week I declared him healthy enough to leave the hospital and oversaw his transfer to the ancestral Carter manse that sprawled southwest of Arkham. I made several visits to Carter while he recuperated and soon concluded that the rambling old house, with its overgrown gardens and dark wooded acres with the accompanying isolation, while familiar, may not have been conducive to his full recovery. Carter had always shunned the wealth he had been born into, preferring to live a more bohemian lifestyle that was more appropriate to his image as a writer. I suggested that it would behoove him to move to an area more in keeping with his needs. Somewhere he could be with more people that might understand the ennui that seemed to be gripping his soul. He agreed, and by the end of February he had packed a small bag and set off for the bustling city that was New York. The change of locale seemed to do him good, for although he complained about the lack of work and money, his writing seemed to flourish and I read with much gusto the draft stories and poems he routinely sent me.

I had apparently been too absorbed in my work, for in March Miss Soames chastised me for failing to notice that someone new had moved onto the street. I had never been much for socializing with my neighbors, the nature of my secret experiments was not conducive to such casual acquaintances;

and the relationship I had with Peaslee and any of his family had long since ceased after Peaslee had recovered from his affliction. Soames knew that I was not very personable, but she also knew that certain modes of decorum had to be conformed to. The neighborhood doctor simply had to introduce himself to the two new bachelors who had moved in down the street.

I put off the visit for a few days, but eventually became annoyed with Soames' periodic badgering, and one fine Saturday morning I wandered down the street to give my regards. From a distance it was obvious that they were still in the process of moving in, for boxes and crates of all sizes, some bearing familiar markings, littered the front lawn. As I drew closer, the markings and shapes of the packing crates grew more familiar, and I soon recognized the brand of a local medical supply firm.

A house away I could hear voices that seemed startlingly familiar, and even though I could not place them, I was suddenly filled with a menacing foreboding and the overwhelming need to turn and flee. I could not, though. Something more powerful drew me forward, and with each step my desire to flee grew but my need to see grew as well. There was no denying this fearsome magnetic force and it drew me to my new neighbors like a moth to a flame. The voices grew louder, and just as I reached the edge of the property the two men who were in conversation appeared in the doorway and sauntered down the flagstones toward the pile of crates.

The sight of them broke whatever spell I had been subjected to, and I casually slipped behind a large elm to conceal my presence. I peeked around the trunk and watched surreptitiously as they maneuvered a large wooden crate up the path and through the door. The one man, the one with ebon hair and a subservient demeanor, I recognized immediately, and I cursed the day that I found it necessary to allow Dr. Daniel Cain to remain free. That the man had not been banished from the city and state for his monstrous acts and horrific medical experiments was wholly my fault, for it was I who had convinced the investigators that his written confession was the result of a drugged-induced hallucination. I had hoped that upon his release, free from the unholy bonds that linked him to Herbert West, Cain might have returned to his native Illinois. Instead, the years of servitude had apparently robbed Cain of any real capacity at self-motivation, and he had fallen back into familiar habits, remaining in Arkham and catering to the most meager and least discriminating of patients. What had suddenly possessed him to move into new more genteel accommodations, and on my own block for that matter, I could not immediately fathom.

It was only after the second man turned slightly that I understood why Cain was here. The slight figure that directed Cain as he carried the various crates into their new abode had changed since I had last seen him. His hair was no longer yellow but had for some reason turned shockingly white. As he moved about I could see that he had suffered some degree of physical trauma, for scars encircled his neck, wrists and shoulders. I thought at first that he must have suffered an injury during the war, but recalling Cain's confession there was no mention of such an event. Not that it mattered much, and despite his change of appearance I had no doubt of the identity of the man who along with Daniel Cain now occupied the abode just a half of a block away from my own. As the two men returned to the interior of the house I caught sight of the sign that had recently been installed on the wall to the left, the sign that in its simplicity confirmed what I had already deduced. It was a simple wooden plaque, with four words painted in white that declared to the world a horror that most would not understand.

Cain and West, Physicians

The prospect of having these two monsters residing and practicing just yards from my own home filled me with dread. I had no desire to engage them socially, but knew that such an encounter was likely. What's more, I also knew that those two were not likely to have abandoned their old practices, despite the fact that Cain had already confessed to a multitude of crimes including multiple murders and grave robbing. I had no doubt that the authorities were watching Cain, and had good reason to believe that if they acquired proof of West and Cain's renewed activities, any investigation would surely expand to include my own practice and residence. Such inquiries were something I surely could not afford.

I considered a variety of options, and will not deny that the act of murder crossed my mind. Other less drastic measures, including trading places with White, closing down my offices on a temporary, or even permanent basis, were evaluated and also dismissed. In the end it seemed that I had little choice but to do as I had done so many years ago. I would shadow these two men, watch them and wait for an opportunity, and when it came I would inflict on them a wound so terrible that they would have no choice but to abandon Arkham and flee. At least, that was my plan.

Whatever had happened to West during his two-year hiatus had changed him and his understanding of medicine and the science of reanimation. Their nightly excursions took us, Cain and West in one car, and I in another, throughout the city and the county acquiring the bodies not only of humans but of animals as well, for not only did we haunt morgues, cemeteries and funeral homes, but stockyards, pet stores and zoological gardens as well. For weeks such material flowed into the basement laboratory that they had equipped, and although I never saw what they produced with such raw materials, the sounds that emanated from the cellar door hinted at things both marvelous and hideous. That none of this organic material ever left the house, while the furnace seemed to run constantly, suggested that West and Cain were not above routinely disposing of whatever they were creating.

Not that the two madmen were particularly cautious. For all their knowledge and medical skill, they were exceedingly sloppy and left a host of clues and trails in their wake, any of which could have easily led investigators back to the two of them. Knowing that if they were exposed I too was put at risk, I was faced with the unenviable task of cleaning up behind them. I swept away footprints and tire tracks left in sawdust, mud and grease. I destroyed receipts that documented their purchase of certain chemicals and equipment. When necessary, I called in false alarms to draw police away from wherever they were. On one occasion I even recovered Cain's billfold containing not only his business card but his identification as well. I returned it to him by depositing it on the back porch of their residence in a location where he would assume he had dropped it as he and West left for their sojourn the night before.

I did these things, knowing full well that I was aiding the very people I had reason to despise. These men through their actions had killed my parents, assaulted dozens, committed crimes against natural and human laws, and through me could be blamed for the deaths of millions throughout the world, though I doubted they were aware of that particular fact. All these horrible things could be laid at their feet, and only a few others and I knew the truth. A good man would have done something about it, but somewhere along the line I had ceased being a good man. My need for vengeance had corrupted me, seduced me, and I had become immune to the morality of life, death and the strange undeath that we in our arrogance wielded. One day I would be free to reveal my reagent to the world, but until then I had to keep it a secret. West and Cain were no longer my nemeses, but rather bumbling fools who through their base actions and crude experiments might reveal my own purer goals before they were entirely congealed. Frustrated, I once more considered a plan of action and resolved myself to doing what I thought needed to be done.

Late one moonless night, one that was unseasonably warm for May, my two subjects casually left their residence and afforded me the opportunity that I had been waiting for. Carefully I climbed through an unlocked second-floor window and with care and speed made my way into their basement laboratory. I quickly found West's logbook and scanned the most recent pages for the formula of his latest batch of reagent. It was a satisfactory concoction, one that I had experimented with myself several years ago, and I could discern what West was trying to gain from this particular direction. Unfortunately, as West had noted, the formulation as it was led to a certain kind of instability in his subjects, and was prone to instances of rejection, particularly at the juncture of distinctive tissues. Thankfully, my own version showed none of the weaknesses inherent in West's and as quickly as I could I went about emptying the contents of the prepared syringes and replacing them with my own formulation. After I finished, I retraced my steps and left the way I came in, secure in the knowledge that I had left no trace of my unauthorized visit. The whole excursion had taken me little more than thirty minutes, and it was easily another hour before West and Cain returned. Where they had been I was not sure, but it must have been nearby. After ascertaining that the streets were clear, the two opened the back doors of their sedan and with no great amount of care unloaded what, even though it was draped in a blanket, was clearly a body, though somewhat small in stature.

The lights of the basement burned brightly that evening, and through the dawn as well. I left soon after the sun rose, not because I believed that whatever the two were doing was completed, but rather because in the light of day I could no longer conceal myself from my neighbors and the tradesmen who would soon be arriving to carry out the business of the day. As I left I noticed a sign on the front door that announced that the practice was closed for the day, and wondered when either West or Cain had mounted it, and how I had missed it, even in the dark of the night.

Whatever they had accomplished that night, West remained out of sight for a week, although Cain actively saw patients. Late one night I watched as Cain carried what appeared to be the same slight body, wrapped in the same blanket, back out to the car and drove off with it. I followed him and was shocked when after a few minutes he slowed and casually parked the black sedan near the back entrance of the University's museum of ancient history.

I quickly turned the corner, secreted my car on a side street, and dashed silently to a spot where I could observe Cain's actions. Furtively, he unloaded the wrapped form and carried it easily onto a loading platform at the back of the museum. Even from a distance I could see the key that he produced from his vest pocket and then used to open the service door. I waited, and within twenty minutes was rewarded for my patience, for he emerged and scanned the streets before exiting the loading dock. Surprisingly, he was still carrying the blanket-wrapped form, though now he seemed less thoughtful, even careless in his manner. Once back at the sedan he opened the trunk and without much thought roughly deposited his burden in the cramped space.

Cain returned home, and was just as careless unloading the body as he had been at the museum, dragging it down the stairs by its feet and allowing it to bang against the runners and wall. After a few moments I heard the unmistakable sound of the furnace firing up, and soon smoke billowed from the stack on the roof. I left for home, concluding that whoever it was that had been hidden within the blanket had been fed to the flames and destroyed.

After a week of inactivity West reappeared, and was soon meeting with University officials both at his offices, and those of the Department of Ancient History. I made subtle inquiries and learned that West had volunteered to serve for several months as physician to one of the University's many expeditions. In particular, he had expressed a desire to join the expedition that was continuing the excavation of a peculiar set of tombs in the deserts of Egypt. Several artifacts, including the sarcophagus and mummy of a hieratic sorcerer, had already been unearthed and were on display in the museum. That West had volunteered to pay his own passage served to assure that he would gain a position with the team.

West left Arkham during the middle of May, leaving Cain to maintain the illusion of their medical practice. I continued my nocturnal observations, but Cain showed no inclination towards solely undertaking the activities with which he regularly aided West. The man seemed generally incapable of even the most common of social activities. One afternoon I watched as he undertook what I considered to be a simple act of shopping for groceries.

He seemed honestly confused on how to select produce and meat or even a loaf of bread. The more time I spent watching Cain, the more I realized how under West's thumb he must be.

By mid-July, West had returned from Egypt, which apparently was a life-changing event. I watched as he moved around town, and even risked peering through windows into his house, and there was something changed about him. He was, if it was possible, even more arrogant than he had been before. He walked as if he had inherited the world, that Arkham itself belonged to him, and all those who resided within were his subjects, to do with as he pleased. At least that is how I saw him. What had motivated such a change I could not say, but I was determined to find out. If I understood West, such a change in behavior was the result of some perceived triumph. Perhaps he had made a breakthrough of some sort or another; perhaps he had made progress on his own reagent. I had to know.

One evening about a week after West had returned from Egypt I decided to spy on the two men as best I could. This was not going to be as easy as it had been when the two had occupied a remote farmhouse, to which I had a key. I had to wait until after dark and then most carefully secrete myself in the rear garden where I could watch them through the windows. Their behavior was almost normal; one would not have thought them monsters as they sat there eating dinner, washing dishes and listening to the radio. At one point Cain made a move toward the cellar, but West waved him off. Cain was puzzled at that, but did not argue with his partner. Instead he picked up the evening paper and perused it for a few moments. The paper must have been uninteresting, for soon Cain put it down, bade West good-night, and then made his way down the hall to his room on the side of the house. I could see his silhouette through the curtain. He moved about for a few minutes, and then the light went out and I turned my attention back to West.

Dr. Herbert West sat listening to the radio and reading a book. Yet as I watched him, I realized that he was doing more than that, he was watching the clock. Every few minutes he would glance up and note the time. I found it very odd, worrisome even. Then, after about an hour, West carefully closed his book, stood up and walked toward the basement door. He opened it slowly and then slipped inside. I took the opportunity to move from the garden toward the foot of the window where I could get a better view. Just as I finished secreting myself, West returned. I knew that something was afoot, for in his hand he bore a syringe radiating green with the tell-tale luminosity of reanimation reagent. The emerald light of the compound cast an eerie glow across West's face as he crossed the room and moved down the hall towards Cain.

I crept along the wall until I found myself beneath Cain's window. There was a gap in the curtains, and light from the hallway allowed me to see West standing over Cain's bed. He lunged forward and clasped his free hand around Cain's throat. Cain woke with a start and struggled, but could not break free of his mentor's grasp. I heard West mumble something, but the walls made whatever he said unintelligible. Cain's body shuddered, ceased its struggles, and then became still. Dr. Herbert West had strangled his long-time companion Dr. Daniel Cain!

Yet as I sat there watching in horror, I knew what was to come. West lifted Cain's head and plunged the syringe he carried deep into the soft spot at the base of the skull. Then, he withdrew and stepped back, a look of supreme confidence and satisfaction on his face. I watched, waiting for Cain to react, keeping time in my head. After ten seconds there had been no response, but West remained still. Twenty seconds, still nothing. Thirty seconds, and I glanced at West, hoping to see some semblance of concern cross his face, but there was nothing. Time crawled forward, unstoppable and uncaring. At forty-five seconds I stood up slowly, careful to keep out of the light. A minute passed, and finally I saw West take action, but it was only to check his pocket watch, and then take a step toward the body.

The bedroom erupted in a horrific, ear-splitting scream that made me stumble back and fall to the earth. The curtains were suddenly ripped from the window and a pain-wracked body rose up from the bed to tower over West's suddenly tiny form. It was screaming, thrashing about in agony. I saw West move forward, and then fly back against the wall like a rag doll. There was a grunting sound, like a pig rutting, and then the window exploded, sending shards of glass showering down on me, while the raging form flew past me and out of the garden. Daniel Cain had returned from the dead!

I climbed to my feet, threw off my glass-covered coat and dashed after the reanimated Cain. It was apparent that he had come back wrong, that West's reagent had failed, that it was somehow insufficient to the task. Part of me wanted to run back and confront West, to demand he turn over his notes and admit his mistake, but I knew there were more pressing matters. Cain was moving down the street toward the University, and I was suddenly reminded of that night so many years ago when another of West's creations had rampaged through this very neighborhood. This time, I was prepared to do something about it. Though it cost me precious time, I ran back to my house and retrieved my medical bag and the syringes full of my own version of the reagent, and the pistol I brought back from the war.

Honestly, I did not know what I was going to do. The gun might be useless, and I wasn't sure what effect injecting a reanimated body with a second, albeit slightly different dose of reagent would have. Yet what were my choices? As I returned to the street, I could see the stumbling form of Cain in the distance. I ran after him, my feet pounding on the worn stones and echoing through the neighborhood. I wasn't fast, but neither was the thing I was pursuing. In mere moments I had closed the distance between us, and left my own home blocks behind. Cain had turned down a side road, one lined with warehouses and tenements, and I could see I was just a block or so behind him.

As I turned to follow I heard a voice cry out and pierce the night. "Dan!" It was West, two blocks behind me, but even from this distance I could see the cheap brown suit and matching hat he was wearing. It was not the light of the moon or the streetlights that allowed me to see these details, it was the harsh, green glow of the syringe that he held in his hand. A syringe full of his own reagent that was whipping back and forth as he ran toward me. I turned down the street and at a mad dash sought to reach Cain before West caught up with us. Still I had no clue what I was going to do once I did catch him, but the gun felt good in my hand.

It was then that I realized that I might be able to have Cain himself help me. Still running, I raised the pistol into the air and fired into the sky. The noise of the shot did what it was supposed to and Cain turned, saw me running toward him, and roared in defiant anger. Like some wounded animal he came at me, growling and flailing with wild eyes and gnashing teeth. I knew as he approached that I would be no match for him physically, so I would have to out-think him. Flipping the gun over, I took it by the barrel, and as he closed I swung the grip at his head. He dodged, but I still caught him across the face, and opened up a gash that ran across his cheek and down his neck. He staggered back, stumbled, and then collapsed to the ground in the middle of the street. Apparently, West's new version of the reagent did not render the reanimated as resistant to physical injury as they were in the past.

Fearing that West, or, even worse, someone else, might come to investigate, I grabbed Cain by the collar and slowly pulled him into an alleyway. Once there I stood up and considered my options. I looked at the gun, and then at the thing that was rasping for air at my feet. It was a monster, one of many that West and I had created over the years, and it was also one of the men I held responsible for the death of my parents. This thing was responsible for ruining my life, and at this moment I could easily exact my long-sought-after revenge. I took the gun and aimed at the thing's head. My finger caressed the trigger and I took a deep breath.

Suddenly my concentration was broken. That damned voice, West's voice, cried out again, and I could hear his footsteps as they came down the street. I ducked back against the alley wall and cursed at being so close to satisfaction. If only there had been some way to destroy both of them at the same time. If only I could find it in myself to shoot the monster at my feet, and the mad doctor that was coming ever closer. It was then that the idea sparked inside my mind. Carefully, I opened up my medical bag, placed the gun inside and withdrew instead a syringe of my own reagent.

I pulled Cain's head back and plunged the syringe into the already reanimated brainstem and injected more than twice the normal dosage. I didn't know what would happen, but I knew there was potential for disaster. As quickly as I could, I retreated deeper into the alleyway. This time there was no waiting for a reaction; Daniel Cain roared back to life and virtually exploded out of the alleyway. I had hoped he would turn right, back in the direction we had come from, and therefore encounter West who was rapidly coming down the street. It was my hope that such an encounter would leave at least one, if not both, dead. Unfortunately, the whims of fortune were not with me that night, and Cain turned left, away from West who once more screamed his friend's name. With some stealth I made my way to the mouth of the alley and watched Cain careening down the streets of Arkham, his screams piercing the night, with West in pursuit.

I had no need to follow them. Somehow or other, my lust for vengeance, which had waxed and waned throughout the years, was suddenly satiated. I returned to Crane Street, retrieved my jacket from West's garden and then went home. Sleep was oddly blissful that night, and if I remember correctly I dreamt of my childhood, of a picnic with my parents and my sister. There were no thoughts of West or Cain that night, nor the next day. Indeed, it was two days before my attention was drawn back to the house just down the road, and I felt the need to investigate the fate of Doctors West and Cain.

Not surprisingly, their practice had closed. A moving van was in front of the house, and I learned from neighbors that the house, and Cain's family property in Illinois, had been listed for sale, which, given the value and location of both, was quickly accomplished. Rumor had it that the two had already signed a contract for a property in New York City, although where no one quite knew. I watched with satisfaction as their personal effects and furniture were loaded into the truck by hired hands.

My satisfaction was suddenly doused when out of the house two figures emerged; both West and Cain were still alive, and seemed to be in control of themselves. As I watched, my satisfaction surged back. Cain moved slowly and his eyes seemed dull and lifeless. If it was possible, the sad subservient Cain had become even sadder and I cannot say that I was entirely surprised by the huge and ghastly gash that ran across his face and down his neck. Even from a distance I could see the fine stitching that would, given time and a modicum of reagent, resolve itself into a scar, a scar that would forever remind both of them of the horrors that they had inflicted on the world and each other!

CHAPTER 21.

QUIRK AT WINTER'S END

It was during the winter of 1924-25, my desire for vengeance sated, or at least satisfied, that I put a hold on my experiments and sealed the door to my sub-basement laboratory. It was about that same time that Dr. John Ramsey organized the Miskatonic University Rural Program. With funding from charitable sponsors, Ramsey's army of interns and seasoned professionals were to travel out into the wilds of the Miskatonic Valley to the small communities that dotted the hundred or so miles of the river and provide some modicum of medical care to the residents thereof. At first I was hesitant to join such an endeavor, having had my fill of the backwoods nightmares that breed in such places, but when Ramsey himself came to my office and all but begged me to join, I reluctantly agreed, though I conditioned my involvement on never having to go near the town of Dunwich. Ramsey acquiesced, noting that there were plenty of other communities that could use my services. On the coast there were Falcon Point, Boynton Beach and possibly even Innsmouth. I could travel north to Madison Corners or Bolton, or west to Witches Hollow. Travel along the Miskatonic River did not mean going all the way to Dunwich; there were plenty of other towns that could use my services, including Foxfield, Misty Valley, Dean's Corners, Quirk, and Zoar.

I cannot say what drove my decision to choose as my destination the tiny hamlet of Quirk. I had only a passing familiarity with the name from its association with Zaman's Hill, a similarly small community that in February

1896 had seemingly vanished overnight. Perplexed officials had turned to the residents of Quirk for answers, but none of the taciturn villagers would admit to having recently been to Zaman's Hill. Indeed save for the rural postal carrier no one could be found that would admit to having been to Zaman's Hill within the last year. Rumors swirled about for years afterward, and the general conclusion was that the locals had long ago abandoned the area, and the postal carrier had failed to report the abandonment of the settlement for his own nefarious reasons, which included pocketing whatever mail had been directed there, and even dismantling the town itself. Others believed more nefarious things, and made veiled references to a series of incidents at the Gardner Farm, but when the carrier hanged himself from a tree at Dean's Corners, folks seemed content with letting the blame lie with the dead.

Only part of the Rural Program was medical in nature; other University departments, including botany, geology, history, and even anthropology, contributed team members to the effort. In many ways the program was like any other expedition to the hinterlands, only these isolated communities existed just miles from our own homes. For the trip to Quirk I was joined by a geologist named Dyer, a biologist named Lake, and a recent addition to the English Department, a young expert in folklore named Albert Wilmarth. The plan for our weekend expedition was simple; the four of us would leave by motorcar early Saturday, January 31st, and reach Quirk that afternoon. Lake and Dyer would explore the countryside, roughing it in the wild or finding shelter amongst the various homesteads. Meanwhile, Wilmarth and I would stay in town, and while I examined patients, Wilmarth would interview willing locals to garner information on local history and legends. Then, on the morning of Tuesday, February 3rd, Lake and Dyer would return and we would drive back to Arkham. The need for subsequent return visits would be evaluated based on our initial findings and the continued funding of the program.

That Saturday morning was cold and crisp, and the scent of burning wood filled the city. As the four of us left Arkham with Dyer at the wheel we immediately fell into conversation concerning our travels in service to our professions. Dyer and Lake were both well traveled throughout Europe and Canada, and both expressed a desire to expand their portfolios with even more exotic locations. There was much banter concerning where they would prefer to travel to first, and such areas as British Honduras, Australia and

Antarctica were jokingly tossed about as priorities.

By the time we passed Foxfield, Dyer and Lake had exhausted the subject and began pressuring me concerning my own history. Initially I begged off, citing doctor-patient confidentiality, but they were persistent, and eventually I gave in and related what tales I could. Still uncomfortable detailing my adventures locally, I focused instead on my time in service during the Great War. After an hour or so of gruesome war stories, my companions seemed to have had enough, and switched their attentions to young Wilmarth.

I call him young mostly because he was younger than the three of us, and had just finished his doctoral thesis, but in actuality he was about thirty-five and the only thing young about him was the last vestige of youthful enthusiasm that lingered from his days as a graduate student at Arkham College. He had little actual work experience, though he had spent a summer interviewing some of the older and more reclusive families of Kingsport. An attempt to do the same in Innsmouth met with failure when the inhabitants of that town less than politely asked him to leave. The residents of Innsmouth, Wilmarth told us, had seemingly rejected Christianity and embraced a primitive faith endemic to the islands of the South Pacific where they carried out much of their trade. Many of the sailors had come home with island-born wives, who like the women of Arab cultures were never seen without a veil covering their features.

Somehow or another, Wilmarth's monologue turned to the significance of the upcoming holiday. Monday was Groundhog Day, which I had entirely forgotten. He had spent some time researching the traditions associated with the event and had traced its origins to pagan celebrations for the change of winter to spring, and whether that should occur in February as the ancients had celebrated it, or six weeks later. The secular Groundhog Day fell at the same time as both the Christian Candlemas and the pagan Imbolc, and incorporated much of the symbolism of that celebration. The groundhog, Wilmarth informed us, was a benign American replacement for the traditional European badger, bear or serpent. Amongst some of the Irish, the day was sacred to the "storm hags", who would emerge from their caves to gather firewood. If winter was to continue, the hag would make the day bright and clear, so as to gather a larger supply, but if winter were over, the hags would make the day overcast, and creep back into their homes without any supplies. Some traditions held that the hags could transform themselves into giant winged birds and would gather wood in their huge black beaks. Wilmarth droned on, filling our ears with the details of dozens of variations of the holiday, including some of the more risqué versions in which the hags were not only the embodiment of winter, but also fertility goddesses that often required significant attention from one or more of their subjects.

With such a subject dominating the conversation, I, Lake and Dyer were relieved when we arrived at the crossroads at Dean's Corners and took a much-needed break. While we were at the roadhouse, I felt impelled to discuss our destination with the proprietor. Dean's Corners sits at the intersection of several roads, some to Aylesbury, another to Dunwich, and others to points near and far. It was imperative that we avoid Dunwich country and so I asked the shopkeeper to confirm the turn-off for Quirk. With a nonchalant gesture he confirmed that the rutted dirt trail I had identified was indeed Quirk Road, but then casually informed me that taking the car into Quirk was impossible. Our destination was on the far side of the river and the unseasonably warm spell had swollen the Miskatonic beyond its banks, washing a good portion of the bridge away. The village had erected an *ad hoc* rope bridge that reestablished foot traffic and allowed some goods to pass, but it would be weeks before the road would be open.

The solution, suggested the proprietor, a man named Addams, was for us to leave our vehicle with him and travel out to the bridge in the back of a farm wagon which ran from the store to the bridge daily. Otherwise, we would have to leave the car unguarded on the side of the road. Such a plan seemed reasonable to us all, and within the hour we had repacked our supplies into the wagon, and rolled the car into a barn. The going down the rutted dirt path was slow and rough, but I was grateful that we weren't trying to traverse this particular trail on our own. It was late afternoon when we finally reached the crossing. The sun was low on the horizon, and long shadows crept out of the thick woods to grasp at us with insubstantial inky grey tendrils.

As Addams had said, the river was swollen, and while the foundations of the bridge were still in place, the bridge itself was severely damaged and unstable. A contraption of scavenged ropes and wood formed a crude rope bridge that clung to the foundations like a parasitic vine crawling up a tree. The four of us cast obvious looks of concern about the stability of such an engineering nightmare, but had little choice but to proceed. As the youngest and most foolhardy, Wilmarth crossed first. The boards were slick but the ropes held, and within half an hour we had moved all of our supplies and ourselves from one side of the engorged Miskatonic River to the other. As we bade farewell to the wagon, its driver reminded us that he would be back for us early on Tuesday morning.

Laden down by our equipment, it was some while before the muddy road leading from the bridge led us to Quirk. By the time we reached the center of town, which consisted of little more than three or four houses clustered together, it was dusk and the air which had been chilly all day was now turning frigid. As we wandered tiredly into the common, a large figure came down off the porch to greet us. His voice was deep, and I was not at all sure he was speaking English. Fortunately, Wilmarth seemed familiar with the dialect, which I later learned was actually English, but with a thick accent and tainted by the inclusion of words and grammar from Manx, the native language of the Isle of Man.

According to this fellow, we had reached the farm of the family Clague, while Quirk proper was several miles still down the road. At this information the three of us let out an audible moan of disappointment, and our supplies made an audible thump as they were dropped to the ground. There followed a rapid exchange between Wilmarth and the young John Clague, which ended with the farmer leading us to primitive but acceptable quarters where we could lodge for the night. While we unpacked and made the bedrolls ready, John returned to the main house. A few moments later a younger man named Joseph joined us with a loaf of bread, some hard cheese and a pot of thick brown gravy. It was a hearty feast for travelers such as ourselves and we were grateful for it, the shelter, and the restful slumber that came later.

The next morning we were invited to eat with the extended Clague family, a boisterous bunch that numbered more than two dozen. We were glad of the company and the warm food and hot coffee, and although I did not speak the language it was clear that John Clague had been reprimanded by both his mother and wife for not providing us with better accommodations. After the meal had ended and only we four and three of the family elders remained at the table, the conversation, which had been facilitated by Wilmarth, turned to what business we had in the area. Through Wilmarth we explained our mission, which was greeted with mild amusement by the elders, particularly Ambrose Clague, who wondered why it was people in cities always seemed to forget their country cousins and then had to mount expeditions to rediscover them. Put that way, Lake, Dyer and I had no choice but to laugh.

For some time after that the conversation was most genial, and we learned that the Clague family had only recently immigrated to the area from the Isle of Man, having inherited the land from a local who had married one of the Clague daughters while recovering from wounds received in the war. The poor fellow had himself inherited the property from his parents, but hadn't survived for long after the nuptials. Though ostensibly part of Quirk, the Clagues seemed uninterested in speaking of the village. Indeed, when we suggested that one of the older Clague boys drive us into town, the faces of our hosts turned suddenly dour and there was no mistaking that such an event was not going to occur. Wilmarth's translation backed up this conclusion, though it seemed that much of the reticence had to do with timing, and that perhaps now was the wrong time to visit Quirk.

It was Wilmarth who came up with a plan that would allow us to carry out our tasks with little additional effort. Rather than traveling on to Quirk and establishing a base there, Wilmarth proposed that instead we establish ourselves at the Clague farm. Wilmarth and I would stay at the house interviewing and examining the family, while Lake and Dyer ranged out into the surrounding countryside to conduct their surveys. It seemed a practical solution, and the Clagues quickly warmed to the idea, particularly after we agreed to a small fee for the privilege of using their property, and hired two of the younger men to assist Lake and Dyer.

Within the hour the field expedition had departed, though they were told in no uncertain terms to return before nightfall. At the same time, Wilmarth had begun interviewing the elders concerning family folklore and history, and I had set up an area in which I could examine patients. It was only a few minutes after I began examining my first patient when the flaw in our design presented itself. Despite good intentions and efforts on everyone's part, the language barrier was simply too great and I found myself unable to communicate with my patients. I described my problem to Wilmarth and together we realized a solution. Using some rope and sheets we were able to create a small area in the sitting room in which I could examine patients in private, while Wilmarth and other family members could sit in the larger area. In this manner Wilmarth could still carry out his group discussions, and aid me in translation as needed. Soon the family, Wilmarth and I fell into a comfortable routine that was both relaxed and genial. My examination of the family men revealed everything one would expect to find in a rural farm family including arthritis, improperly set and healed bones, a missing digit or two and, in the elders, early signs of senility. Oddly enough, there was no sign of conditions that were common amongst my patients in Arkham, such as gout, diabetes, or cirrhosis. Indeed, after spending the morning examining the men folk of the Clague family, I was utterly impressed with their overall state of health and wellbeing.

Wilmarth seemed equally pleased, or at least intrigued, by the conversation he was having. I will fully admit that I understood little of what was said, though the words "Inuto", "Lomar", "Voormis", and "Cailleach" seemed to be common subjects for discussion. At one point, Wilmarth uttered the word "Ithaqua" and the conversation suddenly ceased; the patient I was examining quickly crossed himself, while his heart rate jumped propitiously. Later, over lunch I asked Wilmarth about what he had learned about the Clagues. At first Wilmarth was evasive and seemed unwilling to reveal what the Clagues had told him, but after some further pressure on my part he finally began to speak.

"Dr. Hartwell, the Clagues are a superstitious lot who believe in things long since suppressed by the Church, but once common amongst some of the barbarian clans that were spread amongst the islands and lands of the North Sea. In the mythology of the region, a giant made of ice was used to create the substance of the world. His flesh became the soil, his bones the mountains, his teeth boulders, and his brains became the clouds. Some traditions hold that in the cold places of the world, what was left of the giant called Ithaqua still stalks the skies, bringing winter storms and desolation to the land. At certain times of the year, Ithaqua, like the gods of the Greeks, may enter into a dalliance with a woman and inevitably leave her with child. These children are always female, and are collectively known as the Cailleachan, kind of like the Storm Hags I mentioned to you yesterday. The Cailleachan hide themselves amongst men, secretly spreading the seed of Ithaqua into unsuspecting families." He paused. "At least that's the legend according to the Clagues."

After lunch Wilmarth and I began our work with the women of the family. Unlike the men, the women seemed more reticent, and as a result our conversations, both medically and in terms of family folklore, seemed stilted. Like the men, the women were in extremely good health and seemed strong, showing no signs of disease or illness, though all exhibited a curious trait that I had not noticed in the men. The women of the Clague family, even the youngest of girls, all showed a curious malformation of the feet, which appeared noticeably disproportionate, extremely small, with foreshortened, stub-like toes. When questioned about them as a group they simply looked at each other and giggled about it being an ancestral trait.

Late in the afternoon, as dusk began to draw long shadows and the oil lamps were lit, Lake, Dyer and the two Clague boys returned from their sortie, cold and tired but none the worse for wear. While the two warmed themselves by the fire they described their hike as little more than a pleasant, albeit chilly, walk through the hilly countryside. Much of the land was unremarkable, consisting primarily of hills of the same loose rock and sediment that covered most of the Miskatonic Valley, worn down from the rounded mountains from which the Miskatonic itself arose. The flora too was unremarkable, being primarily conifers with a scattering of maples and a few stands of thick ancient oaks. Animal life was plentiful and the boys had brought home a covey of rabbits for dinner. Lake had taken a casting from a bear print of unusual size, and along a stream bank had found a print he swore belonged to a wolf rather than a dog.

However, the most interesting thing they had found had nothing to do with the natural history of the area, but rather was something the locals had done. Deep in the woods, someone had cleared twenty acres of forest, leaving nothing but stumps and sawdust behind. At first the two learned men had thought that they had stumbled upon an area long in use by some local lumberjack, or woodsman, who had over the years slowly cleared the area. Such a conclusion was quickly rejected, given the lack of new growth, and the prodigious amount of fresh woodchips that spanned the entire area. The only possible explanation for the evidence around them was that sometime within the last few days, a small army had descended on the area and in a furious bout of effort cleared it entirely, leaving behind only a drag trail leading north, deeper into the woods.

The existence of the cleared patch seemed to create much discontentment amongst the family. Window shutters were closed and locked, livestock was rounded up and the barn door barred. We talked at length about the barren area and the four of us agreed that we should mount an early morning outing to follow the trail that led deeper into the woods. In this we would apparently be on our own, as the Clagues seemed unwilling to explore the path any further. Indeed, an attempt was made to dissuade us from going at all. When it became clear that our minds were made up, Ambrose Clague shook his head and then had one of the boys bring forth a valued shotgun and a box of shells, insisting that we take the weapon as a precaution.

It was well before dawn when we four stumbled out of the house and into the yard that surrounded the farm. As we gathered up our supplies and secured our packs, I noted that the women of the house had come to the windows and were watching us. Wilmarth noted it as well, and as the two of us conferred the figures moved away, and the house quickly grew dark. Overnight the air had turned bitterly cold and a wind whipped from the north and gusted strong enough to stop us in our tracks. The sky was dark and any starlight was apparently covered by a thick layer of clouds that rolled like waves through the atmosphere. The ground and grass beneath our feet were frozen and crunched as we marched out along the trail that Lake had mapped out for us. All I could hope for was that with dawn, some lessening of the bitter cold would come as well.

We marched for an hour before we reached the place that had been clear-cut, and it was as Lake and Dyer had described. We paused to rest and assess the site. Wilmarth complained that surely it must already be dawn, and I looked eastward to see a small glow desperately trying to burst through the thick roiling clouds. I turned back to Wilmarth and as I directed his gaze toward the struggling sun I saw his eyes grow suddenly large and his face go white. Wilmarth rushed me, tackling me about the midsection, knocking me backwards into the camera and our colleagues, and carrying us all to the ground. As I struggled to recover, the sky grew suddenly dark and there was a great sound like wind blowing through the grass, or a train rushing past. It lasted a good five seconds and we cowered in the clearing for a few seconds more until we were sure it was past. But what it was, I cannot say, for I saw nothing but the darkness. Wilmarth, who had obviously seen something that spurred him into action, was vague and talked of a whirling mass of black wind that had come from beyond the treetops. Dyer suggested that we had just encountered a snow devil, a tornado generated by extreme cold usually associated with a whiteout. As if to confirm Dyer's hypothesis, from the sky huge flakes of snow began to fall at a rapid rate, and within seconds a thin layer had covered the clearing.

Undeterred by the sudden foul weather, the four of us marched valiantly, and I will admit, a little foolishly into the woods following the trail created by whoever had dragged the felled trees branches and all, north. The trail was little more than a deep rut, and traversing it was no easy task. The accumulating snow made the frozen ground slick, and on several occasions one or more of us slid or stumbled and landed unceremoniously on our posteriors. As we moved away from the clearing the forest grew thicker, and the sky grew darker. I suddenly came into the habit of periodically looking eastward and noting the illumination which weakly penetrated the clouds and lit up the sky. The trail crept through the woods and eventually reached the base of a low rocky ridge. The trail continued up this ridge, and we dutifully scrambled up to the top. It was Dyer who reached the edge first and he quickly ducked down and waved us into a cautionary silence.

The ridge formed the lip of a small valley or hollow that had been modified into a kind of amphitheater with long terraces cut into the hillsides forming a set of concentric rings around a large central plaza easily five acres in size. This vast central space was itself filled with a large ring of fallen trees, obviously those that had been clear-cut further south, that had been stripped of their branches. The branches themselves formed another ring just on the interior of the larger one. All of this seemed to serve as a kind of huge pen, for the interior was replete with cattle, goats and other assorted livestock, all of which seemed on the verge of freezing to death. Outside of the rings dozens of cloaked figures mulled about. Some were climbing the terraces, while others had taken up positions on those terraces and seemed to be waiting for something to happen.

Wilmarth struggled to get a better view. "It's a ceremony of some sort. This is what Groundhog Day used to be. Watch for a wild animal of some sort to be brought out and used to prognosticate the change in season. It'll probably come through there," he said, pointing at a large squared-off cut on the far side off the ridge.

Dyer slid back a little. "What's with the wooden ring and the animals?"

Wilmarth hemmed and hawed a little. "Animal sacrifice using a bonfire probably. I've read of similar rituals in Summerisle off the coast of Scotland."

We sat there for quite some time, and Wilmarth, like those below us, seemed to be waiting for something to trigger whatever was going to happen. Then as I looked back east I saw the sun, still weak behind the clouds, rise up over the trees and cast the first rays down into the valley below. Wilmarth suddenly became agitated, and those below us rose up from wherever they were sitting. They rose up and all at once shed their cloaks. From our vantage point we saw them in all their wondrous glory. They were all women, women of all ages, from teens to haggard crones, and without their cloaks they were all completely nude.

The wind suddenly whipped down over us and into the hollow. The penned animals called out in anguish and fear. Lake, Dyer and I hunkered down and let the wind blow and howl all around us. Wilmarth, however, clung to the ridge and bore witness to what occurred in the amphitheater below. Over the roaring winds I heard snippets of singing, but in a language I had never heard before. I heard a great wailing as well, and the screaming of the animals. There was a horrendous smell, like carrion, or the Miskatonic at low tide. How long Wilmarth watched I could not say, though perhaps it is best to say that he watched for too long.

Of the frantic race away from that haunted place I can say little. Wilmarth maniacally insisted that we stay off the rutted trail, and although we argued with him at first, our protestations ceased when he broke open one of the shotgun shells to reveal nothing more than rock salt. That someone was searching for us as we tore through those thick woods was clear, for several times we took refuge in the thick underbrush and waited until angry, threatening voices passed us by. We avoided the Clague farm as well, taking a long arc to the south, and then working our way back to the dilapidated span just as the sun set. We crossed the rope bridge in the dark and on the far side we crawled into the woods to rest for a while. It took us more than two hours to reach Dean's Corners, and seeing us all wild-eyed and exhausted the shopkeeper offered to let us stay the night. Wilmarth violently refused and at his insistence we drove the whole way to Arkham that night.

Wilmarth has never spoken of that day, at least not to me. We have told no one of what we saw, for whom would believe us? All four of us have since resigned from Dr. Ramsey's project, and we recommended that no one else ever go to Quirk. Of course someone finally did visit that hamlet. In May, a state surveyor found the rope bridge deteriorated, the farm and Quirk abandoned. The state police found no evidence of foul play, and the residents of Dean's Corners have no recollection of any large group of people passing through. Somehow or other, the police learned of our visit, and we were questioned. We told the investigators nothing. Even Wilmarth, who eventually recovered from his mania, was silent on the subject. In time the missing villagers of Quirk were forgotten, the bridge was never rebuilt, and Quirk became just another footnote to be added to the mysteries that haunt that strange country.

I, however, cannot forget the mania that possessed Wilmarth as we drove down the Aylesbury Pike. The road was clear, the stars and moon bright, and the night air was unseasonably warm, and we drove with the windows down and the wind roaring in our ears. Over this we listened, try as we might to ignore him, as Wilmarth screamed into the night. What Wilmarth saw as he watched, and we hid, he could not tell us save in the most obscure and disjointed of rants. He spoke of Ithaqua and of the Storm Hags that were his daughters. He whispered madly of the Windwalker's feet, and of the dark symbolism of the beast in the cave searching for his shadow. All these things he ranted incoherently about, over and over again as we drove down that dark lonely highway. But only once did he speak of the freshly fallen trees, and the gathering of wood by something akin to monstrous birds. He laughed like a madman at this, and he grabbed me by the collar and yelled uncontrollably, "You don't look for your shadow in spring, you look for a mate! And you don't start fires using freshly cut wood. It's not a fire they were building! God help us, it was a nest!"

CHAPTER 22.
UNCORRELATED CONTENTS

After I and my colleagues fled Quirk, there followed an incredible and perhaps well-deserved lull, a period in my life in which little to nothing untoward occurred and I could concentrate solely on my medical practice and documenting the outcomes of my clandestine experiments in the administration of my reagent as a prophylactic against death. I say untoward, but that is not to say that nothing troubling occurred. Miss Soames, my long-time housekeeper and receptionist, passed away in the fall of 1926, a victim of her age and an unrevealed addiction to smoking a pipe each evening. Sometime after that my junior partner, Dr. Randolph White, announced that he needed to either advance in position or move on. Reluctantly I agreed, and the two of us negotiated a price by which he could purchase the Kingsport practice and property from me. It was not a large amount, but it was adequate for my needs and was more than enough to absolve me of any of my own debts with a significant sum left over, which despite the advice of my banker I declined to invest in the stock market, but rather purchased a small bayside cottage in the shadow of Kingsport Head that I could use as a summer retreat.

As time progressed, I became more interested in following the progress of my patients who had been treated with the reagent than with actually maintaining my practice. By my estimation, nearly ten percent of Arkham's entire population had been exposed to some level of treatment or another. This represented a significant number of individuals that I suddenly felt

I was too old to properly handle. I thought about taking on yet another junior partner, but then reconsidered. I had no desire to train yet another doctor and live with the possibility that my privacy and secret life might be invaded once more. In the end I realized that I had spent twenty years as one of the premier physicians in Arkham, and perhaps it was time to slow down. Over the course of several months I negotiated with both my patients and other doctors to reduce my workload.

In the fall of 1927 and into the early winter I began to review, analyze and draw conclusions from the data my experimental subjects were supplying to me. Surprisingly, perhaps because I had for so many years been distracted, a significant number of my patients had obtained advanced age, and though I believed myself and my reagent to be the cause, I could hardly believe the number of septuagenarians, octogenarians, nonagenarians, and centenaries that now called Arkham home. As was the goal, my subjects, even those exposed to the lowest dose of reagent, showed increased resistance to infectious diseases and the ravages of old age, and even trauma. Those that did suffer some kind of cataclysmic trauma, a broken bone for example, healed at an incredible rate. At least this is what the information my experimental subjects, as compared to the control group, told me.

In the interest of science I began to read and take comparative notes on the changing patterns of human lifespan as they related to geographic area, cultural origin and even diet. In almost every case, no matter how I clustered the information, it seemed that my subjects were always significantly above the average. That is to say, in all areas but one, and I was surprised to discover that such a population existed so near to me and yet I had never heard word of it. There existed but scant miles from my own home a population of individuals whose average lifespan appeared equivalent, perhaps even superior to those individuals that I had treated with my reagent. At least they had been. Information on the population of the small and decrepit town had some decades ago ceased to be reported, but near the turn of the century it seemed that the population was dramatically skewed toward individuals over the age of fifty and well into the hundreds. Inquiries with county service members revealed that the last doctor for the town had vanished some time ago, and even before that, his reporting had been spotty at best. Undaunted, I sent an inquiry to the Federal government for details from the national census that had last been carried out January of 1920, and every decade prior to that. If local authorities had no information perhaps the national government could tell me what the demographics of Innsmouth had been over the last thirty years.

The answer to my inquiry came in a manner I could never have expected. One early February morning I opened the paper to discover that Federal agents had descended on Innsmouth. A destroyer had been spotted off the coast, and state police had closed the road. There was talk of a pitched gun battle between revenuers and smugglers, as well as the bombardment of the waterfront by naval vessels. One unidentified source contended that the navy was systematically dropping depth charges along the reef that ran outside the harbor in an attempt to capture or damage a submarine vessel belonging to an unidentified foreign power. This anonymous claim, however, was simply too fantastic, and later editions of *The Arkham Advertiser* disavowed such wild notions.

Over the course of the next few days agents of the Federal government, treasury agents, military men and officials from innumerable other agencies and departments descended not only on Innsmouth, but on Arkham as well. The campus was cluttered with strangers who seemed intent on talking with a number of professors and examining in detail the historical and cultural documents of the area. This made the Miskatonic University Library a virtual beehive of activity, and on the few occasions I found it necessary to visit, I had nothing but sympathy for Dr. Armitage who was spending most of his time supervising the rare book rooms which were now flooded by government researchers who, he complained, knew little concerning the proper treatment of antique volumes.

Thankfully, I needed little in the way of assistance and was fully capable of finding whatever volumes I needed. The din that the strange events in Innsmouth had brought to our fair University was difficult to ignore, and created certain problems with the allocation of reading rooms and private carrels. Thus it came to pass that on one particular day I was forced to occupy a chair amongst the common space opposite the rooms set aside for the review of rare volumes and was in a position to overhear some small portion of the loud discussion that Armitage was engaged with behind closed doors. I was not alone in eavesdropping, for two young graduate students, who from their books I determined were students of mathematics, were with me, apparently keenly interested in what was going on between Armitage and his unidentified partner in conversation. Though it seemed to me they were less interested in the subject of the conversation than they were in gaining access to Armitage.

When several minutes of apparent debate ended, and there came an uncomfortable silence, my two companions rose from their chairs and moved into the hall so as to make their way toward Armitage. Just then the door to the room opened and from it stepped a monster of a man. He was easily over seven feet tall and his vast bulk was barely contained by the worn suit he had stuffed himself into. His face was long, almost goatish, and covered with coarse hair. That thick black hair was apparently endemic over his entire body, for it peeked out from his sleeves and between the buttons of his shirt. His walk was a lumbering gait, and from the way he twisted himself I suspected a significant deformity of the pelvis, spine or both.

Stunned by the appearance of the giant, the two graduate students stood dumbfounded. Even as the monstrous man reached out one of his massive hands they failed to move. Unable to move around them, the giant spoke in a low but deep voice, and said something I could not hear before gently moving one of the young men to the side. His path unblocked, the ogre was quickly gone from my sight. In the distance, somewhere outside the library, a dog howled.

When Armitage himself came out of the room he seemed flustered and mumbling under his breath. "Inbreeding? Great God, what simpletons! Shew them Arthur Machen's *Great God Pan* and they'll think it a common Dunwich scandal! But what thing—what cursed shapeless influence on or off this three-dimensioned earth—was Wilbur's Whateley's father?"

Whatever it was that Armitage said next was lost to me, for I focused entirely on the name that Armitage had given to the thing that had just walked out of the library, for I knew that Wilbur Whateley, the creature that had lumbered past at more than seven feet tall, was no more than fifteen years old, and that I had inadvertently exposed his mother Lavinia to my reagent while Wilbur was still *in utero*. It was I who was responsible for not only his cyclopean proportions but also his congenital deformities that forced him to walk with that horrid gait. Wilbur Whateley was a monster of my own making.

I fled the library blindly. The knowledge that that creature was Wilbur Whateley was stupefying, and the possibility that I was likely responsible for his condition froze me to the core. Soon I was wandering the campus in a daze, unconsciously following the paths and walkways that wind through the University. I shudder at what people must have thought of the blank-eyed mask that gripped my face, and I was grateful that the cold had kept the common areas clear of staff and students.

Somehow or another I wandered off campus and soon found myself wandering through the construction site for the new Tillinghast Building, the pride of Arkham's so-called new skyline. The lower floors of the building were nearly done, and the site was still littered with massive earthmovers, cranes and trucks, mostly concentrated around the great pit that had been dug to construct the tunnel that would connect the railway platform in the basement to the new subterranean railway that the city was building. Each day the project consumed tons of concrete and the trucks that brought it ran through the streets all hours of the day. There was something hypnotically soothing about the construction, and I settled in to watch it and let my mind go blank.

It was sometime later that a familiar, though perhaps unwelcome face disturbed my peace. It had been some time since I had seen Dr. Ambrose Dexter, but suddenly he was beside me, smiling. I should have refused to talk with him, but he waved my request for statistics on the population of Innsmouth in my face and spoke of things that both intrigued and frightened my sensibilities. By that evening I was in my office making arrangements for an army doctor to take over my practice while I was whisked off to a Federal facility in what was left of the village of Innsmouth.

The agreement I signed with Dexter forbids me from going into detail on what I saw and did, but I am not sure that it matters much at this point. I spent six months working for Dexter and his associates, who consisted primarily of military and Bureau of Investigation agents that had seized control of Innsmouth by presidential order. The residents of Innsmouth had not been involved with the smuggling of contraband, but, rather, sometime in the late nineteenth century became enamored with the people and religion of one of their trading partners in the Pacific islands. In fact, the people of Innsmouth had not only married many of the natives of these islands, but had also adopted their religious beliefs incorporating the worship of a triumvirate of monstrous aquatic gods that fit nicely into their seafaring lifestyle. Unfortunately, this miscegenation had resulted in the expression of certain retrograde characteristics that gave the inhabitants of Innsmouth an unwholesome and even somewhat batrachian appearance. Apparently the entire community had been affected by the condition, and the Federal government had found it necessary to reach out and recruit assistance from private individuals such as myself.

Under Dexter's guidance I was responsible for what were designated marginal cases, showing minimal defects. These included cases of ichthyosis, a skin condition that created scale-like patches, webbed fingers and toes, premature balding, and particularly Grave's ophthalmopathy. Given the extensive malformations that my patients exhibited, I was grateful that I did not have to work with the patients that had been classified as having extensive or severe cases.

It was not my duty to develop or even suggest possible treatments for the exhibited conditions, but rather, I was to interview individuals concerning their conditions, behaviors and personal medical history, this being much of the information that I had put forth in my request to the census, and also taking skin, blood and hair samples. On the rare occasion that one of our charges suffered an injury I would undertake the menial tasks of setting broken fingers, stitching lacerations and tending to bruises. Although I will admit that such tasks were unusually rare.

I spent six months at the facility, during which I discerned an incredible, almost miraculous, condition amongst my patients. As with my experimental subjects, those of Innsmouth showed an inordinate resistance to injury and disease, as well as a longevity that was to be envied. This was coupled with, and may have been directly related to, a marked difference in the rate of growth, maturation and aging. As far as I could tell, for I was never actually allowed to correlate the information that I was gathering, the children of Innsmouth grew at an astounding rate and matured quickly, often entering puberty between eight and ten years of age. However, once a state of adolesence had been achieved, individuals, particularly males, seemed to stay in this state for an entire decade, and failed to show signs of physical and mental maturity until they were well into their mid-twenties. Adulthood seemed to span from an average of twenty-five to well into the seventies, with the first signs of age, such as grey hair or arthritis, not appearing until individuals had become octogenarians.

Investigating such trends was irresistible to me, and in July when Dexter made it plain that the compound was to close and the patients to be scattered to other facilities in Utah and Arizona, I schemed to acquire samples of my patients' tissues, particularly blood, for my own purposes. I accomplished this by collecting the blood that remained in the actual needle as opposed to the tube itself. Admittedly, this often left me with incomplete or even compromised samples, but for my purposes it was enough. Examination of these samples revealed an unfamiliar component, a kind of spindle-shaped, nucleated cell. Similar cells perform a clotting function in non-mammalian vertebrates, but this seemed somewhat different in appearance, and reminded me of the experiments Muñoz and I had performed using the extract from the glands of crocodiles and alligators.

I isolated the odd tissue type from several samples and concentrated it in an incubator tube where it seemed to remain stable. After several hours the tube exhibited a strange separation, with the cells settling to the bottom and a layer of pale green fluid floating above them. I extracted samples of this strange excretion, somewhat familiar in color and viscosity, and analyzed its content. As I expected, the cells were secreting a fluid that was in many ways extremely similar to my reagent; indeed, by studying the content and behavior of this organically produced version, I was able to envision ways to modify and even improve my own. Unfortunately, as with many components of blood the cells, despite being nucleated, were not self-replicating, and by the end of July my samples of the unusual cellular component had all ceased to be viable. About the same time Dexter relocated the last of the patients and the facility was shut down. I returned to my quiet and private practice, emboldened by what I had learned in Innsmouth.

I intended to initiate use of the revised formula almost immediately, but my attention was drawn away by a single event, one that would in its complexity lead to a cascading horror which would result in what is now commonly referred to as the Dunwich Horror, and although such events would serve to absolve me of a certain guilt, they would, in the end, precipitate my own personal disgrace.

In his pseudonymous account of those events, rushed to publication following his disappearance in October, Randolph Carter suggests that the Dunwich Horror began in earnest in September, but I tend to agree with Armitage, that the impetus for those later events can be tied to what occurred in the small hours of August the third in the halls of the University library. It was in these unwelcome hours that a great scream had reverberated throughout Arkham, and those closest to the campus had found themselves inextricably drawn to bear witness to whatever had occurred.

I was one of many who gathered outside the vestibule doors to the library, drawn by the whimpering howls of the watchdog that Armitage was known to nightly let roam those hallowed halls. An open window testified that someone had entered in an unorthodox manner, and from the sounds that still emanated, whomever it was had suffered from a vicious and frightful attack. Not long after the crowd gathered, Armitage was there as well, and in the company of his colleagues Rice and Morgan he unlocked the door and ordered the crowd to remain outside.

A few moments after they entered there came an unearthly and unintelligible voice that carried throughout the library and bellowed out of the open window. The sound died out quickly, and with it came a slow but pervasive stench of frightful magnitude. As it leaked out into the campus, the birds roosting amongst the buildings took wing and filled the air with the sound of whippoorwills. A pair of deputies arrived soon after, but Armitage ordered them to stay out for their own good until the medical examiner arrived.

The next day rumors spread like wildfire, and the older residents of Arkham invoked comparisons to certain events that had occurred in June of 1882 following the collection of a meteorite that had fallen on the Gardner farm. Out of curiosity I called the medical examiner and inquired concerning the events of the night before, intimating that perhaps it was one of my patients. My colleague related that Armitage had identified the so-called victim as a resident of Dunwich, though he chuckled at such a suggestion. The coroner was of the opinion that he had been the victim of an elaborate prank, for upon entering the library he had seen no body, but only a large white mass of collagen-like material not unlike the so-called globs of tissue that had been documented in various inlets and beaches, particularly in Florida. That such a mass could once have been a man was ludicrous, and to give it a name, even one as ridiculous as Wilbur Whateley, was simply flummery.

The mention of that name filled me with both dread and relief, for it seemed that the creature for which I had held myself accountable was no more. Still, I felt a measure of sympathy for the life of suffering he must have endured. I was at the same time elated that his passing finally ended any chance that his deformities could be traced back to me. That the end of Wilbur Whateley also closed the book on one of my few errors seemed fortuitous and final.

But it was not to be so simple. On the morning of September fifth I was paid a personal visit by Armitage's wife, Helena, a with as many years as her husband, but as vibrant as a woman much younger, thanks to the effects of my treatments. She came not for herself but rather for her husband. Henry Armitage had become suddenly obsessed with the contents of a ragged journal that had been found amongst the personal effects of Wilbur Whateley, written in some fantastic code. Armitage had finally hit on the basis of the cipher on Sunday, and had since been entirely immersed in its translation, barely stopping for food, drink or sleep. Such a pace was unhealthy for a man of his age, but he refused any overtures made by his wife or friends.

Persuaded, I assured her that I would discuss the matter with Henry that very morning, and before noon I found myself in his office. That my presence was unwelcome was to say the least, but his appearance validated his wife's concerns. His eyes were bloodshot and his speech slow, the pallor to his skin suggested dehydration, while the tremors in his hands were indicative of improper nutrition. I insisted that he cease whatever he was doing, and take some time to rest and properly care for himself. He waved me off, insisting that time was of the essence and promising me an explanation as soon as he was able.

Within hours I was back in his presence, summoned by his wife to their residence not far from my own. The old man had managed to return home and consume a meager amount of sustenance, but he was wild-eyed and almost hysterical. He insisted on returning to the campus, and both his wife and I agreed that some chicanery and a little force were warranted. Using a mild sedative, injected while his wife distracted him, I was finally able to calm him down enough for him to be deposited in his quarters. I spent the night by his side, while his wife retired to a spare room. There was a sense of familiarity as I recalled the time I spent a similar night with the Peaslees so many years ago.

Armitage's sleep was fitful; he moaned and on occasion thrashed about, searching for something that seemed to be eluding him. As the night progressed he began to talk in his sleep, though much of this was unintelligible. What little I could make out hinted at things that I wish I did not know of. Armitage regularly repeated the name Whateley, and the foreign phrases *yog sothoth* and *bug shogog*, though what these meant and in what context they were used I was unable to discern. My patient also seemed overly concerned with what was apparently a metaphorical concept of "The Gate and the Key" and in his fits seemed troubled by the lack or loss of the key. "Without the key," he would whine, "the union is incomplete, the gate shall remain closed. But what of the gate…grow unabated?"

The next morning Armitage awoke delirious, but whether this was because of exhaustion, the medication, the esoteric and eldritch things he had been subjecting himself to, or perhaps some combination is unknowable. I pressed him for an explanation for his actions, but he refused and demanded to return to his office. Denied, he become morose, and at times spoke of apocalyptic scriptures and myths from a variety of traditions. Fearing that he could be a danger to himself or others, I kept him on a mild sedative for the rest of the day, which kept him lethargic and allowed me to return home to bathe and change.

I also used my time away from the Armitage household to summon Rice and Morgan to my office and demand an explanation. The two men were reticent at first, for Armitage had sworn them to secrecy, and they were still unclear of certain details that remained shrouded in innuendo. I reminded the two of them that I was Armitage's physician and that he had over the last few days taken actions that endangered his own welfare. If they would not talk to me, perhaps they would care to testify concerning his mental health before a judge. This dramatic overture seemed to place the situation in perspective for the two professors and they revealed what Armitage both knew and suspected.

In light of what came later, the details of what Rice and Morgan told me need not be revealed. Let it be said that Armitage had gathered enough evidence to convince not only himself, but Rice and Morgan as well, that something of cosmic significance was brewing in the backwoods hills of Dunwich, and had been for some time. The Whateleys had done something obscene, bent the laws of space and time and let something leak into our world. Whatever it was had left its taint on Wilbur Whateley, that was obvious, for Rice and Morgan told me what they had seen as Wilbur had died that night in the library. Whatever that thing was, it had never been human or even remotely related to any species known. Armitage, informed by what he had gleaned from Wilbur's diary, suspected much more, that the worst of it had yet to begin, and he was desperately trying to find a way to disarm what could be a volatile situation. Suddenly the two professors were no longer confessing to me but pleading, desperately begging me to allow Armitage to return to work at any cost. Convinced of the truth of things, for I recalled that fateful night that Lavinia and her father climbed Sentinel Hill, and the strange and disastrous things that had followed, I conceded to the two learned men and agreed that he should return to work as soon as possible.

That night, without informing his wife of my meeting with Rice and Morgan, I administered the first dosage ever of my newly reformulated reagent and once more confined Armitage to bed. He awoke Friday morning clear of mind but in sober spirits. I spoke to him at length, and he agreed to remain calm and avoid stress for the next twenty-four hours. Over the course of the day I checked in with his wife and was informed that the old man was indeed following orders. It was not until Saturday afternoon that he finally left his home and summoned Rice and Morgan to the University.

As has been reported, the three men spent six days formulating plans, gathering supplies and mixing chemical compounds. What has not been mentioned are the frequent visits that I myself made to the three frantic men. They were loath to involve anyone else, and thus it was up to me to make sure that these valiant men were supplied with sufficient food, drink and care. That such preparations included, at their request, periodic injections of a solution of cocaine and other stimulants, I will not deny. Nor will I deny that I used the opportunity to inject Rice and Morgan with the reformulated reagent. It seemed the prudent thing to do, though I had no idea how quickly it would take effect, but I hoped that it would grant them some advantage over whatever forces opposed them.

The three departed Arkham Friday morning and at Mrs. Armitage's request I was once more present to evaluate her husband's condition. Truthfully, I could find nothing wrong with the man, but under the guise of supplying them with an immunization against smallpox, I injected them once more with a solution of stimulants.

That late morning and the rest of the day, I rested, lolling about the house in a drowsy half-awake state that I found extremely restful to both my body and my mind. By evening no word had come from the three, and Mrs. Armitage was in a frightful state. I did my best to calm her down, but by midnight she had worked herself up into a fervor and I found it necessary to administer a sedative. As with the day before, no word from the three adventurers was had on Saturday morning. There was, however, a small article in *The Arkham Advertiser* concerning the inability to locate several state policemen sent earlier in the week to investigate reports of a monster in the hills around Dunwich. This tidbit I kept from Helena in fear that it would incite her even more. Late in the morning, a light rain began to fall, and by the evening it had turned into a downpour. Still we had no word from Armitage or his team, and by evening when the papers detailed the destruction of a Dunwich farmhouse by some powerful force, I too began to fear the worst.

Sunday morning the first definitive report on the actions of Armitage and his compatriots came in the morning paper, which described a terrifying event in the Dunwich hills as being witnessed by many of the locals and three university men. Though the article failed to name these men, both Helena and I took heart that they could be none other than Armitage, Rice and Morgan. At noon a special edition described the devastating effects of what had quickly become known as the Dunwich Horror. The report described how a tidal wave of force had careened through the Dunwich area knocking men and livestock from their feet, and stunning birds dead in the sky. The vegetation, grasses, shrubs and trees had been blanched, turned a sickly yellow by whatever force had ripped through the area. Ancient trees and many buildings had been toppled, and dozens were known to be dead, while dozens more were unaccounted for. A county official out of Aylesbury suggested that the number of casualties might grow as searchers found ways to cross the now damaged bridges and debris-strewn roads.

This news sent Helena Armitage into yet another tizzy, which I forcefully ended by once more administering a powerful sedative. No sooner had I done so when there came a loud and rapid knocking at the door. The messenger came bearing news from Dunwich: Armitage and all his party were well, tired and a little bruised but for the most part uninjured. Overjoyed, I ran to Helena's side to show her the telegram, but try as I might she would not open her eyes. Her breathing was suddenly shallow, and her pulse was wild and irregular. My joy suddenly turned to panic and I ordered the housekeeper to send for an ambulance.

CHAPTER 23.

THE DUNWICH HORROR

The events of September 15th, 1928, the disastrous cataclysm that came to be known sensationally as the Dunwich Horror, galvanized the population of Massachusetts and particularly Arkham into action. Food and clothing drives were organized, and transportation services were arranged by local companies whose drivers volunteered their time. The Miskatonic University Rural Program, still under the leadership of Dr. John Ramsey, organized teams of doctors and nurses to tend to the injured, but their sojourns to the hastily erected camps and crowded hamlets came back with the most sordid of reports. Conditions in and around Dunwich were deplorable, with families and children living in the most unsanitary of conditions, with limited access to clean water, proper food, electricity, gas or education. What's more, the situation seemed unlikely to change. Many homes would require extensive repairs before they could be deemed habitable, wells and bridges had collapsed, roads were blocked and many public buildings were in disrepair. Local public servants were so busy trying to maintain basic services that any attempt to try and rebuild was simply impossible.

By mid-October the Dunwich issue had become untenable and public outcry reached a fever pitch. Dr. Ramsey met with the University president, and then with officials from the state police. A monumental arrangement had been made, one that would serve to relieve some of the difficulties faced by the people of Dunwich and those attempting to help them. Echoing the charitable efforts that had so characterized the University during the outbreak of typhoid at the turn of the century, and more recently the efforts to control the Spanish influenza, under the auspices of the Rural Program, Miskatonic was suspending classes for thirty days, and organizing all staff, faculty and students into a relief army with the mission of aiding the stricken Dunwich community. The Engineering and Architectural departments would be deployed to repair what buildings that could be readily salvaged, while at the same time cannibalizing those structures that simply were beyond hope. Geologists and surveyors were to reestablish drinking water supplies and lay lines for new infrastructure, while the veterinary school worked with specialists in animal husbandry to gain control of the herds of cattle and other livestock that now roamed the hills freely. Chemists and biologists would examine the soil, vegetation and indigenous wildlife to determine if the strange event had had any permanent impact on the area. Students of the law, the humanities, economics and other such studies would be required to help the locals by providing teachers, and accountants, and by helping local officials navigate the vagaries of law, business and custom. It was a monumental undertaking and one that would earn all students who undertook the challenge a satisfactory grade in all course work. The University president and indeed all the staff agreed that this was an opportunity for real-world application that none could afford to pass up.

The University itself would be left with a skeleton staff of just a few maintenance men, security guards, and only the most aged of faculty. St. Mary's, the University Hospital, would discharge as many of its patients as it could and operate with just a few doctors and nurses in an emergency-only mode.

Fortunately for me, my private practice placed on me no obligation to join in such a project, for if asked I could not say that I would have volunteered. My experiences in the wilds of Dunwich and the nearby village of Quirk made my return to the area unlikely, and thankfully Dr. Ramsey knew this. Instead of being asked to travel to Dunwich, I was one of the few selected to stay in Arkham and provide support to the hospital. I made it plain that such an arrangement suited me, for it also provided me with the opportunity to continue my care of Helena Armitage, who, after suffering a minor stroke, was recovering nicely. Her husband, Henry Armitage, one of the heroes of the events in Dunwich, was also recovering, though in his case it was from exhaustion and some bruised ribs, which given his advanced age were nothing to ignore.

The Armitages were not the only patients I had to be concerned about. The author Randolph Carter, one of my long-term patients, and like Henry Armitage a subject of my attempts to immunize against death, had recently vanished under mysterious circumstances, and although I could do little to help find him, the situation weighed heavy on my mind. Likewise, I was also bothered by the behavior of a new patient, one thrust upon me by Dr. Waldron, who served the student body and was like most others deployed to Dunwich. The young man was named Frank Elwood, and had apparently been peripherally involved in some scandal or another in which his friend and fellow graduate student had been killed in one of the less reputable parts of town. Elwood, who had officially completed his thesis, had suffered some sort of nervous shock bought on by witnessing the gruesome death of his friend, which by all accounts had involved an attack by a rat of unusual size and aggression. The details had been the subject of a particularly shocking exposé in *The Arkham Advertiser* that had run early in May. Unfortunately, this had been the time during which I had been in service to the Federal government in Innsmouth, and if I had seen the article I could not recall it. Still, the article in question and the documents it had been based on were readily available in Elwood's medical file, which as his physician I had full rights to review at my leisure. Whatever Elwood had seen, it had left him in a state of nervous shock from which he was only just recovering, and therefore unfit to travel to Dunwich in any capacity.

As he had officially completed his work, it seemed unusual to me that he should remain at the University for a few more quarters, but Waldron assured me that it was best he remain under observation,and several senior staff had agreed that he should continue at Miskatonic until his condition improved. Thus young Elwood was left in my care, and I found myself quickly disagreeing with Waldron's assessment, for I felt that Elwood's nervous condition was severe and I certainly would not have authorized his return to classes. Feeling that some level of candor was required, I explained my position to the young man and was pleasantly surprised when he agreed that his condition was perilous at best. Concerned that it might not be best for him to be on his own, but limited in my ability to find a hospital bed, or nurse to look after him, I did the only thing I could think of to resolve the issue, and with his consent I made the boy my personal, albeit temporary, live-in assistant.

Elwood moved in during the last week in October, and took to shadowing me as I traveled about the city tending to my patients as if he had been doing it for years. Meals for the two of us were at a variety of cafes and diners, and Elwood relished this for it was a delightful change from the meager fare he was supplied at the University dining hall. Each day after visiting patients we would spend our evenings at the hospital tending to whatever maladies presented themselves, whether they originated amongst the few patients still in residence, or presented themselves as emergencies from the greater Arkham populace.

My new assistant showed a skill and empathy that I often felt was lacking amongst those who entered the medical profession, and I suspected that whatever it was that had bought about his fragile nervous condition might also have acted to make him a more sympathetic individual. I felt truly sorry for the young man, and vowed to do my best to aid him as I could. Thus, one particularly lonesome and uneventful night while he slept, I opened his file and read the sensational article and notes that had been written about him.

I found the story scandalous, full of impossible detail and obvious omissions. That such a piece could be published made me question the quality and standards of journalism in our fair nation. Still, if poor Elwood had actually been witness to the horrid circumstances that resulted in Walter Gilman's death, it was no wonder that he was a nervous wreck. Despite my growing sympathy for the poor student, I could see no solution to his condition, at least not a medical one. In my opinion, only the slow passage of time would serve to heal the young man's spirit. In this I believed he was making progress. Over the few days he had been my assistant, he had shown as I have noted an enviable degree of empathy, and had developed a particularly strong bond with Helena Armitage, often sitting with the woman for hours while I saw other patients throughout the hospital.

It was on the last Tuesday of October that the first note of the terror that would come to Arkham was played. That the relief efforts in Dunwich would serve as an impetus to the nightmares to come, and my own professional demise, I would never have suspected. That I blame the events in Dunwich for what occurred in Arkham, and not my own experiments in reanimation, is not entirely fair, for most certainly my use of the population of Arkham as test subjects was a factor. For if I had not done so, if I had not infected the residents of Arkham with my reagent, the horrid events of that night would never have come to pass.

It began innocently enough. The day had been filled with a dreary rain that had, as evening fell, intensified and turned bone-chilling. The streets of Arkham itself had slowly flooded, which made driving in the city treacherous. Whatever challenges the residents of Arkham faced on that night must have been magnified along the pikes and roads that crisscrossed the rural countryside, for as the evening progressed the hospital's radio, tuned to the channel reserved for the state police, reported a steady barrage of vehicles and travelers requiring assistance as a result of complications from the weather. Thankfully, as the clock struck midnight and the thirtieth of October crept over into the thirty-first, none of these accidents had been serious enough to require that the victims be brought in for medical attention.

That all changed rapidly in the wee hours of the morning, when the radio brought word of a car traveling along the Aylesbury Pike that had skidded and struck a tree near Billington's Wood. The three occupants had been thrown from the vehicle and all suffered serious head trauma. The victims had been loaded into a sheriff's car and were being driven with all possible speed to St. Mary's. Sadly, all possible speed meant that it would still be nearly half an hour before these poor souls would reach the hospital. Knowing that once they arrived I might be unavailable for hours, I wandered through the wards to check on Elwood, who was as was his habit sitting with Mrs. Armitage. I found the boy asleep in a wing-backed chair while Helena was busy crocheting. I laughed when she told me that the sweater she was making was for Elwood, for it seemed that even in her convalescence she was more than capable of trying to help even this relative stranger.

As I had predicted, the vehicle bearing the three victims arrived more than a half-hour after we had been notified. As the two nurses and I helped the deputy transfer his passengers, it became obvious that the description of their wounds had been severely understated. Indeed, all three had traumatic head injuries, but one of those had a broken neck, another had been pierced through the eye and brain with a small shaft of metal that had essentially lobotomized the man, and the third was leaking cerebral-spinal fluid from his ears. Though their hearts were still beating, it was clear that their prognosis was poor, and I doubted they would last another hour. Indeed, I was in the process of gathering the paperwork to file death certificates when the deputy called out the names of the three poor souls to the admitting nurse and identified them as my own patients and subjects of my clandestine experiments.

The Fisher brothers were not my favorite people. They lived to the northwest of town and had some years ago taken over the family business of fish mongering from their grandfather Gavin, who himself had come from Innsmouth as a boy back in 1850. Gavin's son Seth had been lost at sea, leaving his young wife alone in the crumbling old house on the cliff overlooking Boynton Beach. Ten months after her husband had died, Rebecca Fisher gave birth to triplets, homely looking boys that she named Edward, Frederick and Godrick. The three men made a modest living selling fish to the people of Arkham, though they also found it necessary to supplement their income by offering their boat for service to any who would pay their modest fee. At one point many years ago they signed a contract with the University to aid in the collection of marine specimens in Kingsport Harbor. The contract required that they obtain medical physicals, and the department chair recommended that they take advantage of my services. Thus they had come to my attention, and knowing that I needed subjects that were of less than perfect health and behavior, I chose to include them as members of my experiment, injecting each with a mild dosage of the prophylactic reagent. It was this exposure that I suspected was keeping them from succumbing to their clearly fatal wounds.

I was not the only one who recognized that the wounds they had received were fatal, and after we had rolled them into an exam room the charge nurse dismissed her junior and, after she was out of earshot, approached me concerning the possibility of euthanasia. She had experience in such matters as these, and was of the opinion that no good would come from allowing these three to linger too long. I thanked her for her comments, and trying desperately not to offend her, falsely suggested that she allow me some time with the men I had known for many years. In a huff she left me alone with the three barely living bodies.

The treatment room that we had placed the bodies in was not without supplies and equipment, and indeed contained all that I needed to carry out the collection of tissue samples and blood that I would need for evaluation. In fact, I was so intrigued by their condition that after collecting samples and storing them in my bag, I found the microscope on the table irresistible. After properly preparing a slide, I examined blood samples from each of them under the light microscope, and in doing so made a startling discovery. Operation of the light microscope requires a modicum of darkness, and as I turned off the lights in the room, I found that the slides I had prepared exhibited a slight but detectable luminescence, not unlike that which was associated with my reagent. Examining the tissues, I found that the blood from each of the men did indeed show traces of the reagent, and more startling, each sample contained a number of the strange, nucleated, spindle-shaped cells that I had first seen earlier in the year in blood samples from the residents of Innsmouth.

At first I thought that perhaps the Fisher boys had a bit of that weird Innsmouth taint to them, that perhaps their father or mother or even grandparents had been thus afflicted and passed the condition down to the triplets. But I soon dismissed such a possibility, for I had years before performed a thorough examination upon the men, including a review for blood-borne parasites, and could not recall seeing anything like the spindle-shaped cells I was now seeing.

Confused, I pushed away from the microscope and ran my hand through my hair. The door opening in the dim light of the room startled me, but I recovered once I saw that it was Elwood who was standing there. He seemed strangely subdued, almost on the verge of tears, and I pressed him to tell me what was wrong. He shook his head in a childish manner and in a stuttering voice announced sadly, "Mrs. Armitage is dead." I was myself stunned for a moment, but was quickly brought back as Elwood handed me a large bundle of handwritten papers. "She was helping me with this. She said that I should give it to you, that you had understood the things that Professors Morgan and Rice had told you, and that you would understand this as well." He left me then, turned and nearly ran down the hall, leaving me with his manuscript and nothing to do but read it.

CHAPTER 24.

THE STATEMENT OF FRANK ELWOOD

My name, though it damns me, is Frank Elwood, and I am a resident of Kingsport, where my family has lived since Thaddeus Elwood first came to that village in 1691. It is true that I was part of the events that led up to the death of Walter Gilman on May the first, 1928. It's true also that the source for the lurid tabloid account of those last days, and of Gilman's possible involvement in the disappearance of Ladislas Wolejko, were my own statements to the police. There seems no point in denying these things. The tale of those first months of 1928, as it has been written, is accurate enough, and I can point to no portion of it and call it fiction. Still, it is only a portion of the whole truth, and it but touches on things that came before. People, particularly city folk, have a strange inclination to say that such a thing begins here and ends there. It is a comfort I suppose, but the truth is that all events can trace their roots beyond the obvious beginnings to seeds and origins that may have once seemed innocuous. I think this is as true in the countryside as it is in the city, but the maddening crowd of urban blight may simply weigh too heavy for such memories and details to be retained for too long. To know the truth, to understand the end, you must know the beginning, but where to begin?

It has been suggested that my relationship with Gilman began in September of 1927 when he moved into the crumbling edifice on Parsonage Street, but I knew of him before then, for like myself, Gilman worked for Professor Upham, delving deep into theoretical physics and mathematics. Our research, as directed by Upham, was equal to that of the latest theories emerging from the laboratories of Einstein, Planck and Schrodinger. Upham regularly corresponded and published with the premier minds of the age. Indeed, his paper providing mathematical proof refuting the Bohr-Heisenberg theory of quantum mechanics won high praise from both Bose and Szilard, and formed the base for Einstein's own later assault on the concept. The paper, published in the summer of 1927, even garnered a note from famed inventor Nikola Tesla, who invited Upham to co-author a paper.

It was this joint paper, between Tesla and Upham, which changed the direction of the work that Gilman had been pursuing. To my knowledge, the manuscript bearing both their names and which bore the title "Historical Evidence for Non-Linear Motion through Fourth Dimensional Space" never saw publication, but I presume that it was for this treatise that in the fall of 1927 Upham redirected Gilman to investigate the linkages between various quantum theories and certain schools of elder magic. Upham invoked his academic standing to gain Gilman access to the medieval metaphysics collection, an act that annoyed a score of history and philosophy students and drew protests from several other faculty members and at least two department chairs. Upham dealt with these distractions, ordering Gilman to wade through the vast holdings in search of evidence that some of the forbidden and secret knowledge of old may have been hidden examples of current breakthroughs in modern math and physics. Gilman took to the work with glee, and by the end of October had filled several notebooks with possible linkages between modern spatial theories and several branches of mystical teachings, particularly those related by John Dee in his treatise *Monas Hieroglyphica*, and to a lesser extent in Prinn's *De Vermis Mysteriis*. Upham was pleased and urged Gilman to delve deeper into the morass of ancient and foreboding texts.

Gilman's studies were not without obstacles. Armitage, the old librarian, put limits on Gilman's access to the rarer texts, particularly Dee's translation of the Necronomicon, to which he was limited to but an hour each day. Here then is the irony of the situation, for it is in the limitations placed on his use of the Necronomicon that drove poor Gilman to peruse other sources. Sources such as the trial journals of Judge John Hathorne, whose details on his encounters with a number of the accused witches would lead Gilman to an obsession with Keziah Mason that would in the end cost him his life.

From Hathorne's papers Gilman learned how in 1692, at the height of the witch panic, court officers seized Keziah Mason on the road from Innsmouth and brought her bound and shackled before the court. It was three days of torture before she admitted to being a witch and revealed to Judge Hathorne her secret name of Nahab. There were places like the desolate island in the Miskatonic River and the dark valley beyond Meadow Hill where she would meet with the Black Man and draw curves and lines that would open doors to spaces beyond space and between space, and to the planets seen in the sky, and beyond. She was, she claimed, a vessel for the Black Goat, and through her had passed the dark hundred, and from them would arise the thousand young, and then the million favored ones. Here Mason broke into a strange quote that Gilman recognized as a translation from Prinn's *De Vermis Mysteriis: "For the Black Goat Mother doth favor her servants with such fruitfulness that would shame even the most fertile of pestilent flies, breeding in the secret wounds of man's misery and pain, like maggots in a slaughter yard."*

Hathorne was so disturbed by Mason's testimony that he ordered her to await execution in a windowless underground chamber, chained to a wall, her mouth gagged, her hands and fingers bound. Despite all such precautions, the next morning Hathorne found the prison guard mad, babbling about a horrid rat-thing that had scurried out of her cell. Of Keziah Mason there was no trace; only a series of strange devices, of angled lines and broken curves, painted onto the cell wall using a viscous red fluid Hathorne refused to identify, remained to mark her passage. As astounding a story as it was, it was Hathorne's skilled renderings of the symbols found in Mason's cell that so intrigued Gilman. Although primitive, and whether that was a result of Hathorne's sketch, or of the original state of the symbols themselves, they bore striking resemblances to the recent geometrically recursive works of Helge von Koch and Waclaw Sierpiński, exactly the kind of thing Upham had been looking for.

Gilman pursued this direction, poring through the antiquated library catalogs for days, but to little avail. The little old ladies who formed the core of the library reference staff, to whom he posed his questions and begged for assistance, would only shake their heads and wander away to attend to other duties. That Walter Gilman was not from Arkham may have had some part in this gentle rebuff. True, he had some family in the area; there were still

Gilmans in Innsmouth, where Walter's grandparents had left in 1846, but this relationship provided no advantage, for the residents of Arkham have no fondness for those of Innsmouth. Possibly, it was not the taciturn nature of Arkhamites, nor their native prejudice against those of Innsmouth that stalled Gilman's researches into Keziah Mason; rather it may have been being from Haverhill itself, easily noticed from the particular accent that Gilman spoke with, that was itself the cause for many to avoid him. For many of the residents of Arkham could not help but blame those from Haverhill for the sickness that had started in that small town in 1926, and which had spread, carried by careless farmers and less than reputable dairy men. The sickness that had swept through the town, an illness of aching joints and low fevers accompanied by strange and horrid hallucinations, was born of unsanitary practices, and claimed a dozen or so lives amongst the Haverhill farms, but that was a fraction of the number it killed in Arkham before it burned itself out. They called it the Haverhill Fever, which was a polite term used by polite people. The older doctors and the less genteel folk who lived and worked amongst the slaughterhouses, factories and wharves of Arkham called it by another, more common name, rat-bite madness.

It was in September of 1927 that Gilman had a breakthrough, and learned that the home of Keziah Mason was still extant. His plodding through local history had turned up a rare and somewhat forgotten treatise, *A History of Miskatonic Valley* by Pr. Everet L. Watkins of the small but respected Arkham College, located mere blocks from the hallowed halls of Miskatonic University itself. Here then was a compendium, not only of the general history of the city, but of its scandals, secrets and rumors. Watkins had succumbed to the 1905 typhoid plague, but before that he had worked for the Historical Society, and before that for the Arkham *Bulletin*. He knew things about Arkham, and the people in it, that most would rather have forgotten. He wrote about the Panic of 1869, during which some of the finer homes in the city were burned down, and also of the young Latimer girl was killed by wild dogs in 1884. Watkins had taken photographs of the man who had built the University observatory, and had filed notice twelve years later when the same man had died in the local madhouse. To him, those dark days of witch hunts and trials weren't just history; to him they were vital occurrences, which still lingered, permeating the landscape and molding events in Arkham even into the beginning of the twentieth century. He had known Arkham like some men know their wives; he knew her joys and beauties, her mercies and loves; but he knew her faults, her weaknesses, her dirty secrets, and the lies she liked to tell herself; and for all of it, Watkins had loved Arkham, her stately homes, her dockside warehouses, her crumbling alleyways, just the same.

It was from Watkins' book that Gilman learned that the old house was just a block away from the University on Parsonage Street. The house itself was nothing of note, a great box of a building with a gambrel roof, and the limited amount of charm that such examples of early colonial architecture hold. Years of neglect had not improved its appeal, and the entire neighborhood seemed blighted by its presence. Finding the exterior of the Witch House wholly unremarkable, Gilman had actually paid the landlord to allow him to explore several of the vacant rooms, and had even gone so far as to crawl up into the attic. It was during this exploration that Gilman inadvertently discovered that I resided in the moldering old edifice, and enlisted, one could even say forced, my aid in researching the legends surrounding the house and its original owner.

Our principal source was Watkins' text, which itself used a variety of older sources, including diaries, journals, and various village and private records to build a brief biography of Keziah Mason. Most of the stories of Keziah begin with the end, with the accusations, the trial and her mysterious escape, but in 1692 Keziah was some fifty years old, and few people tell or even know who she was or what she did prior to the scenario that ended her life. She is remembered as the witch of Arkham, but in those days Arkham was a much smaller place and still in the shadow of Kingsport. Like many of the time, Keziah wasn't even from Arkham, and you can't tell the tale of how Keziah came to Arkham without telling of her sisters as well.

The Mason triplets, Abigail, Hepzibah and Keziah, were born August the twentieth, 1637, in Kingsport, to Elizabeth Talbye and her husband Roger Mason, captain and owner of the brig *Cordelia Ys*. Much is known of the Masons, for they were an active family and well respected throughout the village. A year after the birth of his daughters, Roger Mason met with Arthur Marsh and Benjamin Corey; together the three formed the Kingsport Mercantile Company, which by 1639 maintained a fleet of seven ships plying the Caribbean trade. Even today Kingsport Mercantile maintains vast brick warehouses along the river downstream of Arkham.

In 1640, tragedy struck Kingsport and the Masons in particular, when a great storm blew in from the south, sinking three ships in the harbor, destroying sixteen homes and killing twelve men, women and children. The death of these poor souls, including Keziah Mason, is an established fact documented in municipal and church records. By all accounts, and by my own investigation, the grave of the child Keziah Mason can be found in the old burying ground near the center of Kingsport. There is no doubt that the girl born to Elizabeth and Roger Mason died that day in 1640.

It is from the diary of Dr. Joseph Hillstrom, in an entry dated April the twelfth, 1652, that the story of Keziah Mason begins again. For it was on the morning of this date that a frantic Hepzibah Mason appeared on Hillstrom's doorstep. A violent storm had lashed the coast the previous night, and in the morning the shoreline had been littered with the wreckage of some unknown ship. Combing the beach, the Masons had found, clinging to the debris, the body of a young girl, chilled to the bone, but still alive. Hillstrom found the girl unconscious, cold to the touch and obviously suffering from long exposure to the icy waters of the bay and beach. That she had survived some terrible ordeal was obvious, yet how she had survived was what puzzled Hillstrom the most, for even now, after being wrapped in blankets and set next to the fire, the girl was colder than the doctor thought a breathing person could be. Still, it was the girls Abigail and Hepzibah who noticed the most startling thing about the child, and thus Dr. Hillstrom went about making silhouettes of all three girls to confirm the observation. For the strange unconscious girl that the Mason children had found on the beach had the same features and profile as the Mason twins themselves; indeed, had he not known it to be otherwise, the strange girl could easily have passed for either one of the twins.

It was on the second day that the foundling began to stir and slowly regained consciousness and opened her eyes. It was immediately plain that although she understood the words spoken to her, she herself was unable to speak. Likewise, while she could read, any attempts to have the child write ended in failure. At a loss of what to call the girl, but recognizing that the child needed a name, Elizabeth Mason declared that God had in His mercy returned to them their Keziah. In the village, a meeting was held to discuss the girl's welfare, and whether it was proper to commit her to the Masons' care. While much was made of the burden already carried by the Captain and his wife, none would step forward to oppose Elizabeth Mason's claim on the child.

While her ability to speak and even write words remained lost, she seemed to possess an uncanny skill with numbers and reading. This talent first manifested as she watched Roger balance books and write out missives to those who owed the Kingsport Mercantile Company money. Without the benefit of pen or paper, it seemed the girl was able to carry out complex arithmetic tasks, and even calculate interest in her head. On many occasion she would point to calculations in which Roger had made simple or even complex errors, and then gesture towards numbers that formed the correct answer. It was in this manner that Keziah first learned to write, not with the alphabet, but with numbers. By the end of June, Roger Mason had moved the girl beyond numbers, and by August she had mastered the Masons' entire meager library, including three volumes in Latin and one in Greek.

Much was made of the events that occurred that September when Keziah spent nearly an hour going through the accounts of several local tradesmen. That the accounting showed that the men had been systematically cheating the Kingsport Mercantile Company was apparent, Roger had suspected such a thing; but when Keziah transcribed her mental calculations on to paper, it revealed the most curious of things. While Keziah seemed perfectly capable of handling series of arithmetic calculations including addition, subtraction, multiplication and division in the most normal of ways, it was not the method that she preferred. Going through her notes, Roger would find characters wholly unknown to him. When he confronted the girl about the strange symbols, Keziah was fearful at first, but demonstrated to her adoptive father how each symbol functioned to integrate several mathematical operations into one. That using such notation allowed her to indicate the summation of vast sets of numbers hinted that she was what we would today call a prodigy. Roger and his wife recognized it as a fabulous gift, but warned her not to let any strangers see her use it.

In the fall of that year Captain Mason went to sea, leaving his wife and children behind. It was then that some women of the village complained to Elizabeth about the children's education, particularly in the areas of cooking, sewing, and farming. Without such skills Keziah would never gain a husband, and never have children. When Grace Watkins mentioned as much to Keziah, the girl smiled and shook her head, scrawling out a note that indicated since she never planned to marry, she saw no point in learning such skills. The Watkins woman berated Elizabeth on the subject, and a few days later, after much cajoling, Keziah joined her sisters in household chores, including preparing food and cooking. It was in the process of learning how to cook that the next step in Keziah's development was made, for it was while making a stew that the pot boiled over and scalded Keziah's hand. Thus it was quite by accident that Keziah Mason found her voice and began to scream. Within a week of the accident Keziah was speaking, albeit haltingly. By November, Keziah had joined her family in singing several hymns at church services, and that very same week engaged the Reverend Phillips in an extensive discussion, covering subjects best left to advanced seminary students. That the debate occurred in both English and Latin became the subject of whispered gossip throughout the village. When Roger returned in December, he was greeted by a chorus of song from all three daughters.

By the end of August 1653, the twins had reached their sixteenth birthday, and with them Keziah celebrated hers as well. Over the course of the next several months the girls began working side by side with Roger at the Kingsport Mercantile Company, acting as clerks and doing odd chores about the office and public store, and on occasion with Elizabeth as midwives. The first few weeks of this venture were fraught with issues, the foremost of which were the twins' lack of skill and speed in handling numbers and the inventory. This changed rapidly, and more so than Roger Mason would have thought possible. When Roger discovered that the twins' progress was primarily a response to Keziah teaching the two her strange but efficient mathematical system, he was not surprised in the least.

In September the twins became afflicted with their first bout of the curse. Now normally, such an event wouldn't be worth mentioning in polite company or otherwise, but in this case it had a profound impact on Keziah, who seemed both perplexed and irate over her own failure in the same regard. Both Elizabeth and Goodwife Hillstrom tried to explain the situation to her, and went so far as demonstrating the use of clean rags to capture the flow. Unfortunately, the demonstration seemed to enrage Keziah who grabbed one of her sister's wasted rags and ran from the house. Her family searched for her all that night, finding her just as dawn broke in the woods that dotted Kingsport Head. She was asleep, feverish, and her face and mouth were bloody. She slept the next day away, occasionally moaning and muttering in some strange language. Dr. Hillstrom recorded some of these utterings that he could not identify as any language with which he was familiar, "Ygnaiih thflthkh'ngha n'grkdl'lh buggshugog." The next morning Keziah woke with no memory of the night before but with severe abdominal pains. By noon she had joined her adopted sisters as a woman.

Of what occurred amongst the Masons over the next decade is subject to much rumor and little fact. That each of the sisters became betrothed is well documented. That early in 1656 the *Cordelia Ys* set sail for Jamaica, bearing all three sisters, their parents, the three young men they were meant to marry, and the parents of those men, can also not be disputed. That the vessel reached Port Royal and that the marriage of Abigail, Hepzibah and Keziah Mason to Simon Prinn, Jeremiah Watkins, and Robert Cummings seems also well documented. What happened next is a mystery, for in the fall the *Cordelia Ys* failed to return to Kingsport, and no word was had from any port along the American coast.

It was on the sixteenth of October, 1658, that a black ship sailed into the harbor of Kingsport and a rowboat manned by a short dark-skinned man with wiry hair brought three cloaked figures to shore. Abigail, Hester and Keziah had returned, but the *Cordelia Ys*, her crew and all the rest had been lost. According to the sisters, the ship had encountered rough weather and been forced to seek refuge along the coast of Florida. What had happened there the Mason sisters would speak only in the vaguest of details. Of the Xaeha Indians who they claimed had seized the ship, and of the years they had dwelt amongst them, the sisters would not expound upon. Indeed, when pressed on the issue, the Masons did nothing but turn stone-faced and give quiet thanks to the strange swarthy figure that had brought them to shore, a man whom they fondly called Brown John.

Within weeks of their return, the Masons sold off their properties in Kingsport and moved to Arkham, to the house on Parsonage Street. Here they lived, the three of them; widows at the age of twenty-one, alone save for their man Brown John, a stocky man with brown skin and black eyes, who tended the house and modest garden. Brown John only spoke a little English, but the Masons seemed to speak some of his language too. There was much speculation in the village about where Brown John had come from. Some thought him an African man, and others said he was a hindoo, but according to old Captain Holt, who had traveled some and seen more than others, Brown John was none of these. Holt said he was from a people called the Chau-Chaus, which were little better than savages, living deep in the wilds of central Asia, on a mountain plateau called Liang.

Brown John was not the only addition to the Mason household. In the parlor of their home the sisters had installed a small tree encased in a large masonry pot. Around the tree was erected a cage of thin wrought-iron rod.

Amongst the branches of the tree dwelt Brown John's pet, a small grey-furred monkey that they claimed was from the distant land of Sumatra. Those few who saw it up close claimed it to be in many ways like a large rat or possum, though the hands, face and eyes were peculiarly like those of a man. The sisters affectionately called the beast Brown Jenkin and when the weather was warmer, the beast could be seen traveling about the village playfully riding on Keziah's shoulder.

It was in the fall of the next year that Eliza Abbott sent a letter to her sister detailing the public rebuke of the villagers by one of the town elders, her uncle Ambrose Abbott. The women of the village had noticed that the widows, who had always been slightly built, had all gained weight, and rumors abounded that they were each with child. Some went so far as to point fingers and suggest that Brown John was more than the servant he was made out to be. Whether it was Abbott's chiding, or the sudden onslaught of a bitter winter, little else was made of the Masons, and when May came and went with no birth, all rumors of illegitimate pregnancy were quelled.

That said, there are some curious records that suggest some occurrence that yet still remains unexplained. That spring, James Anable recorded an agreement for a monthly standing order for a significant amount of meat and sundry items. The orders were to be paid by and delivered to Keziah Mason. Now this in itself is not unusual, but that same month, a similar arrangement was made with Harlan Fisher of Kingsport, to be paid for and received by Goody Watkins. Today, the term "Goody" is unused, but in those days it was short for Goodwife, and you would use it like we would use Missus or Ma'am. Thus it is with some assurance that Hepzibah Mason, known in Kingsport by her married name of Watkins, arranged a standing order for large quantities of fish and shellfish to be supplied on a monthly basis.

Over the next years, the Mason sisters entrenched themselves with the citizens of Arkham, Kingsport and Innsmouth, not only as good neighbors and customers to the merchants of all three villages, but also as midwives, a profession they seemed to excel at. They were particularly sought after by some of the older families in Kingsport, the Courts and Fishers, who seemed reluctant to seek medical attention under even the worse conditions. In 1660, much was made of their success in the birthing of Eliza Burke, whose mother had collapsed and gone into labor during Sunday services. The birth had been a breech, causing considerable injury to both the mother and child, which caused some concern amongst the family. That both lived and after several days readily improved seemed near miraculous, and earned the Masons the deepest of gratitude from both parents.

Afterwards the sisters were much in demand, regularly servicing most of the more well-to-do families in the area including the Carters, Pickmans, Whateleys, Marshs, Gilmans, Potters, Latimers and Phillipses. By some estimates one out of every three children born in Arkham was brought into the world by the Masons who, despite the fine quality of their work, charged little if anything for their services. Twenty years would pass, and the Masons began serving as midwives to the very children they had brought into the world. Arkham had begun to swell in size and began to lay down the roads and structures that would guide its growth into a thriving city. The sisters were in their forties and had lost much of the weight they had gained so many years ago. Brown John had left them the summer before, though when exactly, no one in particular could or would say. When pressed on the issue, the Masons would simply say that it was time for him to go, his services were no longer required.

It was the spring of 1685 that the first sour note between the village and the sisters was raised. Arthur Marsh, owner of the Kingsport Mercantile Company, aged but still spry, had come to Arkham to visit family, and after a chance encounter with one of the Masons related the most curious of tales. It was round about 1670 when he as captain of the *Sandra D* took shelter from rough weather along the coast of Florida, and was attacked by natives of the area, which the crew of the *Sandra D* was able to fend off. After some discussion, a militia was formed and the surviving raiders were tracked back to their crude settlement. There the good captain was to behold such sights and acts of indecent barbarism and crimes against God that he quickly ordered the entire village slaughtered. That these natives were the same as those that had seized years earlier seized the *Cordelia Ys*, Marsh had no doubts, for scattered amongst the village were timbers, crates and sacks that still bore the marks of that ship. That the villagers themselves regularly feasted on human flesh, and that this had been the fate of those aboard the *Cordelia Ys,* was for Captain Marsh a foregone conclusion, and it was for this reason that he had ordered the massacre. That he did these things to prevent the villagers from ever again preying on ships in distress seemed to his crew a prudent and wise thing. What they could not understand is why he had taken a sledgehammer to the crude shell-rock temple and collapsed it to the ground. Nor could the crew understand why he had ordered the bodies, the village and the temple doused with kerosene and burned beyond recognition. The crew could not understand these things, for they had not entered the temple and seen the tableau that decorated the walls within. They had not seen the crude but blasphemous paintings that showed the villagers carrying out their religious rites. They had not seen the image of the villagers kneeling before sanctified figures who were gleefully feasting upon human corpses. Marsh had seen these things and he shattered them and burned them in an attempt to blot them from his memory where they glowed like a horrendous beacon. For the figures that feasted in that tableau were a black man and three women dressed in white gowns all with eerily identical features, which despite the crudeness of execution Marsh recognized as belonging to the Abigail, Hepzibah and Keziah Mason, and the fare on the table was unmistakably the crew of the *Cordelia Ys*!

The rumors of Marsh's tale swept through Arkham like a cold wind, turning the town bitter and mean. A summer drought hit the villages hard, crops withered, cows went dry and sows took to eating their own. Food, particularly meat, grew scarce. Rumors spread about strange sounds and violet lights emanating from the Mason house. In September the Derby household woke to the screaming of young Matthew, who had been roused from his sleep, he claimed, to find one of the Masons grabbing at his feet with her claw-like hands. When over the course of the next week Lucy Anable and Jeremiah Upton reported similar nightmares, the townsfolk became restless and there was much talk in the square. Farmers and shopkeepers throughout Arkham refused to do business with them, and it was not unusual to see the three walking on the Innsmouth or Kingsport roads, their backs laden down with dry goods and fish. In late October tragedy struck when Lamar Holt, a boy of just seven years living with his family on the road to Kingsport, vanished. The boy's parents had been called to the barn to attend to a sick horse for several hours, and when they returned, the boy was gone without a trace. A desperate search throughout the night and next day in the surrounding woods found nothing. The parents, fearful and desperate, demanded that the Masons be questioned. The search party quickly became a mob that marched toward Arkham with obvious intent. Only the sudden intervention of a dozen well-armed men prevented the mob from storming the house and forcibly seizing the sisters.

The following years were quiet, for the sisters. Whether out of fear or age, all three ceased to visit Innsmouth or Kingsport. By 1687 their presence on the streets of Arkham was rare, and most of their food and supplies were delivered by members of the Jeffison family who were employed by Ezekiel Chambers, a local man who had taken pity on the sisters. It was the Jeffisons who dismantled Brown Jenkin's cage and sold it to the local smith. What had happened to the cage's occupant was never specified, but it was assumed that the beast had died. Later that year, a wagon appeared in front of the Mason home and the Jeffisons loaded it with a selection of furniture and crates. By noon, Abigail Mason, the widow of Simon Prinn, had left Arkham and never returned.

This began a most strange and rapid exodus that culminated in early 1692. By one accounting, from 1688 to 1692 fully fifteen percent of the villagers had left Arkham, and with them the vast majority of the children delivered by the Masons. Many made clear their destinations as the more urban and civilized cities of Boston, Providence, New York, Philadelphia or even Charleston. Others, such as the Whateleys and Bishops, traveled northwest along the Miskatonic River, settling wherever they could and founding the towns of Foxfield, Zoar, Duxbury and New Dunnich. With the Whateleys traveled Hepzibah Mason, widow of Jeremiah Watkins, who, like her sister Abigail, never again returned to Arkham.

The departure of her sisters seemed to embolden Keziah, who reportedly took to walking through the town and apparently peeking through windows at all hours of day or night. Fisherman and dockworkers, who now seemed to dominate Arkham's growing waterfront, regularly reported seeing her on the marshy island in the middle of the Miskatonic River, though how she reached the island is not known. Children fled and mothers crossed themselves as she hobbled down the road, her days as a respected midwife long forgotten as the town expanded on both sides of the river. The rumors of violet lights and strange noises proliferated. Tales told in roadhouses were retold in inns and exaggerated beyond belief. Any foul turn or ill luck was attributed to Keziah Mason, whether it was lost livestock, a dry well, or a dead child.

The rest of the story is well known. That it was Matthew Derby who accused Keziah of witchcraft, and more than a dozen villagers would testify that they had been molested by her or her demon rat Brown Jenkin is a matter of public knowledge. That after days of torture Keziah Mason confessed, was sentenced to death and mysteriously escaped, driving her guard mad, is also generally accepted. Yet for all this knowledge both common and uncommon that we had uncovered, more was yet to come.

It was the middle of October of 1927 that Gilman cajoled me into traveling out to the island in the river. Gilman had become obsessed with tracking down as much about Keziah as he could. We had already been to Kingsport and gone through the files of the Kingsport Mercantile Company, and while there Gilman had taken a rubbing from the gravestone that marked the plot of the long-dead stepsister for which Keziah had been named. We had even traveled to that dark valley north of Meadow Hill and taken notes on the stone dolmens that lay scattered there. Unwilling to wait for more seasonable weather, Gilman and I made arrangements to borrow a small rowboat from one of the many unsavory wharves that dot the Arkham harbor, and on the morning of October seventeenth made our way out to the low swampy island, braving the flotilla of barges that were endlessly moving up and down the river, transferring bales of unidentifiable cargo. We spent the morning creeping through the underbrush searching for the standing stones that Reverend Philips had described in his text *Thaumaturgical Prodigies in the New-England Canaan*. Gilman felt sure these were what had interested Keziah in the island. It was difficult work, and we found ourselves assailed by vines, creepers and roots at every turn. Thankfully, no insects or snakes seemed evident on the island, and I assumed that such creatures had all taken to their over-winter habitats. Likewise, there were also no birds, waterfowl or otherwise on the island. This I took as curious, as in the last few weeks, Arkham had seemed to be resplendent with the rustle of wings and the harmonious twittering and calls of all sorts including doves, whippoorwills, thrushes and the ever-filthy coterie of pigeons. That such abundance was not present on the island was somewhat unnerving. Moving into the uplands, we thankfully spied our first evidence of animal life on the island: in the bare mud bordering the swamp we could see the tracks of what could only be described as a raccoon or weasel of considerable size. Such a beast could easily and quickly depopulate an island of its resident beasts, and birds, particularly hatchlings, would be easy prey as well. Indeed, given the size of the tracks, Gilman and I both noted that such an animal could likely do us bodily harm as well.

We climbed up the muddy hillside, and discovered three irregularly spaced boulders that sprang up out of the earth, which we estimated at over seven feet tall and four feet wide. Each was covered from pinnacle to base with strange shallow curves and angles, caked with a foul-smelling brown crust that I could not identify. That they were individual stones could have been of some dispute, for as we cleared away mud from the base, so as to reveal partially concealed carvings, we uncovered even more such carvings. Indeed, using some fallen branches as crude shovels, we dug for three or four inches and found no end to them, although we did find that the worn smoothness of the upper portions did not extend to the lower sections. The muddy ground of the island concealed jagged outcroppings and shards of loose rock, upon which I was unfortunate enough to slip against and suffered a short and shallow gash upon my ankle. Ill-equipped to mount a serious excavation, we resigned ourselves to the process of copying the glyphs as best we could. After several hours, the day turned cold, and after some insistence on my part, Gilman finally agreed to return to the mainland. Our trip back was uneventful and we agreed to meet at the docks again the next morning.

We made two more such trips to the island before we resolved that we had to our satisfaction captured all of the stone inscriptions. Though I will admit that our decision was also influenced by the somewhat pointed questions of several unsavory characters who had taken too much of an interest in our outings. It was these drawings and rubbings that Gilman carried with him when in November he burst into Professor Upham's office, disturbing a meeting with the university president, Dr. Wainscott. Despite pleas from both, Gilman proceeded to ramble on at length on the most wild of notions concerning Keziah Mason, the ancient markings and certain things he had gleamed from the Necronomicon. What Gilman had said exactly he never did tell me, but whatever it was, it had earned him an unofficial rebuke from Upham and the department. His independent studies were suspended, all access to special holdings was revoked, and his class work was reduced. He was ordered to visit Dr. Waldron, who after a brief examination and discussion suggested rest and prescribed a light sedative.

It was then, in a disgruntled fit, that Gilman tried to distance himself from the university by moving out of the campus dormitory and into the vacant garret room of the Witch House. That the landlord Dombrowski had not wanted to rent the room to anyone, let alone a wild-eyed student, was forgotten when Gilman offered to pay double the going rate. It was thus that we two came to be sitting around the common rooms of the house and discussing Keziah Mason when we were joined by another resident, Joe

Mazurewicz, who oddly enough had his own tale to tell about the old witch.

Joe's father had been Polish, but his mother had been of the old Burke family that had lived in Arkham since it was founded. According to Joe, the Burke family had long ago split between those that still lived in Arkham, and those that had like so many others left the village about 1690. The split had come between two brothers, the older Lemuel and the younger Thaddeus. Upon the death of their father, Lemuel had inherited the family estate and documents, and amongst the papers he had found a sealed envelope addressed to him from his grandmother, Deborah Zellaby. The matron Zellaby wrote at length about observations she had made and grave concerns that she had, out of respect for her son and daughter, declined to discuss. However, in this letter, apparently written knowing her death was near, she made things plain to Lemuel, going into such detail on matters extremely strange. When Lemuel had finished reading the missive he confronted Thaddeus and under the threat of death ordered him to leave Arkham forever.

The Zellaby letter has long since been lost, but its contents were passed down amongst the Burke family and form the stuff of family legend. Lemuel Burke had been born to Eliza and Thomas Burke in 1657, and like his parents and all his relatives, he was a strapping blonde-haired, blue-eyed specimen of health. Thaddeus Burke had been born in 1660, and it was his birth that the Mason sisters had helped with that gained them such fame as midwives. Thaddeus was the opposite of his brother, with dark hair, dark violet eyes, a pale complexion and a thin wiry build. At his birth, Deborah Zellaby had suspected something, but lacking evidence she said nothing. It was through the course of years that Zellaby watched what was happening in the village; she watched the Masons and noted which children they birthed, which children died, and which children lived. Children brought into the world by the Masons flourished, while those that they did not, tended to struggle to survive. This was particularly noticeable amongst the younger siblings of those children birthed by the Masons, who seemed prone to disease and the occasional lethal accident. All this the old matron wrote about in her letter, and all of it but the most circumstantial of observations. Yet it was the other thing that Burke had noted that had so enraged Lemuel and driven him to banish his brother Thaddeus. For his brother bore no resemblance to his family, and yet bore strong resemblance to the hundreds that had been born and thrived in Arkham since 1660. A whole generation which, regardless of family, had the same dark-hair and dark-violet eyes as the women who had supposedly only helped to bring them into the world, Abigail, Hepzibah and Keziah Mason!

Despite the fact that Mazurewicz was something of a drunkard, the story he told chilled me, and with my mind filled with what Deborah Zellaby had come to believe about her own grandson, and the implications thereof, I found no comforting sleep that night. It was Mazurewicz's tale that drove me to begin my own research into the life and legends surrounding Keziah Mason. November came and went, and December brought us to winter break. Gilman went to visit family in Haverhill, and then to visit a new mill his family had built in Maine near Gates Falls. Given my rather meager finances, I took the bus for the short journey to my home in Kingsport. There amongst my friends and in my family home, I set about initiating my own more personal study of Keziah's dark legacy.

In February our return to the ivory-columned halls of Miskatonic University brought to us the first hint of the supernatural. The incident was so simple, and yet it is undeniably the first in a series of preternatural events that would, in their course, lead Gilman first to madness, and then to his singularly horrid death. Gilman and I had made our way to the great library, cursing the masses that were uncommonly cluttered about the University grounds. It was not merely the student body that milled about the commons, but strangers as well, some of whom wore military uniforms and bore with them firearms and similar such weaponry. Others wore charcoal suits and traveled in pairs, dominating the sidewalks, oblivious to any other pedestrians they might come across. Ostensibly, these hordes had invaded Arkham in response to some secretive government action that had sealed off the aged port town of Innsmouth. Rumor had it that nearly the entire village had been arrested, charged with the smuggling of liquor and other contraband. The streets of Arkham were wild with speculation, and every tidbit of unfounded speculation and gossip concerning Innsmouth seemed to travel across the city like wildfire.

In the library Gilman and I marched defiantly through the marble halls on a mission to persuade Dr. Armitage to restore Gilman's access to the rare book room in general, and the Necronomicon in specific. Unfortunately, both Armitage and the Necronomicon were already occupied. For the better part of an hour the old librarian stood watching as the most curious of characters sat hunched over the ancient grimoire, all the time making seemingly endless notations in an old leather journal. Gilman fumed over what he viewed as an invasion of his personal area of research, and when the stranger finally made to leave, speaking to Armitage in a rough and uncouth manner, Gilman rose to intercept the aged librarian.

It was at this moment that Gilman had his first and cascading preternatural encounter, for as the stranger rose it was to reveal a countenance and stature that brought to mind the ogres and trolls of legend. The man easily stood over seven feet tall, and his bulk was barely contained by his thread-worn suit and broken shoes. That a thin black tie and aged hat framed his face served only to draw attention to the man's huge and goatish head which was covered by a thick beard and eyebrows that created the illusion of fur. That fine black hair was apparently endemic throughout the entirety of his body, for it peeked out at the cuffs of his sleeves, and several clumps were visible between the buttons of his shirt.

As Gilman crossed his path, the lumbering giant paused and stared down at the diminutive man blocking his way. His gaze wandered in my direction and then back to Gilman. A massive hand reached out and came to rest on Gilman's shoulder. With little effort, the monstrous man gently moved Gilman to the side and grunted in a deep and curious way that reminded me more of the bellows made by frogs or whales, rather than a true voice. What was more curious was what he actually said: "Yew should know better than to stand in my way, sir," and then he turned to look at me, "and yew should know better too, little cousin." In those huge violet eyes I saw no empathy, no humanity, and if there was any evidence of emotion, all I could see was pure unadulterated hate. Who the monstrous figure in the library was, and if it was his casual touch that brought on the ensuing events, I cannot say for certain, but it was on that very night that Gilman's bout of brain-fever and strange dreams were to first manifest.

Of the events that followed, of Gilman's dreams, of his ghostly encounters with Keziah Mason and Brown Jenkin, of his involvement in the death of Ladislas Wolejko, and his own tragic death, I have little to add. Some have questioned my whereabouts on certain evenings, and in response to these inquiries I must admit that I was pursuing the course of research that I had begun so many months before in Kingsport. Though my investigation had yielded nothing more than rumor, innuendo and circumstantial evidence, I had, much like Deborah Zellaby, grown to suspect certain things about those early days of Arkham. It was not until that chance encounter in the library that my suspicions began to coalesce and provide a more concrete direction for my delving into history.

It was in April that I borrowed a car and drove madly back to Kingsport. At my request, my brother had dug through the family holdings and there hidden amongst things long forgotten he had found a portrait of the patriarch of the Elwood family, a man who had come to the village in 1691 as a pauper. That I and most of my family bore a resemblance to Thaddeus Elwood was never in doubt. This was not the revelation that my months of research had unveiled. For it was the second painting, the one that made little sense to be amongst our family possessions, that confirmed my worst fears. The painting was more than two hundred and fifty years old, and still bore a note stating that it had been commissioned by Roger Mason to celebrate the twentieth anniversary of his business venture.

For in this painting of the Mason family, I could see the fine dark hair and dark violet eyes, the turn of the nose and chin and the high ridged cheeks that were the most notable features of the young Keziah Mason, features that were reflected in the painting of Thaddeus Elwood, who had once been named Thaddeus Burke. Features I knew well, for I could see them in the face of the monstrous thing we had seen in the library as it played at being human, and in the face of Brown Jenkin as it burrowed out of Walter Gilman's chest and madly chattered at me. Features I madly see in every face around me. For there is I fear no choice but to accept the mathematical certainty that from those dozens of children that Keziah and her sisters brought into the world, those children that fled Arkham like rats in the night, who have had more than two centuries to establish themselves, to marry, and to raise children of their own. Children, with fine black hair and violet eyes, of which, madly I myself may be only one of thousands. *"For the Black Goat Mother doth favor her servants with such fruitfulness that would shame even the most fertile of pestilent flies, breeding in the secret wounds of man's misery and pain, like maggots in a slaughter yard."*

Chapter 25.
Monsters of Miskatonic

The last few hours of that dark morning still haunt my immediate memory. That it has been just days since my arrest on charges of murder seems incredulous, for the pages piled in front of me would seem to have been begun years ago. That my jailers periodically enter my cell to provide me with blank sheets, food and drink seems overly kind. On occasion there have been notes, signed by Dr. Dexter, asking for details concerning certain aspects of my research and formulae. I think perhaps they are trying to re-create my work. Given what has happened, I should try to stop them, but it all seems so pointless, they will find what they need one way or the other. The things that I have done will slow them down a bit, but it will not stop them from trying. Not even the horrors I left behind in St. Mary's will defer them.

As I have previously written, the population of Miskatonic University, its students and teachers, had for the most part volunteered to aid in the recovery of Dunwich following the horror that had devastated that area. Only a scant few remained on campus, and those were mostly concentrated at the University teaching hospital. St. Mary's had been cleared of most patients and only a skeleton crew of medical professionals and a few others remained behind. That night, the night of October thirtieth, only I, my young charge Frank Elwood, and three nurses were on staff, and the early evening had been uneventful, which given the torrential rains that were buffeting the area was somewhat surprising.

After midnight, in the small hours all that changed, and a deputy brought in three victims of a tragic car accident. Their injuries were all severe, and under normal circumstances they would have been fatal, but the Fisher triplets had been patients of mine, and had been subjected to my experiments in immunization against death using a reagent developed in part by Dr. Herbert West, but significantly modified by myself. The exposure of the triplets to the reagent was apparently keeping them from expiring, but there was also something else. All three showed the presence of an unusual cell in their blood, a cell that I had only ever seen in samples from Innsmouth, a cell that appeared to be responsible for generating a natural version of the life-sustaining reagent.

At first I thought that perhaps the Fishers, who had some family history in Innsmouth, had always possessed such a cellular component, but I quickly discounted such a possibility. I would have noticed such a foreign component during my initial examination. The source of the reanimating cell perplexed me, but I had had little time to ponder an alternative explanation. Young Elwood had burst into the room and announced the sudden death of Helena Armitage and then shoved a packet of his own writings into my hands.

The handwritten statement detailed certain facts that had been left out of previous accounts of the death of Elwood's friend Walter Gilman. Elwood's tale, which was the product of his own research, seemed to suggest through the linking of a variety of seemingly unrelated events and facts that something untoward had been occurring in Arkham during colonial times. Though to be honest, I found the idea that over the course of many years, a trio of midwives had systematically replaced the newborn infants of Arkham with their own spawn incredulous. It did however provide me with a possible explanation to my own conundrum.

The strange cells that had appeared in the blood of the Fishers may not have been present when I had examined them initially, but rather may have been triggered to develop as a response to my reagent. That the immune system could respond to a variety of foreign bodies was a well-established fact, and it seemed not unreasonable that my treatments may have perhaps activated some pre-existing component; a cell that naturally produced a version of the reanimating agent, but for some reason had been suppressed by millennia of evolution.

It was a radical theory, but one for which some evidence might well exist within the walls of the hospital itself. I drew my own blood, but as I had expected, there was no trace of the strange spindle-shaped cells to be found. Then, covertly, I took the light microscope up to where the body of Helena Armitage still lay. She was, as Elwood had said, dead, but her blood had yet to coagulate and under examination I confirmed what I had expected. The blood of Helena Armitage did indeed contain a number of the strange cells, though they were not in the numbers that had presented in the blood of the Fishers. Immediately my mind began to develop hypotheses concerning family ancestry as well as reagent dosage and periodic re-administration.

I had no opportunity to document my thoughts, for it was then that the screaming began. It was high-pitched and clearly that of the charge nurse who had helped me wheel in the Fishers. I dashed down the stairs and through a pair of double doors to find Nurse Clemens trapped behind the reception desk, desperately trying to fend off the menacing advances of a large man, half dressed and still dripping from the storm. He was grunting at her and flailing his arms wildly, trying to capture her in a kind of pathetic manner that had little chance of working save for if she were to suddenly panic. With each move Nurse Clemens made, her attacker mirrored it, and it was only when I reached down to pick up a chair to use as a weapon and cried out for him to stop, that he turned to acknowledge my presence. I gasped audibly, for I knew this man, had seen his visage more than I had wished to that evening, and he had no right to be stalking through the hospital after an innocent nurse. He had no right to do such a thing, save for the fact that I had allowed it, or at least made it possible. For the man was none other than Edward Fisher brought back from the dead by my own experiments in death and reanimation.

He charged me, and it was as if a great ape was leaping across the room to attack, and I instinctively thought of the thing that Allan Halsey had become so many years previously. I swung the chair and smashed it across his temple as he dove the last few feet toward me. Blood and teeth flew through the air leaving arcs of crimson on the walls and floor. Edward stumbled back to his feet and roared at me, blood and spittle dripping down his chin. His eyes had gone pale, and I knew then that there was no reason left at all in this creature that was once a man. I lifted up the chair and readied myself for the next attack. Edward crouched down and prepared to strike.

Both of us turned as Nurse Clemens began screaming once more. She was backing away, pointing toward the swinging doors that led to the procedure rooms, doors that had suddenly swung open and remained so. Each door presented a kind of doppelganger to the creature I was fighting, and I swear Edward grinned as the two things that bore his face came through the doors. Those doors swung back and forth, casting wild shadows across the room as Edward's brothers Frederick and Godrick moved to join him. There was a noise from behind me. The doors I had come through had again swung open, and without thinking I swung the chair and smashed the figure that was behind me, sending him to the ground.

The victim of my assault had been the deputy who had brought the Fishers to the hospital, and behind him in the doorway was Frank Elwood. Like myself, they had come to investigate the screaming nurse, and instead fell victim to my panicked attack. The deputy tumbled to the floor, and his gun flew backwards, bouncing off of Elwood's chest before impacting on the floor and sliding to a stop at my feet. Nurse Clemens stood frozen and I screamed at her to run. She stared dumbly at me and then back at the trio of undead that were whipping their heads back and forth between us. I threw the chair at them to get their attention, and shouted once more for the stunned nurse to run. As the chair was casually tossed aside, the woman found her senses and dashed out of the room, leaving only Elwood and myself to face off against the beasts.

I glanced sideways to speak to the young man, but somehow he was no longer where I thought he should be. Instead he was in front of me with the gun in his hand, pointing it at the Fishers. "Stay where you are," he announced, "or so help me I'll shoot." The three paused at the sound of his voice, but it was only for a moment. The three things seemed intent on stalking forward, slowly, stealthily, but inevitably they moved toward us.

I put a hand on Elwood's shoulder. "I don't think they can understand you or the concept of a gun anymore. They're animals, nothing more." I cast a glance at the limp body of the deputy. "We need to get out of here."

Elwood flexed his shoulder and knocked my hand away. He shook his head and in a firm voice he made his intentions clear. "No, Doctor. I'm through running and hiding. I let Walter tell me what to do, and I lost him. I didn't kill him, but I could have saved him, could have gotten him out of that rat hole. Instead I let him die. If these things get loose they'll kill people, maybe lots of people. I can't let that happen."

I took a step forward. "Frank, I really appreciate that, but I don't think the gun is going to do much good. They're already dead, at least as dead as they ever can be."

There was an odd backward glance and then a sudden light filled his eyes. He sneered evilly and leveled the gun at one of the three monsters. "Now there's a theory that needs to be tested," and the sound of three shots filled the hall.

The heads of two of the things that had once been Fishers exploded, coating the third one with bits of brain and shattered skull. Their bodies collapsed to the floor, convulsing violently, but no longer a serious threat. The third one, who I still believed to be Edward, may not have understood the concept of a gun, but he sure enough saw the results. He leapt over the thrashing bodies of his brothers and in an instant was through the door that Nurse Clemens had herself escaped through.

Elwood cursed and dashed off after the escaping thing. I made to follow, but in the flashing light I caught sight of what was hidden in the corner. Clemens had not been Edward's first victim. An orderly, whose name I knew only as Dennis, lay beaten and covered in blood behind the reception desk. He had, given the gaping wound around his neck, been bitten and his throat had been torn out by the deranged thing that had been Edward Fisher. I made to leave, and join Elwood in his pursuit of the Fisher-thing, but as I reached the door an unexpected thing happened. Dennis, the orderly who was clearly dead, moved. His fingers were vibrating madly in a spastic freakish manner that was so fast they blurred. The seizure traveled to his hands and arms, and then appeared in his legs. He bucked wildly against the floor as the convulsions took hold of his torso. It had been years since I had seen such a violent reaction, but I knew it for what it was. At the moment I had no explanation, only a desire to bring the horror to an end. In a daze I ran back into the procedure room and obtained the largest bone saw I could find. It gleamed silver in the light as I marched determinedly back to the hall. As I came around the reception desk, Dennis' reanimated body sprang up and reached for me. I slashed purposefully and in one motion took the saw through the thing's neck. The head fell, bounced against the top of the desk and then fell to the floor, coming to rest next to the body it had once crowned.

Reinvigorated, I careened through the doors and after Elwood and his monstrous quarry. A trail of blood and other fluids led up the main stairwell of the hospital. Based on the footprints that Elwood left behind smeared into the vile trail, he seemed to be not far behind the creature, but I had heard no further gunshots since the first two. I took the stairs by twos and threes, following the spatter past the second, then the third and up onto the fourth floor. There the tile and walls were smeared crimson as if the thing had stumbled or slid. I was grateful that this particular floor had been cleared of patients, but cursed the darkness that came with the lights being turned out.

I took a few cautious steps down the shrouded hall, but before I had gone ten paces it became apparent that the corridor was simply too dark for me to proceed safely. Blindly, I backed up and purposely pinned myself against the wall. “Elwood,” I whispered in desperation.

There was a sound like cloth tearing, and a sweet cloying smell like roses. Something moved behind me. I readied the bone saw, intent on lashing out blindly if I had to. A hand grabbed my wrist and pinned it against the wall. Another came out and covered my mouth just as I began to scream. “Shh-hh,” whispered Elwood. “I think we have it trapped on this floor. All the windows are barred and the door at the other end is chained shut. Maybe we should hold him here and wait for help to arrive.”

I lowered his hand away from my mouth. “That might not be a good idea. I don’t know how but I think that this condition is infectious. The more people that we involve, the more likely that it will spread.”

Somewhere down the darkened hallway Edward Fisher smashed against the door and howled in pain and anger. Elwood dragged me slowly back toward the light. “I have an idea, but you have to trust me.”

With little choice in the matter I took the gun he was placing in my hand and followed him slowly back to the stairwell. “You do know how to use that?”

I nodded; my time in the war had served me well, and I knew how to handle a variety of firearms. “Take the gun and head down to the lobby. I’m going to try and lure him out to a spot where you can get a clear shot. You might only get one chance, so make sure you make it count.”

He barreled down the hallway screaming, while I went down the stairs leaping from landing to landing as fast as I could. I could hear both Edward and Elwood as they finally met and then careened down the hall, one in pursuit of the other. I stumbled down the last few stairs and slid into position.

I watched as three stories above me Elwood suddenly appeared on the landing. He cast a quick glance in my direction, and then let loose with a tremendous and frightening shriek. There echoed back a bone-chilling snarl and the sound of something large pounding down the hallway at breakneck speed. The building shook and once more there was that sound of tearing fabric. I yelled at Elwood to move but he was already gone, and in his place was suddenly the form of Edward Fisher. He seemed to float there for a second, and in that moment he seemed oddly graceful, almost serene, like a leaf drifting in the wind. Then that moment was gone and the creature was flailing, falling, crashing through the stairwell, bouncing off of hand rails and posts as the force of gravity accelerated him down and into the floor in front of me.

The body hit the floor of the hospital, sending cracks through the stone that radiated out until they were lost to the walls. One of Edward's legs turned to pulp on impact, while his other leg seemed to snap at the hip. I stepped back and lowered the gun, for I saw no need to shoot. That was until the thing reared its head and clawed out with a shattered but still functional arm. Panicked, I pulled the trigger wildly and serendipitously blew a hole through one of his dull and lifeless eyes.

Once more Elwood appeared out of nowhere and grabbed the gun from my hand. He carefully took aim and fired once more, this time sending a bullet deep into the center of the skull. I gave him a puzzled look to which he responded simply, "Better not to risk it."

It took us an hour to gather up the bodies of the Fisher brothers and the orderly Dennis. Dawn was not far and we had to dispose of these monstrosities before someone official arrived to take control. We tried to get down into the furnace, but the door was locked and we had no time to search for the key. Instead we loaded the bodies into the trunk and back seat of my car and drove to the construction site that was not far from the University.

In the shadow of the nearly completed Tillinghast Building the construction team was still working on the foundations of the subterranean railway, and freshly poured concrete was everywhere. We took advantage of a driverless concrete truck and, while Elwood poured, I tossed the bodies of our four victims into the pit. In mere seconds the Fisher brothers had sunk into the thick grey composite that would soon solidify and imprison the bodies forever.

As the sun rose, the two of us drove to my home on Crane Street, and for the first time I personally invited someone down into my secret laboratory. Together we piled my notes and research journals into the center of the room. We dumped all of my tissue samples, and smashed any glassware that held any trace of reagent. Then we doused the house with rubbing alcohol, cooking grease and kerosene. As the day began, Frank Elwood wished me well and left me just as I lit the first match. I strolled up the stairs, casually lighting matches and making sure that the flames spread quickly and irreversibly through my home. In my office, I turned on the gas, closed the door behind me and calmly walked down the street.

I hoped that all traces of my work were destroyed in that fire, but I know that is not true. Still, as I walked down Crane Street I realized that for the first time in twenty-five years I was free. Free of obligations, free from the desire for revenge, free to do whatever I pleased. I started to laugh; I was still laughing when the police hauled me away, and three hours later when the doctors finally came. I didn't stop laughing until the nurses at Sefton Asylum sedated me and locked me away in the same cell that Allan Halsey had occupied for so many years.

As I write these final words, as I complete the documentation of the events that led me to this place, I cannot help but look back and wonder. Why is it, exactly, that they think me a monster?

EPiLOGUE

FROM THE FILES OF DR. AMBROSE DEXTER

The incarceration of Dr. Stuart Hartwell in the Sefton Asylum did not last. Following the completion of his so-called confession he entered a state of catatonia and would no longer respond to external stimuli. Beginning in January 1930 onward, despite being under the treatment of four doctors, he remained uncommunicative, and showed no improvement. Attempts to validate the contents and events documented in Hartwell's account have met with mixed success. Inquiries into the whereabouts of Doctors West and Cain continue. All traces of Hartwell's reagent and his notes were lost in the fire that destroyed his home and office.

On December sixth, 1930, two men and a woman entered the Sefton Asylum and demanded to speak to the director. Staff described the woman as small, with an olive complexion and large wide-set eyes. The younger man was described as tall and nervous-looking with strange, violet eyes that held a far-away introspective look. The third individual was perhaps the most memorable, for he towered over the others at nearly seven feet. Swathed in robes and wearing thick white mittens, those who saw him took him to be a Turk or Hindoo based on both the turban he wore and the thick long beard that covered most of his face. Some who saw him up close said that his eyes seemed lifeless and suggested he might have been blind.

According to the hospital staff, the three strangers spoke to the director in private for approximately fifteen minutes, after which he escorted them to Hartwell's cell. Over the objection of senior staff the director ordered the patient placed in care of the visitors whom he said had specific authority to transfer him to another facility. Hartwell was taken to a large black sedan and, accompanied by the three strangers, was driven off. The director of the Sefton Asylum has no recollection of these visitors or of ordering Hartwell's release. As of this writing there have been no credible sightings of Hartwell, and the identities of his liberators remain unknown.

It is my opinion that locating Dr. Hartwell should become a priority of the Bureau. Given the recent departure of agent Hadrian Vargr to private practice, it is my recommendation that another special agent be assigned to the case immediately. The fact remains that Dr. Stuart Hartwell is free and may once more be able to carry out his experiments. It must be presumed that his liberators had just this in mind when they took him. It is even possible that some of his former patients, or victims, collected him to exact some sort of revenge.

Any other intent seems unlikely, but it should not be discounted as a possibility, and an agent assigned to investigating alternatives should be considered. It is possible that Hartwell's associates were more interested in his involvement in the Peaslee Affair, the Innsmouth Quarantine, or even the devastating Dunwich Event. It should also be noted that Hartwell is not the only resident of the area to go missing recently. As noted, the author Randolph Carter has vanished, the mathematics student Frank Elwood is likewise unaccounted for, as are Detective Robert Peaslee, and his wife Megan Halsey-Griffith, the daughter of Hartwell's mentor. That their cases are related seems highly unlikely, but stranger things have happened. If these cases are related, one must ask by whom have they been taken, and for what possible purpose?

Acknowledgements

Reanimators wouldn't exist if it weren't for the people who helped lay its foundations, obviously this includes H. P. Lovecraft, August Derleth, Dashiell Hammett, Earl Derr Biggers, John P. Marquand, Rex Stout and Robert Bloch. Less obvious, are the authors who have served to inspire me including Henry Kuttner, Wilum H. Pugmire, Brian Lumley, Lin Carter, Cody Goodfellow, Charles Stross, Alan Moore, Kim Newman, and Neil Gaiman.

I also need to thank those editors who took a chance and gave me needed breaks: Robert Price, David Hartwell, Kevin J. Maroney, Scott David Aniolowski, Kevin Ross, Brian Sammons, Glynn Owen Barrass, Jean-Marc and Randy Lofficier, Silvia Moreno-Garcia, Mike Davis, and of course Ross Lockhart of Night Shade Books.

Finally, there are family and friends who supported me even if they didn't know it: My son Peter (surprisingly not the third but still a trip), Becky (for immoral support), Mike (ZombieMountain.com), Brad (for editorial comments), Gin and Andy (Formerly of Inhouse, now of 900 Seconds), and of course, my parents Peter and Susan (Thanks for reading me "The Rats in the Walls" as a bed time story).

About the Author

Pete Rawlik was first exposed to Lovecraft when his father read him "The Rats in the Walls" as a bedtime story. He has been collecting Lovecraftian fiction ever since. In 1985 he drove four hours in a "borrowed" Buick Skylark to see Stuart Gordon's *Re-Animator.* Since 1991 he has been active in issues related to Everglades restoration and monitoring, and has published extensively on the subject. For more than two decades he has run Dead Ink, selling rare and unusual books. His fiction has appeared in the magazines *Talebones, Crypt of Cthulhu, Morpheus Tales, Innsmouth* and the *Lovecraft Ezine*, as well as the anthologies *Tales of the Shadowmen: Femme Fatales, Dead But Dreaming 2, Future Lovecraft, Horror for the Holidays,* and *Urban Cthulhu*. His fascination with pulp fiction, secret histories, Arkham, its lesser known residents, and occasional visitors, inspired the creation of *Reanimators*, his first novel. He lives in South Florida.